Dear Jody
I hope you enjoy the story.
With Best Wishes
Ann

SPELLBOUND

Ann Charlotte

authorHOUSE®

AuthorHouse™
1663 Liberty Drive, Suite 200
Bloomington, IN 47403
www.authorhouse.com
Phone: 1-800-839-8640

First published by AuthorHouse 11/10/2008

ISBN: 978-1-4208-2749-1 (sc)

Printed in the United States of America
Bloomington, Indiana

This book is printed on acid-free paper.

To my husband, Ken, who has gifted me with the opportunity to follow my dream.

ACKNOWLEDGMENTS

Many thanks

    . . . to my son, Jeremy, for his companionship and assistance on our research trip to Front Royal, Virginia, and for my back cover photograph;

    . . . to my good friends, Janet and Brian, for proofreading and editing;

    . . . to my cousin, Tim, for refreshing my memory of our childhood haunts in Yarmouth, Nova Scotia, and his knowledge of the fishing industry;

    . . . to Scott Travers Rare Coin Galleries for advice on rare coin;

    . . . to the fine folk at Luray Caverns, Virginia, for their tour script;

    . . . to the many contributors to the World Wide Web from which I was able to glean tidbits of information regarding the Civil War, Underground Railroad and slave trade.

ONE

Clarissa

It is currently the year of our Lord 1863 and I write these words with the hope that the one who follows through the portals of time will know me . . . will know us. I say 'us' for we are one.

We came to be in the spring of 1836 and have been christened Clarissa Margueretta Fontaine. Mama said the moss clinging to the cypress trees dripped heavily with early morning dew as Papa rowed the little boat through the bayou. The sun was just peeking over the horizon to warm its misty waters. The dew droplets sparkled like millions of brilliant diamonds floating in the air. Magical, she said.

Our mother could have delivered us in the comfort of Papa's city house in New Orleans with his physician in attendance, but she chose otherwise. As Papa paced nervously back and forth along the ancient rickety wharf made out of fallen tree limbs and bits of scrap lumber, Grandmama's were the first hands to caress our body in those early minutes of dawn.

❋   ❋   ❋

Brow wrinkled in deep thought, Clarissa paused to chew on the end of her pen before dipping the nib in the ink to continue. Did she really have to write anything at all? If she truly believed in her spell, 'the one who follows' should know. But she was bored. There was little to do. There would be no harvest. The Yankees had destroyed the crops.

Replanting would have to wait for a new year if there was anything left of the valley. There was precious little now.

At least the Montgomerys still had their home. Pettigrew, Roseneath and Tupper weren't so lucky. They lost everything to Yankee torches. Charles had begged her to take the children out of harm's way, but no one really believed the war would last this long. President Davis had sorely miscalculated and the South was now paying the price. It was too late to flee to safety.

Thinking back to a much happier time, Clarissa dabbed at a tear that escaped the corner of her eye. In the ten years they had been married, she had not been separated from her husband for so much as one night up until that horrible day when he recruited. Charles had been gone two years now and she missed him terribly. When the war first broke, they had been fortunate to have the occasional brief visit. Now Clarissa considered herself lucky to receive a hastily scribbled note every couple months or so. She worried. She fretted. She feared for his safety. She tried to keep busy so she wouldn't have to think about it so much. Writing in her journal helped.

Papa is such a kind man. In our younger years, he doted on us to no end. Mama fussed that he would spoil us but he paid her no heed. Perched on his shoulder, we went everywhere with him. Then, when we grew too heavy, we'd ride beside him in his splendid carriage drawn by a pair of stunning dapple greys. Papa raises magnificent horses. For a businessman, with no formal education in husbandry, he certainly knows his horseflesh. His Thoroughbreds take their share of substantial purses at the races which are, to this very day, gaining in popularity. Many breeders seek to buy his stallions to put to stud.

We grew up in the stables. The sweet smell of freshly cut hay—the putrid odor of rotting manure—conflicted our senses. Mama fretted the mammoth horses would crush us with their feet, but each and every one was so exceptionally gentle we could crawl around beneath their bellies with no fear at all.

We thrived on what others of our station would have considered lowly and common.

Mama and Papa allowed us the pleasures of mixing with crowds of all classes. Allowed us to experience the wonders of the multi-cultural society our fine nation has become. We became friends with Soo Lei, the daughter of the Chinese laundress who washed Papa's white linen shirts to the brilliance of new fallen snow. Our bread and sweet treats were purchased from a German baker named Heins Meulker who set up shop just down the street from our city house. Many times our mouth would simply water in anticipation as the gentle New Orleans breeze carried the wonderful scents of his delectable creations to our little nose. His daughter, Ava, became our best friend. She seldom stepped over the threshold of our door without a splendid treat or two. No wonder we were such a pudgy child.

Bertie was our groundskeeper until his untimely death. Must be three winters ago. Dear Bertie. Always introduced himself as 'J—for James— Bertram McKeeg, at your service'. Molly, his wife, is a feisty miss with the reddest hair we have ever seen. From Ireland they were. Immigrated to New York City then eventually found their way to us when they realized the streets of the prosperous new world were really not paved with gold.

So we learned a smattering of a number of languages. Chinese, German, Gaelic and even Sioux.

The manager of Papa's stable is a redskin Indian he found half dead somewhere on one of his travels through the western wild country. Mama nursed him back to health and he has been with Papa ever since.

There is no kinder a human being than Blue Eagle. We love him as if he were our very own blood uncle. He taught us to ride—not using those prissy sidesaddles the gentry ladies have to use for sake of modesty—but with our short legs straddled across Bella's broad back.

Our little lungs exploding with blood-curdling war cries, we'd thunder across the meadow with Blue Eagle by our side. He taught us how to read the signs of the land, how to track game, how to shoot with a bow and arrow. He taught us how to skin a rabbit although that is something we quickly decided we would rather not have to do.

Camped out in his teepee behind the barn, Blue Eagle taught us the ways of his people. He taught us how to cook over an open fire without turning every morsel to charcoal. And his teachings, I'm sure, will not go amiss in this present time of destitution for I fear far greater hardship ahead of us.

❈   ❈   ❈

Thank heavens for Simon, Clarissa thought. He hunted their game. What hadn't been frightened off or already trapped by the soldiers. The Yankees had taken their hogs and what chickens they could catch. They had taken their steers. She was surprised they hadn't taken the children's puppy. Gone was their flour, sugar and coffee. The larder was virtually bare. The soldiers didn't find the root cellar Simon had dug as the warning of their imminent approach spread from farm to farm. Clarissa left just enough in the house as to not arouse suspicion, but the bulk of their supplies were craftily hidden. Martha would be so proud.

❈   ❈   ❈

Martha is our lady of color, as Mama would call her. Several years our elder, she helps with the housework and cooking but she isn't a slave. Papa won't hear of it. Every helper he hires earns a fair wage plus is provided comfortable lodging and plenty good food to eat.

Poor little Martha didn't know where she came from or where she was headed when she landed in town. Mama found the scrawny black child curled up in a back alley, dressed in rags, shoeless, and half starved to death. Mama, just like she would a stray cat, picked her up and took her home.

With plentiful nourishment and bountiful kindness, Martha blossomed into a beautiful, confident woman. Mama patiently taught her to read, write, and cipher.

Once Martha caught on to the written word, she devoured every book in Papa's library. Some books she read twice or even thrice. She'd steal the overseas news journals right from under Papa's nose while he was reading over breakfast coffee. Papa quickly grew to admire Martha's wisdom and insight and still enjoys their spirited debates.

When Mama passed, Martha took over our schooling with such acquired knowledge she could have put to shame the most learned scholar from any renowned university. Mama could not have left anyone a finer legacy than Martha's gift of an education. 'Tis no one's fault but our own that we are still unsure of the proper grammatical usage of 'who' and 'whom'. We were much more interested in the barnyard than the classroom.

Dear, sweet Mama. Margueretta Beaujolais was born in the deep dark backwaters of the Louisiana bayou just like we were. We'll never forget Mama's skin. It was such a beautiful shade of creamy olive. Her long straight hair was so silky and so shiny black it almost looked a dark navy blue. We've been told we resemble her.

Papa met Mama on one of those rare trips Grandmama made to town when she needed supplies. Not looking where he was going, Papa ran smack into Mama knocking her flat on her behind on the dusty boardwalk. Mama was fifteen. Papa was a fair bit older but it was just like in a fairytale. Love at first sight.

How we miss her. We truly believe Papa is still grieving. Mama passed into God's loving arms the winter we turned ten. Influenza, the doctor had said, that turned into pneumonia from which she did not recover. Even Grandmama's spells and potions could not save her.

Now what can I possibly tell you about Grandmama that you don't already know? Mysterious. Eccentric. No word seems to adequately describe Grandmama. Some call her witch. Some enchantress. She calls herself 'High Priestess'.

Grandmama says we have the 'gift'. She introduced us to the art of black magic before we could even talk. Much to Mama's mortification, our first toy was a voodoo doll Grandmama fashioned from rags. Mama tried to dispose of it many times, but we would not be separated from it.

For as much as Grandmama is reclusive, to us she is the most elegant of ladies. She dresses in long flowing white gowns that match the platinum of her hair which sweeps the floor as she walks. Even in old age, her bearing remains straight and tall.

We'd watch as she mixed her potions. We'd listen as she repeated her chants.

But we never really did see anything actually happen before our eyes. Spells can oftentimes span years . . . decades . . . before their effects are known. If something eventually turns out the way Grandmama wants, it is due to her spell. If not, she says whatever was supposed to happen just wasn't meant to be. Like when we lost Mama. Grandmama said God needed her more than we did although we had a very hard time accepting it.

Papa calls it all hogwash. We find it fascinating and have entertained many a folk at gatherings with our readings and incantations. Purely for amusement, mind you, and we are quick to stress that to all who privately seek us out.

After Mama passed, we spent a lot of time with Grandmama in her little shack in the bayou. Although there was a big hole in our heart, I figure we turned out all right. Everyone else said we were wild and willful especially when we rode with Blue Eagle whooping like banshees. Grandmama said we were free-spirited. We preferred the latter.

Papa's father, orphaned at a very young age, stowed away on a sailing schooner and found his way here from Paris, France. Grandmama's ancestry hails from the horrific deportation and exile of thousands of French Acadians from the Atlantic provinces of Canada. One of our favorite bedtime stories follows the tale of Evangeline and her beloved Gabriel.

Papa prefers us to consider ourselves to be Creole. However, Grandmama calls herself Cajun. Both are a melting pot of French, African, and Spanish with a smattering of Indian thrown in along the way for good measure. We have our own dialect, our own vocabulary, and Papa has tried valiantly to train us to speak properly enunciated English. Most of the time we can unless we get overly excited and forget ourself.

From Mama and Martha we learned the skill of Creole cuisine. From Grandmama, Cajun cooking. No difference one from the other. It's just that Creole refers more to the upper class of the city dwellers. Cajun is a term used by country folk who take what they can from the land or bayous. Like crayfish. Both have spicy jambalaya and gumbo. Both have what we call 'Trinity'.

Now most God-fearing people would consider the 'Trinity' to be of religious orientation. Father, Son and the Holy Ghost. But in our culture, it is a culinary masterpiece of onion, celery and bell pepper. The basis of many of our fabulously spicy dishes.

Papa enjoys a special treat of brandied milk punch every Sunday morning. We were allowed to sip a bit from time to time. And Bananas Foster with iced cream. We weren't allowed to try to make that one until we were much, much older. Martha singed her eyebrows clean off one time when the liqueur flared up in her face.

Grandmama's cooking is so hot we have to drink a gallon of water just to put the fire out in our mouth. Her recipes use a lot of onion, garlic, cayenne pepper . . . and even more love.

❄   ❄   ❄

Clarissa wished her children could know Grandmama better. Hopefully the war had not reached her little haven in the backwaters. Maybe the alligator-infested swamps were the only safe places in the whole country right now. She should have taken her family to Grandmama when she still had the chance. Now it was too late. To travel that great a distance would be far too dangerous especially with two small children in tow. And she couldn't leave Breezie and Simon behind with their three little ones. No, they would just have to tough it out where they were and hope for the best.

Corking the ink bottle so it wouldn't spill, Clarissa closed the journal marking her page with the pen. The hammock swayed gently as she moved. The children were playing by the river under Breezie's watchful eye. Simon was sharpening tools. "Never know when a good sharp axe will come in handy," he'd say. Especially with the Yankee threat looming.

They kept close together. Slept in the same room with the adults taking turns on watch. The Yanks could take home owners by surprise in the dead of night. They were as prepared as they could be to defend themselves. How Clarissa wished Charles were there to protect them all.

As the hammock gently lulled her spirit, Clarissa's thoughts wandered to her dear husband. She recalled desperately trying to persuade him not to become involved in this horrid war of hatred.

And when her pleadings had no effect on his resolve, she did the next best thing she could think of—resorted to her grandmother's teachings and put a spell on him. One that would bring him back safe and sound. It just came to her as she was mixing up her potion of plants and roots. Such a simple little rhyme.

> *To span all time, defy the dark; We, as one, will ne'er be part. 'Tis me for thee and thou for me; Be blessed for all eternity. As I wish, so shall it be.*

Clarissa knew it was silly, but she was even more surprised when Charles drank the laced wine she offered without hesitation as she recited her poem.

Had her father not insisted she accompany him to Richmond, would fate still have brought them together?

"Papa, I'm *sooo* excited I could just spit!"

"Mind your tongue, Clarissa," her father admonished sternly. "You are not a gutter snipe. You must act the lady now."

"Yes, Papa. I'm sorry." But Clarissa was too overjoyed to be genuinely sorry. This was her very first cotillion. She was nearly sixteen. Most of the young ladies she knew had already seen two or three seasons. Her father had invited her to go with him all the way from New Orleans, Louisiana, to Richmond, Virginia, just so he could present her at the Merchants' Harvest Ball.

That was what he had told her, but Clarissa knew it wasn't entirely true. Her father was delivering one of his stallions to a business associate and had meetings with bankers in town.

François Fontaine wasn't sure who was more excited, his daughter or Martha. As the train chugged its way northeast, they made their plans. It was abundantly plain to François right from the get go he'd need to set up lines of credit all over town. Sounded like they were going to need it. Women and shopping. They were all alike.

"Don't dally, Missy. You spent too much time with the milliner. Your father will be here to collect you before you're anywhere near ready." Martha swung Clarissa around in front of her and began snugging up the ties.

"Not so tight, Martha," Clarissa gasped. "I can't breathe so trussed up." She was certain she could feel Martha's foot in the small of her back yanking the strings to the corset tighter and tighter nearly cutting her in half.

"You're just not used to dressing like a lady," Martha sniffed. "Land sakes, child, those are the most revolting man trousers you insist on wearing around."

"Just when I'm riding." Clarissa wheezed irritably as Martha gave a little extra tug. "Stop it. My eyes are already bulging out."

"Here. Get your dress on so I can fix your hair."

Such a lovely dress it was. Rich emerald green velvet of a sleeveless cut falling off the shoulder ever so gently to reveal just the slightest bit of cleavage to be considered proper for a young lady of her age.

"I'm *not* putting on those infernal hoops," Clarissa pouted. "I don't care a fig what fashion dictates. They're horrid. Just like crinolines."

"But you are going to wear one or the other," Martha insisted firmly. "The gown won't fall properly without some fullness to the skirt. You'll be tripping over the hem all evening. Your choice. Hoops or crinolines. Make your decision quickly."

"Then the crinolines. At least I'll be able to sit down when these new shoes start hurting my feet." Over her head went layer upon layer of gauzy fluff. The fullness did suit the gown, but Clarissa would have preferred the dress to be more form fitting to show off her slender figure which had finally matured into womanhood. And shorter in the hem.

What a scandal that would create. Her bosom could squish shamelessly over the bodice of a gown, but heaven forbid she should show an ankle. "I swear I'm going to move to Paris and create a whole new line of fashion," she grumbled. "One that's easy to get into and out of. Like trousers for women."

"That day will never happen," Martha predicted. "They have names for women who want to dress like men. They're called . . ."

"*Sensible*?" Clarissa censored with a frustrated pout. "Maybe I'll get Grandmama to cast a spell to change me into a man. Then I could wear trousers any time I wanted to."

"Don't talk such foolishness, child." Martha reached for a brush and tugged none too gently on Clarissa's earlobe until she sat. With a skillful hand, she piled Clarissa's hair on top of her head and held the silken strands in place with ivory combs inlayed with crystal jewels that sparkled like genuine diamonds. No one would be able to tell the difference without having the trained eye of a jeweler. At least she wouldn't have to worry about Clarissa losing them if they happened to loosen and drop to the floor unnoticed.

Just as Martha fastened the last wisp into place, a knock sounded on the outer door. "That will be your father."

Clarissa bounded into the sitting room just as François entered. One look at his daughter and he stood speechless. The spitting image of his beloved Margueretta. His wilful child had matured before his very eyes and he had been oblivious. Words caught in his throat.

"My darling, you are every bit as lovely as your mother." He drew Clarissa to him and kissed her tenderly on the forehead. "Martha, isn't she lovely?"

"Yes, sir, I certainly do agree. You'll have to keep an extra close eye on her tonight. Keep all those young dandies from stampeding a path straight for her." Martha couldn't have been more proud if she had been Clarissa's own mother. She dabbed the corner of her eye with a handkerchief. "Here." Her voice broke as she held out Clarissa's gloves. "Put these on."

Clarissa slowly drew the long white gloves way up passed her elbows with such sophistication then, with the grace of a scullery maid, poked between each finger to make sure her fingertips were jammed all the way to the ends.

With a sigh of frustration, François could only shake his head. Reaching into the pocket of his suit jacket, he withdrew a slim satin-covered box. "These are for you, my dear. I've been waiting for just the right occasion." François opened the box grinning as he watched his daughter's eyes light up.

"Oh, Papa," she squealed with delight. "They're magnificent." Clarissa gingerly reached out to touch the gems with her fingertips. In the box were a matched set of emerald teardrop earrings and necklace. The deep shade of green matched her gown perfectly.

"These were your mother's, Clarry. Now they're yours." Removing the necklace from the box, François fastened the clasp around Clarissa's lovely neck. She positioned herself in front of the mirror to admire the stones then reached for the earrings to try them on.

"A vision, I tell you. A vision." Martha melted into tears and hustled herself from the room.

"Thank you, Papa. Thank you so much. I'll cherish them always."

✳   ✳   ✳

For all her initial excitement, Clarissa was petrified. She knew not a soul at the dance. No one except her father who didn't really count in this case. Clarissa felt awkward. Shy. Out of her element. She didn't belong at a fancy ball. She belonged out in the meadow with Blue Eagle and Bella. She belonged with Grandmama way back in the bayou reciting chants and casting spells.

And she wanted to go home. None of the young men were even glancing in her direction. She perceived herself as a pariah. A leper.

Even though she felt miserable, the musical piece the band began playing was so spirited, Clarissa had a devil of a time keeping her toes from tapping. To keep from swaying with the rhythm.

Her gaze wandering, Clarissa spied her father talking with a distinguished-looking gentleman. Catching her glance, François motioned her over to meet his associate.

Keeping close to the wall to avoid colliding with the dancers, Clarissa made her way around to the opposite side of the room. The orchestra had just begun to play the Virginia Reel. One couple careened too close to the banquet table bumping unceremoniously into Clarissa. Knocked off balance, Clarissa lurched forward just as a young man turned with two glasses brimming from the punch bowl.

With speechless mortification, Clarissa gasped as the cold liquid gushed over her bodice.

"Oh. Oh, m'god," the young man stuttered. "I'm so . . . so sorry." He tossed the glasses on the table. Snatching up a linen napkin, he awkwardly began to dab at the front of Clarissa's gown as she stood frozen in despair. Her pretty dress was ruined. She could feel the sticky punch dribble between her cleavage and puddle at her feet. She could hear the titters of those close enough to witness the spectacle.

And this . . . *clod* . . . had his hands all over her *breasts*.

A frown creased her brow. "Give me that thing," Clarissa snarled as she seized the cloth from his hand and soaked up what she could by herself.

"Please forgive me. I'll see that your gown is properly cleaned. Or replaced."

The offer touched Clarissa. By the horrified look on his face, she could tell he was truly appalled by what he had done. Softening, she replied, "Thank you, but it wasn't your fault. I'm the klutz. I bumped into you. You didn't have a chance."

"My dear, are you all right?" François rushed through the crowd to his daughter's side with his associate on his heels.

"Your father's going to shoot me." The young man whispered so close to Clarissa's ear that his breath tickled the tiny hairs at the nape of her neck sending an unfamiliar flutter to the pit of her stomach.

Startled by the sensation, Clarissa giggled and whispered back. "Oh, he wouldn't shoot you." Deepening her voice, she warned, "He may have you drawn and quartered . . . but not shot." The seriousness of her tone made him take pause. He stepped back.

The other man with François smiled and said to the sodden Clarissa, "I see you've met my son."

"I'm sorry, my dear," her father apologized. "Let me introduce Mr. William Montgomery and his son, Charles. Gentlemen, my daughter, Clarissa."

"My pleasure, sirs." Clarissa dipped into a curtsey as she took each hand politely as it was offered. Her fingers lingered noticeably longer in Charles' grasp.

"Mr. Fontaine, may I request the honor of escorting your daughter back to your hotel so she may freshen up? I'd hate to think she'd miss the rest of the ball on my account."

"Oh, it's really not that bad," Clarissa assured him as she self-consciously tried to blot more punch from the front of her gown. "I'm sure it will dry soon."

"But you must be uncomfortable," Charles insisted. "And the sooner your gown is soaked, the greater chance it might be salvaged."

Turning to Clarissa, François said, "It's up to you, my dear. The lad is right, though. It would be a shame to have such a pretty dress ruined."

❄   ❄   ❄

William Montgomery fell in love with the jet black stallion Papa shipped half way across the country. We fell in love with Charles.

We spent many contented hours together with Charles, under Martha's vigilance of course, and knew very soon we were meant to be together. And we didn't even have to cast a spell.

Much to our delight and Papa's horror, Charles proposed before we left Richmond that fall. After Papa pondered and stewed about it a while, he came around. Charles is well educated and, though too young in Papa's eyes at that time to be settled, is a kind and gentle man. As Papa grew better acquainted with Charles, he could see his potential as husband for us. Papa observed how Charles treated us, how he adored us. Finally, after considerable coaxing on our part, he consented to the match with his blessings.

Papa insisted on a fairly long engagement, we being so young and all, saying these things should not be rushed and it would be best for everyone to wait at least another year before we married. However, it was so dreadfully painful to be separated from Charles. He had unleashed all kinds of wonderful sensations and feelings with no more than a simple brush of his fingertips across our cheek. Feelings we could not wait to explore.

Reluctantly, we had no choice but to return to New Orleans with Papa. Charles remained in Richmond, but was able to visit frequently. It was exciting to make plans for our future and we soon understood why Papa said we should not be too hasty. One simply cannot pull together a proper wedding in a mere few days. I'm sure Charles would have been just as happy to dispense with all the falderal. Lord knows we would have. But Papa dreamt of giving his only daughter an elegant wedding and that was what we were going to have.

How we wished Mama could have been there in the flesh to celebrate with us. But we could sense her presence smiling down on us. She knew our happiness.

Our wedding day was the fulfillment of all our dreams. Everything was perfect if there could be anything at all perfect in this world. Maybe Grandmama had something to do with the sense of magic and fairy dust in the air. Not that we needed any incantations or spells. Our handsome husband is ours forever to have and to hold of his own free will. And we shall cherish him forever.

You must remember our honeymoon in Paris. Suffice it to say it was wonderful. Sensational. Exciting. Most certainly sensual. No one word could adequately describe the new experiences we both shared.

As we no longer had Mama to advise us on what to expect in our marriage bed, and as Papa bashfully declined to explain such intimacies, our blessed Grandmama drew us aside a few days before our wedding and was thankfully frank and most graphic about what to look forward to from our new husband. As much as we appreciated Grandmama's wise words, I think instinct would have proven to be its own educator.

Our love for each other only deepened as the days passed. We relished each other's company. Our bodies meshed together as one. We explored. Touched. Experimented.

Come to think about it, we don't remember much at all about Paris itself, but we're sure the city is quite lovely.

After a glorious honeymoon, our adventure of a new life began. Upon our return, our new father-in-law presented us with a sizable estate in the Shenandoah River Valley of Virginia as a wedding gift. As Charles' father held the mortgage, the land had been claimed by him upon the death of the owner. Now it is ours.

As we examined our property for the first time, it struck us just how at home we felt. Most certainly, this is where we are meant to be for the rest of our lives.

The house is almost hidden amongst gigantic oaks. Their mighty branches intertwine to provide shelter from the stiff mountain breezes and shade from the sweltering mid-day sun. The workmanship that went into building our first home is impressive. Massive stonework forms the foundation. The blocks, three feet thick if they are an inch, must have been chiseled directly from the face of the mountain. How anyone could ever manoeuver them could only be considered a miracle. It puts us in mind of the wondrous pyramids of Egypt. Atop this foundation are beams surely felled from the very oak that grace this estate by the thousands if not millions.

And it is a good thing we have so much free-standing timber. There are so many fireplaces. Ten, if I've counted correctly. It's virtually full-time employment for young Abraham just to keep split wood ahead to feed all the fires.

The previous owner must have been planning a very large family. Unfortunately he passed without fathering an heir. There are six bedrooms and Charles still insists we're going to fill them all. At least the attempt will be most enjoyable.

On the top-most level are living quarters for our colored friends, Simon and Breezie, and their three adorable children, Abraham, Moses and Ruthie. Such dear people they are. How glad we are Charles took us along with him to Richmond that particular week.

I'm certain you will recall that Charles had business to conduct with his father which left us to our own devices for the afternoon. Charles, very generously, had given us quite a large sum of money to order a few new gowns. We did visit some more prominent shops, but nothing really interested us. The styles were old and boring. So, with a small fortune tucked into our reticule, we took to wandering the streets. We will never forget the horror we witnessed in the town square.

As Clarissa aimlessly wandered the streets of Richmond, she unwittingly approached a large wooden platform erected in the center of the cobbled square. Steel cages lined up in rows were off to one side. In the cages were human beings bound, each and every one—even young children—in heavy chains and leg irons.

The condition of some of these poor souls was deplorable. Weeping sores plagued their ebony skin. Welts from recent whippings snaked across their backs. Some had parts of their feet missing, their penalty for trying to escape to freedom. Others stared forlornly through the only eye they had left, the other victim to some sadistic overseer's punishment with a red-hot poker.

Many clung to the closest person in the packed cages. Some wept. Others cowered in fear of the unknown. Those who had given up on life itself stared blankly into oblivion.

It was truly sickening, yet Clarissa could not withdraw. One after another, slaves were dragged to the block to be examined by potential purchasers. Humiliating and degrading examinations. Not only were mouths pried open to check the soundness of teeth like some horse, but also they were stripped naked—both male and female in their prime—the tattered rags they bore rent from their bodies to be judged fit for stud or brood mare.

As respected men jeered and upstanding women tittered, the slave master would tauntingly speculate on the males' ability to produce abundant seed to sire many valuable nigger babies. Yet they stood tall mutely enduring the indecencies to which they were subjected. The anger and hatred burning in their eyes was most justified.

Trembling with fear, innocent young women stood naked before the onlookers and bidders as the master performed his examinations of degradation. Silent tears of shame flowed as the repugnant little man ascertained if their maidenhood was still intact. Then he would invite prospective buyers to do the same. Many esteemed slave owners delighted in deflowering the young ones.

If there was any mercy at all, Clarissa witnessed mothers with suckling babes at their breasts sold together. She was fully aware that many newborns were torn from their mothers' arms and left behind to be nursed by wet nurses. Clarissa could only imagine their despair.

As one buxom black woman was being prepared to be taken to the auction block, in a nearby cell, a man, Clarissa assumed to be her husband, vainly stretched his arms through the bars trying frantically to reach her for one last loving touch. Clinging to his leg was a young boy, barely a toddler, his tearless eyes wide with fear.

She could stand the atrocities no longer. In a voice that sounded foreign to herself, Clarissa shouted above the noise of the crowd, "I will take that entire family over there. Name your price."

She was ignored. Bidding began for an older man already on the block.

The despondency in the eyes of the Negress slave spoke volumes as she stood proudly at the bottom of the block, the next to be heartlessly sold. How much hardship had she already endured? How much pain and suffering? And now she was to be wrenched from her loved ones. Clarissa would not hear of it. Not this time. This family would not be separated if she could at all intervene.

Fighting her way through the crowd, Clarissa climbed onto the block and stood directly in front of the auctioneer silently demanding that he pay her mind. All bidding stopped as one gasp after another spread through the crowd as if she had committed some unspeakable sin by approaching such hallowed domain.

Mouth agape at such effrontery, the auctioneer stared at her. "Madam, kindly remove yourself from the platform."

"I have offered an open bid," she stated stubbornly. "I will be considered."

The smarmy wretch eyed her salaciously. "That item is not the consideration at present. Return with your father, young lady," he said patronizingly, "and he may wager on the merchandise of his choice."

"I conduct my own business affairs, sir, and I demand to be heard."

The crowd began to hoot and holler for her removal so the bidding could resume, but Clarissa stood her ground. "Name your price for the family," she repeated pointing to the woman at the bottom of the wooden steps with one hand while waving toward the man and little boy still locked in the cage with the other.

As she was quite ignorant of the proper procedures for such things, Clarissa should have realized, had she just bided her time and waited a few moments more, she would have had a much better chance at success. Yet there she was, right up in full view of everyone, making a total mess of her good intentions. However, it did not behoove her to slink off stage. Clarissa stuck her chin out just a little further as if the mere gesture would instill fear throughout the auctioneer's sorry soul.

Her plan was not working at all the way she had hoped. The insolent miserable excuse for a human being simply licked his lips and stepped aside pretending Clarissa wasn't there at all. The bidding resumed for the old man. One hundred. One-twenty-five. He mustn't have been considered worth much. The bidding was slow. She realized she would get nowhere until this transaction was complete.

Clarissa stepped to the edge of the platform closest to the woman taking the chance to observe her. Compared with Martha when she first came to them, this black lady had certainly been well fed to say the least. Maybe she had been a house servant. Or more likely, a cook. Her chubby cheeks were flawless, the color of silken ebony.

One-fifty. One-seventy-five. Two hundred. After three repetitions of two hundred dollars with no higher bids, the gavel struck. The old man was pronounced sold and hastily pulled away.

Clarissa would never forget the look on that woman's face as she was pushed up the steps. The sound of chain shackling her ankles rang ominously in her ears. The woman stumbled and would have fallen had Clarissa not reached out to steady her.

"One thousand for all three," she offered shouting at the top of her lungs to be heard.

A slave must not look a white master in the eye, yet the bound woman turned ever so slightly, her imploring eyes meeting Clarissa's for just a brief moment before lowering her gaze once more downward. "Bless you, ma'am," she whispered into her ample bosom.

Clarissa resolved not to fail, yet there were those who would have her do just that. Her plea for the family was ignored as the bidding began for the woman alone.

Three hundred. Three-twenty-five. She could see where this was heading. Her mistake had been to seem too eager and now everyone knew just how much she wanted to win. They would run up the bidding and the person to gain would be the slave owner. Or so she would let him think. It was only money.

Clarissa joined in the bidding. Three-fifty. Another bid the same and was accepted over hers. Three-seventy-five. Again, she was ignored as the auctioneer pointed to a gentleman, a term Clarissa used in the broadest sense of the word, waving his white kid gloves in the air.

"Five-hundred-fifty." Clarissa screamed hoping to squelch a higher offer. The auctioneer, again, didn't even acknowledge her.

Suddenly she sensed a presence beside her. At first she assumed someone had been summoned to forcibly remove her from the square. But as she turned, she realized her dear Charles had come in search of her.

He must have thought we were certainly out of our mind bidding on slaves when he knew just how much we abhorred the practice. Seeing the fire in our eyes, he questioned us not.

"Sir." Charles spoke with an air of dominance. "Is my wife's money not legal tender? Can it not purchase a slave as well as a gown?"

Clarissa was not raised to think herself any better than the next person, however, the name of Montgomery was well respected in the town of Richmond and, as soon as her husband was recognized, the tide turned. Clarissa learned her first lesson that a name could wield considerable influence.

"I believe my wife has offered a most generous sum for this woman and her family. We request that you show them as a lot."

"That's not the way of it, sir," the auctioneer stated smugly. "Bidding's already begun on the woman. No, sir. T'wouldn't be fair to these fine folk here," he insisted waving his hand over the crowd before him like some man of import.

"Then maybe you might ask these fine folk if there are any objections," Charles suggested.

"I don't have that authority, sir."

"Then who does?" Charles followed the direction of the auctioneer's nod to the heavy-set man at a make-shift desk near the cages. With his chair leaned back on its hind legs, the man had been watching the proceedings with a modicum of interest. He seemed more intent on chewing his tobacco and spewing disgusting gobs of slimy brown spittle into the dirt. Charles hopped from the platform and strode towards him with a determined air.

The trader dropped his chair to its proper position then rose as Charles approached. Clarissa did not hear the ensuing discussion and perhaps that was best. She did not care to know how the transaction was decided. Bribery. Coercion. Blackmail. To accept defeat at this point would be a tremendous blow to her pride. Yet she would not have Charles humiliated by a Samaritan action she had innocently set in motion.

The murmurings of the crowd grew louder and more agitated. Clarissa had visions of rioting in the streets of Richmond. Bloodletting. Chaos. But in reality only moments had passed before Charles returned to her side and the trader had the man and boy released from that dreadful cage and brought to the platform. She never did ask what had transpired during that conversation and Charles never did reveal it to her.

The man, in stark contrast to his wife, was poker thin. His naked back showed little sign of scarring, although there was some. The wounds looked old and well healed. Maybe in his youth, he had vainly attempted to run and was captured and whipped as an example to others not to try to escape.

With the little boy clutched in his arms, the man soberly climbed the steps. The child was frightened beyond words, his big brown eyes brimming with tears as he clung to his father. A tremulous smile crossed the man's lips as he slipped an arm around his wife to draw her close enough to brush a quick kiss across her brow. If Clarissa's heart could melt, it would have gushed to a puddle on the rough planks beneath her feet. Such a simple, loving gesture brought tears to her eyes.

Clarissa removed herself to stand beside Charles on the auction block. "We accept the bid from Mrs. Montgomery in the amount of five-hundred and fifty dollars which now includes this fine field worker and boy who will very quickly learn to earn his keep." With a wave of his hand, the bidding resumed. "Do I hear six hundred?"

Anxious not to be outbid, Clarissa almost raised her hand, but Charles held it tightly. "Yours was the last offer," he whispered. Someone at the back of the crowd accepted the six. Another shouted six-fifty. Clarissa bid seven. Then came a brief moment of awkward silence. The auctioneer repeated her bid and asked for seven-fifty. There were no takers. Again, he requested seven-fifty. Clarissa started to shiver, her eyes squeezed tightly closed in anticipation. The words, "Sold to Mrs. Montgomery for seven hundred dollars!" rang in her ears. Clarissa planted an unabashed kiss on Charles' lips and ran to greet their new friends.

As the poor family descended the stairs, Clarissa immediately instructed the overseer to remove all shackles and chains. By the look of horror on his face, she could see that was an order that didn't happen every day. By the look of surprise on the black family's faces, she could see that it certainly wasn't expected yet they readily held out their arms.

"Do you have any belongings?" Clarissa asked.

"No, missus," the black lady responded dejectedly. "Juss wuz on our backs."

"Then we're going shopping," she said as brightly and friendly as she could. "We'll take the little fellow with us. The men can get acquainted."

Shyly, the black lady allowed herself a smile as she dared to glance up. Clarissa could see a twinkle in her eye. Probably the first in many years. Hopefully, if she had anything to say about it, it would not be her last.

Clarissa could hear Charles chuckling as he strode toward them. He had paid the trader with the roll of bills she had hastily shoved into his hands. "He should have taken your first bid," he laughed triumphantly.

Would that we could win the tragic war against the black slave trade, but at what cost? All we cared at that moment was one small victory. Little did we know the whole nation would soon be divided over that same issue.

We can't help but wonder how many Southern Christians still believe that Noah's curse of Ham justifies their domination and enslavement of these people of color.

Clarissa wondered how it all would end. Victory for the South seemed unlikely at this point yet Davis refused to surrender. She feared many more fathers, sons, and brothers would have to die or be maimed for life. She feared the condition Charles might be in when he returned. If he returned at all.

By the bank of the Shenandoah River, Clarissa continued to pen her memories into her journal. Another silent tear slipped from her eye as she waited patiently for any news at all from her precious Charles.

What a blessing it was to have found Breezie that day in the square in Richmond. After overcoming her initial fright and apprehension, she and her family settled into life on the Shenandoah River as if they had been with us forever.

Poor Breezie had been beside herself when we suggested going shopping that first afternoon. Tears of gratitude flowed for days and, at times, she was actually speechless when she paused to blow her nose.

Outfitting the whole family with a few changes of clothing and footwear, we then purchased bolts of fabric to make more. Before leaving Richmond, every scrap of rag the family previously wore was burned to ash in the parlor fireplace of William Montgomery's home.

We said a final farewell to a miserable existence of darkness and greeted the new dawn of freedom. Young Abraham, with God's mercy, will remember little of his days in slavery. And never will any more of Simon's children know the weight of shackles or the sting of a whip.

What we hadn't known for some time was that two older children had been sold away from Simon and Breezie many years ago. It had been too painful for them to talk about until they grew to know us better. They still grieve, but after so many years, little Abraham had been a blessing. A chance for healing.

The first thing we did upon arriving home to Shenandoah was to gather everyone into the parlor and draw up papers of freedom for Simon, Breezie, Abraham, and to guarantee the freedom of any other offspring they may have in the future. Slaves quite often assumed the surname of their master. We would have been honored for them to choose Montgomery as theirs, however, Simon had suggested the name Freeman. It was a good name and fitting under the circumstances. So Freeman it will be for all perpetuity.

Simon proved to be a very hardworking, though quiet, individual. More than likely an acquired trait since he probably couldn't get a word in edgewise when Breezie started in with her chattering. What she found to talk about was truly amazing. Listening to her jump from one subject to the next without so much as taking a breath virtually wore us out. But she certainly is good company. Fussy to the very last detail. Loyal to a fault. And our very best friend.

In the quiet of evenings, we would sit around the kitchen table and teach the Freeman family to make out letters and numbers. Many a night we'd curl up by the fireplace to read little story books to Abraham pointing at the words as we went along. Smart as a whip, Abraham soon knew the stories so well he'd pick up words we'd deliberately skip.

Knowledge can be a dangerous commodity and many slave owners thought a schooled slave might conceivably cause a threat. In some parts it's actually considered illegal for slaves to read and write. Keep them ignorant. Keep them subjugated and they wouldn't rise up to revolt. Maybe so, but the day will come at some point—though maybe not during our lifetime—when they will be free to make their way in the world and they will have to know how to spell and figure to succeed on their own. Breezie, Simon and their children will have that advantage. Their spelling skills will be rudimentary—basic phonetics—but they will fare all right.

Though we doubt all the teaching in the world would help Breezie learn to enunciate her words properly. But that is just one of her many great charms. We encouraged her to practice spelling by starting her own journal. We believe she has done so although we have yet to witness her attempting to write in it. But that is up to her.

An infant's newborn cry pierced the minutes of early dawn. Faint from exhaustion, Clarissa lay back on her pillow, a weak smile crossing her lips as she closed her eyes. Labor had been hard and long, but the painful effort was worth it. Charles finally had his son. And what a fine little lad he was. Plump and pink, the babe filled his untried lungs to capacity and screeched angrily. He was out and now he was hungry.

As Clarissa drew their son to her breast, Charles tenderly stroked the fluffy down on his baby's head and smiled lovingly down on his darling wife. Childbirth was as natural as the air he breathed, but had Charles known just how excruciating the whole experience would be for Clarissa, he would have refused her insistence to begin a family. Had he lost her in the birthing process, he would never have forgiven himself.

The child tugged voraciously at her nipple. Clarissa winced at the unexpected tightening in her womb. "I like this much better when you do it," she whispered to her husband.

"Yo'll git use to it, Miz Clarry." Overhearing the intimate comment not meant for her ears, Breezie laughed merrily as she bustled through the bedroom door to gather the soiled linen. "Dose nipples o' yorn'll tuff'n up an' yo'll like it juss fine'n dandy. Trus me on dis one."

"Speaking from experience, are you Breezie?" Charles teased.

"Yassir, I shurly am. No greater feelin dan sucklin a babe at yo bres. An' I've don my share o dat. Wet-nurst so many babes, caint keep a'count o' dem all. Gud Lord shud'a blest me wit mo teats an' I still wudn't haf ne'r nuf. I'd've younguns hangin' off me like dat ol' sow in da barn an' it'd pleez me juss fine."

"Well, you and Simon are just going to have to get busy and have another one," Charles winked at his wife, "or we just may beat you to it."

Breezie laughed heartily at the look of disbelief that crossed Clarissa's face. "I tinks Miz Clarry juss might haf sumfin ta say bout dat right now, you randy houn'. Shoo yerself an' let dis po wumin git sum ress."

Breezie nudged her ample body in beside Charles to observe the new baby nurse. "Gud latch," she commented knowledgeably. "No starvin' ta def fer dis li'l man."

✳　　✳　　✳

The birth of our first child, William, was indeed a celebration. Papa, Grandmama and Martha arrived just a few days afterwards and, thankfully, we had produced a healthy son for them to fuss over.

Breezie gave birth to another darling little boy, Moses, almost nine months to the day after William. She must have taken Charles' suggestion to heart and had her way with Simon. And at least once more for Ruth came along a year and a half after our sweet Margaret.

Baby Moses was christened on a bright Sunday morning on the bank of the Shenandoah behind our home. As a sympathizer to our cause to abolish slavery, our good friend, Father Francis, was delighted to perform the ceremony for us. In his sermon, the good Father spoke about the first Moses who led his people from slavery in Egypt and also of our present-day Moses, Harriet Tubman.

Harriet was born a slave in Dorchester County, Maryland. She endured tremendous physical abuse but was finally successful in escaping. It's been said that when Harriet crossed the state line into freedom, she looked at her hands to see if she was the same person. As if she had physically changed in some miraculous way.

Making twenty trips back to the South, Harriet risked her life relying on scant knowledge of geography, clever disguises, and her own ingenuity to evade hunters. She succeeded in leading more than three hundred others to freedom using a series of safe houses and routes we call the Underground Railroad. That is an unusual name because it is neither underground nor a railroad.

It is, however, perhaps our most dramatic anti-slavery protest to date. Slave owners regard the Underground as organized theft, a threat to their livelihood.

It is illegal to assist a slave to freedom and, we've heard that in the State of Delaware, a free black person who is found guilty of smuggling slaves is not sentenced to prison but sold into slavery himself.

Punishment is harsh, but we do what we can to help and to honor the Freeman children who have been lost to the family forever.

We probably should not even commit any of this to paper or elaborate on any specifics lest we be found out and unintentionally give away a location of a safe house or escape route. So we will say no more on the subject.

Not for the lack of trying, it was another three years after William before our Margaret was born. Delivery was much easier this time partly, we assume, because we had more of an idea what to expect and tried our best not to become so anxious.

What a little angel she is. Petite. Perfect. Dark hair just like us and our mother. We call her Bijou, *our jewel, which she is. Most of the time. But she can get into just as much mischief as William and Breezie's boys, if not more.*

You must remember the time she took up with Charles' shaving soap and razor then proceeded to shave off her eyebrows, then have a go at the dog and four of her cats. Thankfully, we caught up to her before she reached the horses and cattle. We did have some strange looking animals for a few weeks. And the child does have a tendency to wander off. The next time we go berry picking, the cow bell is going around her neck.

But there will be no berries until the Yankees are well away from the valley and we have no way of knowing when that will be.

Clarissa could almost taste the plump berries she was sure grew ripe along the trestle trail. But she would not chance anyone venturing further than the end of the lane. Not even for one of Breezie's mouth-watering cobblers.

Breezie wanted nothing to do with our little old plot that day Charles left us. It seems so long ago now. While Charles was packing his duffle and Simon saw that Charles' beloved horse, Diablo, had a

good feed of grain and his coat was brushed to a glistening sheen, we mixed up our brew in the summer kitchen. More than a few salty tears dissolved into the mix.

And as before composed, what took us so unaware was that Charles drank of his own will, almost as if he was hoping himself that the spell had merit and would keep him safe to come home to us.

The last we heard from Charles was a note dated the thirtieth day of June of this year. He seemed to be faring well at that time, but much has happened since then. The battle at Chancellorsville. The death of Stonewall Jackson. The news of the horrendous battle at the little town of Gettysburg, Pennsylvania, reached us just this morning. Forty-five thousand good men and boys lost on both sides and we pray to God our Charles is not one of them.

We haven't quite decided whether knowing if Charles is injured is better than not knowing. When he was struck down during the first battle of Manassas, we hadn't received that news until many days later. Long since any danger of death had passed by. How we longed to be there by his side as he recuperated in that dreadful place they call an infirmary. We did manage a brief visit when Charles was finally brought to the hospital in Front Royal.

From head to toe, we inspected his body just to be certain for ourself that no appendage was missing. All fingers and toes were accounted for. Though dreadfully thin, Charles seemed to have regained much of his strength after his ordeal. What caused us the most anguish was the sight of the wound that streaked his chest in the jagged pattern of a bolt of lightning. Had it been any deeper, we're certain our husband would have been sliced in two.

By his own account, we could only imagine the stench of rotting gangrenous flesh causing amputations to be performed in the makeshift surgery on the field without so much as a drop of chloroform.

The screams of those poor souls haunt our imagination. Maggot-infested food if there was any food to be found at all. Patients drowning in their own filth for want of competent nursing care. Charles was adamant he had received adequate attention while he recovered. We are certain he greatly downplayed his discomfort to lessen our anxiety. We pray he never has to endure such conditions again.

*So, until we hear otherwise, we choose to believe our Charles is alive
and well. Any day now we will look up and see him saunter up the lane to
surprise us. Blessed be that day.*

*There is much throughout the years that I am not going to try to record.
Day-to-day happenings and mundane chores. It would fill many volumes.
You will recall everything in time. Open your heart. Open your mind. Open
your soul. You will know and you will remember. I look forward to being
one with you at some future time in our existence. I am as certain of that
as I am that the sun will forever shine. That the stars will forever twinkle
in the heavens. We must have faith. Without faith in these trying times,
we have nothing.*

Clarissa had convinced herself as well to keep faith that the
spell she chanted before Charles left for war was more than simple
tomfoolery. To believe that she, herself, would read these words at
some point in the future, or that someone who had assumed her spirit
would, heartened her.

If nothing else, the children would have something to pass on to
their own children so they would know all about their grandparents.
When this war was over, she'd take them to New Orleans to visit her
father and Grandmama. She'd have Blue Eagle teach them the ways of
his people, just as he had taught her.

Her childhood friend, Ava, had taken over Mr. Muelker's bakery.
Soo Lei had run off to California when gold was discovered in 1849 and
hadn't been heard from since. She was only thirteen years old. Clarissa
couldn't imagine her daughter leaving home so young.

It was nearing the end of November but the sun had warmed the
river bank just enough so Clarissa could write in her journal without her
fingers cramping from the cold. Here she freed herself of worry, freed
herself of concern and dreamt of Charles' return.

Laying down her pen, Clarissa closed her eyes to envision Charles
as he came to her. Arms flung wide to receive her loving body next to
his. Joyous laughter mingled with tears.

Her surrealistic reunion suddenly faded as Clarissa realized all was not as it should be. The distant rumble of wagon wheels, shots and shouting invaded the deceptive peacefulness of the valley.

Rolling from the hammock, Clarissa dropped her journal and started up the incline just as Breezie huffed to meet her with a panicked cry.

"Dem *Yankees*, Miz Clarry! Dem *Yankees* is cummin. We'z gots ta hide!"

TWO

Charles

It would be his first gala since graduating from West Point, but Charles was as determined not to attend as his father was adamant that he should. He was convinced the whole affair would be nothing more than a meat market with him on display for the young debutantes and their mothers looking for a suitable husband. He would much rather sneak out of town and go fishing with a couple of his chums.

It was the perfect time of day. The brush of evening had painted the sky with vibrant shades of pink and gold. With one eye out the window, the other on his new suit which had just been delivered from the tailor, Charles debated whether or not to defy his father, simply climb out the window and shinny down the tree. After all, he was twenty years old. If he didn't want to go to a stupid old dance, he shouldn't have to.

A fish or a pretty girl.

Charles reached for the suit. Not that he wouldn't have stood up to his father if he really wanted to. All his friends would be at the ball. And his father did mention the breeder who delivered his new horse all the way from Louisiana had brought his teenaged daughter along. It would be rude of him not to at least make an effort to meet them.

The orchestra had already warmed up by the time the Montgomerys arrived at the reception hall. A few couples had started to dance. As Charles suspected, young ladies lined the walls. In some places, three deep. He'd have to run the gauntlet just to reach the refreshment table.

Eyeing two comrades from West Point, Charles excused himself from his father to make his way to the back of the hall to chat. Occasionally he'd catch the eye of this girl or that and nod graciously as they batted their lashes flirtatiously at him. Gentleman that he was, he'd dance with a few, but only because it would be expected of him.

Deeply engrossed in conversation, Kent Billings and Jonathan Morrow paused as Charles approached.

"What can I tell you, old boy?" Kent greeted. "Some likely prospects here, don't you think?"

"Can't say I'm too interested," Charles replied absently.

"What?" exclaimed Jonathan. He shook his head with a click of his tongue. "Oh, you're *not* going to tell me you'd rather be *fishing*!" Jonathan sympathetically patted him on the back. "You're just not all there, son. You mean to say you wouldn't like to tap toes with Carol Abernathy over there?"

"Forget Carol," Kent scoffed. "She's got a face like an old shoe. But I'd shuffle a few steps with Mabeline James in a heartbeat."

With a playful shove, Charles pushed Kent out onto the dance floor. "Well, go for it, old man. Be my guest."

After only a moment's hesitation, Kent stuck out his chin and said, "Maybe I just might." He straightened himself up and made his way toward the pretty Mabeline.

Jonathan quickly caught the arm of Maddy Gilmour as she passed by and sashayed her onto the dance floor.

Feeling quite suddenly abandoned, Charles called after them both, "That's okay, I'll just go get myself some punch."

Those guys will be hitched by next summer, you mark my word, Charles thought dejectedly to himself. Shaking his head at the thought of the misery they were both headed for, he solemnly vowed it would never happen to him.

Making his way to the refreshment table, Charles carefully ladled punch into two cups—one for his father if he could find him in this crowd—then turned to try to catch a glimpse of his friends making fools of themselves on the dance floor.

I wasn't looking where I was going and, from out of nowhere, she bumped into me. The glasses tipped in my grasp spilling the punch down the front of her gown. I was horrified. Stammered inane apologies. Then, like a flustered fool, I tried to clean up the mess I had made of her. She just stood there with me making an idiot of myself pawing at her bosom. The look on her face. If I hadn't been so mortified myself, I would have found it comical.

I offered to have her gown taken care of but she insisted it was merely an unfortunate incident of her own making. She said I didn't have a chance.

And she was correct. The instant I laid eyes on her, I knew I was lost. I had fallen in love. Head over heels in love. And the impression I must have made! There before me was an angel and I had just ruined her pretty gown.

From the corner of my eye, I happened to notice a man with Father coming towards us. I assumed the other man was Father's guest, Mr. Fontaine from Louisiana, and this girl I had just sullied would have to be his daughter. And I could only imagine I had just committed grounds for a duel.

"Your father's going to shoot me," I whispered pathetically into her ear.

"Oh, he wouldn't shoot you." Her soft giggle eased my mind until she whispered seriously, "He may have you drawn and quartered . . . but not shot."

Father smiled and said, almost too apologetically, "I see you've met my son."

Mr. Fontaine didn't seem angry. More mildly amused, thank the merciful heavens. He introduced us to his daughter revealing the name of the goddess to whom my life would become forever bound. "Gentlemen," he said, "my daughter, Clarissa."

Clarissa. My Cajun queen. I believed, with her by my side, we could conquer the world. Allowing her name to linger on my lips, it engraved itself indelibly in my mind. In my soul. I was thoroughly enamored by her glowing tawny skin, by her rosy cheeks and sensuously plump cherry red lips. But, most of all, her gentle grace had captivated my soul.

After I had escorted Clarissa and her companion back to the hotel so she could change her gown, we returned to the ballroom to spend the rest of the evening with her held in my arms. I danced with no other which did not go unnoticed by my friends. I endured countless rounds of ragging. But no matter.

Spending the next few days showing Clarissa around town only proved that I was unwilling to live a day without her. She was so sweet. Adorable. Impulsive.

Unique. That's what Clarissa was. How could I possibly let her return to New Orleans without announcing my intentions of undying fidelity?

So much for my steadfast declarations of bachelorhood. It never again entered my mind. The lengthy betrothal Mr. Fontaine imposed seemed interminable, but we finally married and settled in our home on the Shenandoah River. All I could think about was my bride. Blooming with abandon, free of inhibition, Clarissa thoroughly captured my heart.

I could not believe my good fortune. With my loving wife beside me, two wonderful children, a prosperous farm, what more could a man ever hope for?

For ten wonderful years, she slept in my arms every single night. Then came the war.

I reckoned telling Clarissa that I planned to enlist would be worse than any battle I could ever imagine. I was right.

"What do you mean you're going to enlist?" The question was edged with the sharp tone of disbelief and terror. "Why are you getting yourself all messed up in this thing? It isn't our fight. We don't believe in keeping slaves. Why should you help others who do?" Clarissa pouted, a soft drawl crossing her lips in a breathless whisper. "It's all just mass suicide. You know that."

Charles repeated his rehearsed list of reasons why he should join and fight for the Southern way of life. He could feel the temperature of the room drop drastically with each point. He could see Clarissa's eyes narrow just a little bit more with each sentence he uttered until they were no more than mere slits beneath a darkened brow.

Charles turned away to look out over the river. The blazing red sun reflected it's glowing rays on the rippling water. Closing his eyes tightly, Charles unsuccessfully forced back the tears but refused to show Clarissa his weakness. He didn't relish the thought of being away from her. At the same time, he couldn't tuck tail and run.

Taking a deep breath to regain his composure, Charles whispered, "Clarry, I have no choice."

"We can just slip away, Charles. Go where this war can't touch us. Suppose we just pack up and take a trip . . . Europe . . . Paris, maybe, until this whole thing just blows over. General Lee told your father it won't last any time at all."

"I can't just run away, Clarry."

"Run away?" She gave her long curls a vigorous shake. "Nonsense. You'd be taking your loving family on a much-deserved vacation."

She stepped toward him. He stepped away. Charles knew all too well her powerful womanly wiles. Should Clarissa touch him, he'd be lost to her charms and would deny her nothing.

"And what do you think would happen when we came back, if we had anything to come back to at all?" Charles looked at her with downcast eyes.

"Do you think you'd be ostracized if you don't fight?"

"I don't know what to think."

"Oh, Charles. I can live without silly balls and high society. What I can't live without . . . is you."

He chanced an embrace. "Clarry," his voice was barely audible over the lump in his throat. "I have to go." Smoothing back the dark curls from her face, he kissed the hollow of her neck, the place he knew would usually melt her resolve. But not today.

Pushing him roughly away, she said sternly, "Stop trying to change the subject." Then just as suddenly, she pulled him to her. With a strong swish of her long, dark hair, Clarissa angrily shook a finger in his face. "I should turn you into a toad this very minute, Charles Montgomery. Then we'll see just how far you get."

Clarissa refused to speak with him for three whole days. And to have her cold shoulder pressed against him at night rather than snuggling into her femininely softness, was almost too much for Charles to bear. But he knew he had little choice. He prayed she would understand.

So when Clarissa offered him an enchanted goblet of wine, he drank. Not only to mollify his wife, but to ease her pain of separation. To bring her comfort. If she wanted to believe that her mystical brew could bring them any protection and his safe return . . . so be it. He willingly played along. Anything to wipe the tears from her eyes.

We were fortunate to be camped in the Valley where I was allowed to visit the farm from time to time. That seemed to bring some small comfort to Clarissa, although each time I left was pure torture. I often thought of not going home until after the war had ended. That seeing her so often might be worse than not seeing her at all.

Then as I lay near death on the battlefield at Manassas, I feared I would never see my darling wife again. To this day, I know not how I survived. Was it by simple chance the sword that slashed my breast missed my beating heart by mere fractions? Was it the spell she cast that protected me? Faith has all but escaped me. Belief wanes. But at the time, I chose to believe the Good Lord was watching out for me and it was by His merciful grace that I lived to fight another day.

The shroud of good fortune cloaked me from harm. So much so that, on some unconscious level, I may have begun to feel quite invincible. The Second Battle of Manassas at Bull Run, Harper's Ferry, Antietam. I survived them all as thousands of good men and boys fell around me. Then General Lee made an offer I couldn't refuse.

※ ※ ※

The army needed men willing to infiltrate the Union defenses and get as much information as possible on troop movements, campaign maneuvers, anything at all that would be useful to the Confederate cause. Charles could do his country far greater service in this new capacity.

Sworn to secrecy, he was advised against telling anyone of his exploits. He didn't like keeping anything from his wife. Yet Charles knew his silence would be a matter of the utmost importance. Capture by the Federals would be cause for the indictment of treason. Death by hanging. Firing squad. It was a chance he was willing to take for any hope to end this bloody battle between the States.

Charles would not be working alone. Assigned as his accomplice was Belle Boyd, a young spy from Martinsburg, West Virginia. Putting herself in danger many times to bring General Stonewall Jackson pertinent information about Union troop movement, Belle often felt the spit of gunfire as bullets pierced her skirts. For her bravery, Belle had been awarded the honourary rank of Captain.

Charles once asked her how she came upon all the information for which she so eagerly endangered her life. With a laugh, Belle had told him that many of the Union officers she frequently found herself in company with were so arrogant, they simply forgot that a woman could both listen *and* remember. Combined with a little flattery and attention it was *they* who soon forgot who they were speaking to. Belle could practically pick their secrets right out of their pockets. With a cipher Charles taught her, she coded the messages then galloped through the back countryside to Jackson's camp.

Belle collected her information just by being her femininely self. Charles infiltrated Federal camps disguised as a civilian veterinarian to treat their horses. He then found his way back to his own lines with all he could find out about upcoming offensives.

It was in Front Royal that Charles had first met Belle. Installed as matron at the hospital where Charles was eventually taken to recover after being wounded at Bull Run, Belle had amused her patients with her escapades.

Many an evening as the men recuperated, Belle would sit among them telling her stories. Mischievously she'd always threaten to leave them hanging without finishing her tale.

"What happened, Belle?" the men would want to know.

She was leading up to something spectacular as she always did keeping them in suspense just a little longer. Belle paused for effect. With a shake of her head, she stood abruptly and said, "No. I think that's enough for one night. I've talked too much as it is. You men need your rest."

"Aw, come on, Belle," one man after another complained.

"You can't just leave us on the edge like that," Geoffrey Bates groaned.

"Yeah, Belle," Russell English added. "You've got to finish the story. I might be dead by tomorrow. Then I'll never find out what happened."

With a heavy sigh, Belle would relent. "Well, all right. But just a little more." With a swish of her skirt, she would take her seat and continue her story.

One that struck a nerve in Charles remained in the back of his mind throughout the early years of the campaign. Belle had shot to death a Federal soldier who had ransacked her home and threatened her mother.

Charles wondered what Clarissa would have done under those same circumstances. Both she and Belle were feisty. Both were protective to a fault. Would Clarissa have the same fortitude to place herself in danger to protect hearth and home? Surely she would. Charles had no doubt.

That thought frightened him beyond anything he had yet faced.

Their little war of espionage was short lived. In the summer of 1863, Belle was arrested while visiting her home in Martinsburg and found herself jailed in Carroll Prison.

With forged signatures copied from captured documents on his passes, Charles followed Belle to Washington to help her escape, but she was too well guarded.

Reassigned a new partner Charles resumed his duties of espionage though it wasn't nearly as exciting. His thoughts often slipped to the flamboyant '*Belle Rebelle*' and wondered how she fared.

Weary weeks of waging war took their toll on everyone with the loss of many a fine man. Food was sometimes plentiful. Sometimes not. Sometimes they slept warm and dry. Other times they spent days in pouring rain soaked to the skin without a stitch of dry clothing to put on. It was little wonder disease took more lives than enemy bullets.

Cold weather was beginning to set in and the troops would soon be preparing winter quarters. Charles filled his lungs with frigid air and watched his warm breath exhale in a cloudy puff. Attached once more to the Thirty-eighth Virginia Regiment, Charles awaited his next assignment which he hoped would be soon. The challenge of being a spy was certainly far more exciting than sitting around a boring camp all winter. Perhaps he could use his furlough and get home for Christmas. The perfect surprise for Clarissa and the children.

How he longed to tuck his children into their beds at night then curl up in front of a blazing fireplace with Clarissa snuggled beside him.

Mail call interrupted his daydream. Hoping for a letter from home, Charles was disappointed. But there was one from Henry Francis, their priest. Although that did surprise him somewhat, he thought it kind of the Father to think of him and send a letter. Charles pulled up a block of chopped wood intending to sit by the fire, but curiosity got the better of him. Ripping open the envelope, Charles read the first line.

My heart stopped. I couldn't breathe. I was suffocating. Holding that letter in my hand, my legs crumpled from beneath me, unable— unwilling—to hold me upright. The shock was just too great to bear. If I had the strength at that moment to reach for my pistol or saber I would have ended my life right then and there. I am unashamed of the tears that fell as I wept against the breast of the private who came to my aid when I collapsed. He gently pulled the letter from my hand and, as he could read nothing but his own name, handed it to another.

"Good merciful heaven," the Lieutenant whispered as he scanned the letter. "Cap'n's family done all been wiped out by the Yanks."

Jubal Hennessy folded the note and tucked it into Charles' breast pocket with a friendly pat. "Someone go fetch Chaplain Meredith," he ordered helplessly. "Maybe a word from God will help ease Cap'n's suffering."

But no 'word from God' could ease my pain. My brain could not absorb any sound over my own thought as I recited every single word of that letter until I had committed it to memory.

The 26ᵗʰ day of November, 1863

My dear Charles, wrote Father Francis. *It is with the utmost sorrow that I must inform you of the unfortunate passing of your dear wife, Clarissa, and both your darling children. If murder can be a more apt term, so be it.*

Troops of treacherous Federals have been taking it upon themselves to ransack each farm along the river valley to, not only gather supplies for the Union larder, but render the fields useless to produce further crop. This task is surely being accomplished. Smoke and flame can still be seen for miles.

From what I could gather from the Freemans, as the force drew near your home, Breezie gathered the children into the cellar so, if need be, they could escape by means of a tunnel Simon had the foresight to dig from the root cellar to the river bank.

Ignoring Breezie's pleas to join them in hiding, Clarissa took up watch with the men. As the Federals came within sight, your wife met them at the end of the lane imploring them to take what they wanted and leave them in peace.

Unbeknownst to Clarissa, the troops had consumed many jugs of whiskey which they had confiscated along the way.

The house was searched. Breezie and the children were discovered before they could escape.

Half a dozen or so soldiers dismounted and pressed upon Clarissa. Breaking free, she reached into the pocket of the overcoat she wore, pulled out one of your pistols and shot dead the first soldier to approach her.

The others drew their weapons and fired upon her just as William pushed passed his guard and ran between the men and his mother. He was struck in the back and perished in Clarissa's loving arms.

Even though she was severely wounded by the same bullets that passed through William, she snatched up the axe Abraham had dropped nearby and began swinging at anything and everything—man and beast alike.

Margaret began to scream and fight for release from the man who held her. The more she struggled, the more insistent the soldier became that she remain quiet and still. As her outcry added to the melee, the soldier became more agitated, drew his pistol and silenced the child. An instant later, as the axe cleaved his skull in two, Clarissa drew her last breath.

Your dear ones are laid to rest on the knoll overlooking the river where the oak saplings grow.

You have my deepest sympathies dear friend. May you find comfort in the knowledge that your loved ones are forever at peace in God's tender embrace.

We pray for your safe return. May God be with you.
Henry Francis

Charles did not feel the presence of God. He felt nothing for anyone or anything lying forlornly on his narrow uncomfortable cot, unable to talk, unwilling to eat. In unrelenting torment, days passed one after another. His only thought was to plot revenge, risk desertion, and hunt down the murderers who took his family . . . his life . . . from him. As the chill of night descended, he felt no cold. The burning fires of hell raged deep within his soul.

The Yankees would pay for this. With his dying breath the Yankee dogs would pay. If he had to kill Lincoln with his own bare hands, Charles would find a way to avenge the murder of his precious family. But he could not accomplish anything mourning in his bed.

Rising one bleak morning, Charles threw back the flap to his tent and stepped out into the crisp winter air. Snow had fallen through the night blanketing the ground. The sun was just beginning to peek over the horizon. Making his way to the campfire where the cook had a pot of coffee brewing, Charles poured himself a cup and squatted before the fire. The enlisted men were just rising and started milling around waiting for mess call.

"Good to see you up and about, Cap'n." Jubal Hennessy regarded his friend closely but did not mention the dark circles that had appeared under his eyes. Or his sunken cheeks. Or the sickly pallor that had replaced his ruddy complexion.

Jubal was a good man. A few years younger than Charles, a bit on the short side, but wiry, strong, and agile as an alley cat, he had made his mark in the ranks as the best sharp shooter in the army.

"I'm going after them," Charles declared viciously. "I'll find them. First them, then Lincoln."

The twenty-sixth day of November. The day Lincoln had unwittingly been sentenced to death. By the twenty-sixth day of December, the President would be dead. Charles would benevolently grant him Christmas day to spend with his family. A privilege that had forever been stolen from him. Then Lincoln would die.

"I understand your grievin', Cap'n, but you might want to do some rethinkin'," the Lieutenant urged. "You ain't gettin' anywheres near Washin'ton. Security's so tight the Federals are arresting everyone and everything."

"I've done it before. Many times. I'll get through or die trying." The fire sizzled as he tossed what was left of his coffee onto the hot coals. Charles rose and arched his stiffened back.

The ferocity in his voice took Jubal by surprise. Captain Montgomery had always been regarded as a gentle man, fair and decent. But the death of his family had hardened him. Made him cynical and vengeful. Hennessy didn't blame him. Probably do the same thing had the same cards been dealt to him. There'd be no reasoning with him yet. Perhaps in a few more days. Or a few weeks. But not just yet.

Maybe if he went along he could eventually knock some sense into his friend's skull before he got himself into too much trouble. Jubal's parents were already gone. He had no wife or children. His farm had already been burned to the ground. Hell, he had nothing to lose.

As Charles turned to leave Jubal blurted, "Cap'n, to my way of thinkin', you shouldn't be agoin' alone. Take me. Someone's gotta watch your back."

With or without permission, Charles was bound and determined to head for Shenandoah. Demanding the furlough due him, he was packed and saddled within the hour. It took little persuading to have Jubal accompany him. With Jubal's wiles and Charles' knowledge of the valley, if anyone could locate the Yankee bastards, they could.

It took a week of steady riding to reach Front Royal by little traveled roads and back trails. As dusk fell, they were home.

Home. That word meant nothing to me anymore. As I pulled Diablo up beside the gate to the property, I simply stared at the house that was now

no more than a few sticks of lumber nailed together. No longer did it hold any promise of a future for me and my family. There would be no more laughter here. No more love.

Charles circled his horse at the end of the lane.

"We going in, Cap'n," Jubal asked quietly, "or beddin' down out here?"

A dark frown creased Charles' forehead as he struggled for the strength to answer. Finally he said, "We've come this far, guess we'd better go in."

Candlelight could be seen glowing from the windows as the two bedraggled soldiers rode up to the house. Lamp oil had run out months ago. Simon heard riders coming and was waiting suspiciously on the porch, rifle in hand.

Raising the weapon Simon took aim and shouted, "You fellers hold it right there. If'n yur lookin' fer trouble we don' want no mo' here dis house. We'z had 'nuf."

A weary voice answered, "It's Charles, Simon."

Squinting into the rapidly darkening night, it took him a moment to recognize Charles. "Lord have mercy," Simon whispered as he lowered the rifle. "Breezie, Breezie," he called through the door. "It's Mista Charles. Mista Charles is home." Propping the gun against the wall Simon hobbled down the steps and took the reins of both men's horses. "It's good to have ya home, suh. I'll ten' to da hosses. Yous juss go on in and git yurselfs warmed up."

Just then Breezie appeared on the veranda. Wringing her hands in her apron, tears began to flow as she met Charles at the bottom of the steps. Flinging her arms around him, she almost toppled them both to the ground. "Oh. Mista Charles. You dun cummed home safe an' soun'. Oh, mercy. Blessed be da Lord. He dun bring y'all back to us. We pray'd long an' hard fer dis day. Yassuh, we shurly did."

Suddenly overwhelmed, Charles could not stop the tears. Through the sobs he managed to say, "I got Henry's letter."

"I know, suh," Breezie cooed as she held him tightly. "I know. You cum in dis house now an' git sum gud hot food."

Jubal mumbled something about helping Simon bed down the horses as Charles allowed Breezie to lead him into the house. The children swarmed over him. Breezie's children. Simon's children. Not his own.

The house seemed dreadfully somber and quiet. Lifeless. Even with Breezie's and the children's incessant chatter. And as he plodded up the stairs to his room . . . their room . . . Charles' heart was heavy with grief. He didn't want to go in. Shadows from the fireplace played against the walls as he stood in the doorway. Charles set the candle on the bureau.

The room was void of life. Empty. Closing his eyes Charles tried to conjure up the image of Clarissa. If she were there with him, even in spirit, sleeping in their bed may just be bearable. In his mind's eye she came to him. Lovely beyond words. Soft. Feminine. Delightful. When he opened his eyes though, she vanished. If only he could keep his eyes closed forever.

Snatching a blanket and pillow from the bed, Charles curled up on the braided rug unwilling to sleep in the bed without his beloved wife. As exhaustion finally overtook him Charles once more felt Clarissa nestled in his arms.

❊   ❊   ❊

Morning brought no more peace of spirit than when he had gone to bed the night before. Sun shone through the window. Bright red coals glowed in the fireplace. Birds braving the winter to come twittered cheerily from the treetops. It should have been a happy day. Would have been a glorious homecoming had his family been there to greet him. But they weren't there and Charles could find no spark of happiness.

Pulling on his boots, Charles joined the others already waiting in the kitchen for breakfast. Bacon sizzled in the pan. Breezie's buttery biscuits filled a bowl on the table. The children had hunted up a few eggs from the chickens the Yankees hadn't run off with.

"We'll be leaving today," Charles stated heavily as he poured himself a strong cup of coffee.

"Mista Charles," Breezie objected. "Caint yous stay juss a li'l longer? Yous muss be dog tir'd. Yous needs ta res up."

"Can't Breezie. We're going after the Yankees who came through the valley. Simon, what can you tell me about them? Have you heard which way they went?"

With tears glazing his eyes, old Simon fiddled with his fork before answering. "There wuz a gud doz'n or so, suh. Maybe mo'. Din't take no speshul note of em. But they's headed wes from here."

Abraham stepped forward. "I remember one, Mister Charles. He had long hair. Greasy, yellow hair. And his teeth were bad. And I remember he wore a red bandana around his neck."

"That could be almost any of them, Abe."

"Then take me with you," he said bravely. "I can tell you when we see him."

Smiling for the first time in days, Charles tousled the boy's black curly head. "I think you'd better stay here, son. Help your mother and father." Young Abe was a good boy. Trustworthy and loyal. Thanks to Clarissa, Abraham's speech and diction were almost as proper as his own.

"But Moses is getting big enough. I want to help. For Miss Clarry."

Charles looked to Breezie and Simon for guidance, but all he saw was the boy's father nodding in agreement. "He'd be a gud help, suh. My boy's very sharp. Don' miss much."

"I can't say how long we'll be gone," Charles argued. "It won't be safe. I'd hate like hell for something to happen to him. I'd never forgive myself."

"Please, Mister Charles," Abe begged. "I'm not afraid. I can do it."

Jubal pulled Charles aside. "He might get to places we can't, just because he's colored, Cap'n."

Charles pondered the possibilities. He still didn't like it, but he relented on one condition. "You'll not put yourself in danger for any reason," he stated adamantly. "If I tell you to skedaddle and hide, you'll do it."

"Yes, sir. I'll do whatever you say."

"Then go saddle up the old mule. I suspect she's all we've got left."

"Yes, sir. The Yanks thought she was too old and tough to be good eating."

❋   ❋   ❋

Charles sat on the knoll overlooking the river among the stones that marked his family's graves. It would be a pretty spot when the leaves returned in the spring. Now it was just bare and forsaken. He'd plant roses. Yellow roses. Clarissa would like that. He had to force himself to climb the hill in the first place. Now he couldn't pull himself away. All Charles could think of was the day his reason for living was taken from him. Over and over he relived the scene as Father Francis' letter had painted for him. Anger seethed from every pore. Hatred toward the vigilantes who stole his precious family from him grew by the minute as did self-loathing for not being there to protect them all.

A rustling noise behind him drew his attention. Breezie had come to find him.

"Mista Hen'sey says he's a'ready, suh. All saddled ta go. I'za filled a bag wit' food from da cellar. Dem so'jurs di'nt git it all."

"Thank you, Breezie. Don't make yourselves short, though. I'm sure we can scrounge up what we need on the way."

"No, suh. Miz Clarry made shor we hid plenty, bless her lovin' heart." Breezie dabbed her eyes with the tip of her apron. "We miss em sumfin awful, suh."

"I know, Breezie," Charles said softly as he wrapped his arms around her comfortingly. "I do, too."

Young Abraham was fairly dancing with anticipation as Charles returned to the house. With one look at the old mule he'd be riding, Charles had his doubts the poor thing would make it two miles down the road. He'd buy the boy a horse if they could find a decent one anywhere along the way. In the meantime, the going would be slower than he'd bargained for.

"Don' you worry 'bout nuthin' Mista Charles." Breezie still dabbed at her eyes.

"Thank you, Breezie. I appreciate that."

"Take good care o' my boy, suh," Simon pleaded. "Y'all come back safe."

"I'll do the best I can, you can be sure of that." Maybe it was a good thing the boy was going. Charles would have a reason to stay alive if only to protect Abraham.

With a wave they were off. They'd head west following the signs of destruction. There was no telling where the Yankees may have gone once they left the valley. They'd follow all the way to the California coast if they had to.

The magnitude of destruction stunned Charles. Skeletal frames of burned-out houses and barns littered the countryside. Crops, fields, devastated beyond redemption. What sparse food there was to share was freely given. The trio was fortunate to gain shelter at many of the remaining homes and farms along the way though most nights it was in hay lofts. Nonetheless, it was out of the cold and the wind. Had any livestock been left it would have been warmer, but the Union forces had seen fit to take all but the good-for-naught.

When they came to a town, spending a night in the local hotel became a luxury. A hot bath. More substantial meals where they could get them. A soft bed. But even in pro-abolitionist communities, young Abraham was more often than not banned from all but the stable.

"The boy stays with me," Charles would argue vehemently. Overprotective to a fault, he seldom let the boy out of his sight. Bribery worked at some places. Most times he and Jubal just snuck him up the back stairs. At one point, exhausted after a long, wet day in the saddle, Charles angrily resorted to pulling his pistol. That only proved to provide them with uncomfortable quarters in the local jail for the night.

Christmas came and went with no celebration. As did the new year. Further and further west the three ventured in search of the murdering band. They hadn't caught up to them yet, but they knew they were on the trail of the Jayhawkers. The pro-Union guerillas had left a trail of death and destruction in their wake.

Weeks turned into months as Charles led his weary followers through Kentucky then into Missouri.

Stopping just inside the State line, Charles and Jubal visited the saloon below the rooms they had rented for the night. Abraham was safely fast asleep but the men found themselves in great need of a stiff drink before they turned in themselves.

The barroom was smoky and noisy with a fellow playing poorly on a tinny piano. The bartender poured them two shots. Jubal scooped the bottle from the counter and followed Charles to a table. It was a busy spot for such a no-account town.

Men all around eyed them suspiciously. They hadn't been wearing their Confederate uniforms since they were unsure of where many towns' sympathies lay. But as they sat, they noticed a hodgepodge of rebel uniforms in various combinations. Some wore uniform tunics. Some striped trousers. Others only caps. Many wore long duster coats hiding their clothing underneath. As Charles had hoped, they had chosen a pro-Confederate town.

All chatter ceased as two of these men sauntered toward them. Charles rested his hand on his pistol at his side just in case. Jubal did the same.

"Mind if we join you, gentlemen?" the older of the two asked. Not waiting for a reply, they both pulled out chairs on either side of Charles and Jubal. The wooden legs scraped along the floor making an annoying grating sound. Charles cringed.

"Barkeep!" the man shouted sharply. "Let's buy these gents a round." The bartender quickly brought two more shot glasses to the table and poured drinks from the bottle Jubal already had taken. His nervousness had not gone unnoticed by Charles.

The older of the two slammed back the first shot. "Ahhh." He smacked his lips and refilled his glass. The man seemed rough around the edges although he couldn't have been more than twenty or twenty-one. A slightly receding hairline revealed a prominent forehead and strong facial features. A full mustache circled his upper lip.

More suspicious than curious, he asked, "What brings you fellers to town?"

Not taking his eyes from Jubal, the younger played with his drink swirling the whiskey around rather than gulping it down. Not more than a teen himself, he was of slight build. His narrow face and elongated forehead made his dark, sinister eyes seem closer set.

"Business," Charles replied curtly.

"What business?"

Charles didn't have a mind to respond, but thought better of it. They were severely outnumbered if these men decided to take a disliking to them. Through clenched teeth, he answered truthfully. "Tracking the filthy, yellow bastards who killed my family."

A slow whistle escaped the man's lips. "Sorry to hear that." He stretched out his hand. "Frank James. This here's my brother, Jesse. He's joining up with us today."

Charles accepted his hand. "Captain Charles Montgomery, lately of the Thirty-eighth Virginia. My Lieutenant, Jubal Hennessey."

Frank gestured toward the others in the room. "And this motley crew of reprobates belong to Quantrill's Raiders."

Now Charles understood why the bartender was skittish. William Quantrill was the leader of perhaps the most savage fighting unit of the Civil War. He had developed a style of guerrilla warfare that terrorized civilians and soldiers alike. And now Charles and Jubal were smack dab in the middle of the most feared men in the country.

"We're not looking for trouble here," Charles said quietly.

"Not about to give you none. Hell, we're probably chasing the same outfit." Frank stood and searched through the smokey haze. He hollered, "Hey, Bill. Come on over here. You'll want to meet these fellers." Bill was followed by most of the others.

Frank started the introductions. "Bill Anderson. His brother, Jim. Peyton, Buster Parr, Jasper Moody, Snowy Jenkins, Archie, Moses. And this grisly old sod is Socrates."

Charles noticed a youngster slightly behind the others. He would have guessed he was even younger than Jesse. The hardened look in his eyes made him seem years older. "Does that boy ride with you, too?"

Frank nodded solemnly. "Afraid so. That's Riley Crawford, Jeptha's boy," as if the name would mean anything to Charles. "Jeptha was dragged from his home near Blue Springs and outright executed by Jayhawkers. The boy's mother brought him to Quantrill when he was fourteen. Had his own gun, so he let Riley stay. Damn shame, too. He'll probably be dead before the year is out."

Charles suspected that somber prediction would most likely hold true for the majority of Quantrill's men.

"You want to ride with us?" Anderson offered.

Contemplating his whiskey which he had yet to taste, Charles took his time to answer. He didn't particularly want to associate with such ruthless vigilantes. The man who stood glaring down at him waiting for an answer struck fear in the hearts of many a lesser man. Bloody Bill

Anderson, Quantrill's vicious lieutenant, was known to wear a necklace of Yankee scalps into battle.

Even more cold-blooded, was seventeen-year-old Archie Clement. Small, blond and grey-eyed, Anderson's lieutenant was his executioner and scalper. With a perpetual smile, he mutilated his victims when it pleased him.

Shuddering at the mere thought of such barbarous actions of this band of renegades, Charles surmised the same tactics were employed by the Jayhawkers from the North. However, the pro-Union forces murdered innocent women and children, something Quantrill, it was said, would not do. Charles had heard otherwise from all accounts of the massacre at Lawrence but he wasn't about to debate it.

It didn't take Charles long to make up his mind. Four hundred guns had much better odds than three. "We'll go with you until we catch up with them. Then we're heading back to Virginia."

"Fair enough," Anderson nodded in agreement. "We head out in the morning to join up with Quantrill this side of Independence. We hope to trap the bastards in the middle. You men get some rest. It'll be a long, hard ride."

❊ ❊ ❊

Charles didn't sleep much that night. A nap here and there maybe but nothing restful. By daybreak they were saddled and headed out of town at a gallop.

Three days of hard riding, with brief stops to rest the horses, brought them closer to their goal. Anderson's goal. Quantrill's goal. Possibly not his. There was no way of knowing if the vigilantes they tracked were the same ones who killed his family and others throughout Shenandoah.

With Abraham's help, he'd find out soon enough. As much as he needed the boy to identify the murderers, even more so was he conscious of the danger he was placing him in. Charles made Jubal promise to take the lad out of harm's way should they run into trouble. And to take Abraham all the way back home should anything happen to him.

On the morning of the fourth day, Quantrill's scout came riding hard into camp. Pulling his horse to a quick stop, he hopped from the saddle and hurried to the fire where Anderson sat on a nearby rock sipping his hot black coffee. The Union outfit was a good four, five hours ahead. Quantrill, a half-day further, was heading fast their way. Anderson would let the Jayhawkers run into the devil himself, then box them in from the rear.

"Any man I catch sneaking a drink will see the business end of my Winchester," Anderson warned his men. "There'll be no skaggin' here."

"Skaggin? What's he mean by that?" Abraham asked Frank James who was packing his saddlebags close by.

Frank laughed. "Bill started saying that after Quantrill took the town at Lawrence last summer. Old Larkin Skaggs got hisself so dumb drunk he couldn't git back on his horse so he just stayed behind after we all lit out of there. O' course we didn't notice he wasn't with us 'til we were well away and we weren't stupid enough to go back ta git him. Nothin' to go back for anyways. Townsfolk we left standing took care of him right quick like. So now no drinking's allowed before a battle. You a drinking man, son?"

Abraham shook his head. "Never tasted the stuff," he stated seriously. "My mamma says it makes a man do foolish things."

"Listen to your mamma, boy. She's a wise woman."

Charles insisted Abraham ride at the back of the raiders with Jubal so they could get away if need be. After what seemed like intolerable hours in the saddle, faint gunshots could be heard ahead. Quantrill had met the Jayhawkers head on.

Swinging his horse around, Charles galloped to the back. He had to yell to be heard over the sound of pounding hooves. "We'll circle around through the brush and come up from the side. Maybe we can get Abraham close enough to see if he recognizes any of them without getting ourselves shot."

Jubal had his doubts. "Things'll most likely be moving too fast to get a good look."

"We'll give it a try, anyway. Least ways he'll be out of danger."

Charles led the way through the trees, up hill and down, until they found a decent vantage point. A craggy knoll overlooking the battle field provided a good cover of undergrowth and rocks. The scene before him reminded him a great deal of the many skirmishes he was involved in. Fewer men, but just as savage nonetheless. A flurry of swords and bayonets blurred in the smoke from the rifles. Yelling, shouting and screaming horses added to the confusion.

Abraham rested his elbows on the jagged edge of a large boulder and peered through Charles' field glasses to carefully study each soldier in the fray below. Making one man out from the other was virtually impossible. The only distinguishing mark of a few Union guerillas was the red sash belting their tunic or bandana around their throat. Yet one man stood out from the others. One the lad would never forget.

Abraham handed the glasses to Charles and shouted, "That's him." He pointed to a soldier wearing a scarlet scarf. Scraggly yellow hair hung beneath his tattered cap. As he barked orders to his men, Charles could see spaces from missing teeth. Others, rotten and black. "That's the one, I'm sure of it."

"Okay, son. You get yourself well back behind those trees with the horses and high tail it out of here if they get passed us. You hear me?"

"Yes, sir."

"Jubal," Charles ordered. "Take your mark and pick off any Yank wearing red."

"With pleasure, sir," Jubal smiled in anticipation. He'd been itching for just this moment for weeks. Taking his time, he took aim and fired. One Yankee fell to the ground. Then another.

Charles joined in and took out a third. Two more Jayhawkers came down before someone realized where the shots were coming from.

"Snipers!" Half a dozen Yankees broke free of the battle and swarmed up the knoll toward the trio hiding in the rocks.

Deliberately avoiding Charles' man who lead the charge, Jubal picked off two. Charles killed one and winged another. Just as they were about to crest the hill, Charles rose from behind the outcropping of rock and aimed point blank at the man who murdered his wife.

Abraham did not have to run.

So you were avenged, my darling Clarissa. Our obligation complete, we were back in the valley by spring. The weather had grown warm. Buds were forming on the trees. Wild flowers were popping up here and there. Life was being renewed at every turn, yet my heart remained dead. Abraham

was home safe and sound. Jubal returned to the Thirty-eighth. I resumed my duties of espionage although there was no longer any enjoyment in the challenge.

As weeks wore on, Charles grew more despondent. Loneliness consumed him. Anger controlled his every move. Charles took to drink to mask his perennial pain. He became sloppy in dress and attitude. Well on the road to self-destruction, Charles was put on report for disregarding orders on more than one occasion. If he went looking for trouble, he found it.

Sneaking out of camp one evening, Charles swung himself up on Diablo's back and reined the horse north toward the Potomac. He missed Lincoln last winter because he was chasing the Jayhawkers. By God, he'd get him this time before the year was out.

Whiskey burned his throat with each swallow. With each swallow his plan to assassinate the President became more daring. Outlandish plots played around in his mind one after another. Charles became invincible.

Before long, the strong liquor began its numbing effect. Charles' brain fogged. His eyes blurred. He swayed sharply from side to side throwing Diablo off stride. The bottle slipped from his hand shattering on the rocks at the horse's hooves. Diablo skittered away from the splintering glass. Charles tumbled to the ground as darkness invaded his consciousness.

I came to realizing I was tied up jostling around in the back of a supply wagon. My head pounded unmercifully. My stomach emptied on more than one occasion. There was nothing left to do but endure unrelenting dry heaves. It was my own fault and have no one but myself to blame. The devil's elixir. That's what Breezie calls it. I should have listened to her. To make matters even worse, there was no sign of my Diablo.

Under suspicion of being a spy, Charles was taken to Forrest Hall in a nearby suburb of Washington. He stated adamantly to all who would listen that he had regrettably just got himself plain drunk between camps and fallen off his horse. Since when was having a bit too much to drink a crime?

"And where's my horse?" Charles demanded boldly.

The sergeant in charge laughed and shoved him roughly along in front of him. "Probably roasting over a camp fire by now, fool."

Forrest Hall, 'The Last Ditch,' as it came to be known, without exception was the most fearful realization of a prison that Charles could have imagined. Picking his way through dirty groups of sleeping men or puddles of tobacco juice the floor was saturated with, Charles took stock of his surroundings. Four grated windows looked upon the street. He had already been warned. Anyone presuming to look from these windows would be shot dead on the spot.

In a space not more than eight hundred feet square, over five hundred dirty, ragged and filthy wretches of all conditions and color crowded together forlornly on the floor. The place swarmed with vermin, the corrupt air vile with disgustingly nauseating odors.

It was early Sunday morning when Charles entered this cesspool after undergoing a rigid examination of his person. It was so late that only nine or ten out of the whole number that lay huddled together on the floor were awake. One or two stared at him for a short time, then went back to playing cards.

After processing, Charles was allowed to go with the others to breakfast. Although he was famished, he could eat nothing. The coffee was a mixture of . . . what? He couldn't describe it. The hard tack was the flintiest kind of flour that was ever baked. His mouth watered at the thought of Breezie's biscuits which just made him even hungrier.

Charles spent his first two weeks at Forrest Hall without so much as an interview with the superintendent. He did manage to get his hands on a piece of paper from the sutler and wrote a simple note of denial to the charges brought against him. After three days, a judge sent for Charles who dismissed him with the assurance he would attend to his case in due time.

Due time dragged into six months with no end in sight. New prisoners came. Old prisoners were released in exchanges, died from disease, or were executed. Even if he was suspected of being a Confederate spy, surely he should have been released, or exchanged at the very least, after all this time.

It was almost Christmas. Charles had an engagement with Abraham Lincoln which he was loath to miss. Even in all the time he was held in prison, it did little to dampen his resolve to carry out his plan.

He had to escape.

But he had no money for bribes. Nothing to barter. His pleas for freedom fell on deaf ears. No one knew where he was.

Languishing in misery, Charles sank further into despondency.

It was then, when all hope was lost, when all expectation of release vanished, that I found one ray of light in the darkness. I remembered the spell my darling Clarissa cast on me the day I foolhardily left her side. I allowed myself that little glimmer of trust in her faith that it would bring us together once more.

I don't know how it would ever be possible. But I will pray that it will be so. I'm not certain to whom I should be praying. I know that all things are possible to our Good Lord in Heaven. So I shall pray to Him even though I strongly doubt Christianity condones the craft of magic.

My cell mate managed to get this booklet for me from the sutler. It cost me dearly. Two moldy slices of bread and my cup of coffee for a whole week. But no matter. I no longer have an appetite.

Breezie had shown Charles the journal Clarissa had been writing when the Yankees came upon their farm. As he skimmed through the pages, he had silently scoffed her ridiculous notion that making up a little poem would keep them safe. It certainly hadn't kept herself and the children from harm. But maybe the final chapter had not been written for them. She was no longer alive. He barely was. Maybe they would be reunited in death. It gave him a glimmer of hope.

I have taken Clarissa's lead and started a journal of my own. If ever I shall be released, I will put it with hers to be read at some future time. If I die here in this prison, no matter. With God's mercy, they'll not find and confiscate it beforehand.

Charles remained in prison although he and several other prisoners were transferred to Fort Delaware after the new year of 1865. Taken to Philadelphia by rail, they arrived in the city about midnight and were escorted under guard to a dismal windowless slave-pen. This would be their quarters for the night. Their beds were hard boards, their blankets what they stood in. Sleep was out of the question. Charles felt sore, stiff, cross, out of temper, and indisposed in every way. Even more so the next morning when breakfast was unidentifiable. But not knowing when the next opportunity for food might arise, he ate and drank anyway.

After arriving in Wilmington, Delaware, they had to walk eight miles to the harbor at Newcastle. The roads were very bad and almost all of the way they were over their ankles in mud and slushy snow. The steamboat, *Osceola*, took them the twelve miles down river to the fortress.

Spending another miserable night, Charles awoke more dead than alive due to excessive cold. He contemplated escape but knew it was fruitless. Escapes during the summer months were not infrequent. But in winter all such attempts were given up. The floating ice in the river and the utter impossibility of anyone living any length of time in the water, however strong a swimmer he might be, was a most effective deterrent. Even for Charles. He would bide his time and wait for just the right moment when success had better odds.

Unrelenting coldness. Unsanitary conditions. Poor nourishment. Death from illness took many more lives from the prison pens than execution for attempts to escape. And Charles was not immune to the savagery of dysentery that spread like wildfire through the entire compound. Struck down as the sun gained just enough warmth to begin melting the snow, it was two full months before Charles recovered enough strength to stand unaided for any length of time.

Word of the war effort was not very reliable as most of the guards took great enjoyment in passing false information—all to the detriment of the South—to the prisoners. Few letters from family and friends on the outside were allowed through. Those that were received with any news, were often censored and cut up. So when it was bandied about that General Lee had attacked Grant's forces near Petersburg, but was defeated, then unsuccessfully attacked again, the Confederate prisoners did not know whether there was any truth to the information or not.

Then, to add insult to injury, word spread through the barracks that General Lee had evacuated Richmond. Grant called upon Lee to surrender. The two commanders met at Appomattox Courthouse and agreed on terms.

Mixed emotions ran through the prisoners held at Fort Delaware. Some lamented the loss for the South. Others rejoiced in speculation that the war would soon be at an end and they would, at last, be granted freedom. Charles abandoned all thoughts of escape. With renewed dedication, he once more concentrated on his plot to assassinate the President of the United States.

Tired, dirty and alone, Charles hobbled his way south toward the Shenandoah Valley. He relied on the kindness of strangers as he had no money for food or lodging. Thankfully he found many sympathetic people willing to take him in. Only a saint would have given him any mercy at all by the look of him. A crownless felt hat topped his head. A tattered blanket kept the cold from his coatless body. A pair of horribly threadbare underwear covered his lower extremities. With a soleless boot on one foot and the other wrapped in old rags, Charles limped home though nothing was left there for him.

The war was over. Richmond had fallen. Lee had surrendered.

John Wilkes Booth had beaten him to Lincoln.

Charles stopped at the end of the lane and looked forlornly at his empty, lifeless house. He longed to say he came home, but there was no longer a home without his family. His wife and children were gone.

With a heavy sigh and a heavier heart he trudged onward.

❋   ❋   ❋

It is said time heals all wounds, yet, as time wore on, his suffering did not ease. Charles merely existed for the next thirty years praying for some life-threatening illness or accident to end his misery. He mechanically trudged through his daily chores. Many times he sat vigil in the tiny cemetery plotting his own demise, yet hadn't the nerve to carry it through. Not that Charles lacked the courage. He was, however, reluctant to jeopardize any path to Heaven, for he was certain Clarissa would be waiting there for him. In fact, Charles was certain he had held her angelic hand in his as his spirit mercifully escaped its mortal prison.

THREE

Claire — 2007

That one almost got her. The next would surely soak her through. In furious succession, powerful waves pounded against the craggy fog-dampened shoreline of Cape Forchu. They could not frighten her. Perched atop a massive jagged rock, Claire remained undaunted, head in hands, contemplating her decision.

Looming behind, the lighthouse lent its sense of comforting childhood familiarity. Across the harbor, she studied the brightly painted buildings of the quiet fishing town's reconstructed waterfront that was ravaged by the violent Ground Hog Day storm a few years back.

Claire had come here to think as she had done many times since her husband had died. The pain of his loss cut deeply even after all this time. Oftentimes taking her breath away. A freak fishing accident. Sudden. Senseless. Shattering.

She watched Billy and Maggie scramble agilely over the same rocks she had as a child. Slickly covered with seaweed left behind by high tide, they were the cause of many a scraped knee and elbow. But a little injury didn't impede the thrill of the race to beat the soaking spray from the next wave to slap its fury against the barren rock wall.

Lifting her head toward the mouth of the harbor, Claire bent an ear toward the low thrumming sound of powerful engines. The spewing wake splitting the salty ocean water eased to a mere ripple as the captain of the passing ship cut throttle.

Tomorrow this same ferry would take them to Bar Harbor, Maine. The new high-speed catamaran, *The Cat*, would cut nearly four hours from the time it previously took to cross the Bay of Fundy. A good thing, too, since this stretch of water was considered the roughest in the world.

Claire was born with salt water in her veins but the thought of spending even a few confined hours on board a pitching vessel with no *terra firma* under her feet threw her stomach into queasy spasms. With the number of motion sickness pills she'd popped over the years, she should have included a pharmaceutical company in her investment portfolio. She could have been rich by now. It had become the family joke. Claire grasped the small bottle in her pocket. She had saved two little pink pills for tomorrow. That would be enough.

Armed to the teeth with road maps, and a compass for good measure, Claire planned to drive from Maine through New England then south to Virginia. Directionally challenged, she relied on her maps. Liked knowing where she was. Where she was going.

Claire couldn't help but smile as she recalled how her husband would make fun of her little fetish. Ethan had been competent to steer his big lobster boat by the stars if his GPS equipment failed. But spin her around three times, he would laugh, and she'd get lost in her own kitchen.

Ignoring his teasing Claire would study the maps that were tucked into his copies of *National Geographic*. Maps to exotic places like Egypt and Greece. Places she'd never expect to go unless the company paid for it.

Tomorrow would be the start of a long journey alone with two young children. Claire shook her head once more doubting the logic behind this hasty decision. Virginia landscapes would probably hold no interest for the magazine's readership even with the article plastered with award-quality photographs for which she was rapidly becoming known.

Was she doing the right thing?

That very same question had relentlessly knocked around in her head the past couple weeks as Claire doggedly pressed her editor for this particularly bizarre assignment.

It was fast becoming an obsession and even today she was no closer to an answer as to why it should.

He felt no concept of time anymore. Days and nights, they were all the same. It didn't matter whether the sun rose or the stars shone. He was waiting . . . waiting to be released from this limbo. This no-man's land. She was near, now. He could sense her closeness. He knew she would come. Some year. Some century.

"Well, let's remember never to stay in this town ever again," Claire muttered as she sleepily tried to pull a brush through her tangled curls. Looking up at the ceiling of the tiny bathroom, she could only shake her head. A hole much larger than it needed to be gaped at the top of the wall through which the heating duct passed into the adjoining motel room.

It was late when they arrived. Too late to find a room in a more respectable establishment. Especially, they had been told, with all the tournaments in town. And it was too late to travel on. The children were tired and cranky. She had been driving almost non-stop for the past two days and could simply go no further.

The room didn't seem all that bad when they first checked in. But all she was interested in at that point in time was a place to lay their heads. And in spite of everything else, the beds looked invitingly clean and comfortable. The pillows cushy.

Claire ignored the burn marks in the carpets and drapes. She closed her eyes at the peeling wallpaper, the rust stains in the sink, the mildew around the tub.

All she wanted was sleep.

Claire tucked the children under the covers, crawled into her own bed and switched out the light. Nestling deeply into the soft pillows she closed her eyes for welcome respite.

Abruptly she was jolted out of near slumber by the slamming of the door to the room next to theirs. Then came the screaming and cursing. Rudely awakened and afraid, Maggie started to whimper.

"It's okay, sweetheart," Claire assured her.

She picked up the phone and dialed the front desk. When the clerk answered, Claire asked as politely as she could that he call the next room and ask them to quiet down.

In a moment she heard the phone ring and a man answer. He paused, listened, then hung up. "Look what you've gone and done now," he bellowed at his companion. She screamed a torrent of obscenities back at him. Someone hit the wall with such force it knocked the mirror off on Claire's side of the room and shattered on the dresser below.

Claire called the front desk once more. "Listen," she said more forcefully. "We've driven a long way today and have even further to go tomorrow. We're exhausted. The children are crying. We need to get some sleep. Either you call the police or I will," she threatened. "Someone's going to get hurt in there."

But he didn't. And she didn't. Claire wasn't one to turn her back on a woman in distress but, truth be known, she was afraid if she caused too much of a fuss she'd go out in the morning and find their tires slashed.

She guiltily tucked the children in again and shoved a pillow over her head to muffle the noise.

Claire hoped their drunken neighbors would pass out soon and be quiet but the battle raged on. Nearing midnight, she threw back the covers and switched on the light prepared to pack everything up and move on.

"That does it!" Claire snarled. "We're out of here." But when she looked over at the children, they were sleeping so peacefully she didn't have the heart to wake them. How they could actually sleep through all that noise totally amazed her. Knowing she'd never be so lucky, Claire pulled a novel out of her suitcase, shoved the pillow behind her back and began to pass the time reading.

The minutes ticked by painfully slow. Somewhere through a murky haze, Claire heard the thud of a car door closing then gradually became aware of the hum of steady traffic on the busy street outside. Coming to, she realized she must have eventually dozed off, still sitting up, her book falling to rest against her chest. All was quiet in the neighboring room. They had passed out. Or killed each other. She really didn't care which.

Rubbing a kink at the back of her neck, Claire tiptoed around pieces of broken glass still scattered on the shabby carpet. Stopping in mid-step, she reached back and tugged the bedspread off her bed to throw over the shards on the floor before the children got up and cut their feet. "No way are they charging me for that," she stated firmly as she stumbled into the bathroom. If she hadn't already paid by credit card she would have demanded her money back. Maybe she still would.

Staring through gritty eyes at her grim reflection in the cracked mirror, Claire wondered if the black circles would ever disappear. Her eyelids were puffy, her eyes red and bloodshot. The bathroom didn't look any better in the morning than it had the night before. And nobody was getting into *that* tub. The towels were so threadbare it would have taken a dozen or so just to dry themselves. She'd wash the children's faces and hands. They couldn't be too dirty from sitting in a car. The showers would have to wait until they reached Virginia later that day.

Billy crawled out over top of Maggie waking her up in the process. "When can we leave, Mom?" he asked grumpily. "This place is a dump."

"Watch your feet," Claire cautioned. "You want breakfast first?" They had packed hampers with them in the trunk of the car.

"*No*," they shouted in unison.

"Then let's get out of here." Quickly they dressed, packed up and drove off without looking back. The motel office wasn't open yet, so she left a note about the mirror, along with the key, on the top of the dresser beside the television that didn't work.

Spotting a McDonalds not far from the motel, Billy asked, "Can we stop, Mom?" Figuring the children deserved a treat after what they had just put up with, Claire pulled into the parking lot.

"We'll even go inside," she said with a smile. Usually they'd use the drive-through and continue on. Today they wouldn't be quite so rushed. She had a special stop planned along the way.

Claire sat quietly watching the children inhale their breakfasts of hotcakes and sausage. They pretty much talked non-stop planning what they were going to be doing all summer, how many friends they would make.

But that little spark was missing from their voices. The twinkle in their eyes just wasn't there.

The unexpected death of their father had been difficult for all of them. Especially hard on the children. That 'resilience of youth' Claire had heard from countless counselors, family members and friends just didn't seem to apply to Billy and Maggie. They missed their father terribly.

Hoping a holiday would lift their spirits, Claire finagled her editor into making this a working vacation. Her job as photojournalist allowed her to travel extensively to all sorts of wonderful places. The children deserved a change of scenery and the Shenandoah Valley in Virginia sounded like the perfect spot. It had a soothing, comforting name. Like Zanadu or Shangri-La. So that's where they were headed.

Back on the Interstate, the miles zipped by. To stretch their legs and take a break, they stopped at each rest station along the way. There were only so many times they could play *Eye Spy* before they ran out of things to spot. Billy had tried to get his sister to sing *Ninety-nine Bottles of Beer*, but she couldn't count that high let alone count backwards.

The back of the car was loaded with pillows, blankets, games and books. Maggie and Billy both had their own little CD players with earphones but listening to the same songs over and over had worn thin three states ago. Once in a while, Claire would start a movie for them on her laptop. The children were understandably getting tired of being cramped up in the car.

They were well into Pennsylvania when Claire started spotting signs for their next stop. A trip through the Hershey's chocolate factory would be a perfect distraction. For her anyway.

A bona fide chocoholic, Claire was probably more excited than the kids. Her stomach growled in anticipation. Claire could taste it already. Afraid she'd buy the store out if she went while hungry, she pulled the picnic hamper out of the trunk of the car and prepared a hasty lunch of sandwiches and tangerines.

Claire had no idea it was an amusement park complete with a roller coaster and Ferris wheel. Promising the children a few rides, they quickly took the tour which cleverly routed them to the outlet store. She felt totally foolish, but all Claire could do was stare at row upon row of chocolate. Never before had she seen so many delicious calories in one spot.

Laden with heavy shopping bags, they struggled back to the car and stowed most of their treats in the trunk well out of reach hoping it wouldn't melt in the heat of the waning afternoon. Justifying they had to keep up their strength for the long drive ahead, Claire kept some out to munch on.

The blinding sun had sunk to eye level by the time they crossed the Virginia line and turned off the highway at Front Royal. Claire stopped for gas, picked up a few groceries, and made sure she was heading the right way. Within a few minutes, they turned off and bumped along a rutted wagon track through a farmer's field.

"Look," Billy yelled excitedly. "A water slide. And mini golf." He jumped from the car with Maggie close behind.

"Don't go near the pool yet," Claire warned as she went to check in. She had reserved a small cabin rather than try to cope with a tent, two young children, and rain.

When she made the reservation, they told her the cabin was rustic but that didn't really adequately describe it. The furnishings consisted of a double bed, a set of narrow bunks and a small shelf. Nothing else. It was cute enough and would do for a day or two but Claire had expected a few more basic comforts. Maybe a chest of drawers so they could unpack their clothes and not leave them crumpled in their suitcases. An inside table and chairs would have been a nice touch in case it rained. The only place to sit was on the bed or the picnic table on a porch so small one could barely squeeze around it.

Thoroughly disappointed, Claire only hoped she could convince the children it would be an adventure. She wrestled open a bag of Reese's Pieces and tossed back a handful. Tomorrow things will look better, she promised herself with a heavy sigh.

But all morning brought with it was a miserable drizzling rain. There would be no pool or water slide. No mini-putt. Claire had really hoped for just a day or two to lounge around and rest but it just might be the day to explore since there wasn't much else to do.

A couple brochures she had picked up at the office caught her eye. Virginia had a number of scenic caverns not too far from Front Royal. Luray Caverns, just a bit south of the campgrounds, were the closest but Claire decided to go further to Endless Caverns then work her way back. These caves were near a town called New Market.

They arrived at the caverns just in time to join in with the next tour. Camera slung around her neck, Claire made sure the children pulled on heavier sweatshirts. It would be much cooler down below.

Mysteriously beautiful, formations such as Santa's Sleigh were appropriately named. Claire wished she had brought the camcorder from the office to capture the beauty of the light show in the Cathedral.

It was hard to believe such natural wonders existed and that these caverns weren't discovered well before 1879. Two young boys out hunting cornered a rabbit beneath some limestone boulders. They moved the rocks aside only to discover their prey had disappeared into a dark hole in the ground with a cool breeze blowing out. Scurrying to find candles and rope, the boys soon found themselves deep inside an endless complex network of underground passageways.

Many expeditions through the years have tried to find an end to the caverns. Over five miles of cavern passage have been mapped with no end in sight.

The boys who found the caves missed so much beauty with only light from candles. Now the caverns are lit with white light which shows the breathtaking magnificence of the calcite formations.

Their tour guide kept them all in stitches with his dry sense of humor, but when he turned out the lights to give everyone a taste of what total darkness was like, Maggie was anything but amused.

"It's okay, sweetheart," Claire consoled her whimpering daughter. "It's just like when you close your eyes to go to sleep. You can't see anything then either." The pitch blackness lasted but a moment. "Look, they're back on."

"Scaredy cat," Billy taunted. "I wasn't afraid."

"Me neither," Maggie bit back.

"Then why'd you cry, baby?"

"Did not."

"Enough, the pair of you." Claire silenced them both.

The sun was doing its best to peek through the mist as they made their way back over the mountain. So close to Shenandoah, Claire turned south to take pictures of the town that had given the valley it's name. She had envisioned the peaceful serenity of a little town nestled deep within the protective shadow of mountains. A sense of history. Magic.

They found a grocery store, pharmacy, school. Claire didn't see any sign of a museum and she didn't take time to ask. They picked up a few groceries, ice for the cooler and were off again.

Though the town itself held little allure, Claire gazed over the valley, over the river winding its way between the fields and houses built up beside it. She felt a profound sense of belonging. Of peace.

It was still early afternoon and the drizzle had cleared to a steamy, hot day. Since they were already there, Claire decided to take to the back roads and work their way around. Turning off the main road, she took a side street that seemed to lead toward the base of the mountain ridge.

It proved to be a photographer's gold mine. Just the subject Claire was looking for. Putting on her signal, she pulled as far to the side of the road as she could and reached for her camera.

A magnificent stone wall complete with arched gates and iron work still intact ran down a stretch of road. Moss and lichens had spread through the years nearly obliterating sections of stonework entirely. Wind and rain had softened the edges of visible blocks to a smooth roundness.

Trying different locations to get just the right vantage point, Claire walked the length of fence several times focusing her camera and snapping shot after shot.

At one point she stopped to examine the abandoned acreage searching for other points of interest. As thoughts often do, hers drifted. She visualized horse-drawn carriages. She heard the music of a lively minuet. Saw people dancing. Heard their laughter. Saw a . . . *face.* Blinking, it vanished.

Although the buildings were gone, Claire envisioned, with stark clarity, the mansion that once stood just behind that grove of trees. To the right was the stable, barn and other outbuildings. To the left and far behind the house were slave quarters, a jumble of ramshackle cabins in serious disrepair. The crack of a whip followed by a foul curse stung her ears.

The familiarity of it all startled Claire. Where did that come from? she wondered. She shook her head to rid herself of the mental imagery. Taking a deep breath to calm her nerves, Claire backed away and hurried toward the car.

The road twisted up and down skirting the base of the mountain. Its height loomed over them. Following the road, a babbling stream flowed to the river. There were precious few road signs. Their map didn't show many of the lesser-traveled roads and, after taking a few turns, Claire was left a bit disoriented until they came to a stone train trestle at the next stop sign. Across the road was the Shenandoah River.

"Okay," she unconsciously whispered aloud. "Now I know where we are."

After following the river a few hundred feet, Claire became edgy. It was such an odd feeling. Like anxiousness and anticipation all rolled into one. Maybe she was getting tired. Maybe she was hungry. The children weren't complaining. If anyone should be hungry it would be them. But they still seemed quite satisfied after their lunch at the caverns.

Cresting the next rise, Claire suddenly slammed on the brakes and swerved to the side of the road provoking the driver behind them to lay hard on his horn. But Claire didn't notice. Her attention was drawn to the property down the drive. For there on the knoll overlooking the river was the sorriest excuse for a house she had ever seen.

"Why'd we stop here, Mommy?" Maggie asked, her nose pressed to the window. "Do you want a picture of that ugly house?"

"Come on, Mom, let's go," Billy urged.

But Claire couldn't move. She just stared at the house with a sense of longing she couldn't explain. "I'll just be a minute," she said as she grabbed her camera and got out of the car. Focusing her lens on the dilapidated structure, Claire began snapping.

If the siding had ever seen a drop of paint, it had all peeled away to weathered bareness. The veranda sagged. The shutters were falling apart. The screen door was held on by only one hinge. Someone had taken pot shots at the attic windows breaking out some of the corners. Birds were nesting up there. Two flew out.

"Come on, Mom," Billy called impatiently.

"In a minute." Claire wandered closer. The house had to be vacant. Creeping up on the veranda, she tried to peek inside but the windows were too dirty. She couldn't see a thing. Venturing around to the back, the land sloped gently toward the river. Prickly brush and creeping vines had spread their tentacles to such a degree any easy access to the water had been concealed.

Overwhelming sadness swept through her. In great need of a vast amount of tender loving care, that poor house reminded her of the little Christmas tree in the Charlie Brown cartoon. Claire couldn't understand how anyone with property so lovely could let it get so overgrown.

It didn't used to be like this. The orchard was pruned. The meadow was always scythed. Breezie's garden was . . . over there.

A violent shiver made the tiny hairs on the back of her neck stand on end. She distinctly felt that someone was watching her. Swinging around, Claire saw no one. Nothing. But as her eyes lifted toward the roof line of the house, she thought she saw a shadowy figure disappear behind the tattered cloth covering the attic window. Staring for a moment, she realized just how foolish she was being.

More than a little uneasy, she quickly retraced her steps to the car. By the road, Claire spotted a lopsided real estate sign tacked precariously to a rotting fence post. She couldn't resist jotting the name and number down in her notebook.

"Just got time to get back to Luray before they close," she said lightly. "Let's go."

"Mommy," Maggie whispered hesitantly. "I'm not so sure I want to go down underground again. Are they going to turn out the lights?"

"Probably, you chicken," Billy cut in. "Nothing happened last time, did it?"

"Just this one more time, please, Maggie," Claire coaxed. "I'd really like to get some more pictures. Last time. Promise."

The final tour of the day had just left, but the group waited at the bottom for them to catch up. If it were possible, these formations were even more spectacular than the ones they had seen earlier. Their guide, Christy, was a pretty little thing, no bigger than a minute, with long, curly auburn hair, a twinkle in her eye and a giggle in her voice.

"On the morning of August 13, 1878," she began brightly, "Andrew Campbell, the town tinsmith, his thirteen-year-old nephew, Quint, and three other men set out exploring for a cave. When cold air rushing out of a limestone sinkhole on top of a big hill west of Luray blew out the candle Campbell was holding, they spent four hours digging away loose rock. Campbell, followed by Quint, slid down a rope and found themselves in the largest caverns in the East, an eerie world of stalactites and stalagmites sparkling in the candlelight."

Claire wondered if any of these tour guides ever lost their train of thought and forgot their scripts. It was a lot to remember . . . facts and details about each formation. They continued on.

"With no more than eighteen to twenty inches at its deepest point, Dream Lake is the largest body of water in the caverns." It looked like tiny formations were growing up from the bottom of the pool. With such clarity, it made a perfect mirror image of the stalactites hanging from the ceiling. Beautifully deceiving.

"The original point of entry was down that tunnel." Christy pointed toward a darkened passageway. "That entrance hasn't been used for many years. But when Campbell and Quint first started poking around in here, that's how they got in. Now remember. All they had to see by were candles and you can't see very far ahead with just a candle. They slid down a skinny rope, crawled on their hands and knees, even on their bellies. They didn't know where they were going or what they were going to find. Imagine what they thought when they came upon a giant chasm over five hundred feet long. That's about the size of two football fields, and about seventy to ninety feet deep. About the height of a ten-storey building.

"It's all that's left of the main horizontal channel of water that created Luray Caverns. See how it looks like it just goes down underground forever? It's all dark and eerie. Just like what we might think a path to the center of the earth would be. They called this Pluto's Chasm. At it's heart is the ominous figure of Pluto's Ghost, a column named after the Roman god of departed spirits and of the underworld. And I'll tell you why they called it Pluto's Ghost as soon as everyone catches up." Christy paused for a moment.

Maggie and Billy squeezed themselves closer to the railing so they could see better. "With the candle light flickering, this column looked spooky, like a ghost. Everywhere the men went, there it was. Just like it was following them. They were pretty scared, these big, strapping men. But they never let on to each other they were scared. Finally, after a couple hours, they figured out they had been going around in circles." Laughter echoed through the cavern. "Actually, even today we can say it's following us, too. We'll see the formation three times at different points during the tour."

"Who's Pluto, Mom?" Billy asked.

"Well, you know in your video, *Hercules*? He's the bad guy, Hades. Pluto's just another name the ancient Romans used."

"I didn't like him," Maggie sniffed. "He was mean."

As the group started moving on ahead, Billy said, "I wish we could go down there. It'd be fun." He called out to Christy. "Can't we go down there?"

"I'm afraid not," Christy explained. "It takes a lot of practice and hard work to be a caver. But when you get bigger maybe you could join a club and learn how to be a spelunker."

"Sp'lunker?"

"That's just a fancy word for somebody who crawls around in caves," Christy laughed.

Billy peered deeply into the chasm, his mind already set on someday climbing over that railing and finding his way to the center of the earth. "I'm going to be a sp'lunker, Mags!"

"Come on, Billy," Maggie said pulling at his arm.

But a slight movement caught Billy's attention as he stared at the brightly lit column in the center of the chasm. He pointed. "*Look, Maggie.*"

A smoky haze was beginning to emerge from the side of the formation. Their curiosity gluing them in place, neither child budged. Wide eyed, they looked on as the obvious form of a human took shape inside the column. The apparition, larger than life, stepped out into the chasm just as easily as if he had walked through a door.

"What . . . Who is it, Billy?" Maggie whispered shakily. The man smiled and waved at them with a wink of an eye.

"*Mom!*" Billy hollered, fear filling his voice.

"*Mommy!*" Maggie sounded just as scared as they ran ahead and grabbed their mother's hands to make her stop.

"*Mom. Look. It's Pluto's Ghost!*" Billy pulled her around and pointed to the column. "*Look. There he is.*"

"Billy . . . " Just as Claire lifted her eyes to examine the column, the shape vanished. "I'm sorry, guys, I don't see anything."

"Awww. He's gone." Billy whined, disappointment showing on his face. "Honest, Mom, we really did see him," Billy insisted. "Maggie saw him, too, didn't you, Maggie?"

"It was *him*, Mommy. It was *Pluto*."

"Hush now." Claire took a last look down the chasm as a thought came to her. "You know what? It was probably just a trick they play on us tourists." She took them each by a hand.

"I don't think so, Mom," Billy insisted. "I'm pretty sure it was Pluto."

The children kept pulling back straining to see behind them as the group made their way along the pathway. Suddenly the sweet strains of music filled the cavern.

"What you are hearing," Christy explained, "is the Great Stalacpipe Organ. We'll see that in the Cathedral in a couple minutes." It suddenly dawned on her. "Wait a minute. That's strange. We're the last group." She shrugged and said, "Must be one of the other guides joking around."

"Bet it's that Pluto guy's ghost," Billy shouted. "We saw him."

Everyone turned and laughed. "Children have such vivid imaginations," a woman next to Claire said.

"They certainly do," she agreed. To Billy she whispered, "Stop that now, Billy. You know there's no such things as ghosts."

"But Mom . . . " he pouted.

"Listen. No more," Claire repeated sternly with a shake of her head.

As they entered the largest room discovered so far in the cavern, Christy began her recitation once more. "Here in the Cathedral is the world's largest musical instrument. Stalactites covering three and a half acres of the surrounding caverns produce tones of symphonic quality when electronically tapped by rubber-tipped mallets.

"This unique organ was invented in 1954 by Mr. Leland Sprinkle of Springfield, Virginia. Mr. Sprinkle was a mathematician and electronic scientist at the Pentagon. It took him three years to search through the chambers of the caverns and select stalactites to precisely match a musical scale. Electronic mallets were wired throughout the caverns and connected to a large organ with four rows of keys." They all drew closer so they could see. "When a key is pressed, a tone occurs as the rubber-tipped plunger strikes the stalactite.

"We've had many weddings here and sometimes we have an organist come in to play the console manually, as Leland Sprinkle did for many years. But most of the time, the organ is played by activating an automated system." Christy reached behind a boulder and flicked the switch. Music seemed to be coming from all directions.

"Does anyone recognize the piece that's playing?" Christy asked.

Claire thought the music sounded familiar. "Sounds like the theme from the old Sunday morning cartoon *Davey and Goliath*."

"Well, I don't know about that," Christy giggled. "Guess that was a bit before my time, no offense intended. It's actually a hymn by Reverend Martin Luther, *A Mighty Fortress Is Our God*."

Almost to the end of the tour was the Wishing Well, a large subterranean pool of water over six feet deep. Lit from the bottom, its cool blue water reflected the thousands of coins that had been tossed in. Once a year the coins are removed and donated to charitable organizations.

Claire reached into her pocket for some loose change and gave some to the children. "Close your eyes and make a wish."

Maggie scrunched her eyes and tossed in her coins. They plunked against a stone reef along the side of the pool. Billy threw his farther and watched them sink out of sight to the bottom.

"What did you wish for, Maggie?" Billy asked curiously.

A slight frown puckered her brow as she lowered her eyes. "I wished Daddy was here," she whispered sadly.

Her wistful words broke Claire's heart. Bending down, she drew her little daughter into her arms and held her tightly. With a catch in her voice, she said softly, "I wish Daddy were here, too, sweetheart." Throwing in her own coins, Claire hoped that her children and herself would soon be able to move on with their lives.

With a brighter tone, Claire asked Billy about his wish. Bubbling with anticipation, he said, "I want to see that ghost again."

FOUR

Thunder rumbled in the distance as rain pelted the tin roof of the tiny cabin with a deafening melody. It was still dark outside. The children were so deeply asleep they hadn't been disturbed. Claire, on the other hand, had spent one more restless night. For the last week, she couldn't get the sight of that house by the river out of her mind. It was no different from any other dilapidated old house. But this one plagued her.

Unzipping her sleeping bag, Claire swung her legs over the side of the bed and slid bare feet into her waterproof ducky boots. Good thing she tucked them into the trunk as an afterthought along with an umbrella and rain slickers for them all.

The beam from the flashlight suddenly dimmed. Claire tapped it against her leg then stared into the lens. "Batteries," she muttered groggily. "Must get batteries." She nearly tripped over the extension cord strung across the room to the little heater they used to take the dampness from the room. When the heater wasn't on, they had brought along a light they could plug into an extension cord to see to read by. The pig-tail ceiling light practically blinded them with the brightness of a twenty-five watt bulb.

Claire tugged at the towel they had used to plug the gap under the door. She didn't mind crickets out in the back yard where they belonged. But chirping from some invisible crevice in the floor boards under her bed in the middle of the night didn't impress her one bit.

Opening the door to a torrent of water draining off the roof, Claire tried to convince herself she really didn't have to go. The late-night trek to the restroom had lost its sense of adventure days ago. She could wait until the rain let up. But the sound of water wasn't helping the situation. Shielding herself behind the umbrella, Claire sprinted down the lane. This had all the makings of a flood. By the time she made it back to the cabin, the legs of her sweat pants were soaked through. She left a trail of puddles on the plank floor with each step.

Unable to get back to sleep, Claire huddled deeply into her sleeping bag until daybreak. When it was light enough to see, she pulled out her notebook to work on the article she was planning to go with the pictures she had already taken. Opening to the first page, she noticed the realtor's phone number she had jotted down for that sorry house by the river. An idea popped into her head. A plan began to formulate.

❄   ❄   ❄

"What place was that?" It took only a moment for the agent to recall which property the caller was talking about. "Oh, yes. The old Montgomery place. On the river. You say you want to see it? Are we talkin' about the same place here, honey?"

She had finally unloaded that property, again, and hadn't shown it for a number of years. "I've got some much nicer homes I could show you. Closer to town." The caller was insistent. "No? Well, then, I'd be happy to show it to you. Meet you there in about an hour? Fine. I'm looking forward to meeting you, too."

What kind of nut case do we have here? she thought to herself as she hung up the phone. Constance Jenkins hoisted her ample body out of her chair and fairly waddled over to a shelf in the corner of her office. Slapping dust from the lid of a cardboard banker's box, she rustled through and finally pulled out the dog-eared folder.

"Don't worry, baby," she chuckled addressing the file. "You'll be back with your friends in no time." This was going to be a thorough waste of a good morning, but it was a nice day for a drive. Maybe she'd be able to steer this potential client toward a more profitable commission.

Arriving a few minutes before the agent, Claire and the children roamed around the hayfield that used to be a front yard. Virginia creeper had spread down the entire fence line. Wild flowers bloomed brightly in oddly placed patches throughout the yard, probably spread from seed dropped by birds.

Claire had no idea if the vendor would agree to her proposal, but she had nothing at all to lose by asking. As soon as she saw the house again, the pull was so strong she knew she just had to have it. Even for a short time. There was no explaining it.

When the agent drove up, Billy and Maggie were playing hide and seek in the heavy brush beside the house. Neither one had thought much of their mother's idea until she mentioned running water and a bathroom. But as they took another look at the house when they drove up, both had very serious misgivings.

"Let's not judge a book by its cover," their mother had urged. "Let's see what it looks like on the inside before we make a decision."

Constance squeezed out from behind the wheel and puffed her way up the drive. She was a very attractive black lady. In her fifties, Claire guessed. Her dark eyes held a mischievous sparkle enhanced by a jolly laugh as she held out her hand and introduced herself.

Claire took an instant liking to the rotund agent. "Claire LePaige. And my children, Billy and Maggie."

"I'm going to be totally honest with you, honey. Why would you even consider looking at such a place? This property's been back and forth on the market as long as I can remember. Since I was a babe in diapers. I'd like to get rid of it for good but can't keep it sold. Nobody stays." In a hushed tone, she whispered, "It's *haunted*, you know."

Her bluntness took Claire completely by surprise. "Aren't real estate agents supposed to sell you on the good points about a property?" she laughed. "Just how many houses have you sold?"

"Don't get me wrong, dearie," Constance tittered. "I'm all for getting my commission. But you look like a sweet little thing. I just don't want you to be getting into something you'll regret."

"You haven't heard my proposition yet. Let's look inside."

Reluctantly, Constance cut a path through the long grass to the veranda, balanced open the rickety screen door and unlocked the inside one. Stagnant air hit them full in the face taking their breath away.

"I'll just leave the door open," Constance suggested. "Needs a little airing out."

With only one step inside, an overwhelming sense of peace flooded deeply into Claire's soul.

Starting in the cellar, Claire wasn't surprised to see the quality of the workmanship that formed the foundation. The stonework alone had to be at least a yard thick. The timber beams were the size of massive tree trunks.

Claire caught sight of a section in the back corner of the cellar that appeared to have a raised wooden frame buried into the earthen floor. Concealed under a few broken-down cardboard boxes was a trap door. Curious, Claire reached toward the ring used as a handle to raise the door.

"Oh," Constance waved her hand. "That's just the old root cellar. Nothing but dirt and spiders down there."

Claire looked back at Constance, hesitated, then slowly withdrew her hand. With a sharp intake of breath, she straightened and stumbled backward a step or two. *Panic. Fear.* The sudden urge of flight or fight was numbing. It took a moment for her legs to move. Slightly bewildered, Claire followed Constance back up the old wooden steps.

As she thoroughly inspected each room, every nook and cranny— several times—an even greater sense of familiarity filled Claire as if she caught a glimpse of a life long past. The parlor, dining room, even the smell of the pantry. Vanilla. Cinnamon.

Vague experiences flitted through her mind. Laughter, happiness, sorrow. As she entered the upstairs front bedroom, the exhilarating joy of children being born.

Shaking her head, Claire forced the images to disappear. Had to be her journalistic ability that had her making up stories in her head, she convinced herself. She could make up a story about anything.

The house was in surprisingly good shape for being vacant so long. Everything, of course, needed a good washing down, a little paint and wallpaper. But the structure seemed sound enough. There was even furniture in each room covered with heavy sheets.

"I tell you the place is haunted," Constance repeated. "The last people in here were in such a hurry to get out they just left all this behind. Nobody's stayed more than a few days. Old Charles just runs them right on out."

"Who's Old Charles?" Billy asked.

"Charles Montgomery was a Confederate soldier years ago. Some folk swear his ghost's still roaming around here. His wife, Clarissa, was raised in Louisiana mostly by her Cajun grandmother who practiced magic, voodoo and the like. Story goes Clarissa conjured up a spell to put on him when he left for war and now he's been waiting all these years for her to come back for him."

"That's ridiculous. We don't believe in ghosts. Please don't go putting such foolish thoughts into the children's heads," Claire begged. "No wonder people keep running off. You've been psyching them out with all your wild stories. Must be an old creaky pipe or something. Or bats in the belfry."

Billy couldn't have been more happy. "Mom, if there really is a ghost here, maybe he knows Pluto?"

Exasperated Claire said, "Mrs. Jenkins is just teasing, Billy. It's just a story, right?"

"If you say so," Constance grinned with a wink at Billy.

They had made their way up a steep narrow staircase to the attic. Claire wanted to make sure the floor was good and safe if the children wanted to play on rainy days. Then she'd be able to check for the holes where birds were getting in.

But try as they might, there was no way they were going to get that door open. It was either locked or jammed up tight. They couldn't tell which.

"Guess I won't have to worry," Claire said. "If no one can get in, no one's going to fall through the floor."

"But that's where ghosts live." Billy was disappointed. "Everyone knows ghosts live in attics."

"Then he won't bother us if he can't get out."

Getting tired of all this ghost nonsense, Claire hustled the children down the stairs and out into the back yard. The porch needed a little shoring up but nothing she couldn't manage on her own. She'd become quite handy with a hammer and saw this past year. And they wouldn't be there that long. Hopefully things wouldn't fall apart more than they already were.

"Things have really been let go," Constance explained. "The present owner lives in D.C. Bought this place as a summer retreat. Wife and kids high-tailed it after one day. I think he managed to stay a whole five or six days out of sheer stubbornness. He's never been back."

Claire had wandered over to what she assumed had been a garden plot. "Breezie would have a tizzy fit if she saw this," she absently whispered.

Her words stopped Constance short. "What did you say?"

Claire looked at her quizzically and shook her head. "I didn't say anything."

"Yes, you did." Constance nodded adamantly. "You said something about *Breezie*."

Totally confused, Claire denied it. "Why would I say that? There's not even a hint of any breeze today."

"Well, I have no idea." Constance regarded her suspiciously. "Maybe I'm just hearing things. It's just that *Breezie* was my great-great grandmother's name. She worked for the family who owned this property. The Montgomerys."

"Montgomery . . ." Claire whispered to herself as if trying to place the name. "She was a slave?"

"Not with the Montgomerys. No, ma'am, the Montgomerys refused to own slaves."

The fleeting image of scarred backs, shackled hands and feet, the bang of a gavel, came to mind. Intrigued, Claire wanted to know more. It had given her an idea for another article. "I'd love to research it, Mrs. Jenkins."

"Please, call me Connie. I'm really not the formal type."

"Okay, Connie. How much do you know of the family?"

"Well, not too much. Mostly only what's been passed down by word of mouth." As an afterthought, she added, "My brother Rudy has some old writings of Granny Breezie's. Not much left of the book now, but he'd probably let you have a look at it if you're interested."

"That'd be a good start. Now let's see if your guy will agree to my terms. You have a cell phone, right? Use it, please."

"All right, but personally I still think you're crazy. Darlin', he should be paying *you* to stay here." Reluctantly, Connie fished through the giant satchel she called a briefcase.

Claire didn't know what she'd do if the vendor refused. There was no way she could outright buy this property even at the listed give-away price. Not and keep their home up north, too. Anxiously, she watched Connie gesture wildly as she spoke to the owner then finally hang up. The expression on her face was not encouraging.

"Well, he thinks you're nuts, too," she stated glumly. "He doesn't expect you'd last one night."

"Oh." Disappointed, Claire hung her head. They didn't want to stay at the campground. Couldn't afford a motel for the rest of the summer. Their only other option would be to go home.

"Now don't look so down in the mouth," Connie continued, a smile growing on her face. "He's thrown out a challenge. He doesn't think you'll stay. But you prove him wrong and the place is yours for the rest of the summer."

Squealing with delight, Claire danced around Connie giving her the biggest bear hug she'd ever had. Claire was squeezing so hard she was cutting off her air supply.

Tickled at her enthusiasm, Connie pried Claire's arms from around her neck, and said, "He figures it won't move anyway and will agree to a short-term lease on your terms. Of course it didn't hurt that I told him a house is more sellable when somebody's living in it."

"I can't thank you enough," Claire laughed. Waving to the children, she shouted, "We have a bathroom!"

❋　　❋　　❋

The maintenance crew was still tackling the grounds when Claire and the children drove up two days later. The tractor was huge and the bush hog it dragged behind almost as big as a hay bind. "You kids will have to stay inside until they're done," Claire warned. "You can help me get your rooms cleaned up."

"That's no fun," they pouted.

"We can play in the attic," Billy suggested as he bounded up the stairs with his sister close behind. "Maybe we'll see Old Charles."

With a heavy sigh, Claire called after them, "Cut it out guys. There's no ghost. Anyway . . . you can't get in there." Billowing dust wafted into her nostrils as she plunked her box of cleaning supplies onto the filthy table. Sneezing, she fanned the cloud away.

Fine help the kids were going to be today. She had Constance Jenkins to thank for this latest round of nonsense. Ghosts! The very idea. Fantasy. That's all it was. Not that she had anything against childhood fantasies. Santa Claus. Tooth Fairy. Easter Bunny. But ghosts? Claire had to think of a way to nip this one in the bud quickly before the kids had her up all night with nightmares.

❀   ❀   ❀

"How're we going to get the door open, Billy?" Maggie panted as she raced her brother to the attic, her little legs always two steps behind. They stared up at the door as if it were some impassable obstacle to conquer.

"I don't know. Maybe there's a key someplace." Billy stretched to reach the top of the door frame but he was far too short. He huffed in disgust. "Mom put the axe in the trunk. We could chop it down."

"Maybe it's just stuck. Push harder," Maggie suggested as she grasped the door knob in her tiny hand and gave it a twist just as Billy put his shoulder to it. Without any effort at all, the door flew open and both children toppled into the attic.

"*Whoa!*" Billy shouted with glee. "We're stronger than Mom and Mrs. Jenkins put together."

"Yeah," giggled Maggie as she picked herself up from the floor.

Sunlight shone into the attic through the eight dormer windows around the roof line making the room bright and airy. The entire level was open now, but you could see where walls had been dismantled. It didn't even seem stuffy for being shut up so long. The children inched their way in not quite sure if they should be there after all. It didn't seem scary, but Mrs. Jenkins' story about Old Charles made them just a little leery.

"I don't think he lives here, Billy," Maggie whispered. "There's no bed."

"Ghosts don't sleep in beds, silly," he retorted. "They just kinda float around in space."

The room was full of boxes, old trunks, plastic garbage bags. Each successive owner had added to the clutter abandoning it in his haste to leave.

"Wow, Maggie. Look at all this stuff," Billy said tearing open the first box he came to. "Come on, let's see if we can find some toys." Maggie pulled at the next box toppling it off the pile.

"*Your dolls are over here, Margaret. Here in this box.*" The voice of a man filtered through the noise the children were making just as a small wooden crate scooted into clear floor space. Startled, they both stared at each other then furtively peeked over their shoulders. Behind them by the window, was the same figure they saw in the caverns.

"*It's Pluto!*" Maggie yelled. She dropped the box she held in her hands and took off down the stairs screaming for her mother. Billy was at her heels.

"*Mom! He's here. Pluto's in the attic.*" They raced into the kitchen almost bumping into Claire as she was coming to see what all the commotion was about. Each child grabbed one of her hands and began pulling her toward the stairs.

"*He's here, Mom. Up in the attic. We found him.*" Billy's mouth was running away with him. "*Come on, Mom. You've got to see him. He's there now.*"

"Slow down, slow down. Who's where?"

"*Pluto. He followed us. He's up in the attic.*"

"Oh, for heaven's sake, you guys. Cut it out. I'm really busy here. I don't have time for your nonsense. I'm trying to get this place cleaned up so we can sleep here tonight." Claire tried to shake them off but they held fast.

"*Come on, Mom. Just come and look. He's there. Honest.*" They persistently dragged her to the bottom of the stairs.

Exasperated, Claire gave in. "Okay, okay. I'll look." The children pushed at her backside as if she couldn't get up the stairs under her own power. "Hey, wait a minute." She stopped in mid-step. "How did you two get into the attic? The door wouldn't open."

"I turned the handle," Maggie stated with her little chin proudly jutting in the air, "and the door just opened up easy as pie."

"Yeah, after *I* pushed on it," Billy added.

"Really." Claire just couldn't understand that after the fight both she and Connie put up the other day. Maybe a change in humidity had dried the door out shrinking it enough to open more easily. There had to be a logical explanation. Connie certainly had enough weight behind her to knock it right out of the frame if she put any real effort into it. But there it was, open, just as pretty as you please. Claire ran her hand along the edge of the door and the frame but found nothing unusual.

Billy was just about beside himself as he burst passed her. Twirling around, he looked all over the place. Pluto was nowhere to be seen. "Pluto?" he called. "Are you still here?" There was no reply. The anticipation drained from his face. "Aw," he whined dejectedly. "He took off." Sinking to the floor, he pouted. "Now you don't believe us."

"I believe Mrs. Jenkins has you seeing things," Claire laughed as she tousled her son's silken hair. "Sometimes when you want to see something badly enough, you think you really do."

"Mommy, he said there were dolls in that box." Maggie pointed to the crate in the middle of the room. "He put that box there. Just slid it across the floor without even using his hands."

"Is that a fact?" Bemused, Claire took a closer look. "Are you sure you two didn't put it there?"

"No way, Mom," Billy's face lit up. "We were over here." He showed her the boxes they had started to rummage through.

Quite seriously Maggie told her, "He said 'Margaret, your dolls are in this box.' He called me *Margaret*, Mom."

"Oh, come on now," Claire said skeptically. "This is really going too far." But curiosity got the better of her and she lifted the lid from the box. A look of genuine shock covered her face as she let the cover slip from her hands. Stunned, she lifted doll after doll from the small wooden chest. Beautifully crafted, well preserved, these dolls had to be antique. Well over a hundred years old. Hand-painted porcelain faces. Hands and feet. Curly hair from the finest silk. Velvet dresses.

Speechless Claire just looked at Maggie. "But . . . But . . . " was all she could stammer. Had she seen these dolls before?

"Can I keep them?"

Finally her mother found her voice. Still very confused she managed to say, "These are very precious dolls, sweetheart. They're really too old to be played with. They're so fragile, they'd break easily. And they're not ours. They belong to someone else." They belonged in a museum, not some dusty old attic. Why would someone leave something so valuable behind?

"But he said they were *mine*," Maggie cried.

Thoroughly convinced the children had regressed to their story-telling stage, Claire anguished not knowing how to help them. Should she play along? Should she get them therapy, again? She wished she had someone to talk with.

"Well, maybe we can say they're yours while we're staying here," Claire compromised. "How about we set them up in your room so you can look at them?"

That seemed to satisfy Maggie. Picking up the box, Claire carried it down to the room Maggie had chosen for her own. There was a lovely built-in bookcase in the corner that would be a perfect place to display the dolls.

After the shelves were washed Maggie carefully placed the dolls in just the right spots. Each one had a name. Annabelle, Victoria, Grace, Rebecca. Old names so totally opposite to what Maggie had named her own dolls at home.

Claire handed her a black mammy rag doll. It was dressed with a bright green plaid dress, blue kerchief and apron. Big white eyes and exaggerated ruby lips were embroidered on her face. "What's her name?" she asked.

"Mammy," Maggie replied without even thinking about it. Shocked, Claire wondered where she had ever heard a reference like that. Certainly not from herself or Ethan.

"Why did you call her that?" Claire wanted to know.

Maggie shrugged. "Cuz that's her name."

Billy sulked in the attic—head in hand—sitting in the middle of the floor.

"William." Charles spoke softly. Billy didn't turn around.

"Mom doesn't believe me," he whispered sullenly.

"She will, son."

FIVE

Tackling one room at a time, Claire finally thought the old house was quite livable. Cleaner at least. Most of the first day she spent just on the kitchen. She swatted the cobwebs down from the ceiling. The stove and fridge were a virtual nightmare. Every cupboard, wall, floor and window was washed down with antiseptic cleanser. The washing machine leaked, but a couple new rubber washers in the hoses fixed that.

The oak trees surrounding the house provided protection from direct sunlight and, with the windows open in all the rooms, the cross flow of air kept the second storey surprisingly cool. At least they wouldn't have to use their hot sleeping bags for bedding. The children discovered three garbage bags full of sheets and blankets in the attic. Claire didn't imagine anyone would complain about using them.

Quite pleased with herself, though thoroughly exhausted, Claire tumbled into bed. They had clean sheets, clean beds, a clean bathroom. The hot shower felt extremely relaxing. She would have absolutely no trouble sleeping tonight. They were settling in quite nicely. No disasters they couldn't handle. No noises that went bump in the night.

No ghosts, she convinced herself as she drifted off into dreamless slumber.

He stood over the bed watching her sleep. Peaceful. Childlike. She was so beautiful. Her tawny skin glowed flawlessly with all the vitality of her Creole ancestry. Just as he remembered. Long, dark curls cascaded over the pillow. He longed to reach out and stroke her hair as he did years ago, but he didn't dare. Not yet. He didn't want to frighten her should she awaken. That would ruin everything. He had been waiting. Forever it seemed. But now that she was finally here, there would be time.

Charles leaned over. Her scent was intoxicating. He drank it in. A wisp of breath whispered across her ear. "Soon, my darling, Clarissa. Soon."

Snuggling deeper into her pillow, Claire smiled.

Billy waited impatiently in bed until he heard his mother and Maggie go downstairs. He wanted to see if Pluto had come back. Running up the stairs to the attic, he pushed open the door peering inside. "Pluto? Are you up here?" The sun was just beginning to peek through the dormer windows spotlighting the tiny particles of dust he had stirred up.

"Are you here?" Billy whispered again. His tummy fluttered in anticipation. He was hoping to see the ghost and, at the same time, not really certain he did want to see him. Not sure if he was just making it up like his mother suspected. Tiptoeing through the maze of boxes and castoffs, he peeked here and there anxiously inspecting each and every nook and cranny.

"I'm right behind you, William," Charles spoke with a chuckle.

"*Whoa!*" Startled, Billy swung around to see the apparition, large as life, leaning up against the back wall. The glow of sunlight illuminated the friendly smile on his face. He looked pretty normal for a ghost. Except for his clothes. They looked really old, Billy thought. His grey woolen pants had red stripes down both legs. Broad brown leather suspenders strung over his shoulders held them up. Billy thought his shirt looked like the underwear top his grandpa used to wear with the sleeves pushed up over his elbows and buttons undone at the neck. A ruffle of soft down peeked from the gap at his chest. Hazel-green eyes twinkled when he smiled. Just a hint of grey at the temples speckled his sandy-brown hair. The full mustache drooping around the corners of his mouth was streaked a reddish tone.

"And my name's not really Pluto."

Billy's brow puckered. "Then how come we saw you come out of Pluto's rock in the cave?"

Charles shrugged. "I just couldn't wait any longer to see you."

Billy's eyes widened in amazement. "How did you know we were there?"

"I just knew," he said with a smile.

Quite satisfied with that answer, Billy pulled a box out to sit on. Looking up at his ghost, he pondered for a moment. "If you're not Pluto, then are you Old Charles?

Charles chuckled softly. "I guess I would be pretty old by now."

"Mrs. Jenkins told us about you. She said you scared people away."

"I only scare those people away I don't want here."

"So you want us to be here?" Billy asked hopefully.

"Very much so," he said sincerely. "You're not scared are you, William?"

"No way, you're not scary," Billy assured him. "I think it's really neat. Bet none of the kids back home have their very own ghost." There were so many questions Billy wanted to ask, but they were racing around in his head so fast he couldn't get his tongue around a single one.

Maggie called from the landing, "Mommy says breakfast's almost ready, Billy."

Billy wasn't thrilled about sharing his ghost with anyone, but he couldn't think of a way to hide him from his sister for the whole summer. "Come up here, Mags."

Skipping up the attic steps, Maggie hesitated at the door fully expecting her brother to jump out from behind something to scare her. But all she saw was Billy sitting cross-legged on the box and Charles beaming back at her. She sucked back a deep breath to scream.

Charles held up his hand to silence her. "Don't be afraid, Margaret." His voice was kind. Friendly.

Maggie clamped her mouth shut. Her face broke out in a broad grin. Spunkily she stuck out her chin. "I'm not scared." If Billy wasn't, she wouldn't be either. Maggie warily tiptoed closer and examined him up and down. "You don't look like a ghost. How come you're not flying like Casper does?"

"Who's Casper?" He tried to get the question in but Maggie just rambled on.

"How did you get in that rock? How come you looked so big? How come you dress so funny?" She fired questions at him fast and furious leaving precious little time for him to answer a single one.

Waving his hands in the air, Charles managed to squeeze in, "Hold on there, *Bijou*," as Maggie gasped for a breath. Charles sat her down beside her brother. He tugged on his suspenders. "This is how soldiers dressed when I was in the army. When we didn't have to be in full uniform, that is. And I'm afraid I don't know why I can do a lot of the things I can do," he said with an honest shrug. "I can't really explain it. I just think very, very hard about what I want to make happen and somehow it just happens."

"I'm glad you're still here," Billy said. "Mom got so mad yesterday I thought she scared you away."

Charles laughed heartily. "It would take a lot more than your mother to scare me away, son. I think she just needs some time to get used to the idea. That's why it's really important you two don't say any more about me being up here for a little while. She might really get fed up and want to leave. Let's just keep it our little secret."

❊   ❊   ❊

Stretched out in an old hammock, Claire closed her eyes and let the breeze float over her. Great find, this hammock. The kids discovered it stuck behind a pile of boxes in the attic. The green-and-white striped canvas was still quite pliable, though filthy. Spreading it out on the floor of the veranda, Claire mixed detergent and bleach and scrubbed the daylights out of it with a stiff bristle brush. At least it didn't smell quite so musty.

In a small copse of trees down by the riverbank, Claire created her very own private retreat. It took a little oomph, but the trunks were just close enough together to force the ropes from one to the other. Now, swaying in the breeze, she'd just take a moment and close her eyes before heading back up to the house.

❋   ❋   ❋

Dreamily, Clarissa snuggled deeper under the afghan drawing it cozily under her chin. Spinning rabbit fur with the wool, Breezie made the yarn soft and warm. Perfect for snuggling on a cooler afternoon.

On the verge of drifting off, she hadn't heard him approach. Suddenly the hammock tipped. Startled, she grasped the side to keep from spilling to the ground.

She could feel him crawl in behind her. Feel him snuggle into her back. Feel him nuzzle his nose playfully into the nape of her neck. Clarissa giggled. His stubbly beard prickled.

Molding his body against hers, Charles draped an arm across her chest drawing her into him even closer.

"This hammock isn't going to hold the both of us," she warned.

"You think I should leave?" Charles whispered his breath tickling her ear.

"Hmmm . . . I don't think so." He began nibbling at her earlobe, his tongue warm and wet. "Where are the children?"

Not answering right away, Charles tugged at the ribbon lacing her bodice closed. One side of her sleeve slipped freely away revealing a creamy shoulder just begging to be caressed with his lips. Mumbling against her skin, he said, "Simon and Breezie took them into town."

"You don't say." She could feel his head nod.

"We're alone."

"You don't say," Clarissa struggled to repeat as he loosened her ties even more and slipped his hand under to cup an ample breast, his fingers rolling her nipple into a taut peak. He could feel her shiver right down to the tips of her toes. A hushed groan escaped her lips. "You're the devil incarnate, Charles Montgomery."

"You think maybe I should stop?"

"Hmmm . . . I don't think so."

Charles grumbled, "You wear too many clothes, woman," as he slid his hand down the length of her long cotton skirt.

Clarissa said, "I do believe I am adequately attired."

"Never seen any God-given reason to be trussed up so. Corsets, bloomers, a thousand and one petticoats." Finally reaching the hem, Charles was surprised to feel no impediment. No slippers. No stockings.

Stopping short of her knee, he propped himself up on his elbow sending the hammock into another wild swing. All the way up, nothing but velvety smooth leg. "What's all this?" he asked in amazement.

"It's too hot," she insisted petulantly.

"Too hot for undergarments?"

"It will be."

✳   ✳   ✳

A strange contentment swept over Claire as she woke from the nap she really hadn't intended to take. Catlike, she arched her back in undeniable satisfaction. A warm sheen of perspiration slicked her body. She lazily glanced at her watch. Connie had picked Maggie and Billy up for a play day with her children, but they'd be back before too much longer. Maybe she'd have just enough time to put a second coat of paint on a wall or two before supper.

Rolling out of the hammock, her legs felt oddly weakened as she tried to stand. Giving them a shake to get the circulation going, she straightened to make the climb back up the steps to the house.

The landscapers had just finished mowing the grounds for the third time since they'd moved in. The owner generously agreed to pay, which pleased Claire to no end. It would have taken her weeks to mow and prune a property this size.

The roses she planted were already blooming profusely. Red, pink, white. She bent to sniff a fragrant yellow blossom.

"Yellow always was your most favorite shade of rose."

Claire dropped the bloom as if she held hot coal in her hand and looked around in confusion. No one was near. The men were in the driveway loading their equipment into the trailer.

Yes, she did prefer yellow roses, but that certainly wasn't the sound of her own voice rattling around in her brain. Someone . . . some *man* . . . had spoken to her. Out loud.

She felt a touch. With a catch in her breath she raised her hand to her cheek. She pictured a face. It vanished as quickly as it had appeared.

For just a second Claire wondered if Connie was right and she had just had her first paranormal experience.

Once her heart stopped thumping, Claire clicked her tongue. "Oh, get a grip, LePaige." Rolling her eyes at her own gullibility, she shook her head and briskly brushed off her hands effectively casting out even the remotest possibility she could have heard a voice from beyond the grave.

Muttering to herself all the way to the house, Claire stalked haughtily through the back door. No way on earth was she going to be taken in by a stupid legend of a haunted house. No way on God's green earth. She didn't care how many people before her actually believed that nonsense and ran for their lives. Claire vowed she wasn't going to be one of them. Anyway, there were no such things as ghosts. She'd prove it to them all.

The mixing stick received the brunt of her frustration as she unmercifully whipped the can of paint. Her foul mood carried over through supper. Billy and Maggie escaped upstairs to the attic before their mother had a chance to sentence them to an early bedtime.

"Don't worry about your mother," Charles told them with a grin. "I reckon she'll feel much better by morning."

The twitter of birds wheedled their way into her fading dream. She didn't want to wake up. She wanted to stay right where she was, warm and safe, snuggled in the arms of the man she loved. Fighting against the inevitable, Claire squeezed her eyes closed praying morning would never come. Willed the sun to slide back down behind the mountain.

Still stretched out beside her, Charles leaned up on an elbow to watch as she began to stir. He should leave, he knew, but he just couldn't force himself to disappear. Not quite yet. Reaching over, he brushed the tumble of hair from her face. A faint smile appeared on her lips. The lips he dared to kiss one last time.

Wrapping her arms around him, Claire threw a leg over his thigh pinning him against her warmth. Charles, aware she was almost awake, held her close. Stroking. Soothingly. Lovingly.

Arching against him, Claire's breath soon came in ragged gasps as he teased unmercifully. Pressure mounted relentlessly—beyond the breaking point—as sparks of sheer delight exploded from deep within. A low, guttural scream burst from her throat waking her instantly.

The dream vividly etched in her memory, Claire found herself without a stitch of clothing on. Arms and legs were tightly wrapped around her pillow. In a heap on the floor was the tee-shirt she was positive she wore to bed.

On the shirt lay one delicate yellow rose.

The ecstasy of the dream blanched. Someone had been in her room. Someone had taken off her shirt. She didn't remember doing it. If she had, it would have been the first time *ever*.

Grabbing another shirt from the dresser drawer, Claire pulled it on then shimmied into a pair of shorts. The rose remained untouched where it lay.

Racing down the stairs to the phone, Claire frantically dialed 9-1-1.

"What'cha doing, Mommy?" Maggie asked sleepily as she trudged down the stairs behind her mother.

"Go wake up Billy," she ordered briskly, "and both of you come down here with me."

"What's wrong?"

"Just do as I ask, please. *Now.*"

Maggie scampered back up to get her brother. Billy was not happy to be wakened. Especially by his pesky sister. He complained, loudly, all the way to the bottom of the stairs. They came in just as Claire was reporting an intruder to the police.

"Someone was definitely in my room last night." Her voice shook as they heard her explain. "There's just myself and my two children here. All the doors were locked. I'm sure of it. No, I haven't checked everything yet but I will."

Billy and Maggie looked at each other wondering what all the fuss was about. Tugging on her sleeve, Maggie tried to get her mother's attention. When Claire ignored her, she turned and whispered to her brother. "Maybe it was Charles."

"Maybe. I don't know." Billy shrugged petulantly. "I was asleep. Anyway, you can't say anything about him. We promised."

"Oh, yeah. But Charles wouldn't let anyone hurt us would he, Billy?" Maggie asked.

"It's the old Montgomery place on River Road . . . Oh, I don't know. South, I think . . . Thank you. I'll be watching for somebody."

Claire hung up the phone and gathered her two children to her. She tried not to frighten them as she explained why the police were on their way. Before long they heard the crunch of tires on the gravel driveway. Claire met the officer at the door.

"Sheriff Harper, ma'am," he drawled lazily as he stepped toward the house. Removing his khaki Stetson as he nodded to Claire, the sheriff took a cursory glance around before he slowly entered the house.

"Thanks for coming so quickly. I'm Claire LePaige. These are my children, Billy and Maggie." The sheriff tousled Billy's head as he walked hesitantly into the room.

He took off his sunglasses. Claire tried not to stereotype, but with the cropped hair, dark glasses, mustache, he looked like most every other policeman she had ever met. His skin was richly tanned as if he spent a lot of time outdoors rather than in the office doing paperwork. Muscles well toned, she doubted he ate too many donuts either. And he certainly didn't resemble most of the southern sheriffs portrayed on television.

There was a mischievous sparkle in his eye when he said, "I didn't really believe the dispatcher when she told me this is where the call came from. Didn't think anyone was living here now. Place is haunted, you know."

"So I've heard." Claire laughed at the expression on his face and couldn't resist chiding, "Oh, come on. A big strapping officer of the law like you doesn't believe in ghosts. Do you?"

"Hell no, ma'am," he said a little too quickly. "That's for simple-minded folks." Yet he didn't seem too anxious to search further than the foyer.

"Do you want to have a look around?" Claire prodded only slightly amused by his reticence.

Pulling himself upright, Sheriff Harper nodded and simply said, "Sure." Sticking his head through the archway to the parlor, he asked, "What makes you think you had an intruder? Any indication of forced entry? Anything disturbed, broken or out of place?"

"Just one thing. Actually two." A definite blush tinged her cheeks as she motioned for him to follow her upstairs to her room. "I know this is going to sound really, *really* strange. But look at this." She pointed to the little pile of clothing adorned by the pretty yellow rose. Taking a deep breath she continued even though she knew she'd probably be the joke of the squad room by noon. "I wore that shirt to bed last night. This morning it was on the floor with the flower on top."

She could feel his eyes bear down on her. His eyebrow arched.

"I didn't put it there," she shook her head adamantly. "I know I didn't."

"Ever take a notion to sleepwalk?"

"Never."

"Just a thought." He turned to check the window.

More than a little embarrassed, Claire hung her head suddenly wishing she hadn't made that call. She could tell he didn't believe her. But Sheriff Harper was very professional, she had to give him that. He didn't come right out and laugh at her but she bet he was bursting his gut trying to hold it in. Claire caught a fleeting smirk on his lips when she summoned the nerve to glance up at him. He was tall. She had to look up a long ways which made it all the more difficult.

Diplomatically, Harper suggested he check the rest of the windows and doors. Inside and out.

While he was investigating outside, the children dashed to the attic. "Charles, a policeman is here," Billy called excitedly.

"*I know, son,*" he spoke invisibly.

"Somebody broke in the house last night."

"*Nobody was here, William. I would have known.*"

"See, Billy," Maggie chortled. "Told you Charles wouldn't let anyone hurt us."

"Well, then," Billy wanted to know, "how did the flower get there?"

"*I left the rose for your mother,*" Charles admitted. "*It's her favorite. But I hadn't counted on her calling the authorities.*"

It didn't take the sheriff long to make a superficial tour around the property. He couldn't determine any sign of entry, forced or otherwise. Claire waited for him on the veranda. Thoroughly humiliated, she endured his questioning so he could complete his incident report.

As he drove off, Claire was no closer to an explanation than she was when she first woke. Maybe she did take her tee-shirt off. Maybe subconsciously she thought it was too hot.

Or, as the sheriff had suggested, perhaps she had taken to sleepwalking. He'd seen it before. New surroundings could trigger them, he'd said.

Sleepwalking down the stairs, out the door, across the lawn to the garden and snipping a flower . . . She'd take that under advisement.

The only other possibility was that the children had something to do with it. Claire jolted at the thought. Why in heaven's name had she jumped the gun and called the police before asking the children? She probably could have saved herself a lot of embarrassment.

Claire called Maggie and Billy down from the attic. "You guys didn't put the rose in my room sometime last night, did you?"

Maggie opened her mouth about to spill their secret, but Billy stabbed her in the back with his finger. "Ow," she squealed and punched him in the arm.

Normally Claire would not have overlooked the childish spat, but she was too upset to come down hard on them.

"We didn't put it there, Mom. Honest."

Billy certainly seemed sincere, Claire thought. But as she intently studied her daughter, Maggie peered a little too innocently back up at her mother. "Hmmm . . . " she hummed skeptically. Something in Maggie's eyes told Claire that she knew more than what Billy was saying. Maggie couldn't keep a secret. Sooner or later she would crack and Claire would have her answer. All she had to do was bide her time.

SIX

Rinsing the last dribble of paint from the roller and brush, Claire hung them to dry over the laundry tub. The kitchen was now a sparkling snowy white, bright and fresh. But the fumes were still a bit strong even with the windows open. And it was so humid, she'd be surprised if it even dried. Tomorrow she'd tackle the dining room and parlor. But, for today, she'd had enough. After all, they were on vacation.

"Okay, guys, we need a break," she called from the bottom of the stairs. "Let's go for a drive."

"Just a minute, Mom," Billy hollered. To Charles he said, "We've got to go, now," and hurried out the door. "We'll come up when we get back."

Maggie was already half way down the stairs. Without thinking she turned, ran back to the landing and shouted, "Bye. See you later."

"Who are you talking to?" Claire asked.

Both children stopped dead in the middle of the stairs and stared mutely at each other. They did promise. "Nobody." Billy spoke for them both. "We were just playing." They pushed passed their mother without another word.

But the looks on their faces didn't fool Claire. They were hiding something but she didn't press it. Glad they were having fun and keeping out of her wet paint, Claire knew she probably shouldn't let them play in the attic with so much other people's stuff stored up there.

The temptation to snoop a bit herself one day gnawed at her sense of respecting other people's property. She quickly justified they couldn't have considered anything remaining to be of much value. She still hadn't figured why the box of dolls had been abandoned. Maybe there were more treasures to be found.

"Where're we going?" Maggie asked excitedly as she sat on the bottom step struggling with the laces of her sneakers.

"We're going to climb a mountain."

"No way!" Billy exclaimed. That was one of the things he had on his to-do list this vacation.

Claire checked the hamper to make sure she hadn't forgotten anything. They'd be gone for lunch. Maybe supper, too. "Take your jackets just in case."

Hearing the drive through Shenandoah National Park was magnificent, she made sure she had lots of film in her camera case. They should have gotten an earlier start to make it all the way around the parkway, but they'd go as far as they could today. Maybe go further another trip.

The park entrance wasn't far from the campground where they had stayed. Claire didn't give it another thought as she sped by. She didn't miss anything about that cabin. The arrangement she had made was working out quite nicely.

Deer calmly grazed by the side of the road. Stopping to take a picture, Claire almost wished they'd bolt away but, unfortunately, most had lost their fear of humans. Humans meant treats of juicy apple and, despite frequent warnings, people continued to feed the animals.

The whole Skyline Drive along the Blue Ridge was supposed to be one hundred and five miles. Massanutten Mountain alone was forty miles long.

From the scenic turnouts, one could see forever over a carpet of luscious green trees, meadows, and winding rivers. The autumn colors would be spectacular. Claire wished she could come back to see. Maybe another year she'd visit later in the season.

"Honk the horn, Mom." They were heading through Marys Rock Tunnel and its six hundred feet of eerie darkness.

There were many hiking trails throughout the park but they would have to explore them another time. Particularly interested in the one to the highest point, Claire checked the brochure one more time to see how much further they would have to drive. "Keep an eye out for a sign that says Hawksbill Mountain," she told Billy. "I hope it's not much further." The day was rapidly wasting away.

After another excruciatingly slow forty-five minutes stuck behind a tourist bus, Billy pointed. "Is that it?" Sure enough, the sign pointed the way to Hawksbill Mountain with an elevation of 4,051 feet. Claire swung the car into the parking lot and they all clambered out. The children ran to the beginning of the trail while she paused a moment to read the information marker. After making a quick calculation, Claire now was having second thoughts. When she read the elevation in fine print in the brochure, it didn't seem like much, but it just dawned on her that the peak of the mountain was only about twelve hundred feet shy of one whole mile, practically on a forty-five degree angle all the way to the top. She looked warily up the steep trail and groaned silently to herself. This was supposed to be a pleasant walk in the park, not some endurance trial.

"Come on, Mom," Billy pulled on her hand.

"Okay, let's do this." She didn't want to disappoint the kids. "Race you to the top," she challenged.

The kids took off in a flash. "Stay where I can see you," she called after them as they disappeared around the first bend in the path. Claire had to admit she did pretty good to keep up with them. For the first couple hundred feet. Then her energy drastically petered out to barely a crawl. Her thighs began to burn. Her calves cramped. Each and every step a struggle, she literally forced one foot in front of the other.

The going was painfully slow. Forever up. No plateau. No downhill respite. Each fallen log, every stump and craggy rock became a welcome resting spot. For a brief moment. Just to give her legs a bit of a break.

Thankfully the children had slowed down, too. Maggie was busy collecting acorns, her little pockets already bulging. Testing out his aim, Billy pelted pebbles into the tree branches.

Upward they trudged. Passed the half-way marker. Claire was finding it more difficult to breath.

Another marker said ten minutes to the peak. It lied. Ten minutes dragged into another ten. Then another. But finally, after well over an hour of nothing but uphill climb, they conquered the peak. And it was worth every angry muscle, every wheeze of ragged breath.

Fine mist spritzed their faces. Strong wind forced Claire to hold onto the children's hands as they made their way up the final grade to a stone-walled lookout.

"Why is it so wet up here?" Maggie complained swiping her hand over her face. "Is it raining?"

"No," Claire explained pointing out to an adjacent mountain. "Look over there. See that? We're so high up, we're in the clouds."

"*Awesome*," Billy exclaimed.

"I'm cold. I want to go down now," Maggie whimpered.

"We just got here, you baby," her brother sneered.

"That's enough," Claire intervened. "I'm just going to get a few pictures."

Suddenly Billy scampered from the tower. "Take one of me over here." In a heartbeat he had climbed over the rocks and teetered dangerously near the edge of the mountain trying to look over.

"*Come away from there!*" Claire screeched as she raced after him. The soles of her sneakers slipped perilously on the greasy rock. Billy wasn't very heavy. A strong gust of wind could easily whisk him over the side. Frantically, she grabbed his arm and dragged him roughly back from the precipice.

Wincing, Billy tumbled onto the rocks. "*Mom*," he whined.

"Don't you *ever* do that again," Claire warned cradling him in her arms. "You scared me to death."

"I was all right, Mom," he sniffed. "I'm not a baby, you know."

Trying to make him understand why she was upset, Claire explained, "I know you're not. But you're not a big, heavy-weight wrestler, either. The wind could have just picked you up and flown you away. And we forgot to pack your parachute." She gave him a peck on the cheek which he immediately rubbed off.

The downhill pace was much quicker. The angle of decline practically forced them into a jog. They made it back to the car in only fifteen minutes.

Claire was just about as tuckered out as she had ever been in her life, but instead of turning back the way they came, she drove on looking for a faster route back to the house. According to the map, they should soon come upon a junction for a road heading back north.

But before they had gone too much farther, she spotted the sign for Dark Hollow Falls. It was supposed to be the waterfall closest to the drive. Cascading only seventy feet, surely it wouldn't take long to snap a few photos. The sun was still at a decent angle.

Ignoring her aching legs, Claire chatted cheerily to the children as they started down the path at a good clip. She missed the marker that showed the trail to be a mile and a half round trip.

Photographing waterfalls was a skill she had acquired over time. Colleagues she knew would do just about anything, oftentimes putting themselves in danger, for the perfect shot.

Claire set her limits, but she had to confess she was one of them. She told the children to keep away from the edge of the churning water. Balancing herself with outstretched arms, she tiptoed across a fallen log and hopped from stone to stone into the middle of the current to get just the right vantage point. So far she'd been able to keep herself and her camera dry. As invincible as she felt, Claire also knew there would eventually be that first time she'd get a cold wet awakening.

From the middle of the stream, the water roiled and frothed at her feet. Claire squatted on the rock, raised her camera, focused and took her shot. As she looked back up at the falls, she suddenly realized the parking lot was a very long ways away. Uphill. All the way. The waterfall might have dropped only seventy feet, but that drop stretched out over a good half mile or more.

She could have cried if she had any energy left to make the effort.

The path had leveled out. A narrow bridge crossed the stream connecting the pathway with a fire trail that led to the main road in one direction, and into the forest on the other side of the stream.

One more shot and they'd head back. Claire changed the lens and aimed her camera to get the full view of the falls from top to bottom.

Spotting a school of small fish sunning themselves in a shallow pool, Billy pulled off his shoes and socks. "This water's freezing," he sputtered as he gingerly waded toward them.

Laughing at him, Claire said, "Then you'd better get out of there before your toes turn into ice cubes and fall off."

The sun was floating low on the horizon. There would be no more pictures today. Slinging her case over her shoulder, Claire bolstered herself for the dreaded miserable climb to the car. Promising herself a long, hot soak in the tub when they got home, she turned to go. "Come on, guys. Let's get out of here."

Billy struggled to get his wet feet into his socks. Claire looked around behind her. "Where's Maggie?"

✳   ✳   ✳

A fluffy grey squirrel with a bushy brown tail scurried into the brush just in front of her. With pockets full of acorns Maggie followed it for just a little ways beyond the bridge. Taking one plump nut in her outstretched hand, she clucked at the squirrel. It stopped for a moment, drew up on it's hind legs, whiskers twitching, then bounced a few more steps away.

Maggie followed a few more steps hoping to entice it to take the treat from her fingers. She tossed one toward the little furry animal. It took no notice of the nut but just stared at Maggie with idle curiosity. With a shake of its tail off it went. But not so far that Maggie lost sight of it. She tossed it another. Then another.

Further and further into the woods the little squirrel scampered with Maggie right behind. Suddenly it disappeared and she was alone.

✳   ✳   ✳

Panic seized her. Tears blurred her eyes. Running up and down beside the stream, Claire searched for any sign that her daughter may have slipped unnoticed into the water.

It was getting late. There was no one else around. Everyone had already headed back up the trail. Maggie might have followed the others to the parking lot thinking she and Billy were right behind her.

Nearing hysteria, Claire wandered aimlessly back and forth along the fire trail. Her haggard face betrayed her fear. Her long brown curls hung in strings wet from her tears as Claire continually brushed it back out of her eyes. Distraught, she couldn't decide what to do.

"*Maggie*," Claire screamed over and over until her throat was raw.

❋   ❋   ❋

Huddled at the base of a giant pine, Maggie shivered. With her arms wrapped around her bare legs, her little shoulders slumped forward as she rested her head against her knees. She sobbed for her mother. It was cold in the forest. And dark. Hungry and scared, she wailed harder with each passing minute.

"Don't cry, *Bijou*. It's all right."

The man's voice startled Maggie but not as much as the sensation that she was floating upwards into the air. "Aaawww," she squealed holding her arms out to steady herself.

Out of nowhere Charles had appeared beneath her. Maggie found herself cradled in his lap his strong arms wrapped around her enveloping her with instant warmth.

Twisting around she stared into his smiling face. Tears vanished and were replaced by sheer amazement. "How did you do that?"

Charles just shrugged. "Why did you wander so far away from your mother, Margaret?"

"Why are you calling me Margaret?" she asked quizzically.

"That's your name, isn't it?"

"Really. I guess. But everybody calls me Maggie."

"Margaret is the name you were christened and that's what I'll be calling you. Just like William is William not, God forbid," he shuddered, *"Billy."* Eying her sternly, Charles waited for her to answer his first question.

"I was feeding the squirrel," she admitted with downcast eyes knowing by the look on his face she had done wrong.

"And was the squirrel hungry?"

"Nooo," she whimpered her bottom lip again beginning to quiver.

"But I think maybe you are." Giving her a reassuring squeeze Charles rose with Maggie still held protectively in his arms. "Let's get you back to your mother." With long strides he stepped over brambles, brush and fallen branches quickly returning her to the fire road.

Shadows lengthened. The late afternoon sun was nearly spent.

Standing her down on the road, Charles took Maggie by the hand and led her toward the falls.

"How did you find me?" Maggie wanted to know.

"I've been keeping my eye on you. Making sure you kept out of mischief. Just like I saw your brother at the edge of the cliff."

"You were there?"

"Hmmm, hmmm. I was standing right in front of William to make sure he didn't fall."

"Why didn't we see you?"

"I didn't let you to see me."

"How come?"

Charles chuckled. She always did have to know all the answers. "Well, because if you saw me you'd probably talk to me and that would have just upset your mother."

"Oh." She guessed that made sense. "Are you ever going to let Mommy see you?"

"Sometime." They were nearing the bridge. They could hear Claire frantically calling out for Maggie. Her voice sounded hoarse, almost demoniacal. He bent down to look Maggie in the eye. "I'm going to go now. Your mother's just a little ways down the road. You keep on going and call her. She'll come get you." Maggie held fast to his hand not wanting to let go.

He gently pried at her fingers. "It's all right, sweetheart. I'll be right beside you watching. You just won't see me."

Maggie relented and released her grip on his hand. He vanished before her eyes. Turning, she began to run toward the sound of her mother's voice. "*Mommy!*" she shouted as loudly as she could.

Hearing Maggie's cry Claire bolted down the road with Billy close at her heels. Tears of relief flowed down her cheeks as she swept her little girl up into her arms. Overjoyed beyond words, Claire set her down and quickly began to check her all over to make sure she wasn't hurt. No obvious cuts or scrapes.

"I'm okay, Mommy." In her excitement, Maggie forgot all about her promise to Charles. "Charles found me."

Claire stopped her inspection and asked curiously, "Who's Charles?" Looking around she wanted to thank the person who rescued her daughter. "Where is he?" She thought it strange a person finding a child would not make sure she actually got safely back to her parents.

"You know. Charles. Up in the attic."

Billy had just caught up with them. "Shut up, Maggie. We're not supposed to say anything."

Tilting back on her heels Claire stared at both her children. "What man in the attic? What's going on here?"

With a heavy sigh Billy hung his head and said, "We promised we wouldn't tell you."

"Made a promise to whom you wouldn't tell me what?" Claire asked sternly.

"Pluto. I mean, he's not really Pluto. He's Old Charles. Just like Mrs. Jenkins said. And he really is living up in the attic. And he talks to us. And we can see him."

Claire stared at her children and shook her head. "I really don't know *what* I'm going to do with the two of you," she said crossly. "I've *had* it with your stories."

"But we're not making it up, Mom. He's real," Billy insisted. "And he's a friendly ghost, Mom. Not like Mrs. Jenkins said at all."

"Oh. Mrs. Jenkins." Claire nodded knowingly. "I've got it all figured out now. Your ghost and Mrs. Jenkins have a conspiracy going on. He scares everybody off. The more times she sells the place, the more money she gets. She must have made a fortune by now."

"But he's *not* scary, Mom." Billy assured her. "And he *wants* us to stay there."

"*He* wants *us* to stay?" she repeated incredulously. "*He* told you this?"

"Well," Billy hesitated. "Yeah."

The trip back to the house was quick. Definitely quicker than Claire should have been driving. She was bound and determined to prove once and for all to her imaginative children that there was nothing up in the attic. No Pluto. No Charles. No ghost.

Ushering Billy and Maggie up the steps to the attic, she flung open the door and switched on the overhead light. All was quiet.

"So where's your ghost?" she demanded.

Billy peeked around her and pointed. Slowly, not really wanting to make her even madder, he whispered, "He's right over there. By the window."

Claire critically examined the spot he indicated. "That's nonsense. There's nothing there."

Amused, Charles leaned against the wall, arms folded across his chest, a broad grin on his face. *"Tell her she can't see me yet. And she can't hear me. She doesn't believe."*

Billy swallowed hard and nodded. "He says you can't see him or hear him cuz you don't believe."

"I don't . . . *what?*" Thoroughly exasperated and vexed by such an exhausting day, Claire finally lost what little was left of her patience. Shooing them to the door, she ordered, "To bed. *Now.* The both of you!"

Before she followed them down the stairs, Claire couldn't keep herself from turning back to glance by the window.

✳   ✳   ✳

Fluffy white bubbles tickled her chin. Claire leaned back into her steaming hot bath thoroughly enjoying the peace and quiet. Her legs ached. Her whole body ached right down to the core of her soul. Feeling like a rotten mother, she just couldn't send the children to bed without any supper. But it had taken every bit of what little energy she had left to fix them something to eat.

He sat on the edge of the tub watching as he used to do years ago. With a black velvet ribbon, her long dark curls were piled on top of her head to keep from getting wet. Like he remembered. She stretched her legs out to rest her heels on the side of the tub, the suds clinging to her skin. Just to tantalize him. Charles longed to take the sponge and drizzle soapy water the length of her silky body. From the tip of her nose to the tips of her toes. The fragrant foam would part just enough for him to be teased with a glimpse of her luscious curves hidden beneath the bubbles.

She did love her baths. To Clarissa it was a luxury she had coaxed for ever since she saw the lady-slipper tub displayed in the mercantile store in Richmond. How could he have refused her anything?

Glossy white porcelain. Pretty pink hand-painted roses all around the sides. Brass feet. Tiger paws, she'd called them. It remained, still in perfect condition, some owner along the way braving Charles' presence long enough to allow his home to be adapted with modern plumbing. He had no quarrel with tradesmen.

And now his darling Clarissa lay in front of him once more, relaxed, drawing the warmth from the water to heal her aching muscles. Closing his eyes, he imagined the thrill of her flushed body stretched against his own. Skin to skin. Thigh to thigh. He couldn't wait much longer.

He had to make her believe.

SEVEN

"Don't be too hard on them, my love. They're only children." Charles leaned over to whisper to Claire while she slept. Murmuring gently, his breath fluttered the fine soft hair feathering around her ear. It was all he could do to keep from touching her.

"You must believe them, my darling. They tell you the truth." She stirred. Rocking back on his heels, Charles remained still. Why, he didn't know. Claire couldn't see him. Not yet.

Charles did not understand this business of afterlife. All he knew was that he was somehow caught up in it. He would not have thought a ghost, a phantom, would have substance or solid form. Should not be able to grasp or be touched. Should not possess the ability to breathe or feel the warmth of his blood coursing through his veins. Yet he did.

"Clarissa. You *will* know me once more." After all, it was her spell that sentenced him to this incarceration in the first place.

Charles had not believed in her black magic. Had not believed in her childish incantations. Seeing no harm in her potion, he had partaken. Willingly. Anything to humor her.

"Remember, my love? Remember the night you brought me into this world?" Closing his eyes, he could hear her words.

> To span all time, defy the dark; We, as one, will ne'er be part. 'Tis me for thee and thou for me; Be blessed for all eternity.

Drinking deeply of the wine she offered, Charles gave no heed to what might actually be in the brew. Dragons blood from the dracaena plant, lotus, orris root and sandalwood. Clarissa made no attempt to hide from him her little vials and charm bags filled with herbs and finely ground powders. Doves hearts, sparrow livers, swallow wombs, rabbit kidneys. All necessary ingredients for her potions of love and protection.

Although claiming her mystical powers had been passed to her through her Cajun grandmama, Clarissa did not religiously practice the Craft. It was more an amusement for her. A parlor game. Entertainment for the lovesick swains and bashful southern belles attending the countless balls and cotillions they attended throughout the year.

Clarissa let them know, in no uncertain terms, that her practice was purely for fun and only matchmaker's sport. Frivolous amusement with no promise or guarantee. If they believed her spells had brought them the happiness they sought, what harm was there in that? If the object of their affection spurned their advances, even after they had sipped of her potion, then, as Grandmama said, it wasn't meant to be. They would surely have lived a life of misery and discontent had they pursued the match.

A true romantic, Clarissa would have nothing to do with rendering potions of revenge or demonic ritual. There was already far too much evil in the world. To dance with the devil would bring no peace and she severely admonished anyone coming to her with such a request threatening them with a curse of her own. With a sinister giggle, she'd warn she hadn't found the need to turn anyone into a toad . . . yet. But there could always be a first time.

A few pious old biddies tried to have her arrested for witchcraft, but the town justice laughed them off. He hadn't heard of anyone since the time of Salem being hung or burned at the stake, he had told them, and he wasn't going to start up that persecution again. Clarissa was just playing up the romanticism of her ancestry. She made no bones about it. He, himself, had been thoroughly entertained on many occasions with her palm readings and tarot card predictions. No one took her seriously.

No one except Charles who now found himself wandering alone in a no-man's land called the hereafter. As he gazed at his sleeping bride, he couldn't help wondering what had kept her from joining him at the time of his death. Her own spell had not affected her in the same way it had protected him.

When that final night had overtaken his own earthly body, his spirit rejoiced. To be in this world without his beloved wife and children had been hard enough to bear. To wake on the other side still alone was torture beyond words.

He told her this while she peacefully slept. Charles hoped she would hear him. Hoped she would somehow absorb what he was saying and know it to be true.

✸   ✸   ✸

It had all the makings of a glorious party. The troops were marching out in the morning.

Charles had worn his new uniform as did all the other officers. The women looked resplendent in their gowns.

The atmosphere of the whole affair struck Clarissa as being outrageously festive. Was she the only person in attendance who had any inkling at all of the severity of the situation about to face them? Their men were being sent to war and all these women could do was bat their eyelashes and flutter their fans.

The strains of *The Blue Danube* could be heard from the ballroom. This would be Clarissa's last chance to persuade Charles to rethink his decision, yet she already knew no amount of pleading on her part would ever change his mind once it was set.

Clarissa did her best to keep her spirits bright if only for Charles' sake. She did not want his last day with her to be melancholic, yet it was painfully hard to keep the sadness from showing in her eyes.

He held out his hand to lead her onto the dance floor. She buried her face into his shoulder to hide the tears.

✸   ✸   ✸

She could hear her own voice. The laughter. The music.
She could see herself. The gowns. The uniforms.

She was there in that ballroom. There dancing in a long flowing gown of royal velvet trimmed with delicate Victorian lace. The voluminous skirt spread wide with those despised wooden hoops. The very same hoops that hung from a spike in the roof truss in the attic.

Claire had been dancing with a tall handsome man in his freshly pressed uniform. With a thin black leather thong, his shoulder-length sandy hair was pulled back into a queue that bounced against his broad back as he twirled her around the dance floor. Rimming his full lips, a respectably trimmed mustache hinted a few strands of red mixed with wiry whiskers just a smidgen darker than the hair on his head. Laughing green eyes gazed adoringly into hers.

Sparkling eyes that betrayed just a hint of fear.

The dream had continued and, as dreams oftentimes do, turned disturbing. Claire turned fitfully in her sleep. Her legs thrashed although they seemed leaden. Movement was slow. Burdensome. She ran yet got nowhere.

Horses. Soldiers. People shouting. Screaming. A gun shot.

Hide. Take the children to the cellar. You'll be safe in the cellar.

Claire woke as her bare feet hit the cool dampness of earth. Disoriented and confused, she could feel her heart pounding against her rib cage. Its deafening pulse throbbed in her ears.

Claire turned to get her bearings. This sleepwalking business was getting completely out of hand. The thought of handcuffing herself to the bedpost flitted through her mind. Had she not been so disconcerted, Claire may have found the notion humorous, but she was anything but amused. One minute she was snuggled sound asleep in her bed. The next she was . . .

Where was she?

It gradually dawned on her that she hadn't wandered outside into the yard. The floor under her feet was hard packed and there were stone walls all around her. She was in some kind of pit. A dungeon.

There were lights. Somehow she had managed to turn on the overhead lights but all she could see in front of her was a bright yellow halo surrounding a big black spot that blocked most of her line of vision.

It took a moment for her eyes to adjust. Squinting, she rubbed a hand over her face.

As she became more focused, Claire realized she was in the basement. Wooden steps behind her led back up to the first floor. And there was the trap door in the corner Connie said was the root cellar.

Claire's attention riveted on the trap door. She pulled back, yet she was powerless to stop her feet from inching closer. She reached for the ring and pulled up on the door.

Musty air filled her lungs. She coughed then sneezed as an eerie chill swept over her body. Reaching for another light switch, Claire peered into the hole before her.

The pit wasn't more than six feet deep. Maybe ten by ten square or even twelve feet she guessed. Claire wasn't very good at judging dimensions.

A rickety ladder sloped against one side. Claire gingerly placed her weight on the top rung. She bounced lightly to test its soundness then scrambled down.

Dirt and spiders. That's what Connie had told her. There was certainly no doubt about the dirt. And spiders the size of walnuts bungee-jumped from their sticky webs to look her over. Old paint cans. A bit of rotten rope. Dusty Mason jars. Rusty jar lids and nails were scattered here and there. A bashed-in bucket with holes in the bottom. Moldy harness straps with buckles tarnished a turquoise blue.

Claire moved closer to examine a plank wall which seemed out of place. The others were nothing but dirt.

She reached out to run her hand over the rough wood. As her fingers grazed the surface, a wave of paralyzing fear clamped her eyes shut.

In her mind's eye, Claire saw herself raise a weapon and fire upon a blue-coated soldier. She felt a child lifelessly slip from her arms. Another shot rang out and a young girl crumpled to the ground. In frenzied anguish, she swung the axe that took another's life.

The horrendous scenes sped through her memory flash upon flash. The repetitions accelerated into a blur. The momentum reached the breaking point as numbing pain drilled into Claire's chest, the force so powerful it slammed her back against the ladder.

A void dark as death descended upon her.

Charles held her trembling body as she endured her hell. Nestled in his arms, Claire had cried out in fear and torment.

As she threw back the sheet and sat up in bed, Charles was aware she still slept. He followed Claire to the basement of their house. Stood silently by as she woke. Witnessed her pain as she relived the darkest day of their past. Caught her as she crumpled in unconsciousness.

Charles carried her back to their bed. She lay so motionless, so deeply asleep, he had to assure himself she still breathed. His tears fell onto Claire's flushed cheek.

"*Charles!*" she whispered aloud then abruptly awoke.

After treating the children to a feast of pancakes and sausage, Claire took her time cleaning up the breakfast dishes. The dream had disturbed her so much she couldn't help but think about it.

It had frightened her. And she couldn't explain it. It had felt all so—familiar. Like *déjà vu* or something.

Maybe her subconscious was reliving a book she had read or a movie she had seen at some time in the past. Yet that didn't explain the dirt on her feet.

Pretty well sick of painting, Claire wasn't too anxious to get back at it. She had planned to start on the attic storey, but thought better of it. It was too hot to be out on the roof today. Besides, there was always tomorrow. The birds were singing. It was a perfect day to take a break.

With a picnic lunch packed, bathing suits and towels thrown in the back seat just in case, off they went to explore parts unknown.

Claire expected to be caught up in the anticipation of discovering and exploring new places, but down every road, around every corner, seemed familiar. As if she had been there before.

And to top it all off, unless her memory was failing her terribly, the upper levels of the house seemed to have been painted while they were gone. A whole five-gallon pail of paint had been emptied. The brushes, clean and dry, hung where she had left them.

That, combined with the dream the night before, was all too unnerving. With a queasiness in the pit of her stomach Claire couldn't define, she tucked two exhausted children into bed then went to draw herself a well-deserved bath.

He leaned back into the corner and watched as she untied the cord that snugged her nylon wind pants around her trim waist and let them fall to the floor. Fascinating. Undergarments were appreciably more fetching than in his day. Today they were lacy and red. What there was of them.

She slipped the panties off flinging them by one delicate foot into the corner where he stood. Like waving a red flag in front of a raging bull. Teasing. Taunting. He almost reached out to snatch them in mid-air. Struggling for control, Charles bit his lip.

Her breasts bounced as she pulled her shirt over her head. Long dark curls tumbled into her face hiding for a moment the gentle curve of her nose. Her cheeks. Bared from head to toe, Claire reached for her brush. One breast then the other would peek from under the cover of her swaying locks as she stroked her long hair until it shone.

Just as entranced by her beauty as he was over a hundred and fifty years ago, Charles followed as she freely strolled around the room totally unconcerned about her nakedness.

From under the pillow Claire snatched a longer tee-shirt pulling it roughly over her head breaking the spell that held Charles' gaze. Barely covering the swell of her bottom, the night shirt did precious little to protect her modesty.

As Claire switched off the light and climbed into bed, Charles whispered huskily so only he could hear. *"Sleep now, my darling. Sleep so I may come to you."*

Soon her chest rose and fell in soundless rhythm. Sitting on the edge of the bed, the mattress dipped under his weight. Risking a touch Charles brushed a tendril from her cheek. She didn't stir. His lips brushed across hers. Sitting back he waited to see if she would waken. She didn't. Bending toward her once more he kissed her. Fully. Deeply. Passionately. Then reluctantly he withdrew.

Honeyed breath escaped her lips in a gentle sigh as she rolled over to make room for him. "What took you so long?"

For over a century, he had waited— hungered—for this very moment. Sliding his body next to hers, Charles shivered as the silky smoothness of her legs touched against the hairy roughness of his own.

Turning into him Claire unconsciously squirmed out of her shirt and tossed it onto the floor. Holding him close in her arms she pressed her breasts into his chest. Nuzzled her lips into his neck. Ran a finger down the ridges of his spine to the bottom of his tail bone then back up again sending him into convulsions of delirium.

"It's been so very long, my love," he whispered hoarsely. Searing heat spread through his loins. There was no controlling it. No holding back now.

He could see her there in the dark. See her in all her splendid glory. Daring to explore, Charles spread his hands over her firm breasts. Kneading. Teasing. Arousing. Thirsty heat scorched as he suckled one. Then the other. Just how she liked. With a whimper of pure delight, her hand grasped the back of his head pulling him closer. Closer still.

As she held his head firmly, his hands searched lower. Arching her back, Claire welcomed his touch. Reaching around, Claire grasped Charles' buttocks pulling him toward her moaning seductively as the strength of his maleness pressed deliciously against her inner thighs. She opened herself to him.

He took her gently. As gently as on their first night together.

EIGHT

A warm glow washed over Claire as she leisurely stretched. As vividly as the others, she remembered—*everything*—about this dream. The facial features of her leading man. The sound of his voice. The way she imagined him touching her.

Claire knew she had always dreamt but seldom remembered much, if anything, when she woke. To her knowledge she had never before had a recurring dream. Although the scenes playing in her nocturnal dramas were always different—some event or other from a time long past—the finales were, without a doubt, worthy of a thousand encores. The thought sent a thrill of delight directly to her lonely heart.

With a groan of protest Claire reluctantly rolled out of bed. She wished she could just stay where she was all day long. But there was still too much to get done to keep her end of the bargain with the owner of the house. She was almost finished her room. Just had one more wall and the closet to do. Maybe she could get it done before breakfast.

One side of the closet was floor-to-ceiling shelves, empty except for a heavy box she discovered shoved to the back out of sight at the very top. The chair rocked precariously beneath her as Claire stretched on tiptoe. "What's in this thing, lead weights?" she groaned as she tried to slide it within reach. All of a sudden the shelf gave way and the box plummeted to the floor with a resounding crash. The floorboards shattered.

"*Oh, no*!" Claire cried as she gaped at the damage she caused. "How am I going to fix that?"

Hearing the smash, Billy and Maggie ran into the room. "What happened, Mom?"

"Oh, I dropped that box," Claire explained miserably. "It was so heavy it broke the floor."

Billy took hold of it. "Be careful," she warned. "It weighs a ton."

"No, it doesn't." Billy easily lifted it off the cracked boards. "There's nothing in it," he said peering inside the opened flaps.

"*What?*" Claire exclaimed. She hopped down from the chair and had a look herself. Sure enough there was not so much as a fluff of lint inside.

Meanwhile, Maggie had crawled into the closet to check out the hole the box had made. Squinting in the darkness to see under the boards, she said, "There's something down there, Mommy."

Claire lifted the chair out of the way over top of her crouching daughter. "Billy, go get me the hammer, please." The boards were still fastened tightly at the edges, the cracked ones not broken enough to pull apart.

With a little effort, Claire pried off the loose boards. Hidden underneath was a good-sized metal box. Covered with dust it obviously had sat undisturbed for many years. Heaving it out from between the floor joists, Claire moved into the light.

The children huddled in anticipation as Claire cautiously lifted the lid. It was not padlocked but the rusty hinges creaked eerily sending a chill up her spine.

"Just a minute. Just a minute." Claire swatted their hands away as the children each tried to reach in and make a grab. Feeling she had just made the discovery of the century, Claire took a moment to bask in the moment quickly taking stock of the contents before removing them.

Gingerly, she first removed a bound packet wrapped in stiff cotton. Probably a flour sack or maybe even a sugar sack at one time. Inside she found a number of hardcover books, the pages brown and brittle with age. With only a cursory glance inside, she would have to say these books were someone's journals. Along with the journals were bundles of old letters tied up with red satin ribbon.

Setting them aside, she reached for a dark brown leather pouch. Very heavy, it was obviously what had given the box its weight. Carefully pulling apart the thong that held it together, Claire gasped in disbelief as she looked inside.

Now she knew exactly how the old prospectors felt when they made a strike. With a jubilant cry of victory, she tipped the bag spilling a few hundred golden coins through her outstretched fingers.

"Holy smokes," Billy yelled.

"What are they?" Maggie squealed jumping up and down clapping her little hands mirroring Billy's enthusiasm even though she had no idea why.

"It's money, stupid," Billy jibed.

"That's enough," Claire interceded, still stunned by the brilliant glitter she held in her hands.

"Can I have a pony?" Maggie asked hopefully.

"It's not our money," her mother tried to explain.

"Why not?" Billy demanded. "We found it."

"Well, it's not our house, for one thing. It doesn't belong to us. So this doesn't belong to us either," she said with a twinge of disappointment as she scooped the coin back into the pouch.

"Well, that's not fair," Billy grumbled.

The money already forgotten, Maggie pulled the last package from the box. "This is pretty. Can I open it?" Wrapped in a remnant of soft crimson velvet, it was small and very thin.

"Carefully."

Holding the packet as if it were rare treasure, Maggie painstakingly unwound the fabric, fold after fold after fold.

"Hurry up," Billy said impatiently.

Claire shot a warning glare at her son. Just as anxious to see what was inside, she didn't want Maggie to break whatever it was by being overly rough.

What looked like three pieces of thin metal were tucked into the last fold of velvet. Carefully turning them over, Claire recognized they were old tintypes. The first was a woman and two children.

"That's *me*," Maggie pointed excitedly.

Billy bent to get a closer look and laughed aloud. "That's me, too."

"Oh, don't be silly," Claire scolded gently as she tilted the photograph to the light. The background was quite dark and grainy and the image of the people not very clear. But her heart skipped a beat as she stared into the dark brooding eyes of what appeared to be her very own reflection.

With a shaky hand, Claire carefully set aside the mysterious photograph of someone who bore a striking resemblance to herself and her children. The next was a photograph of a group of people posed in a rather formal setting. Rich brocade drapery provided the backdrop. Potted ferns sat atop waist-high Grecian columns on both sides of the group. Smaller children were seated in the foreground of the photo in ornately carved chairs. Studying the picture intently, Claire could make out the people who resembled herself and the children. Catching her breath, her eyes riveted on the man dressed in a captain's uniform of the Confederate Army. Standing straight and tall, slightly behind the others, was the image of the soldier she had danced with in her dream.

Shaking her head, Claire dispelled *that* ridiculous notion from her thoughts. Of course it couldn't be the same person, but the coincidence of the resemblance—or what she imagined the man in her dreams looked like—was staggering.

There had to be a logical explanation for all these look-a-like photographs. Then Claire remembered how much her own mother looked like a photograph she had seen of her great-grandmother. They could have been sisters. Possibly there was a familial connection way back somewhere. It's said everyone has a twin someplace. But a twin for all of them at the same time?

Claire forced herself to look away from the dashing soldier and concentrate on the black couple standing proudly behind three young black children. "*Simon and Breezie.*" The names slipped from her lips in a barely audible whisper.

"Don't dawdle, children. And don't get yourselves all mussed up." Clarissa herded all five of them in front of her out of the dusty street and onto the slatted board side walk. Just like a parade of little stair steps, they were so close in age, but had just enough difference in height to be comical. Abraham, then William, Moses, Margaret, and little Ruth trotting along at the rear of the line, all spit and polished in their Sunday best.

Darling little Ruth, so excited, her chubby cherub cheeks were about ready to pop with the biggest smile she could muster, her dark chocolate skin in stark contrast against the snowy whiteness of her frilly gown. The boys, each and every one, tugged miserably at their stiffly starched collars uncomfortable and itchy in their new woolen suits.

The pendulum clock on the wall chimed its eleventh stroke as Clarissa ushered everyone into the room. "Just on time," she sighed with relief. No other clients were in the studio.

The photographer emerged from a curtained alcove in the back saying, "I'll be right with . . . " He looked up, his jaw dropping, his face draining instantly of any and all color.

"What is it, Mr. Rainsford?" Clarissa rushed to his side, steadying him by the arm. "You've become frightfully peaked."

Desperately trying to compose himself, Mr. Rainsford motioned to Charles who, dressed in his newly issued Confederate uniform, hurried to support the photographer's other arm. "Anything we can do, Mr. Rainsford? Should we call for the doctor?"

Mr. Rainsford waggled his finger for Charles to come closer. Lowering his voice, he bobbed his head toward Breezie and her family. "Captain Montgomery, I don't allow coloreds in my establishment."

Clarissa gave Charles no time to respond. "Mr. Rainsford, I made an appointment weeks ago for a family portrait and a family portrait is what I intend to have."

"Mrs. Montgomery, with all due respect," he implored impatiently, "I was not aware your family was so . . . diverse . . . so to speak."

Slowly sidling toward them, Simon nervously twisted his hat in his hands. "Miz Clarry," he murmured, "we don' wants to cauz you no trouble. We'll jus' go on outside an' wait fer y'all."

Not taking her blazing eyes from Rainsford's, Clarissa shooed him back. "You'll do nothing of the sort, Simon. Mr. Rainsford will be taking our photograph in just a moment."

With that she clutched Rainsford by the arm and dragged him toward the curtained alcove.

"Captain, please," the photographer pleaded. Charles threw up his hands and backed away. Better his wife to deal with this situation.

Once partitioned from the others, Clarissa turned angrily. She slowly perused the little man up and down. Rainsford was a gaunt man not a fraction taller than Clarissa herself. A bead of sweat trickled from his brow under a shock of greased-down black hair. His horn-rimmed spectacles slipped to the tip of his nose. With a quivering finger, he pushed them back into place. His suit was finely cut, she observed, but the cuffs were just beginning to fray.

Rainsford cleared his throat. His Adam's apple bobbed apprehensively. "Mrs. Montgomery . . ."

"Mr. Rainsford," she interrupted. "I didn't realize you were so affluent that you could afford to refuse an engagement."

With nervous hesitation, he raised his nose ever so slightly. "I'm quite successful."

"You don't say," she said with arched eyebrows as if she didn't believe a word. "Well, now, isn't that just the cat's meow. Then I guess you really don't need my money after all. Or my father-in-law's. You're acquainted with my husband's father, are you not, Mr. Rainsford?"

The little man swallowed hard. "I do believe so, madam," he croaked.

"And I do believe he holds the mortgage on this fine establishment, does he not?"

Rainsford did not answer. By the pallor of his face, one would think he had just been stricken with apoplexy.

"I believe we have just reached an understanding, have we not, Mr. Rainsford?"

The last thing the photographer needed right now was more financial woes. He barely made his last payment. This month, as well, would be a tight squeeze. Fact was, he needed the money from this sitting. Desperately. Bad publicity would destroy his faltering business and he had no doubt Mrs. Clarissa Montgomery could effectively ruin him with just a few well-chosen words.

This could be the beginning of a very lucrative season for him. Many of the enlisting soldiers were making appointments for a photograph for their families or sweethearts before they headed off into battle.

Finding himself in a total quandary, the photographer could only suggest a compromise. "One consideration, if you will, Mrs. Montgomery."

"I'm listening, Mr. Rainsford."

"I do understand where your sympathies lie, ma'am. Really I do. But you have to realize these aren't the times to make enemies. With the war and all . . ."

"Your point, Mr. Rainsford," she said impatiently tugging at the fingers of her white kid gloves.

Rainsford swallowed hard. "I still have to make a living in this town. If anyone saw you all coming in here . . . if anyone sees you leaving the studio. No offense, Mrs. Montgomery, but my business— my livelihood—could be wiped out. You'll have your photograph, but I would ask that you afford me the courtesy of leaving by the rear door. That's all."

Clarissa frowned at the little man and stubbornly shook her head. "I won't hear of it, sir. We came in the front door, we'll be leaving the same way." Her conviction was strong, but she did understand his position. He was afraid, just like everyone else in town.

She had no intention at all of trying to ruin his business. It was just a ploy to get what she wanted. Nothing more. However, the stricken look on his face softened her resolve. "May I make a suggestion to you, sir?" Rainsford raised his eyes. "As you say, with the war and all, you may want to consider changing your, um . . . policy. I dare say many Negroes will be joining up and would more than likely appreciate services such as yours."

"It is a consideration, ma'am." One he had not thought of and could see as profitable.

"And to address your concern of a moment ago. I can assure you no one saw us come in here. What I would be willing to do for you this one time, Mr. Rainsford," she proposed, "is to make sure the street is clear before we leave. But we will be leaving by the front door."

With a heavy sigh, Rainsford knew that would be the best he could hope for. With downcast eyes, the little man nodded assent. "Then we have an understanding, madam." With that, he shot through the curtains clapping his hands, barking sharp instructions, just wanting to get this whole procedure over and done with as quickly as possible before anyone else chanced by.

"Okay, now," he ordered crisply. "Let's pull these chairs into the center. The two little girls sit in front. Women behind the chairs. Gentlemen on either side of your wives. Boys, squeeze in around your parents."

Clarissa took her place beside her husband in front of the richly woven drapery. With an affectionate squeeze of her hand, Charles leaned over and whispered, "What did you do, threaten to turn him into a warthog?"

With a smug giggle, Clarissa responded, "Worse than that. I threatened him . . . and enticed him . . . with the almighty dollar."

With practiced efficiency, Rainsford slid a prepared plate into the camera and tossed the dark-cloth over his head. He peered through the lens. "Now don't move."

Rainsford was just about to remove the cap to let the light hit the plate when he noticed a gap between the Captain and the black couple. Suddenly, he felt the edge of the dark-cloth lift. "Mrs. Montgomery, please take your place."

"Just one more thing, Mr. Rainsford," Clarissa whispered with just the slightest hint of suspicion. "I do trust these photographs will develop properly."

❋　　❋　　❋

The scene swept vividly through her mind in a split-second flash. As though it were tainted by the devil himself, Claire flung the metal plate from her fingertips.

"What's wrong, Mom?" Billy asked as he rescued the picture from the floor to take a look. His face broke into a broad grin. "Hey, Maggie. It's us again with a whole bunch of black kids."

"How did we get in the pictures, Mom?" Maggie asked innocently.

"It can't be us, sweetie," Claire tried to explain. "It's just people who looked a bit like us a long, long time ago." What else could she say?

With just a hint of trepidation, Claire hesitantly reached for the last photograph. Turning it over, she found herself gazing into the solemn face of the Captain. His eyes seemed to lock with hers with a look of sheer devotion. Yet the camera caught a hint of sadness. The obvious outpouring of love reached the very depth of her soul. With a gentle fingertip, Claire traced the outline of his cheek.

"Who's that one of, Mom? Let me see."

Claire cleared her throat along with her mind. "Well, I don't really know. I'm guessing it just might be Charles Montgomery."

"Yup, that's him," Billy said as he bent to look closer at the picture. "Isn't it, Mags?"

"Yup. Let's go tell him we found his picture." They scooted off to the attic.

Stammering some incoherent nonsense in reply, Claire was too mesmerized by the photograph to fully grasp what the children had just said. She was positive . . . almost . . . maybe . . . that this was the image of the soldier she had dreamt about.

Could it be possible? Was something—someone—truly haunting her nights? Was she dealing with a ghost?

NINE

The river was swollen from a heavy rain the night before, but that didn't stop the children from wanting to swim. With a watchful eye, Claire stayed close by wading up to her thighs in the shallows putting herself between the children and the faster-running current. The cool water lapped at the bottom of her bathing suit. That was as wet as she intended to get. She wasn't much of a swimmer any more.

They had found the little cove further up from the house where the flow calmed and the river bottom was covered with fine gravel and sand.

Letting her eyes roam, Claire took in the scenery around her. It was such a pretty spot, she thought. The sound of the water trickling around a tangle of fallen branches here—over a jumble of rock there—made it peaceful. The land rose in a gentle slope up towards the top of the hill which was amass with giant oak trees. Fine grasses blew in the breeze. Wild flowers adorned the hillside.

Straining to see the top of the knoll, Claire could have sworn she saw a shadow pass behind one of the trees.

She thought no more of it as Maggie cried out, "No *splashing*, Billy."

"Then stay out of my way."

"Wasn't in your way." Maggie scooped her little hand through the water and shot a feeble spray toward her brother.

"Was too." Billy's splash was bigger.

"Was *not*!" Water stung Maggie's eyes. *"Mommy!"*

"That's enough." Claire stepped between shooing them toward the bank. "Let's go. Get out and dry off."

Billy just had to get one last shot at his sister. Dipping his hands deeply into the water, he let loose a huge wave drowning his mother instead as she stepped into his line of fire. "Whoops. Sorry, Mom."

Claire looked like a drowned rat, her hair hanging in tangled strings down her face. Sputtering from water that had filled her mouth, she glared at her mischievous son. "You're in for it now, kiddo." Springing toward him, Claire knocked Billy off balance playfully trying to dunk his head under water. "Say *Uncle*."

"Uncle. Uncle. *Uncle*," Billy gasped between fits of laughter. Claire took him by the hand and dragged him to shore.

Maggie was already toweled off and heading up the hill. "Let's go home this way, Mom." They hadn't explored this far yet and the children were still looking for a good spot to build a fort.

"Race you, Mags," Billy challenged. He shot passed her and was half way up the hill before she could even turn around.

"No fair, Billy." Her brother had already disappeared over the crest, but she chased after him anyway. Claire straggled along behind loaded down with towels, water wings and floaters.

"Hey, Mom!" Claire could hear Billy shout. "There's a cem'tery up here."

"What?" she hollered back not sure if she heard him correctly.

"Dead people are buried here."

Claire finally reached the top just in time to hear him more clearly. Billy was pointing to a small square of white picket fence nestled among a stand of oak trees. Prickly brambles had grown to such a height they all but obscured the tiny plot. It was a wonder Billy could see it at all.

"Who's buried here, Mommy?" Maggie tried to find an easy way to the gate.

"Wait, honey. There's too many brambles. Let me go see if there's any names left on the stones." It was a shame that so many old grave stones were damaged by decades of erosion and exposure to the elements. What a story they could tell.

"I should have brought my camera." Always an afterthought. "This would make a great shot for my article." An abandoned grave site, long ago forgotten by descendants through the passage of time.

Picking her way through the thorns, Claire was surprised to see the picket fence wasn't rickety or falling down. She gave it a firm shake. It seemed sound enough and in such good repair it made Claire think it wasn't so old after all. The paint, not peeled or weather worn, seemed quite fresh.

Abandoned, perhaps, but not totally forsaken.

As she lifted the latch and pushed open the gate, it struck her odd that the grass had been carefully cleared from around all four stones. Claire might have assumed an animal, maybe a dog or coyote, had jumped in and taken a nap in the sunshine matting down the long blades.

But someone was taking very good care of this little cemetery. And someone had planted yellow roses which now rambled wildly among the stones.

Suddenly uneasy, Claire gingerly touched a bloom. "Yellow," she whispered.

The blossom slipped from her fingers as her attention was drawn to the names chiseled on the markers. A silent cry caught in her throat. Claire crumpled to her knees in front of the gravestones. Very clearly one bore the name Clarissa Montgomery. To her left lay Charles. To the right, their children. *William* and *Margaret.* The very names and ages of her own children. And the date of deaths, except Charles, was the same day.

Tears stung her eyes as she tenderly touched the stones of the children.

"They're not there, my darling." A calming sensation came out of nowhere. *"Look behind you. The children are alive and well."*

Claire looked around. With wild flowers fisted in her little hand, Maggie watched her. Billy was climbing a tree.

"We are all here, my love. We shall be together once more."

"Why are you crying, Mommy?" Maggie had followed her as far as she dared. Prickles grabbed at her bare little legs. "Did you get jabbed?"

Clearing her throat, Claire dabbed her eyes with an edge of a towel. She sniffled and wiped her dripping nose. "I'm okay, honey. It just made me sad to see children's names on the stones."

"Who is it, Mom?" Billy swung from a tree limb and scampered over beside his sister.

"It's the Montgomery family that Mrs. Jenkins told us about. Charles, his wife and their children, William and Margaret."

Maggie's little brow furrowed as she tried to put two and two together. "But Charles . . . "

Billy shoved her. He knew she was about to say that Charles was up in the attic. And they were still sworn to secrecy. Even though Maggie forced him to spill the beans that day they were at the waterfall, their mother hadn't believed them. So Billy figured they better not aggravate her any more than they normally did.

Maggie took the hint and said instead, "That's our names."

"Yes, it is." Claire's voice softened with sadness for the little ones buried behind her. "A real coincidence, isn't it?"

❉   ❉   ❉

"Lord have mercy, girl. Look what you've gone and done with this place." Connie Jenkins stopped in on her way by to see how they were making out.

Claire was busy in the attic replacing the broken window panes with new tiny glass squares she measured and had cut at the hardware store. She had watched her father fix their windows many times years ago and figured it couldn't be too difficult. Prying off the trim and pulling the window out was the hard part. Broken shards had to be tapped out and the old, hardened putty scraped off. The fun part was warming up the fresh putty getting it nice and squishy.

"This stinks," Billy said, his nose scrunched as he squirted the gooey stuff through his fingers.

"It's just like Play-Doh," Maggie giggled.

Toenailing the glass into the frame with glazing points, Claire had smoothed the putty around the edges and propped the window against the wall until it hardened.

"It's coming along." Pleased with her efforts, Claire wiped her hands on a rag and cleaned up her mess. "I'm ready for a break. How about a cup of tea?"

In the kitchen, Claire dropped a couple bags in the pot to steep. She was quiet for a moment trying to decide whether or not to confide in Connie. She felt she had to tell someone about what was going on.

Claire was afraid she just might be going crazy. After all, it was Connie who brought up the subject of ghosts in the first place.

"I'm glad you stopped by," Claire finally said. A slight tremor of nervousness quickened her voice. "There's something I want to show you. I'll be right back." Before she lost her nerve, Claire ran up the stairs for the strongbox.

"I thought maybe I wouldn't find y'all here. Thought maybe Ol' Charles would have scared you off by now." Connie laughed as Claire set the box on the table. "What's this?"

"Well, Connie, that's the funny thing," Claire said quite seriously. "The kids told me he wants us to be here."

Connie stared at her then broke out into a full belly chuckle. "The dickens, you say."

"They believe it wholeheartedly. But they haven't said much just lately after what happened the other day."

"What happened?"

"I'll get to that in a minute. Take a good look at these. They're unbelievable." Opening the box, Claire lay the tintypes out in front of Connie.

One by one, Connie picked up the photographs examining each in turn. "Sweet Mary, Mother of Jesus," she said under her breath more than once. Shoving one of the pictures under Claire's nose, she giggled with delight. "Look, I'm the spitting image of Granny Breezie."

Not quite as enthused as Connie, Claire politely compared the two. "That's because you two *are* related. My parents were French Canadian but I can't see how we could be related to these Montgomery people." Claire studied the photos thoughtfully. "But come to think of it . . . " Her brow furrowed with speculation. "Clarissa was Cajun. Maybe she was descended from the Acadians. My mother's people were from the Annapolis Valley. The Acadians were exiled from there and we know some found their way back."

"For sure, those poor unfortunates moved around a lot. Bloodlines have a tendency to get muddled up along the way at times. It's possible, I suppose."

"But not very likely." She still couldn't accept a potential link. Claire tucked that thought away and tapped the photo of the soldier with her index finger. "I've been dreaming about that man. Before I even saw this old picture of him. It's the same person, I'm sure of it."

"Are you serious? You think it's Charles you're dreaming about?"

"Well, I can't be one hundred percent positive, but this sure looks like the same guy. It hasn't just been once or twice either. It's all the time. Whenever I fall asleep he's wheedling his way into my brain."

"I never really took much stock in all those old ghost stories, but maybe there is something to it." Connie helped herself to another cup of tea. "Then again, there has to be some reason this poor old place changes hands so many times."

"Well, according to the kids it's all true. Charles is here. Up in the attic. They say they can see him all the time. They're always talking back and forth." She choked on a big gulp of scalding tea and rambled on. "Maggie wandered away in the park the other day. She swears it was that—*ghost*—who brought her back." She waved her hands in frustration. "They've got me so wound up with their stories maybe that's why I've started dreaming at night."

Enthralled with the whole idea, Connie asked, "What are you dreaming about?"

"Well, mostly about things that seem to have happened a long time ago." Claire stammered a bit, her cheeks blushing with embarrassment. "And they're really quite . . . *realistic* . . . if you know what I mean." She giggled suggestively. "Maybe I've just been alone too long and I'm making up these wild fantasies," she supposed. "But it's getting so weird, you know? Like someone's playing with my head.

"We found the old cemetery where the family's buried. I've never been so upset to read inscriptions on headstones like I was those ones. It was just *weird*. I can't think of any other word to describe it."

Taking a chance, Claire forged ahead. "And when I saw that group picture, I thought I could imagine the day it was taken. I even came right out and called these people Simon and Breezie. Just how bizarre is that?" Claire laughed in spite of herself afraid Connie was going to think she had gone completely nuts. "I've never seen these people before in my life."

Taking up her spoon, Connie concentrated on stirring her tea. "Well," she began slowly, "I've got the same picture in an old family album at home. There's no doubt. This *is* Breezie and Simon." Wagging a finger at Claire, she chuckled, "When we first met, I knew there was something familiar about you. Now I know why. It's like you've been plucked right out of the photograph. Maybe the children *are* seeing something. Or someone."

Frowning, Claire leaned back in her chair. "You've *got* to be kidding me."

Shaking her head, Connie continued. "Seriously. My brother wrote his thesis on the paranormal while he was studying in New Orleans. Studied the voodoo occult and all that black magic stuff. What actually got him interested was an entry in Granny Breezie's journal." She thought for a moment. "Listen, we're having a little get together Saturday afternoon. Just a backyard barbecue. Nothing fancy. Rudy's coming down from Washington. Why don't you bring the kids and stop by?"

"Oh, Connie, I don't think so. This is just far too *Twilight Zone* for me. It's got to be just a coincidence that we look similar to these people in the pictures. Maybe you're right and our bloodlines have gotten crossed way back somewhere."

"That's very possible, but it doesn't explain," Connie adamantly poked the table with a chubby black finger, "why you called these folk Breezie and Simon?"

Claire shrugged. "I haven't the slightest idea," she said truthfully.

"You did the same thing the day I first showed you around this place. You said the name Breezie. Remember?"

"Vaguely," Claire admitted hesitantly though she wasn't sure she wanted to admit anything at the moment.

"Well, something's obviously going on here, don't you think?" she huffed indignantly.

In spite of the folklore, Claire just couldn't force herself to believe that the house she was living in was invaded by spirits and she, herself, could be somehow caught up in the whole fantasy. But not wanting to offend, she said reluctantly, "Leave me your brother's number. I'll think about it."

❀ ❀ ❀

Claire had intended to leave the box untouched. The letters and journals unread. But curiosity got the better of her. Maybe it was the journalist in her. Maybe the researcher. Chiding herself for figuring she was just being outright nosey, she finally recognized it to be more than that. It was an overwhelming *need* to know what was written.

Someone had arranged the letters in chronological order. From the dates on one of the journals—the one written by a masculine hand—it carried on from where the packet of letters left off.

Curled up in the chair by the front window in the parlor, Claire pulled the top letter out from under the ribbon that held the stack together and eased the brittle pages from the envelope. She may as well start at the beginning.

> *June 7, 1861   My Dearest -*
>
> *I have only been away from you, my darling, for one day and that is one day too many. I miss you fiercely already. We have not heard yet when we will leave Richmond and I don't know whose brigade I will be attached to. The wait is almost unbearable. I say let us get on with it or let us go home. I long to see your beautiful face. Perchance there will be opportunity for me to get a brief furlough, but I am not counting on it.*
>
> *I don't think this whole thing has been thought through all too well. General Beauregard certainly opened a can of worms when he fired on Fort Sumter. The scramble is on for men, weapons and enough officers who know what they're doing to train this motley crew of green recruits. God bless them. Their hearts are in the right places but a lot of them coming from shops in towns and cities have never even seen the business end of a rifle, let alone handled one. If they don't shoot themselves, it will be a miracle.*
>
> *The attitude of the volunteers is depressingly festive. I fear they have not the faintest idea of the magnitude of the task facing them. Their swaggering gait shows that none doubt the outcome of this campaign. They are in for a very rude awakening.*
>
> *Old Diablo is faring well. There is no lack of ration for neither man nor mount . . .*

Breath caught in her throat. Had she read those words before? Not possible, she told herself with a shake of her head. But in spite of that conclusion, her hand trembled with anticipation as she finished that letter and opened the next envelope.

July 18, 1861   Dearest Clarry -

I was never so thankful as to be assigned to Johnston's Brigade here in the Valley. At least I'll get to see you once in a while. Had I been forced to stay here in camp day after day, I would surely go mad. After reveille and roll call, the order is usually drill, drill, and more drill sometimes lasting passed sunset. If we're lucky, we get to stop for a meal. Sometimes I think I would just as soon be a private. Then at least I'd get some change of pace. Maybe gather firewood or go to the river and collect water. Even dig latrines or fortifications. But they frown on officers doing such mundane duties. I don't see why we can't lend a hand. It's exercise and would break the monotony.

I'll have to finish this later. Just got called to Johnston's quarters.

July 19, 1861

It was too late to write any more last night, my darling. We'll be finally marching out this morning. Looks like we're headed for our first fight. We've been ordered to support Beauregard at Manassas Junction. He's holding off McDowell's army at Bull Run. There's Union troops nearby us so we're going to try and give them the slip and use the Manassas Gap Railroad and head on up to see what's going on. We've got 10,000 men here in the Valley. It's going to take a while to get there. Good Lord willing, we'll be back soon. Kiss the children for me.
Love to you all, Charles

July 30, 1861   My Darling Clarry -

Claire could see by the handwriting that something was terribly wrong. The boldness of the script of the previous two letters she had read had been replaced by a shaky hand and she could only imagine the words had been painstakingly written.

By now you will surely have heard of the unfortunate time we had of it at Manassas. I will spare you the details, my love, but suffice it to say I was one of the lucky ones.

Word is the losses totaled nigh on to nine hundred good young men. Fear not, my sweet. I am healing well and will be back in the field very soon. My wound, though somewhat painful, is not serious. More blood loss than damage. You'll have a pattern to trace with your finger along my chest . . .

Claire set the letter aside. With a gentle stroke of her fingers, she brushed it lightly, reverently, across the fading ink. For the life of her, she couldn't explain the strange feelings flooding through her.

Connecting her laptop computer to the phone line, she searched the internet for information on the Battles of Bull Run. Manassas was an easy trip from Shenandoah. With a little background under her belt, camera and notebook in tow, Claire set off for Battlefield Park.

The grounds seemed eerily quiet when she pulled into the parking area. One RV was taking up a good five spaces. There were only two other cars besides her own. But it was still quite early.

Overlooking the peaceful landscape of gently rolling fields and patchy woods, Claire wondered how much the country side had changed over the years since the battle. She could imagine bustling farms dotting the land with people toiling in the fields, cattle grazing, garden plots, corn crops and peach orchards.

A monument to the memory of the patriots who fell at Bull Run was erected near the rebuilt Henry House where the walking tour began. Also nearby was the grave of 85-year-old Judith Carter Henry. Refusing to leave her house for a place of greater safety, she was the only civilian killed in the first battle. In the end her fallow fields were bathed in blood and she lay amidst the wreckage of her house which was destroyed by a stray shell.

Leaving Henry House, Claire followed the trail north towards the Confederate artillery positions overlooking Matthews Hill, a vital location during the morning phase of the battle.

As she climbed over the knoll, the sun disappeared behind a cloud. Mist hung low in the little valley swirling in eery wisps along the path. The grass was slick after a steady rainfall the night before. Not watching her step, Claire slid precariously down the slippery slope wildly flailing her arms to keep from falling on her backside in the sticky red mud.

Catching her balance, she groaned as she realized her feet had become mired in the mucky ooze.

The mud made an unearthly sucking noise as she pulled her feet free. Claire stared at her shoes. Never before had she seen dirt this red anywhere in her travels. Balancing on one foot, then the other, Claire tried to scrape it off. Her mud-splotched face twisted with disgust as she flung globs of sticky muck from her fingertips with a flick of her wrist.

Considering she was in a battlefield, Claire imagined the mud stained with the dark red blood of the hundreds of fallen soldiers forever soaked into the earth.

That thought had little more than crossed her mind when deafening shots rang out. Instinctively, Claire ducked and covered her head. The acrid sulfuric odor of gun powder filled her nostrils. Her eardrums throbbed from the blasts.

Daring to look up, Claire could not believe her eyes. Out of nowhere, a battle was raging around her and she was caught in the middle. She spun wildly in all directions. Artillery, cavalry, infantry. Smoke. Carnage. Men falling as they cried out in agony and terror. Horses screaming as bullets bore into their flesh. Blood. *Death.*

She threw herself to the ground. Looking at her feet, Claire cried in horror. On her shoes was no longer mud but real blood that also streaked her arms and legs. Crawling to a small clump of trees, Claire hid in the bushes as soldiers fought to their last breaths right in front of her. Tears streamed from her eyes. No one heard her cries.

Inveigling its way into her mind, a voice carried through the din. A soothing caressing voice saying, *"Don't cry, my darling. No harm will come to you."* An aura of safety enveloped her. Claire sat up and dried her eyes looking around to see who had spoken. No one was near.

The more Claire calmed down and thought about it, the more she came to realize just how bizarre this whole scene was. This couldn't be real. She must have stumbled onto a re-enactment put on by some historical society. Or maybe it was a visual illusion, some brilliant special-effects show.

Concluding it was all just play acting, Claire swung up her camera and began photographing the images that appeared before her. Kudos to the actors and make-up artists. Oscars all around for authenticity and special effects.

Keeping well hidden in the underbrush, Claire skirted the performance trying to remember what she had read in her research that morning. As she watched in awe, the battle played out before her.

Bugles blared as more Confederate brigades marched in to assist. But even with these reinforcements the thin grey line collapsed and the Southerners fled in disorder toward Henry Hill.

"Stand and fight, men." Loud and clear, an order was bellowed from a general brandishing a sword, his mount dancing on staccato legs beneath him. "There stands Jackson like a stone wall! Rally behind the Virginians!" The famous cry of Barnard Bee gave General Thomas Jackson his nickname, "Stonewall," and turned the tide for the Confederate army.

The shattered brigades rallied and the battle continued for ten long hours. Just after four in the afternoon, fresh Southern units crashed into the Union right flank on Chinn Ridge. The tired and discouraged Federal soldiers withdrew.

Glancing at her watch Claire was amazed that it was already past four. Time had flown by. It didn't seem like she had been here that long.

Claire remembered reading that quite a few people from Washington brought wine and picnic baskets out to the battlefield to watch the spectacle. The Federal soldiers retreating across Bull Run found the road jammed with carriages. Panic seized many of the soldiers and the retreat became a rout.

The Confederates, though bolstered by the arrival of President Davis on the field just as the battle was ending, were too discouraged to chase the Yankees.

"What a show!" Claire, surprised she was still the only spectator, applauded as the actors straggled off the field. Some carried or dragged their comrades. Hundreds remained, Union and Confederate alike, where they dropped.

The majority of the boys weren't moving at all, Claire noticed, but lay prone in the dirt. They mustn't have realized the show was over. One young man lay on his back within a few feet of her. "Hey, buddy," she called out in a loud whisper. No response.

Claire crept out from behind the brush where she had been squatting and edged toward the fallen soldier. "Hey, you . . . " Leaping back, Claire gasped. The young man stared blankly toward heaven. His mouth gaped open. A large gash from a bayonet had torn through his neck. This man was really . . . *dead.*

Filled with revulsion, Claire hung her head to vomit. As rancid bile emptied from her stomach, she couldn't imagine how something so staged and choreographed could go so wrong. Was this poor boy a victim of some terrible accident? Did somebody's enthusiasm get so out of hand in his desire to make this performance realistic that he forgot this was all an act?

In a haze of shock, Claire stumbled from body to body, staring white-lipped into each face frozen with the grotesque expression of pain and agony. Of death.

A low moan of suffering caught her attention. Heading in the general direction of the sound, Claire searched for any sign of life. Anything at all.

Catching a slight movement out of the corner of her eye, Claire ran to a fallen soldier and fell on her knees beside him. Blood soaked through the front of his tattered grey uniform. The captain's stripes were virtually obliterated by filth. His eyes fluttered open as he sensed her nearness. A weak smile crossed his lips as he attempted to reach up and touch her face.

"*Clarissa* . . . " he hissed through clenched teeth.

Instantly recognizing him as the man in the tintypes, Claire instinctively reached to brush the hair from his forehead. "*Charles!*" Stifling a cry of terror, Claire shrank back as the essence of his body dissipated into thin air at the touch of her fingertips.

All the soldiers had disappeared. Each and every one. The field lay before her lush and green just as it had been from the moment she set foot on the grass earlier. She sat in the same spot in the path where she had slipped. The back of her head throbbed.

And her clothes. *White*, she grumbled. Of all the practical colors in the world, why would anyone pack white clothes to go camping? For the same reason, she guessed, they'd pack frilly red underwear. Sheer stupidity.

"You okay, ma'am?" The voice startled her. Claire stared mutely at the man. What could she say? She had just witnessed the first major conflict of the War Between the States.

Claire stammered something about falling and hitting her head. No need to see a doctor. Probably no concussion. She'd be just fine.

"Is there anyone I could call for you?"

"No. No one," she said flatly. "But thank you anyway." At least she could try to be polite. Really she would rather be left alone to try to make sense of what had just happened to her.

With the man's assistance, Claire shakily got to her feet but leaned on him more heavily than she had intended as he walked with her back to the visitor's center. He tried to keep her talking but Claire was in no mood for conversation. He left her at the door to the restroom.

Every nerve in her body vibrated as Claire tried to clean herself up. The experience had shaken her more than she would have liked to admit. She could have sworn she had witnessed the battle through to its conclusion late in the afternoon. Yet her watch read just ten thirty.

TEN

The scene that had just played out before him was so bizarre Chase wasn't quite sure what he had witnessed. He could have just passed her by. Could be just another bystander not wanting to get involved. But there weren't many people here so early. If she were in trouble he couldn't simply ignore her.

Chase had seen her slip and fall backwards onto the muddy slope. Looked like she gave the back of her head a good knock. Before he even had time to react, she got right back up again. Didn't seem to be hurt at all, just filthy with mud from head to toe.

A disgusted look crossed her face when she noticed the mess she was in and tried to shake the sticky mud from her fingers. Ducking suddenly, she covered her head like she was trying to avoid being hit from above.

Chase studied the sky. Hit by what? There wasn't so much as a bird in sight. Then she fell to the ground screaming as if something had frightened her. No, she was terrified. He had seen enough horror during his stint in the Marines to know terror when he saw it.

Chase never knew anyone could crawl so fast. The hounds of hell were snapping at her heels as she fled to the bushes. There he could see her cower in fear, could see the tears stream down her cheeks leaving muddy smudges where she tried to wipe them away with her dirty hands.

Then just as suddenly the tears stopped. Swinging her camera up in front of her face, she picked her way through the undergrowth of the tree line taking pictures of the empty field. Then, of all the crazy things, she started clapping. If the whole thing wasn't so strange, it would have been funny.

She wasn't laughing.

When the woman stepped out of the bushes, knelt on the grass and threw up her guts, Chase started to run. It probably wasn't such a great idea to be running so soon after his surgery but there wasn't time to call security.

The girl began running around the field like a madwoman. She'd stop for a split second here and there then swing around and take off in a new direction frantically calling for help.

The whole episode barely lasted a minute, two at the most, Chase guessed, when she ran back to the same knoll she had slipped down just moments before. Crouching on her knees, she stretched her hand toward . . . nothing . . . and passed out. He thought he heard someone's name slip from her lips. He wasn't sure.

On medical leave from Quantico, he planned an overdue visit with his parents. Spending the first few days after his release from hospital in D.C. visiting buddies probably wasn't the wisest thing to do considering the carousing reprobates they were. Too much booze. Too many late nights just about knocked the stuffing out of him.

But that was the last hurrah. No more alcohol. No more cigarettes. One bypass surgery was enough, thank you very much. The devil-may-care lifestyle he had known for the last twenty years had taken a drastic turn. For the better, he promised himself. He was too old for that kind of foolishness.

After two days in a hotel room sobering up, Chase finally felt well enough to get himself back behind the wheel. It was a long way to Arizona.

Continuing his trek meandering along back roads, he would keep to no particular route or schedule. He'd get there when he got there. With a new lease on life, he planned to take his own sweet time.

Manassas wasn't far from either DC or the Marine base at Quantico but he had never been. It was to have been a break, a pleasant stroll on a sunny day.

But Chase hadn't bargained for this when he pulled into Battlefield Park. Puffing from such slight exertion irritated him as he was now constantly aware of every surge of blood flowing through his arteries. The beat of his heart pounded like jackhammers in his ears as he bent to catch his breath. Chase realized it would take time to overcome the temporary limitations but this was ridiculous. The Corps had given him twelve weeks before he would be reassessed for active duty. He darn well better be fit by then. Any longer and Chase figured he would go nuts just like this poor creature lying in the mud.

Coming to, the woman sat up rubbing the back of her head. She hadn't heard him approach.

"You okay, ma'am?"

Catching her breath, the sound of his voice had taken her by surprise. Squinting up at him, she looked totally baffled and Chase wondered for a moment whether she saw him at all.

"I . . . hit my head . . . I think." Her voice sounded weak. Fragile. Confused.

"Can I get some help for you? Should we call an ambulance?" She did go down pretty hard. "Maybe you've given yourself a concussion."

Shaking her head adamantly, her response was quick enough. "No. Thank you. Really, I'm fine."

As she forlornly sat there in the mud, Chase had a chance to observe the woman a little more closely. She probably was a pretty little thing underneath all that dirt. Not much younger than himself he guessed.

She waved her hand toward the field whispering haltingly as if she really didn't want to broach the subject at all. "Did *you* see anything, *anyone*, you know, out . . . *there*?" She looked up at him her eyes almost pleading for validation of what she thought she had seen.

Following her gesture, Chase took a moment before he spoke, then countered with a question of his own. "You mean something else besides you?" The most pathetic look washed over her face. He thought she was going to cry. Averting her eyes, she nodded her head ever so slightly biting her quivering bottom lip.

He looked out over the empty field once more. Chase was at a loss how to respond. He wasn't about to tell her she was out there running around in circles, all alone, acting like some crazy person. Instead he asked, "Like . . . what?" hoping to get some idea what he was supposed to have seen.

Chase could almost see the wheels turning in her mind as she stared up at him. She was having great difficulty trying to decide whether to say anything at all. Finally, after a deep breath for courage and arms waving for emphasis, she blurted out, "Like soldiers. And horses. And . . . *shooting.*" She buried her face in her hands as if the recollection was just too painful to think about.

"Yeah, well, they're still fighting the Civil War down here," he muttered more to himself than to her. Then he saw the stricken look on her face. "No, there's just you and me out here," Chase spoke calmly. Shrugging his shoulder, he offered a simple explanation. "You know how the mind can work. You're in a place where something horrible has happened. If you blacked out for even a brief time, maybe your subconscious pictured the actual event since that may have been what you were thinking about when you fell."

Absorbing that possibility, she nodded acceptance. "I guess. Maybe." Still, she examined her arms and legs. "Do I have any blood on me?"

"Not a drop."

Brow furrowed in confusion, she whispered, "Strange. I could have sworn this whole hill was covered. It was so . . . *real.*"

"Pardon?"

Shaking her head the woman said nothing. It was a comment she hadn't intended anyone else to hear.

Since she didn't respond, Chase didn't press the matter. "Is there anyone I could call for you?"

"No. No one," she said flatly. "But thank you anyway."

At least she was trying to be polite. Chase reached out to give her a hand up. Just as she was about to grasp his hand she withdrew her own and looked at it with repulsion. "Oh, I'm so terribly filthy. I'll get you all dirty."

"I'm a big boy." His lip curled into a grin. "My mom taught me how to wash myself." Did he see a hint of a smile crease her lips? "Come on. Give me your hand. Or I could pick you up and carry you. What do you weigh? Ninety pounds?" He stood back, arms crossed, and gave her an overall appraisal. Were his eyes deceiving him or was that a blush creeping out from under all that grime?

"I don't remember *ever* being ninety pounds." She giggled in spite of the obvious discomfort. Wiping as much dirt off her hands and onto the grass as she possibly could, she relented and allowed Chase to help her up. A bit woozy from the bump on her head, it took a moment for her to regain her balance.

She twisted around to try to see the back side of her. "I should have known better than to wear white," she complained lightly. "It's going to take a gallon of bleach to get all these stains out."

"No matter. You're still beautiful."

She lowered her head bashfully at his compliment. Chase reached into his pocket for a handkerchief. "At least that's what I imagine you must look like under all this." He gently dabbed at her nose. His eyes suddenly locked with hers. The brief contact sent an electrical shock shooting up his arm scrambling his brains. He stepped back and handed her the handkerchief.

"I'm sorry. I shouldn't have done that," he stammered self-consciously. He, a confirmed bachelor, a career officer in the United States Marine Corps, was coming on to a strange . . . *very* strange . . . very *dirty* . . . lady. Present detour from reality notwithstanding, Chase could tell with one look she was far above the caliber of woman he was used to spending time with. Relationships he had of late were the kind you'd forget the girl's name by morning if you ever asked it at all. Even with her odd behavior of a moment ago, this was no one-night-stand kind of gal. No, she was one classy dame under all that muck. The kind you should ask before you touch.

"Well, I'm not going to break," she insisted as she plucked the handkerchief from his fingers and scrubbed it across her forehead. After a look at the mess she left behind she added, "You realize you won't be getting this back until I can wash it for you."

Here was his perfect opportunity to see her again or at least get her number. "Don't worry about it," Chase said instead. "My mother keeps me well stocked. One of those Christmas gifts you never have to ask for." Never before had he passed up a chance like the one that had just been practically dumped in his lap. What did those bloody surgeons do to his libido? It wasn't that she wasn't attractive enough or would be after she got herself cleaned up.

"Yeah, I know. With my mother it was cashews. I really looked forward to it. It was great because it was a real treat I wouldn't have gone out and bought for myself." Her voice softened. "I miss it."

"Your parents are gone?"

She nodded. "It's just me and my kids now."

Kids. Red flags suddenly waved in his face. No way were kids in his future. Chase blew out a long breath of relief. Good thing he hadn't tried to start anything. "Well, let's get you back so you can wash up a bit. Can you walk okay?"

"I hit my head. Didn't break my legs." Yet she swooned heavily against him. Catching her balance, she apologized. "Sorry. I guess I am a little dizzy."

"That's okay. Hold on to me. We'll take it slow."

"At this rate I won't make it home before dark." She glanced at her watch. "Oh, great," she muttered miserably. "It's broken."

"Let's see." Chase checked it against his own. "No, it's okay. That's the right time."

Again a look of total disbelief washed over her face. "It *can't* be." But she said nothing further.

When she came out of the restroom, Chase noticed she had tried to rinse out her hair. Though damp and tangled, at least it was no longer caked with mud. Her arms and legs were clean. There'd be no saving the clothes.

She didn't see him there in the shadows by the display of heavy artillery. Chase thought it best all around to keep out of sight. He'd done his civic duty just helping her back there. But the deep frown cratering her forehead, for some reason, bothered him.

Following at a distance, Chase watched as the woman unlocked the trunk of her car and reached in for a blanket. This she used to cover the driver's seat.

Almost forgetting his resolve, Chase's heart went out to her as she took a minute to rest her head on the steering wheel before starting the car. He had pretty well convinced himself it was the knock on the head that had her acting so weirdly. Another place, another time, and he would have probably given thought to pursuing her.

But he had places to go, people to see. And getting involved with a ready-made family was definitely not on his top-ten list of things to do.

Yet as she put her car into gear, he felt a yearning he couldn't quite explain. It took him by surprise.

Whatever it was he wanted, needed, craved from this woman was on a different level than anything he had ever known. She was different from any woman he had met.

Pushing through the door of the visitor's center, Chase found himself hurrying towards her vehicle. If he could have kicked himself in the ass he would have for he hadn't even asked her name. But it was too late.

As she pulled out of the parking lot, Chase noticed Canadian plates on her car. She wasn't even from around here. A tourist, like himself, just passing through. Chances of their ever crossing paths again were virtually slim to none.

Though it wouldn't hurt to see where she was heading.

Confident she hadn't noticed him following her, Chase pulled his Jeep out onto the highway. It didn't take long to catch up with her. She was driving slowly. Cautiously. Chase caught a glimpse of her reaching to rub the back of her head from time to time. At one point she pulled into a gas station, filled up, then took a minute to study a map.

Not wanting her to know he was near, Chase watched from the opposite side of the street. Letting a couple cars get between them, he once more followed at a safe distance.

Deep in thought, he recalled the strange events of the day. The minutes ticked by. He should have been well on his way west by now, but Chase rationalized it away. He was on a mission.

"It's a mission you want, is it, young Tanner?"

Chase jumped. A woman's voice came out of nowhere startling him.

"Stay true to your heart."

He glanced beside him. Chase could almost picture a hazy apparition riding shotgun with him. He did a double-take to the passenger seat. Another blink and the vision was gone and forgotten as Chase once again caught Claire's vehicle in his sights.

Claire made it home from Battlefield Park. How, she'd never know. Oblivious to everything but the pounding behind her eyes, she didn't notice the vehicle behind her slow at the end of the drive and inch along until it disappeared out of sight over the knoll.

She eventually managed to untangle herself from the car. Locking the door, more out of habit than anything, Claire clutched the car keys tightly in her hand hoping the sharp edges would cut through the pain in her head and shock her out of the stupor that threatened to scramble her sanity.

She didn't know what made her look up, why she couldn't resist lifting her eyes to the attic. Just as she did, her breath caught. A shadow flitted passed the window. She was sure of it.

Claire stumbled passed the sun-drenched flowers she had planted around the front steps. Passed the wind chimes tinkling their cheery melody in the breeze. Unlocking the door, she shoved it open. Silence.

Flashing through the crack of the open door, a splash of sunlight spilt across the old wooden floor to the bottom of the stairs. With only a slight sense of propriety, Claire stripped off her filthy sneakers and socks tossing them aside.

Then, standing at the foot of the staircase, she let her eyes drift toward the upper level. Totally convinced she had lost her mind somewhere out there on the battlefield, Claire timidly mounted the stairs to the attic. Slowly pushing the door open, she stepped warily inside. The haze of daylight still brightened the room. Claire let out the breath she had been holding in one quick whoosh. The attic seemed empty. Totally empty.

"Are you here?" she whispered nervously then suddenly realized the absurdity of what she had just done. Giving her head a shake, she said aloud, "I can't believe I just did that," and turned to leave.

Something warm and moist brushed her cheek. It put Claire in mind of a kiss. She knew better, yet instinctively touched the spot with her fingers.

"You have the power to see me any time you want." Strong and clear his voice startled her.

Spinning around, Claire saw him. Without a doubt. The same dashing uniformed soldier who shared her dreams.

"Who—?" But of course she knew who he was and asking was simply a waste of her dwindling energy. Yet she refused to believe he could be a ghost.

"I've waited a long time for your return."

Claire shook her head. It was impossible. A person couldn't chat with a ghost. The man had to be flesh and blood. And he was an intruder.

"Who are you?" she repeated. "What are you doing here?" Someone, for some sick reason, was playing games. Maybe he was some local trying to scare her away to keep up the legend of a haunted house. Or maybe some land developer thinking he could get the owner to drop the price of the house even lower so he could get a better deal.

"Get out of my house," she ordered. With little thought for her own safety, Claire strode forward reaching out to grab the man by the arm. To forcibly remove him from her house. Throw him down the stairs . . . *out the window* . . . if need be. "I'm not afraid of you."

Charles could have allowed her to touch him in solid form, but it would have defeated his purpose. So, by his choice, her hand passed through his arm as easily as it would through water. Claire could have sworn she saw a ripple effect.

The keys she grasped so tightly slipped through her numbed fingers and clattered to the floor. Claire's knees failed her. Speechless, she slid to the floor.

Charles quickly caught her and eased her onto a wooden box. Breath squeezed from her lungs. Her brain prickled threatening her consciousness.

"Is it so impossible to believe that more exists to life than what you can see and touch?" He said it graciously because he now knew what it was to accept the unknown. "You already feel it in your soul. In your mind. It's only a matter of allowing your heart to follow."

"I dream of you," Claire whispered. The sound echoed flatly in her ears.

"I know, my darling."

He reached for her. Suddenly alarmed, Claire summoned a burst of adrenaline. Throwing her arms up in front of her to ward off his advance, she closed her eyes and shouted, "No!"

The image vanished.

Heart pounding, Claire flung herself down the stairs and out the front door chanting, "*This isn't happening. This isn't happening. It's a dream. It's all a dream.*" She shot across the lawn until sharp stones of the gravel driveway brought her up short.

Despondent, Charles watched her from the attic window. His little appearing act hadn't played out the way he anticipated. Claire obviously needed just a bit more time. A bit more time and persuading to realize they were meant to be together. Charles rubbed the heel of his hand over his heart. He didn't care for the ache he suddenly felt. She'd come around. Eventually. She just had to.

❋　　❋　　❋

Barefoot in the middle of the driveway, Claire forced herself to take a couple deep cleansing breaths. She tried to think rationally.

The scene at the battlefield?

She did fall at the park. Had a witness. Also had the lump to prove it. Claire touched the tender spot on the back of her head just to make sure it was still there. Maybe she had been unconscious long enough to imagine a wild dream. A hallucination. Just like that guy said.

The voice in the attic? The apparition?

Maybe she had passed out again in the attic and was just experiencing more delusional effects of a concussion. More likely it was simply her own overwrought imagination playing tricks on her after a taxing day.

Reasonable. Logical. Decisively explainable. And it made perfect sense to her.

There was no man in her attic.

With a determined shake of her still-throbbing head, Claire marched back toward the house. No way were they going to chase her out of there. Not the children with their stories of ghosts and goblins. Not Connie Jenkins and her multiple commissions.

Certainly not any old spook.

Yet her resolve waned drastically the closer she neared the house. Disembodied voices. Phantoms in the light of day. Erotic dreams in the still of night.

Second guessing herself, Claire glanced apprehensively over her shoulder as she snuck into the kitchen and pulled a little slip of paper from beneath a fridge magnet.

Time had come for help.

With trembling hands, Claire picked up the phone and dialed.

"Dr. Rudy Freeman," the deep voice stated formally on the other end of the line with a tone of annoyance at the interruption.

"Um . . . Dr. Freeman?" Her voice quivered. On the verge of tears, Claire bit her lip to gain control. "This is Claire LePaige. Your sister gave me your number." With a deep breath she managed to whisper the words that would change her life. "Can we talk?"

ELEVEN

She was more nervous than a mosquito on a lily pad.

Connie tried to reassure Claire that her brother, a noted psychologist and university professor, lived and would die for the paranormal.

Claire was sure he would think she was a complete wacko.

Not wanting to show up at Connie's barbecue empty-handed, Claire and the children stopped for ice cream on their way. Not knowing what everyone liked, she picked up a variety of flavors. Arms loaded with enough containers to keep all the kids in Virginia hyper for the next week, Claire pushed open the grocery store door almost running headlong into Sheriff Harper. A tremor of quiet humiliation coursed through her veins.

"Good morning, Sheriff," she greeted hesitantly not able to prevent her eyes from intently studying her scuffed sneakers.

"Fuzz, ma'am," he said with a chivalrous tip of his hat. "I'd be pleased if you'd call me Fuzz."

"Only if you'll stop calling me ma'am."

"Fair enough." He held the door for her.

"So you won the election? Congratulations. I saw the campaign signs and kind of wondered what a person named Fuzz would look like."

"I know it's a little different, but it's a long sight better than my real name."

"Oh? And what would that be?"

"I could tell you, ma'am, but then I'd have to kill you." He laughed at his own joke.

"It can't be all that bad." Claire smiled as she tried to imagine a name so horrible he'd be embarrassed to tell her.

"You're right. It's a family name. And a good one. But when you're a kid in a small town and you've got a handle like Fusselman Harper, well, you tend to keep clear of the dark alleys." He took a bag from her as he turned and walked with her toward the car.

"You chose to be called Fuzz?"

"I can live with that one. Darn sight better than some I'd been called. Started into sports in school and the team sort of took care of the decision for me. Kind of stuck."

"You certainly don't look any worse for wear. Now look at you. Shiny badge and all."

"I've been sheriff in this county going on fifteen years now."

"That's quite an accomplishment, isn't it?" Claire opened the car door for the children then popped open the trunk.

"Guess the good people of the county must have thought I was the lesser of two evils. You know, go with the devil you know over the one you don't."

"I'm sure the job must be pretty demanding."

"Can be at times," he nodded in agreement. "Doesn't do much for a private life, I can tell you."

"I'm sure your wife is understanding." Claire could have bitten her tongue off. She hadn't spotted a ring and normally wasn't so blatant. But the words were out before she could stop herself.

Fuzz arched a brow. The corner of his mouth bowed slightly. "Well, ma'am, can't say I've met anyone I've thought of pursuing on a permanent basis yet," he stated matter-of-factly. "But there's always hope now, isn't there?"

Claire was sure she saw a twinkle in his eye. A twinkle that had her stomach doing a little flip. She took the bag he handed her and turned to put it in the trunk so he wouldn't see the blush creeping over her cheeks.

Changing the subject, Fuzz asked, "Any more intruders?"

Claire's warm fuzzy feeling chilled.

"Oh, you know," she said nonchalantly waving it off as an everyday occurrence. "No more than usual. I still don't know what happened. Maybe I am starting to sleepwalk. I just can't explain it. The kids swear up and down they didn't have anything to do with it. I apologize again for bothering you. You must have had many more important things to do than placating a hysterical woman."

"Then I wouldn't have had the pleasure of meeting you." Fuzz flashed her a dashing smile. "Ma'am." Touching his hat with a two-fingered salute, he turned to walk away.

Claire was flattered. Two men in two days who actually said something nice to her and she had totally humiliated herself with both.

❋　　❋　　❋

Rudy Freeman was a tall, heavy-set man. Except for the balding head and neatly trimmed beard, he resembled his sister in many ways. Quick with the wit and always ready with a hearty laugh or two.

After their fill of hamburgers and hotdogs, Rudy ushered Claire to a quiet spot away from the frolicking children and barking dogs. Holding out a patio chair for her, Rudy took an opposite seat and sat pensively studying her for a moment. His sister would see they weren't disturbed for he was thoroughly intrigued by Claire's story.

"Connie's told me tidbits about the children and what you're experiencing. This is just so fascinating," he began with a Cheshire-cat grin of anticipation.

"Well, I'm sure you're going to think I've gone completely crazy," Claire said with a nervous giggle. Swallowing hard, she hesitantly recounted her experiences over the past few nights. The sense that someone had been in her room. Watching her. Talking with her. Messing with her mind.

"I thought maybe it was the kids playing practical jokes, you know, with the rose. But imagining the battle was the last straw. And, of course . . . these. It's been worse since I found these." Claire reached for the little velvet-wrapped package in her purse and slid it across the table toward Rudy. Her fingers locked at the knuckles pressing the little packet tightly against the tabletop just out of Rudy's reach.

"I wasn't sure if I wanted you to see them or not." But she slid it just a little further and quickly pulled her hand back.

"Are these the portraits?" Rudy asked as he nabbed the red bundle before she had a chance to change her mind. She didn't answer. He unwound the fabric until he came to the tintypes.

"They were in the strongbox with the journals and letters. They're the ones I showed Connie." She hadn't mentioned the leather pouch filled with golden coin to either Connie or Rudy. That was still hidden under her mattress.

Rudy put on his glasses to examine the fading images. More than once he lifted his eyes to examine Claire's features then looked back at the pictures. "Uncanny," he muttered. "Absolutely unbelievable. You, or I should say, *Clarissa*. The children." He chuckled as he flipped the one photo around. "Connie was right. She's the spitting image of Granny Breezie."

"Yes, she is." Claire could now see the resemblance between the two women as Connie pointed out, but when she first saw the photo, all she was thinking about was the flashback she had to when the pictures were taken. Mustering her jumbled nerves, Claire recounted all she could remember about her experience.

Regarding her with a look of wonder, Rudy nodded but kept silent and let her speak. While he was thoroughly enjoying himself, he did understand it must be more than a little bizarre for her.

Rudy was basking in the revelation of a lifetime while Claire was on the verge of tears. She was experiencing so many mixed emotions, she didn't know which one to let take control at any given moment. Trepidation. Anxiety. Skepticism. More than just a little curiosity, she reluctantly had to admit.

With barely a whisper, Claire said, "I didn't tell you this before, but I think I *did* see him." With a furtive glance over each shoulder, the words were spoken in fear an outsider would overhear.

"Where?" Rudy was intrigued. "Up in the attic?"

"There. And in . . . " *Bed*, she almost said but caught herself. "I think it may be him I'm dreaming about," she finally said. A faint blush tinged her cheeks. "But I'm not sure."

"Can you tell me more about your dreams?" Rudy prompted.

Claire instantly flushed such a bright red she was sure her skin would spontaneously ignite. She composed herself enough to stammer, "All I remember is that they seemed very . . . " Erotic, sensual, exciting, she wanted to say, but said instead, "Very real. Like he was right there with me. A *part* of me."

How could she tell a man she didn't even know about a dream so intimate her own body could respond the way it did. Instead, she told him of the dance at the officer's ball. Waking in the cellar. The voice in the garden. The yellow rose she discovered on the floor beside her bed that was still sitting in a glass of water in the center of her kitchen table.

"Did you sense the images might be from different periods of time?"

"No. Not that I could tell. They all seemed to revolve around the Civil War time frame." And in the same breath, she leaned forward and whispered furtively, "Have you ever been in a place or heard a conversation that you're positive happened before?" Rudy nodded. "It's like that. The dreams were all so *familiar*. Like I've lived it all before."

Claire shook her head and laughed. "I feel so foolish telling you this. I even called the police when I saw that blasted rose. That certainly was a mistake. Now they've for sure got me pegged as a crazy woman."

Claire paused to take a breath. She had to have some answers. She hoped Dr. Freeman would have a suggestion. "What do you make of all this? Am I going mad?"

Rudy shrugged as he leaned toward her. "I guess it's all a matter of what you're open to believe. Did you feel threatened at all?"

Adamantly, Claire shook her head. "No. Not so far, anyway." Then as an afterthought, she added, "That's not entirely true. In the battlefield, I was scared to death, but I heard this voice come out of nowhere telling me I wouldn't be harmed." Pulling another package from her bag, Claire placed it in front of Rudy. "There's more." Her hand shook as she pulled the photos from the envelope. "These are the pictures I took during the battle."

Rudy flipped through one after another. Trees, grass, meadow. No fighting. No soldiers. No cannon or artillery. No horses. Just lush parkland, green and serene.

"What do they say about vampires?" Claire asked. "They can't be seen in photographs or mirrors? Does that apply to ghosts?"

Rudy shrugged. "Some people say they've captured images on film, but Lord only knows if they're real or just hoaxes."

"Well, I *know* I took those pictures. If I hit my head when I fell and was unconscious for a minute or so, my hands wouldn't be focusing the camera and shooting, would they?"

"Not very likely," Rudy had to agree.

Throwing up her hands in exasperation, Claire exclaimed, "This just blows me away. I can't make hide nor hair out of any of it."

"And your children swear up and down they actually converse with the spirit of Charles Montgomery?" It was more statement than question. Wanting to get their mother's take on the situation first, Rudy had not yet spoken with the children. Claire merely nodded.

Rudy contemplated what she had told him. Maybe she'd blow him off as another crackpot or maybe she was just curious enough in what he suspected was happening that it would be worth throwing out the possibility. He'd take that chance.

"You know, there's really no possible way known to science yet that can truly, one hundred percent, confirm or deny the existence of ghosts or the spirit world. All we have are the personal accounts of real live people. Ordinary people who have had encounters and experiences with—*beings,* if you will—from beyond death."

Tapping a finger against the top of the plastic patio table, he thoughtfully continued. "I've interviewed hundreds of subjects claiming to have lived a former life. Some swear they've lived multiple times."

"And you don't think they're just making it up?"

"How can we disprove it? Call them all liars? I'd say it was all a matter of what you are *willing* to believe."

"And what do you believe, Rudy?"

"Personally," he said bluntly, "I believe anything is within the realm of possibility. Like I said, I've interviewed countless people who'd swear on a stack of Bibles they've seen apparitions, ghosts, whatever you want to call them. And, believe it or not, a good majority of them are young children."

The happy screeches of her own children running through the lawn sprinkler drew Claire's attention. The Jenkins' three children were very close in age to Maggie and Billy. It didn't take any time at all for them to become fast friends. Like they had known each other all their lives.

Claire had such good kids. She didn't want to think they were lying to her. "Why would children see ghosts easier than most adults?"

"One can only surmise," Rudy said lightly. "My theory has been that children's minds are so innocent. Uncluttered. They haven't closed themselves off to new concepts or ideas. Haven't learned to be cynical like most adults." He gave a hearty chuckle. "They don't know they're not supposed to see ghosts."

Skeptically, Claire said, "Maybe they're just influenced by all the television shows their parents let them watch. All the Saturday morning cartoons nowadays—monsters and creatures from outer space. They're certainly not like Yogi Bear and Mickey Mouse any more."

"True enough," Rudy admitted. "But what about all the kids who play with imaginary friends? Very real to them. Can we, as adults, see them? No. Maybe they're really spirits not just make-believe playmates. Who knows for sure?" He tapped more forcefully on the table stating emphatically, "We have to keep an open mind. Just because we can't see them doesn't mean they don't exist."

With crinkled brow, Claire's head shot up. Those words. They sounded familiar.

Rudy continued. "That's where faith comes in."

"You mean like believing in Christ even though we can't see Him?"

"I don't think I'd quite put Jesus Christ on the same plane as paranormal beings," he said thoughtfully. "But you're on the right track. Let me ask you something, Claire. Why did you come here?"

Taken aback, Claire replied defensively, "Connie asked me."

"No," Rudy chuckled. "I meant why, of all the places to vacation, did you come to Shenandoah?"

"Oh. Sorry. I don't know. I guess it felt like I was being pulled or drawn here. Like this was where I was supposed to be somehow."

Rudy nodded as if he were pleased with her answer. Pulling a tattered old book from a worn leather satchel, he said, "I brought something to show you. Connie said you were interested." Held together by a thick elastic band, the little volume practically fell apart when he opened it.

"There's not too much left," he said sorrowfully. "Real shame, that is." Tenderly lifting each brittle brown page, he pushed the book closer so Claire could see. "This was our great, great, great, I don't know how many greats. Doesn't matter anyway. It's Granny Breezie's journal. My grandmother passed it on down to me." He flipped more crackled pages. Many pages were torn in two. Others missing altogether. "Connie told you Granny worked for Charles and Clarissa Montgomery. Where you're staying now."

"Yes, she did," Claire replied hollowly.

"There's just one entry I'd like to show you myself." Scanning each page with his finger, Rudy finally found the passage. "Here. Read this if you can make it out."

Queasiness suddenly rising up from the pit of her stomach, Claire thought maybe she really didn't want to know more about this after all. But she pulled the fragile book toward her anyway tilting it out of the sun's bright reflection. The thick black script, now faded and smudged, was very difficult to read.

> *"Mista Charles iz gonna be leevin in da mornin. Tis a sad sad day fo shor. Po Miz Clarry iz amopin arown eer sumfin awful. I sez to her cher up Miz Clarry. Mista Charles be back reel soon. But her eyes juss filt up wit thoz grat big gator teers o hers an she rund off. Fown her in da back kichen cukin up one o her wikket brooz. I sez to her Miz Clarry wat ya cukin up now? She sez to me Breezie Ima gonna make shor he cums back to me. Ima gonna make shor weez always be tageder. Alluv us. I sez to her Miz Clarry I shor don wanna be apart from yall, but don ya go doon nun o dat voodoo mumbo jumbo on me, ya heer me Missy? Wen Iza ded an gon Iza wanna stay ded an gon."*

Visibly shaken, Claire wordlessly closed the cover and replaced the elastic band. "Just like in one of the first dreams," she whispered. "I dreamt Charles—or whoever it was—told me about casting some spell on him. I didn't remember that until just now."

Face paling, Claire felt on the verge of passing out. She pitched sharply to the side.

"Put your head between your knees," Rudy ordered grabbing her arm to steady her. He jerked her chair away from the table, placed his hand behind her head and forced it down. "Deep breaths. Deep breaths," he crooned fatherly patting her back.

As she gulped for air, Rudy tried to explain. "Really, it all fits. We know Clarissa dabbled in black magic. You've told me about your dreams, about the children, and—if my suspicions are correct—I, for one, would really like to believe you are the reincarnation of Clarissa Montgomery."

TWELVE

The hammock had become her refuge, her special place for trying to get her thoughts together. Keep her wits about her. But the kiss of the cool breeze, the ripple of the river below, and the gentle sway of the hammock, would inevitably lull her to sleep. With sleep always came the dreams. Sometimes the same. Sometimes a little different. But always she woke filled with a sense of profound love and well being. And just a little pang of regret she couldn't stay asleep forever.

Although certainly not convinced the dreams were connected to the paranormal, Claire could not explain what may be prompting them.

Never before in her life had she experienced the same intense reaction when making love as she did in these dreams. They were so real. So vivid. So unbelievably fulfilling. Okay, it had to be possible. Males have wet dreams. Females must be able to climax in their sleep, too. It's only fair.

Clamping her pen between her teeth, Claire snapped her notebook closed and let it fall against her chest. How she could ever possibly explain all the things that were happening this summer she'd never know. As far fetched as it all seemed, she promised Rudy she'd jot down what she could remember of her dreams, her thoughts and feelings.

What she felt like was a human guinea pig for some wild, outlandish science fiction experiment. The very idea—reincarnation. Black magic. Why, it was just plain ludicrous. He was so totally full of crap. She had told him so and laughed at him—once she had stopped hyperventilating—right in his face.

Planning to make a special trip from Washington the next day, Rudy wanted to check out the attic, she guessed, to see if he got any vibes from good old Charles.

Skeptically, she had agreed. Why burst his bubble all to smithereens? Maybe he'd bring some fancy spirit energy detection gizmo with him. In any case, it'll keep the kids occupied and happy. Someone finally believed their tall tales.

Although disturbed, Claire was really not at all very surprised by this latest turn of events. Too many coincidences. Too many unexplainable things happening to deny the possibility that maybe—just maybe—Rudy may know a little bit more than she did. She was beginning to admit, grudgingly, that she wasn't privy to all the secrets of the universe. Didn't have all the answers. How could she believe in the probability of the existence of life forms on other planets far off in distant galaxies but be so close-minded to the possibility of a spirit world? Maybe she'd just have to re-evaluate her whole philosophy.

"Mom!" Billy called from the woodshed at the back of the house. "We can't reach the shovels."

Gathering her notebook and pen, Claire rolled out of the hammock. So much for reflection and speculation. It would have to wait. Life in the present beckoned.

Claire shouted back as she crested the river bank. "What do you need shovels for?"

"We're on a mission."

Claire barely suppressed a laugh. "A *mission*?"

"Yup." As Maggie bobbed her head, her ponytail bobbed with her. "We're digging for china."

Claire arched a brow. "Are you now?" Every kid had to at least try to dig to China. She'd done it herself but finally gave up after three hours and two palms full of broken blisters. Claire opened the shed and handed them each a small garden spade. "It's going to take a long time so you'd better get started. It will be supper time soon."

The children dragged their shovels to the bottom of the hill around the far side of the house. As Claire weeded her flower bed, she could hear them happily chatter away as the sound of dirt whooshed across the ground.

Forcing herself to clear her head from all Rudy's ghost nonsense, Claire began to daydream. Began to visualize life as it may have been at the time of the Civil War. Property owners in the valley taking precautions. Hoarding food. Hiding valuables. Scrambling to stash whatever they could possibly save from the invading Yankee army.

Caught up in the thoughts of it, Claire pictured herself packing crates of special treasures and burying them deeply under ground. No sooner had the notion flitted through her mind, the dull thud of metal hitting wood snapped her back to reality.

"Come quick, Mom," Billy shouted excitedly. "We found it!"

Dropping her fistful of weeds, Claire scurried around the corner to where the children had a pile mounded beside a large square hole. It hadn't taken them long at all to dig that much dirt. In fact, it seemed impossible that two little children could have dug so quickly. Confused, Claire looked around fully expecting to see that someone had helped them. But they were alone.

Peering into the hole, Claire could see the top of a wooden box. Words escaped her. Of all the square footage between the fence lines and the river, how had they known to dig in that particular spot?

"How did you . . . ?" Bewildered, the rest of the sentence trailed off. She really didn't want to know.

It was a struggle, but Billy helped her drag up the crate. The lid pried off easily as if someone had already loosened it.

Nestled between layers of tightly packed straw, Claire found a treasure. A complete set of the prettiest china she had ever seen. Each piece was rimmed in gold. Tiny bouquets of delicate hand-painted yellow roses adorned a shimmering white background.

Claire turned a plate over. 'Made in England' was the only identifying mark. No manufacturer or pattern name. Yet it looked very old and very expensive. And very . . . *familiar*. A design she may have seen someplace before.

Claire could do nothing but stare at her children. Digging *for* china, not *to* China. The breath hissed from her lungs. No, she didn't want to know.

❋   ❋   ❋

"I'm not sure I want to read any more of them, Rudy," Claire stated emphatically as she carefully placed the journals and letters back into the strongbox. Not sure at all she wanted to delve any deeper into the lives of these people who possibly—somehow—held the key to her past. "Do you want to take them?"

"Not now. Maybe later." Rudy regarded her intently. Her hands shook nervously as she closed the box. Her teeth almost bit through her bottom lip she was clenching her jaw so hard. She had already told him about finding the crate of dishes.

Rudy had arrived before breakfast. Before she had even managed to pull a brush through her hair.

More excited than the children, Rudy raced them to the attic. As soon as they pushed open the door, Billy called for Charles. He called again, but no image appeared.

Disappointed, but not discouraged, Rudy explained to the children that maybe their friend just needed to learn to trust him, that there was nothing Rudy would ever do to hurt him or betray him.

These words spoken, an overwhelming sensation suddenly coursed through his body—a pacific sense. A definite feeling of something unseen. Rudy nodded quietly toward the point where the presence seemed strongest, an unspoken signal of understanding. Charles may never reveal himself, but he was there. Observing. Listening.

Many years ago, Rudy had discovered he had the ability to sense beings from the spirit world. How he had developed this—*skill*, if you could call it that—he would never know. There was no explaining it. It just happened and it had fascinated him ever since.

They spent over an hour in the attic, Billy and Maggie each vying to tell their stories. Rudy opened himself to absorb a myriad of feelings. A powerful sense of pride as each child spoke. Of love. Of grief. The sensations were so mixed and overpowering, Rudy finally had to tear himself away if only for a few minutes.

Coffee was ready when he came downstairs. Intent on wiping a dribble from the table, Claire asked blandly, "Did you see him?" She didn't dare look him in the eye.

With a shake of his head, Rudy admitted, "No, I didn't."

"Have you ever seen a ghost . . . spirit . . . whatever it is?"

"Thought I did once, but I'm not really sure. It happened so fast." He took a sip of coffee and added more milk. "It's more like I can *read* them."

Claire concentrated on stirring an extra spoonful of sugar into her coffee. For courage, she told herself. "Well, did you *read* anything in the attic?"

"Without a doubt," Rudy said bluntly.

Slumping back in her chair, Claire stared at his serious expression. A look of begrudging acceptance gradually spread over her face. Unless Rudy was a total fraud, she now had to admit her house was possessed by a being from another dimension. Something was certainly going on. But a husband from another life? She had yet to be convinced of that.

"Now what?"

"I wish I could tell you more." Rudy pondered a moment. "Maybe you should just come right out and ask him what he expects of you?"

"*Ask him?* You want me to *talk* to him? You mean . . . like you and I are talking?"

"Sure, why not? Either you'll get answers or you won't. The children see and hear him all the time. He's starting to let you see and hear him, too. I figure he's just waiting for you to accept the *possibility*."

"The possibility that he might actually be . . . who you say he is?" Claire's mind began whirling in all sorts of fantastical directions. "Oh, Rudy, I don't know about that. I'd feel so—*foolish*—just talking to thin air."

"Well, really no different than singing to yourself or rehearsing a speech out loud, I would think."

"I guess that part wouldn't bother me too much," Claire speculated. "I'm just not quite sure what I'd do if I got an answer."

❄   ❄   ❄

Suspiciously, she peeked into the closet, behind the curtains, under the bed. Satisfied she was alone, Claire climbed into bed and settled down to read for a while. If her little nightshirt found its way to the floor so easily, Claire couldn't imagine she'd get the track suit off without waking herself up.

It was a hot night. She'd swelter for sure but at least she'd be fully clothed.

The heat from the lamp just made everything worse. Perspiration gathered on her brow. Squirming to get more comfortable, Claire scrunched the pillow up more behind her back. She waved the thin sheet over her legs and feet trying to create a breeze.

Ignoring the river of sweat running down between her shoulder blades, Claire tried to immerse herself in one of the journals. By the look of the writing, she could tell it was written by a woman's hand, Clarissa's hand, which was amazingly similar to her own script.

> *"I write these words in the hope that the one who follows*
> *through the portals of time will know me . . . will know us.*
> *I say 'us' for we are one."*

Claire shuddered. "*The one who follows through the portals of time,*" she breathed aloud. "*We are one.*" The words rang with an ominous tone of *déjà vu*.

Scanning the first few pages, it dawned on Claire that it all seemed eerily too familiar—as if she had written the words herself. Turning from page to page, Claire could not put the book down. She could almost anticipate what was penned overleaf and often caught herself whispering the very words before she read them.

Clarissa began at the beginning, with her childhood, concisely hitting the major events in her life. Painstakingly, she had copied her grandmama's recipes for potions and elixirs, clearly indicating what each was for and where to find the ingredients.

On a separate page, all by itself, was the incantation Clarissa had used the night before Charles left for war. The instigation of all this chicanery.

But, as intrigued as she was by what she was reading, Claire could not force her eyes to stay open. Finally, her chin drooped heavily against her chest.

He left the light on even though he didn't need it to see her. He knew every sensuous square inch of her body by heart. Snuggling in beside her, Charles snuck his arm under her back and drew her toward him. Claire molded herself to his body just as she had done so many times before.

Having known her as Clarissa since—forever—Charles had to force himself to think of her as Claire now. She was her own unique person. Yet undoubtedly she carried the same spirit of the woman he loved years ago. Loved still.

Though deep in sleep, Claire's subconscious could no longer control the yearnings of hidden desires suppressed for so long. The same ardent passion for the man she loved and lost over a century before ran eternal. Each touch, every taste brought back memory after memory. Sensual. Scathing. Torrid.

Never had Clarissa considered herself so prudish as to look on her marriage bed as duty rather than pleasure. Freely, she enjoyed her husband just as thoroughly as he enjoyed her. The hindering clothing was quickly removed.

Running his tongue from her ear to her breast, Charles drank the saltiness of her skin, inhaling her glistening scent. A more potent elixir he had never experienced. Taking her nipple in his mouth, he rolled his tongue gently around the taut peak.

Just that simple touch of his lips brought an earthy moan from deep within Claire's throat. She needed more. She needed all of him. Exploring his firm body, Claire ran her fingers lightly over Charles' buttocks, down his legs and up his inner thighs sending waves of electricity through every fiber of his being. Nerve endings ignited as she stroked that special spot sending him to the brink and almost over the point of no return.

With a sudden twist of his body, Charles positioned Claire over him, lowered her down. With slow, determined rhythm, Claire moved with him. Bending over she whispered raggedly into his ear, "How I've missed you, my darling." Their bodies, slick with sweat, slithered steamily against each other, her breasts gliding seductively along his chest.

"Soon you will know me, my love. Very soon." How he wished she were fully conscious as his wife to know they were making love together.

For now he would have to be satisfied with unconscious memories of time long past. She would eventually remember. She had to. He had to trust that the spell Clarissa had cast would not leave him in this hell of suspension forever without being with him as she had promised.

Liquid heat seared through Claire's veins as she neared her release. Never before had she experienced such passion. Breath came in ragged gasps. She was *so* close . . .

❇ ❇ ❇

"Mommy, I can't sleep." All sensation evaporated as the little voice woke her instantly.

Claire squinted groggily as the brightness of the light, still on, hurt her eyes. The track suit she was determined to keep on was heaped on the floor beside the bed. Between sodden sheets, she lay naked.

Claire remembered the dream precisely. Every moment. Every movement. An overwhelming sense of disappointment drained her heart. To be abandoned on the verge of climax with such abruptness felt like someone had plunged her into ice water. She wasn't quite convinced who this mystery man of her dreams was, but he could come back any time. His face . . . his touch . . . his taste . . . would be etched in her memory forever.

Maggie stood in the doorway rubbing her sleepy eyes. "Who were you talking to, Mommy?"

Getting hold of her faculties, Claire pulled the sheet up to her chin. "I must have been dreaming, honey." Quickly changing the subject, she cooed as Maggie crawled up beside her, "What's the matter? Why can't you sleep?"

"It's too hot," her daughter whined. Claire agreed but for a totally different reason. Just the thought sent a wave of pleasure deep into the pit of her stomach, the reaction burning her cheeks.

"You go splash a little cold water on your face, and I'll get you a drink." She had to wait for Maggie to leave the room before she could get out of bed.

Throwing a light robe over her bare body, Claire figured it was just no use fighting to keep clothes on. They obviously were coming off no matter what she did. Either she was disrobing herself in her sleep or her nightly visitor was stripping her bare. Didn't matter which. She was beginning to enjoy it.

Claire had loved her husband dearly, but there was something— *different*—in the way she responded to the man in her dreams. Lovemaking with Ethan had been satisfying but, quite frankly, there was just no describing the thrilling sensations she had just experienced. Claire couldn't wait to get back to bed. Perhaps she'd get lucky and be able to continue the dream from where it left off.

But try as she might, she was far too wound up to drift off. Sleep didn't come leaving her frustrated and miserably irritable as dawn broke.

She got out of bed and trudged down to the parlor. The sun was just beginning to peek through the front window. The birds were chirping. It should have been a glorious beginning to a wonderful day, yet her mood blackened.

Claire couldn't get a grip on what was happening to her. She was turning into a nymphomaniac. A pervert whose overactive mind had to dream up an imaginary man to get her jollies.

Curling up in the overstuffed easy chair, Claire leaned her head back and closed her eyes. Warming sunlight hit her face as the brightness flooding the room bathed her in its glow. Her body relaxing, Claire remembered what Rudy had said about talking to the . . . *ghost*. She felt rather stupid, but after last night, she decided she needed to settle this fallacy once and for all.

She whispered just under her breath, "Who are you? Why are you doing this to me?" Silence.

Just a hint of anger crept into her tone as she spoke a little louder. More forcefully. "Come on, Chuckie baby, show yourself, you coward." Nothing.

Then she thought it probably wasn't such a good idea to try and coerce a ghost. With a heavy sigh of resignation, Claire leaned back. She spoke softly, "I'm sorry. Forgive me. I'm new at all this. It's just that I've never been seduced by a spirit before."

She glanced around the room and waited for some kind of response. A sign. Anything.

"Oh, this is pathetic." Shaking her head, Claire laughed at herself with more than just a little embarrassment. If anyone had heard her they'd have her locked away for a long, long time. Then what would become of her children? Maybe they should just pack up, go home and forget about this little bit of heaven in the Virginian countryside.

Rudy's suggestion hadn't worked. Now she was right back to square one still not knowing what to believe. Actually, truth be known, Claire felt quite disappointed. Maybe she had been alone far too long without loving male companionship. Surely her mind was just playing tricks on her. Wishful thinking, that sort of thing.

Yawning sleepily, Claire climbed back up the stairs to her bedroom. It was still far too early to be up and about. Snuggled deeply into the soft mattress, she decided to give it one last shot. Stifling another yawn, she whispered, "Just to let you know, if you really are my long-lost husband, I sure do enjoy making love with you."

In the blink of an eye the atmosphere in the room shifted. Lighter, somehow. Little sparks of energy fluttered over her skin like tiny fingertips. Tingling. Scintillating. Arousal was quick taking her by complete surprise. She could imagine his mouth on hers. His hands on her breasts. The delight of his manhood merging deeply inside her body.

Convinced she was fully awake, she *knew* she was not in that bed alone. Not even *her* imagination was *that* good.

Freeing herself to accept his spirit into her own, Claire immersed herself—willingly—into a thousand different sensations each one more intoxicating than the one before.

"Charles, come to me," she pleaded, her whimper heady. "Please . . . let me see you. I need to feel you in my arms."

Claire caught her breath as a translucent form began to take shape over her yet she didn't cry out. As the bed sagged under the added weight, the being molded itself into a human male figure. Firm sinewy muscles rippled down his chest and back. Sandy-brown hair gathered at the nape of his neck. A red-flecked mustache nearly hid his entire upper lip. His eyes—soft and green—captivated her heart.

All Claire could do was stare back at him in silence. There was no fear in her heart. Just pure astonishment. This being was no threat. He wouldn't hurt her. She believed that now just as she believed he was her soul mate from another time and place.

Searching deeply into his eyes, Claire hesitantly reached up to cup his face between her hands. Solid, warm flesh. Arms, chest, legs. All there. All very real to the touch. Every masculine square inch of him. She hadn't known exactly what to expect. Maybe that she would put her hands right through him like the gossamer apparitions depicted in movies. Like she did in the attic.

"How can this be?" Claire whispered as she slid her hands over his taut body. "I must still be dreaming." Tangling her fingers in his long, sandy hair, she drew his mouth to hers and ran her tongue over his top lip.

His mustache tickled as he curled into her devouring her sweet mouth. Reluctantly, Charles pulled back to regard her intently. "You have no fear, my darling?"

"No, of course not," she whispered. "But that's only because I've gone completely mad. Or I'm so deeply out of it I can't tell if I'm dreaming or awake."

"It is no dream, my love," he moaned into her ear. Charles began moving ever so gently within her. "You drive me to distraction. You always have."

Sensations mounted beyond any hope of control. Her head fell back as she arched against him. "Then it's true?" Claire managed to ask. "It's true you're my husband?"

"Without a doubt, my love."

"How can I be sure?" she whispered breathlessly.

"You know it, my love. Deep in your heart you know." A groan of bittersweet pain rattled in his throat. "Tell me," he demanded gently. "What do you feel?"

It took a moment for Claire to put together the words. The more she thought about it, the more she was sure. "I feel like I've known you—*forever.*"

The primeval moan hissed from her lips with such a need for fulfillment neither could hold back a moment longer. Release was swift and powerful leaving them both sated and pleasantly exhausted.

Their entwined bodies glistened with the heat of spent passion. As Claire basked in the afterglow, she dared to open her eyes. Stroking his face to make sure, she whispered dreamily, "You're still here. You didn't disappear."

"Not yet," he assured her. "Soon I'll have to leave you."

"Why? Why can't you stay?"

"I wish I knew. I can't seem to keep human form for any great length of time."

"How much time do we have?" Panic riddled her voice. Would he be able to come back to her?

"Not much now."

She was too inquisitive to let him go just yet. Claire hitched herself up on an elbow. "I don't understand any of this."

"There's no point in analyzing. I don't have many answers for you. Actually, I don't think I have *any* answers. I'm just thankful I can be here with you now."

Rolling over onto his back, Charles cradled her into the curve of his arm. She nestled her cheek onto the soft down of his chest. Claire couldn't believe just how familiar it felt to cuddle up beside him. She should have been running down the road screaming for help. But she wasn't.

"How is this possible?" His skin was warm to the touch and she could feel a heartbeat under her hand. "I have to admit I haven't known any ghosts up close and personal, but I wouldn't have thought you would actually feel . . . *human.*"

Chuckling, Charles accused playfully, "Well, it's all your . . . Clarissa's . . . fault. And that accursed spell. I should have met my Creator eons ago. But no. I'm left to wander this earth alone for well over a hundred years waiting for you to show up. And you sure took your sweet time doing it, I might add. "

"Well," Claire laughed. "Had I known what I would find, I would have been here years ago."

He kissed the top of her head. "You're here now. That's all that matters."

"I just can't understand how a ghost can seem so real. Especially when we . . . you know." Sliding her hand along the side of his face, Claire was still amazed by the warmth of his skin.

"We shan't underestimate the power of love."

Snuggling deeper into his embrace, Claire played with strands of his hairy chest. Twisting some around her finger, she asked with a hint of jealousy, "So do you romance all the women who try to live in your house?"

Feigning indignation, Charles answered haughtily, "I'll have you know, madam, I do not practice adultery. Neither do I consider myself a coward."

Claire instantly regretted her earlier challenge. "Oh. You heard that."

"Of course I heard. I've heard every syllable that has passed your lips ever since I became aware you were near. And *who*, on God's green earth," he continued, "is *Chuckie*? I've never been called *Chuckie* in all my born days."

THIRTEEN

Claire woke alone. As she roused herself from slumber, a contented sigh escaped her lips. As with all the other dreams, the experience was so unmistakably realistic. Had she, once again, just dreamt she had been awake? Did the hot moistness between her legs prove nothing?

Yet, as real as it seemed to be, now she wasn't quite so sure. Charles had vanished. He had explained he would not be able to stay with her. She understood that. But on his side of the bed . . . where she could have sworn he had lain his head as they drifted off to sleep entwined in each others arms . . . there was not so much as a wrinkle on the pillow.

Struggling for the energy to pull herself out of bed, Claire began to prepare for another day. An edge of ambiguous disappointment shadowed her spirit. Thoroughly perplexed, she tried to make sense of the emotions whirling around in her mind.

Foremost, Claire was again quite convinced she was going insane. What in the world possessed her to actually expect to wake with a ghost in her bed let alone believe in them at all? Just because Rudy did didn't make it so.

Was she so terribly lonely that only a phantom spirit could provide comfort through the long, dark nights? What was so wrong with her that she couldn't attract a real live *human* male?

On the plus side, maybe a ghost for a lover wouldn't be so bad after all. Wouldn't have to feed him, do his laundry, clean up after him.

Shaking her head at such a ridiculous thought, Claire concluded they'd be gone soon enough and they could leave all the ghost nonsense behind. It wouldn't be long before school would start again and they would have to be on their way home. It wouldn't take much longer to put the house in half-decent shape. She couldn't believe it wouldn't sell quickly. Her part of the bargain upheld, Claire could walk out with a clear conscience.

But a pang of despair tore through her heart. How could she just up and leave a place where she felt so much at home? Her whole history was here.

"There I go again," she muttered angrily to herself. Waffling between belief and skepticism, Claire let the spray from the shower hit her full in the face. Maybe she should just let it drown her then she wouldn't have to think about anything anymore.

Maggie spilled her glass of milk just as her mother walked through the kitchen door. Billy had tracked mud in from the back yard. A trail of caked footprints led from the door to the table where her son blissfully shoveled cereal into his mouth. Each time his swinging heels hit the legs of the chair, little fragments of hardened clay flew in all directions.

"Good morning, you two." Claire obliviously poured herself a cup of coffee and took it out to the veranda. Sitting on the top step, she lifted her face to the sun. It felt good. Warmth infused her body as did each sip of the steamy brew.

Suddenly Claire felt the distinct impression of another presence by her side. Although she could see nothing, the soft flow of heat radiating through her body felt just like being enveloped by strong arms . . . loving her . . . keeping her safe.

It never occurred to Claire to try to explain the sensation she was feeling. Without even thinking about it, she simply relaxed and allowed total peace to fill her soul. After the journey into ecstacy last night, she was certainly tempted to accept the possibility.

Reaching into the pocket of her robe, Claire pulled out another letter. She sensed a need to learn more about Charles and Clarissa. If she was his wife from long ago as Rudy suspected, maybe some more of the entries would seem familiar. Maybe she would remember something if she could only open her mind and be willing to accept the past so there may be some hope to face whatever uncertain future lay in store for them.

Deep inside she somehow knew in her heart of hearts that Rudy was right. What other explanation could there really be? She remembered Breezie and the photographs. She had vividly pictured the ballroom and Charles' last dance. But there was still that little niggling stubborn streak that needed proof beyond the shadow of a doubt. Perhaps she held it right in her hands, there in smudged black and white. All she had to do was open the envelope.

> *August 7, 1861 My Darling Charles*
>
> *Not knowing how you fare is sheer torture. My desire is to be by your side so I can nurse your wounds and see with my own eyes that you are safe and sound. My arms ache with emptiness. I long to hold you even if it's just for one night.*
>
> *The children ask constantly when you will be coming home. I fear I am at a loss as to what and just how much to tell them. I am of a mind, as you are, that this conflict will not end soon. How that disheartens me.*
>
> *Margaret baked you a cake—ginger spice, your favorite. She thinks you may not get enough to eat in hospital. Unfortunately, it may not survive delivery . . .*

Claire could imagine the look on the child's face as she proudly took the pan out of the brick oven in the back of the summer kitchen. More likely it was the power of suggestion causing her to think of a young girl the spitting image of her own Maggie laughing with glee as she admired her creation. She could picture hair pulled back with pink ribbons to keep the child's long curls out of the batter, and not only was her face and smock dusted with flour, but the entire kitchen floor was coated in a slippery white film.

Carefully wrapped in a sugar sack, Margaret had packed the cake tightly with the hand-knit woolen socks Clarissa was planning to send to her father anyway. The price of clothing had skyrocketed and most soldiers had to depend on whatever garments family members could provide for them.

The crunch of tires on gravel made Claire break her concentration and look up. A police cruiser pulled to a stop inches away from her veranda. Sheriff Harper unfolded his lanky form from behind the steering wheel as he whisked his hat from his head.

"Mornin', ma'am." His smile was bright and cheery. It wasn't yet nine o'clock. Suddenly realizing she wasn't quite dressed for company, Claire futilely combed her fingers through her snarled hair then modestly drew her robe tighter across her chest.

"Good morning, Sheriff Harper," she greeted pleasantly. "What brings you by this morning? Is there a problem?"

"No, no problem. At least there won't be if you'd consider having lunch with me. The children, too, of course," he hastened to add. Fuzz placed a polished black boot on the bottom step and leaned forward, his elbow on the bent knee.

Taken aback at the invitation, Claire didn't know quite how to respond. "Do you have time for a cup of coffee?" she asked instead stalling for time. "I've got a fresh pot on."

"Sounds fine, ma'am. Thank you."

Stuffing the note she was reading into her pocket, in her haste to get up Claire failed to notice one of the other letters slide from her lap. Fuzz picked it up examining the envelope curiously. It was creased as if it had been folded and refolded many times over, dirty and grubby, with a faint pattern of a fingerprint he could have sworn was left behind by . . . what? Blood? So his gut was telling him.

Stepping up on the veranda, Fuzz listened at the door for Claire coming back then deftly pulled the page from inside. What he read intrigued him.

> *April 27, 1862 My sweet Clarry*
> *I have just received new orders. Apparently I am to become the generals' special envoy to deliver secret dispatches back and forth between command posts. General Lee is suspicious that many of our couriers have been intercepted and at times it seems the Federals are one step ahead of us. They must think a more senior officer will be stealthier and not as likely to get captured. And seeing as I know the backwoods so well, I might just take a detour along the trestle trail some time soon, sneak over and steal a kiss or two.*
> *We're near Yorktown and facing a large force. The troops have started shooting bombshells back and forth.*

It's bound to be a bloody battle when all is said and done.

We have had hard times for the last two weeks. Marched about one hundred and eighty miles. Many of our boys have worn right through their footgear and now have nothing at all to protect their feet. We laid out three days and nights in the snow and rain without so much as a blanket.

I long for my home and the haven of your tender arms. But a soldier is at home wherever he stands so long as he has his hat for shelter.

Speaking of home, Clarry, I trust you are using the gold . . .

He turned the page but it was too late. She was coming back. Fuzz quickly folded the letter and tucked it back into its envelope. He had just bent to put it back where he found it when Claire pushed open the screen door. Straightening, he handed the envelope to Claire making it look as if he had just picked it up.

"You must have dropped this," he offered with outstretched hand.

The edge of guilt to his voice went unnoticed as Claire balanced a tray on the railing. Her hair now pulled back into a ponytail, she had made a quick change into shorts and a tee-shirt.

"Thanks." She said it almost too curtly as she thrust the letter into her pocket volunteering no explanation. "How do you like your coffee?"

Claire tried not to look too embarrassed as she poured him a cup. Her poor excuse for a serving tray was the old cookie sheet they used as a drain tray when she washed dishes at the cabin. The coffee mugs were old plastic castoffs picked up at a yard sale somewhere.

"Black's good. Thanks." Fuzz barely noticed the battered old mugs anyway. He was too busy looking at her. She sure was pretty. Hoping he wasn't being too obvious, Fuzz was having a hard time not staring and making his desire known. He couldn't remember ever meeting a woman with eyes that big and dark. Or hair that silky and shiny. Or flawless creamy skin the texture of the finest satin.

And he was waiting for an answer. "So how about lunch? I know a nice little place not too far from here that's got pretty good burgers if you're into that sort of thing. Home-made ice cream, too."

"What makes you think I like ice cream?" Claire laughed regarding him curiously.

"Well, your arms were pretty loaded the day I met you coming out of the grocery store. Detective stuff, you know. Deduction. That sort of thing."

"Oh. Right."

Claire had considered the invitation while she was getting dressed. Drastically out of the loop, she hadn't been on a date since Ethan died. Granted, it was only a year ago. How much could possibly have changed on the singles scene in that short a time? He seemed like a nice enough guy. What could it hurt? After all, it was only lunch.

"Lunch sounds like fun. Thanks." She handed him a cup. "I'm sure the kids will enjoy it as much as I will." Claire had refilled her own mug and motioned him to a lawn chair.

"That's great." Fuzz took a seat and regarded her admirably. "You've done a great job here. Place looks like a million bucks." He eyed the corner of the veranda. "How did you get this straightened up?"

"Well, let me tell you, *that* was fun. Used the jack from the car. Figured if it could lift up a ton or so of metal, a few sticks of wood would be a piece of cake. Still needs some work but it's a far sight better than it was."

"If you need any help, just let me know. I've been known to be pretty good with a hammer. Paint brushes, too."

A thought occurred to Claire. "Speaking of paint brushes, we came home the other day and everything above the veranda was done while we were gone. You didn't, by any chance, do it, did you?"

Fuzz shook his head. "Wish I could take the credit, but I've been pretty bogged down with paperwork the past few days. Maybe the owner took pity on you and had it done."

"No, I called him. He didn't know anything about it."

"Well, it must have been a Good Samaritan."

"Maybe I did it in my sleep," Claire laughed. "But thanks for the offer. You may be sorry. I asked the owner about clearing out the attic sometime but he wasn't too thrilled with the idea of coming to do it himself. Said to help ourselves to whatever we could use and trash the rest of it. I really don't want to rummage through stuff that isn't ours."

"Oh, I don't know," replied Fuzz. "You never know what buried treasures you can find in old places like this." He eyed her intently. Fuzz was more than just a little curious about where she had come upon those old letters. He wondered what else might be hidden away in some dark secret cubbyhole.

The comment took Claire by surprise but she recovered quickly. "Well, I can only assume any buried treasure would have been discovered long before we came on the scene. Did find an old hammock, though. That's turned out to be priceless."

She didn't take the bait. But the way he was looking at her made her uncomfortable. Claire cleared her throat and took another sip of coffee.

Fuzz sensed her agitation and changed the subject. "I'm really surprised you've lasted this long in the old house with it being haunted and all."

Claire laughed. "I still don't know what all the fuss was about with all those other owners. We've had no problems," she lied. Maybe she was getting a little too good at fibbing. She just didn't want to raise suspicion and have anyone else snooping around the house. Rudy being here was enough. "At first I guess I was just spooked by all the ghost stories. There's been no noises going bump in the night or anything like that."

No noises. Just a mysterious lover crawling into her bed every night. Passing it off as a joke, Claire added, "The kids say the ghost must like us since he's not scaring us away like he did everybody else."

"Well, I can't see why he would, you being so pretty and all. What man in his right mind would kick a lovely lady like you to the curb?"

Claire ignored the bristling sensation behind her. "Why, you're sweet to say that." So many compliments in such a short time. Her cheeks flushed a soft pink.

Draining his cup, Fuzz said, "Guess I'd better get back on the road. Tough job, this fighting crime."

"I wouldn't think you'd have too much trouble around here." Claire couldn't imagine there'd be much crime in a sleepy little town like Shenandoah.

"Not a whole lot normally," he agreed. "Seems to pick up more once tourists start coming through in the summer. We try to keep as visible as we can as a deterrent."

Following him to the cruiser, Claire couldn't help but notice just how well Fuzz filled out his uniform. It certainly did seem to fit snuggly enough in all the right places. The breadth of his chest strained the buttons of his shirt almost to the point of gaping, though it didn't seem to be too small a size. Muscular thighs tightened his trousers against his upper legs. His gait was confident as he held himself erect.

There was no doubt he was a fine figure of a man.

But he wasn't the man of her dreams.

❋　　❋　　❋

Fuzz picked them up as promised just before noon. Claire was waiting on the veranda and called to the children when he pulled into the drive. As Fuzz strolled toward the house, Maggie sauntered out the front door with Billy not far behind.

"All set?" Fuzz asked cheerily. All of a sudden the sound of a door slamming reverberated through the house. "What was that?"

Startled, Claire said, "Sounded like a door. Breeze must have caught one."

"We were in the attic." Billy admitted. Drawing his sister aside, he whispered, "Charles isn't too happy. He thinks maybe we shouldn't go."

Billy thought he was speaking just loudly enough for Maggie to hear, but Fuzz was closer than he thought.

"Who's Charles?" he asked curiously.

Wide-eyed, the children clamped their mouths shut.

Claire narrowed her eyes in warning. She had to admit her resolve was slipping, yet she was in no mood today to explain a ghost to Fuzz or anyone else for that matter.

"Nobody." They all spoke at once shaking their heads.

"We were just playing," Billy said innocently.

"Yeah," Maggie echoed. "Just playing."

"Oh, they're just being silly," Claire responded a little too casually as she took the children by their hands and headed towards the car.

Fuzz glanced quizzically at the house for a brief moment then followed.

As Claire checked that the children's seatbelts were secure, she wistfully looked up at the attic window. Was that a shadow she saw pass behind the curtain? Was he watching them go?

If she didn't believe what Rudy suspected—if she didn't believe the possibility that she had a ghost for a husband—then why did she suddenly feel so unfaithful?

Claire looked back at Fuzz. No, this man she was getting into a car with certainly was not the man of her dreams.

FOURTEEN

Even though he is not visibly in the room, his presence envelopes my body, consumes my very soul, in warmth and love. I can feel his fire as if he were stoking the very flame inside me.

Claire read the notation she had just written in her own journal and sighed deeply. No one would ever in a million years believe any of it. She couldn't see him, but she sensed Charles was there in the room with her. Watching. Waiting. She could almost smell the muskiness of his scent.

Putting down her notebook, Claire looked about her. "I can feel you're here," she whispered nervously. "You're in the room. Will you let me see you?" For just an instant, a hazy mist took shape beside her chair. The obvious shape of a man whose hand reached for hers, his head bending to place a tender kiss on the back of her own. Then he was gone. The dampness of his lips remained.

It happened so fast, yet there was no question he was there beside her. She tried to calm herself enough to speak again. "I remember you saying you can't stay in human form for long at a time. Can you speak with me?"

Listening intently, Claire was almost certain she heard the words, "*Yes, my love.*" Did she actually hear something or just imagine it? She was wide awake. She pinched herself just to make certain.

"Are you Charles Montgomery?"

The answer was unmistakable. "*Yes.*"

✳   ✳   ✳

Each letter took on an entirely new perspective. A chronicle of life as a Civil War soldier. The frequent hardships, occasional respite, glorious victories, heartrending losses.

Sitting at her laptop, Claire keyed snippets from some of the letters to later be molded into an article.

> December 15, 1861 . . . *The Colonel has promised to let the married men go home for Christmas once we settle into winter quarters.*
>
> *. . . Met a man just released from prison in Washington. The Yankees took him prisoner on the 13th of July and just released him last week. He said his fare was very rough and that there were 60,000 sick Yankees in Washington.*
>
> *. . . Many of our soldiers were ill earlier in the fall . . . typhus, rheumatism, measles, mumps, syphillis.*
>
> *. . . There were two men shot in Centreville last week for trying to kill their commanding officers. I understand they gave the priest twenty-five dollars apiece to save their souls. Men are getting desperate and the war has just begun.*

> February 18, 1862 . . . *You must write me all you know and everything that is funny, for there is certainly nothing funny here.*

> April 19, 1862 . . . *Conditions are miserable; our men are in the trenches, standing knee-deep in water enduring torrential rainstorms, trading fire with the Union troops. The Yankees are shooting at our men constantly though it is very seldom they hit any of them. They sent a flag of truce this evening to bury their dead.*

> August 3, 1862 . . . *Some of the boys are getting very anxious to put in substitutes. I don't blame any man for putting in a substitute if he can, though I think if it is kept up much longer, it will ruin our army. It is enough to make a man want to get out.*

. . . Took a look at our flag that we carried in the last battle. There were six or seven men shot with it in their hands and there were forty-five holes pierced through it. The staff was splintered in two.

September 30, 1862 . . . *Have not seen a paper in a month so don't know what the public opinion is.*

. . . We've had to wade every stream we come to that has no bridge across it. We have waded the Potomac three times. The men are grumbling. They hadn't been given time to take off their clothing to cross the creeks and rivers, so had to march with wet clothes on.

October 17, 1862 . . . *I think I can stand the service better if they would give us enough to eat. And we do not get near enough salt. I am glad that we are going to leave this region soon. The people through here are mostly Quakers. The Federals will sell us anything cheap. The Quakers will sell anything they have when the spirit moves them, though we can't catch them right half the time.*

April 27, 1863 . . . *I think the prospect for peace is very gloomy now. It doesn't look like either side is making any preparation to end this conflict. There are greater preparations for fighting than ever. This is a rich man's war and a poor man's fight.*

October 1, 1863 . . . *This is quite a pleasant morning. I was very surprised indeed to receive a letter forwarded from none other than President Abraham Lincoln himself declaring the war over and releasing me to Shenandoah just as soon as I can get myself there. I was pleased to say the least, but the next one he sends to me, he had better not get you to write it.*

Charles sat unseen by her side as Claire finished the letters. The most disturbing was the final one from Father Francis informing Charles that his beloved Clarissa and both children had perished by the hands of the Union army in the fall of 1863.

Claire sobbed as she fought to draw the experience from a forgotten past. The memory was devastatingly genuine as it had been in her dream. The paralyzing fear. The suffocating grief as she was forced to watch her precious babies take their last breaths before her very eyes. The excruciating pain of the bullet piercing her breast. The black endlessness of death.

Suddenly he appeared beside her. Wrapping his arms around his inconsolable wife, Charles crooned solace as Claire wept into his shoulder.

The fact he had materialized failed to shock her as she found comfort in his embrace. Through her tears, she whispered bitterly, "They murdered our babies."

Holding her tightly to him, Charles cradled her as he whispered into her ear. "We are all here, my darling. Our family is together once more. We are one."

Realization dawned as Claire pushed herself back and stared at him. Gradually a smile spread across her lips as she vainly tried to dry her eyes. "Oh, Charles," she cried anew flinging her arms around his neck. "I've missed you so."

❋　　❋　　❋

She remembered. As if someone had flicked a light switch, each memory came flooding back. Her carefree youth in the bayous of Louisiana. Traveling to Richmond with her father. Being introduced to Charles for the very first time at the Merchants' Harvest Ball.

Stretched out beside him in the hammock by the river, Claire snuggled closer into his embrace. Charles cradled her lovingly drinking in the scent of her hair as he buried his nose deeply into her luscious dark curls. "Soap smells appreciably better than it did a century ago."

"Lots of things are better now. Electricity. Indoor plumbing," she chuckled. "Refrigerators. I could go on and on."

"I'm sure you could. There's much you'll have to teach me."

Sliding a finger down the long, jagged scar snaking to his navel, Claire shuddered at the thought of the injury that caused the whitened trail. "I'm thankful the saber didn't cut any deeper."

"As am I."

Pensively, Claire ruffled the golden down covering his chest. "Where do we go from here, Charles?"

"I wish I knew, my love," he replied sadly. "I wish I knew."

❋   ❋   ❋

"Madam, why do you insist on naming the children after a barnyard goat and a squawking magpie?" It had been a bone of contention with Charles since they arrived at the house. "Their christened names are William and Margaret. Always have been. Always will be." Pacing a path in the hardwood of the parlor floor, he waved his arms to emphasize his point.

Claire had been trying to read one of the journals from the strongbox, but he kept interrupting her. Laughing at his attempt at righteous indignation, Claire explained calmly, "If you prefer to call them by their proper names, you go right ahead. But if I start calling them William and Margaret, they'll think they've done something wrong and I'm upset with them."

"It's an abomination, I tell you," he grumbled.

"You'll get used to it," she cajoled. "Anyway, when they get older and out working on their own, they'll probably want to be called William and Margaret or something totally different like Megadeath and Moonbeam."

"What do you mean? They could change their names?" The shock in his voice was amusing. "Children can just up and do that?"

"Nowadays kids can do just about whatever they please at the drop of a hat."

"Well, I've never heard of such foolishness. Where's the respect? The discipline?"

"It's obvious you haven't been around teenagers lately." Claire tossed the journal aside. "You know, it would save me a lot of reading if you could just tell me what you've written in these journals. Or would the memories be too painful?"

Charles shrugged. "No more, I guess, than reading it again over your shoulder."

"I would much rather hear your voice. Your Southern accent is so cute."

"*Cute?* I don't have an accent," he laughed in denial. "But I can still hear the Cajun French in yours when I listen very closely."

"Maybe a bit. I've been pegged for an Easterner more than once. But my accent isn't nearly as distinctive as some Maritimers."

His voice smooth, almost hypnotic, Charles recounted some of his experiences during the war. Curled up in his warm, strong arms, Claire closed her eyes as he spoke though it seemed like an illusion that might disappear the instant she opened her eyes and blinked.

He had been through so much. Seen so much. Agony. Death. Yet he shrugged it off explaining most soldiers found that war was ninety-nine percent boredom and only one percent sheer terror.

Many days and weeks—even months—were spent either in camp between engagements or marching from one place to another. The major skirmishes were well publicized. They were few and far between considering the total length of the war.

Keeping busy was a chore in itself. There wasn't too much to do after drill but read, write letters or play music. Some men brought their harmonicas or jews harps with them or even guitars and banjos if they were lucky enough not to get them smashed somewhere along the line.

Even though most commanders forbade card playing, some men passed the time gambling. They'd only get eleven dollars a month in pay, but most times they'd do without any money at all for months at a time. But a really good poker player could send money home to help in the hard times shared by many.

"We tried to get as much sleep as we could," Charles recalled, "because we never knew how long it would be until the next time we could catch a good night's rest. When the order came down to cook three days' worth of rations, we knew a long march was ahead. Most times we'd eat the rations before the march ever began. We figured it would be easier to carry the food in our stomachs than in our haversacks. And when we did get to stop, most of us didn't bother to pitch tents. We just fell asleep where we stood.

"Sometimes we got lucky and won a battle or captured some Federal supply wagons. A lot of the men were pretty good foragers. It wasn't considered legal but sometimes morals had to go by the wayside when you've spent days with no food in your bellies."

Charles couldn't help chuckling. "Rode into Hood's Brigade one afternoon. Joined some of the lads for mess. They were all named John but two . . . and the others were both Bill. Had to distinguish between them by using their middle names. Johnny Frank was quite a character. Fat as a bear and sassy as a panther. Bragged about killing Yankees. Hadn't got one yet but he'd nicknamed himself Yankee Hunter. Vowed he was going to kill himself a Yank and eat him raw with salt."

"Sounds pretty barbaric," Claire commented with a shudder.

"All big talk, believe me. He was wounded in the fall of '62 at Second Bull Run and spent most of the war as a nurse in the hospital. Lost track of him after that. Johnny Frank was planning to stay in Virginia and marry. Kept saying we had some of the prettiest girls here that he'd ever seen. Kind of agree with him about that." Charles gave Claire a squeeze. "I was pleased to tell him I already had the prettiest one."

"What a flatterer you are, Mr. Montgomery." She snuggled deeper into his arms. "I can't imagine the horrors you went through."

"Of course you can," he pointed out with a tender kiss to her cheek. "You went through it just as much as I did. Paid a greater price."

"I guess I did," she reflected solemnly. "When you're telling me about it, I can picture it all happening in my mind, but I can't be sure if I'm actually remembering or just imagining it as you're describing it."

"After all, my love . . . it's been well over a hundred years. Memories tend to fade over time."

"Some do," she agreed. "But you never forgot."

"Once I realized I still had consciousness after passing, I had something to look forward to. The hope of your coming back to me kept the memories alive."

"Do you know what happened to my father? Martha? Breezie's family?"

"Yes, my dear. Your father and Martha visited me a number of times over the years. Even persuaded your grandmother to leave her bayou once. François wrote me your grandmother slipped away peacefully in her sleep. She was one hundred and five. Neither your father nor Martha recovered from your death. They passed within days of each other. I imagined from broken hearts. And to be left alone . . . well, the grief was too much to bear."

"They really loved each other, I'm sure of it," Claire whispered haltingly, "but, of course, could never show it openly." She could feel Charles nod behind her.

"After I was gone, Breezie and Simon stayed here until they could no longer keep the property in good repair. Abraham sold the farm and they moved on. Little Ruthie married a fine young man and moved with him north into Canada."

"And Moses?"

"Ah, dear Moses. You'd be so proud, Clarry. Moses went to school and became a teacher in a Negro university. Your Rudy and Constance are descendants of his lineage."

"Maybe they could have all been here with us today if Breezie hadn't been so stubborn. You must have been so lonely with everyone gone."

"The passing of time meant nothing to me," Charles assured her. "But I managed to keep myself occupied."

She arched a brow. "Like painting the house for me?"

"Certainly. No wife of mine is going to be dangling out of dormer windows thirty feet in the air for the sake of a little white-wash," he said chauvinistically.

"I should have known. I am surprised you let the property get so run down. You always took so much pride in the way it looked."

"With you gone, I really didn't have any reason to keep it up. Then, when I felt you coming back to me, I wish I hadn't been so quick to lose faith and had taken better care. Then again, it wasn't like I could go out and buy paint myself. I had no money but the gold. Had to wait for someone to bring it."

"Well, the inside of the house is in good shape."

"Thanks to you. But you almost lost your tub. I put a stop to that right quick like. Usually I'd allow someone just enough time to make a few improvements, but more often than not, they'd start to annoy me in a day or two. And chasing people away was the only amusement I've had for a long time."

FIFTEEN

As the opportunity arose over the next few days, Charles continued his recollections of his time during the war.

"It wasn't quite as bad for the officers. We had a few more comforts. Better tentage. Some furniture. My heart went out to the enlisted men, but there was little I could do. Policy prevented us from intervening to any great extent. Each man was issued only half a tent. They'd have to pair up to make a full-sized one. The odd man out was on his own. When we captured Federal camps, we'd take their canvas."

Food was plentiful. Food was scarce. At times they'd only be issued a pound and a quarter of cornmeal a day. That would have been plenty if they had anything to go with it. They pretended to give them coffee and sugar though it was as near to nothing as anything at all. Then some physician decided sugar was not good for them and the quartermaster stopped rationing it.

"I suppose I shouldn't have even been associating with the enlisted men, with me being a Captain, but they were a darn sight more interesting to be around than most officers. Some of the escapades they'd tell you about! It was a wonder they weren't all court-martialed.

"When we weren't marching or in a fight, there'd be a lot of free time to get into trouble. There was Bobby Crowder from Tennessee. Met up with that lot after Shiloh. Bobby had put himself on the outside of some moonshine and that got him hankering for some good old down-home Tennessee applejack. He and his buddy, Sparrow, got caught after checking out all the distilleries within ten miles. General Bragg's escort asked them if they had any liquor and Sparrow made the mistake of telling them they had some of the best apple brandy he ever had the pleasure of tasting. Well, if they weren't ordered to dump it out. Near broke their hearts. But Crowder had a Yankee canteen full still hidden under his coat." Charles chuckled. "You talk about a good forager. That lad played many a mean trick on poor unsuspecting folk."

"So it wasn't so totally miserable all the time," Claire observed.

"We took our laughs where we could find them," agreed Charles. He had to pause to wipe his eyes. It felt good to laugh. "There was this one lieutenant from Missouri and about twenty of his mates from school who formed their own little army. If there ever was a natural-born storyteller, he was it. Spent a few days with him at Matson's spread. Clemens had sprained his ankle quite badly falling out of a hayloft and was laid up there for a few weeks."

"Clemens?" Claire's curiosity peaked when she heard the name. "Samuel Clemens from Hannibal, Missouri?"

"Lieutenant Sam Clemens." Nodding in recollection, Charles arched an eyebrow. "Yes, I do believe that's where he said he was from. Why? Do you know him?"

"Not personally. But everybody knows Samuel Clemens. Actually, he's better known as Mark Twain and he is . . . *was* . . . a very famous storyteller. Billy has a couple of his books. They're classics."

"Huh. You don't say."

Intrigued, Claire asked, "Well, what stories did he tell you? Do you remember?"

"I don't recall offhand. There were so many."

"So how did he come to fall out of a hayloft? Didn't you say that's how he sprained his ankle?"

"That's right. They left camp foraging for food and finally came to Matson's farm. It was late. The place was dark so they figured everyone was already asleep. Bedded down in the barnyard. Some of them climbed up in the hayloft. It wasn't long before one of the men took to smoking and set the hay on fire.

"The commotion woke Clemens. He rolled away from the flames and right out the big hay-window into the barnyard below. The other fellows tossed the burning hay out the same window right on top of poor Sam.

"His buddies found the whole event hilarious, but for old Sam it was the last straw. He cursed and swore and announced, in no uncertain terms, just what he thought of them all, the war, the Confederacy, and the whole human race in general."

"He must have been terribly interesting to speak with."

"He was quite the character."

Chances for respite were few and far between. Occasionally, the soldiers would be welcomed into private homes for a meal of whatever could be scraped up from hidden supplies.

So often the tragic stories were told of friends on opposing sides killing each other. Brothers killing brothers. Fathers killing sons.

"There are so many horrific stories I could tell you," Charles said quietly shuddering. "Terrible memories." He ran a hand over his face pausing as if trying to find the strength to continue.

"You don't have to tell me any more if you don't want to." Claire put her hand on his arm.

Charles drew her close and kissed the top of her head. "I'm all right, my love. I know it all happened so long ago. But it seems like it was just yesterday. I didn't think it would still affect me like it does.

"I think the most heartbreaking incident I heard about was near Harrison's Landing. It was in 1862, not too long after the war began. Our troops were on one side of a field. The Union army was holed up across the way. A Yankee heard a soldier moaning during the night. Didn't know if it was a Confederate or Union soldier. All he knew was this man was hurting out there on the field.

"This Yankee risked his life to bring the fallen soldier back for medical care. Crawling on his stomach through the gunfire, he reached the soldier and began pulling him toward his camp. When the Yank finally reached his own lines, he saw it was actually one of our boys, but the lad was already dead. The Yankee lit a lantern and saw the face of the soldier he had just risked his life to save. It was his own son."

Charles' voice hitched as he continued. "The father was heartbroken. His boy had been studying music in the South when the war broke out and he enlisted with the Confederate Army without his father knowing. He asked to give his son a full military burial despite his being on the enemy's side. He found a piece of paper with some musical notes on it in the pocket of his boy's uniform and asked permission for the army band to play the tune at the funeral. His request was turned down but they did allow him a bugler.

"We could hear it all the way to our lines. I'll never forget it." Charles hummed a bit of the haunting melody as if he were reliving the memory.

"I know that tune," Claire exclaimed. "We call it *Taps*. It's played all the time now at military funerals or memorial services. At least in Canada it is."

"I'm sure the father would be pleased to know that."

Curled up on his lap, Claire nuzzled into Charles' neck as he continued to reminisce. "Do you remember the photographer giving us so much trouble when we had those photographs taken? Not wanting to let Simon and his family into his studio?"

Claire giggled. "That was a fun day. I swear I would have had the whole town boycott if he had turned us away."

"I have no doubt. I'm glad it didn't come to that. But do you remember what Simon said afterwards on the way home?"

Claire's brow puckered as she tried to recall the rest of that day. "I'm not sure."

Doing his best to imitate Simon's voice, Charles said, "You white folk . . . when you's a babe, you's pink. When you's all growed up, you's white. When you's been in da sun too long, you's red. When you's been bit by da cold bug, you's blue. When you's got a fright, you's yellow. When you's feelin' poorly, you's green. When you's got a good whack on da shins, you's purple an' a whole lotta other colors. And when you die, you's grey. Us darkies . . . why we just stay darkies our whole life long. And he's gots the nerve to call us colored?"

All of a sudden, Charles' head jerked up and he vanished leaving Claire suspended in mid-air. They hadn't heard the knock.

"What the . . . ?" Fuzz had rapped briskly on the door, but didn't wait for it to be answered. He strolled into the parlor just in time to see Claire floating precariously above the edge of the sofa for the briefest instant, then land unceremoniously on the floor.

SIXTEEN

Rushing to her side, Fuzz gave Claire a hand to her feet. "What happened?" he asked. "You must have jumped two feet in the air." It was so comical he couldn't hide the smile. "Are you all right?"

"Sure, I'm fine. Must have fallen asleep." She avoided his gaze by looking around for any tell-tale signs that Charles had been in the room. "You startled me."

"Just dropped in to see if you and the kids would like to come riding with me. My friend has horses for hire but the ranch is a ways away. We could make a day of it tomorrow if it doesn't rain," he suggested.

Smiling sweetly, Claire did her best to ignore the scorching breath that tickled her ear. *"Get rid of him, Clarry. I don't like his being here in the house."*

Giggling nervously, Claire brushed her fingers through her hair inconspicuously shooing Charles away. She took Fuzz by the arm and led him toward the kitchen. "Got time for a cup of coffee? Or cold drink?" She might as well at least try to be hospitable. "I think there might be some lemonade left if the children haven't drained the jug."

"Thanks, but I'm on my way to a call."

"Good . . . leave . . . now!" The men stood practically nose to nose. No one but Claire could see.

"Nothing serious, I hope." She couldn't help but smile. Certainly not appropriate behavior if the call was urgent.

"Don't expect it will be."

"Clarry!"

With a start, Claire turned toward the voice. Charles beckoned her to the parlor. Nervously, she glanced back at Fuzz. He gave no indication that he had heard anything out of the ordinary. "Then I'll walk you to your car. Just give me a second to find my shoes." Claire left him at the door and hurried into the parlor.

"I don't want you to go with him, Clarry. He's up to no good. I can feel it."

"Shhh," she whispered as quietly as she could as she bent to pick up her sandals. "He'll get suspicious if we don't go now that we've been out together a few times."

"You don't have to go. Just throw the miscreant out." He waved his hands in exasperation. *"There's nothing that says you have to keep seeing him. Besides,"* his tone softened suggestively as he swept a finger along her cheek, *"we can find much better use of the day."*

Nuzzling into her neck, Charles' kisses tickled as she giggled, "Behave yourself."

"Who are you talking to?" Fuzz had followed closely enough to hear only her muffled side of the conversation.

Swinging around, she practically ran right into his steely chest. "No one," Claire stammered guiltily. "Just muttering to myself." Avoiding his scrutiny, she held up her shoes in front of her face. "Found them."

❋   ❋   ❋

He was quiet as he held her in his arms. Brooding. Jealous. His wife of a hundred-and-forty-odd years was still insisting on going on yet another date . . . *being courted* . . . by another man. A man he didn't trust.

He realized she was capable. Strong. She had tried to convince him she was going for no other reason than to treat the children to a horseback ride. Nothing more.

"Just think of it this way, sweetheart. I'll be saving about two hundred dollars just by letting Fuzz take us. And Billy has his heart set on riding this summer. I've already promised him. I can't go back on my word now."

"If it's the money you're worried about, take some of the coin I left for you. That should be more than enough to pay for a day."

Claire brushed the hair from his eyes and smiled. "No doubt it would be. But I can't walk up to just anybody and hand them old Confederate gold coins. I've been meaning to try to find someone to ask, but I thought I heard years ago that it was illegal to own gold. We may not be able to use it at all unless we sell it as collectable coin."

"I do not understand how gold cannot be legal currency in any century. But if we can't dispose of it legally, then I'm sure we can find a less legitimate way."

❈   ❈   ❈

"Wait until we've been gone a while before you go in." Fuzz leaned through the window of his deputy's squad car. "Then have a good look around."

"Just what am I supposed to be looking for?"

"Not really sure. Anything unusual. I just got a feeling there's something going on in there. Check out the attic, too, but make sure you put everything back where it was. Don't want her filing another break-and-enter complaint."

"She won't know one little frilly's been disturbed."

Fuzz would have much rather gone in himself, but he figured he could trust Claud. He had been his deputy for the last ten years and had helped him out with more than one less-than-lawful deed.

The local coffee shop was still buzzing with rumors about the lady who rented the haunted house by the river being the only one brave enough to stick it out for so long. She hadn't been scared off. He had to find out what was so different about her living there.

The morning turned out to be bright and sunny. Billy excitedly crossed off one more line on his summer wish list. Claire brushed Maggie's long curls into a ponytail and pulled it through the hole in the back of her ball cap.

"Why can't we buy cowboy hats to ride the horses?" Maggie asked, her lip sticking out in a pout.

"Because they're expensive and you're growing so fast you wouldn't be able to wear it for very long," Claire explained.

Fuzz had advised them to wear long pants so the leather of the saddles wouldn't rub the inside of their legs raw. Their jeans would be pretty warm on such a hot day, but Claire insisted they do as he asked.

Each of the children packed their backpack with a swim suit, towel, and bottled water. Into Claire's larger one, she added a picnic lunch and snacks to keep the children happy along the way. She also cut up some carrots and apples to treat the horses.

Banishing himself to the attic, Charles sulked as he listened to the cheerful voices of his wife and children getting ready for their outing. Was this how Clarissa meant for them to be forever together? He left behind stuck in the past while she, in flesh and bone, was able to take full advantage of all the wonders of the present? He was here. They were here. Yet he couldn't be with them as he had envisioned. Not how he had prayed to be.

There had to be a missing piece to the puzzle. Clarissa may have forgotten some critical ingredient in her potion. Maybe there was another incantation they were supposed to perform to complete the process of his reincarnation.

"We're ready to go." Claire had come up to the attic, but couldn't see him. "Please don't be angry. Come let me say goodbye."

Even though he was still a tad put out, her tone was so gentle and alluring Charles could not resist. He appeared in front of her. Wrapping her arms around his neck, Claire pulled his head down for a long, sensuous kiss.

The beat of his heart quickened as Charles fervently returned her affection. "I still don't trust this man," he cautioned when he finally released her.

"I'll be careful," Claire promised with a hasty peck to his cheek. "Don't worry."

He watched from the window as they drove off.

Claud waited a good fifteen minutes after he received the all-clear signal from the sheriff. Boldly pulling up the drive, he figured the neighbors would be so used to seeing a police car at the house by now they wouldn't give it a second thought. He did glance around, however, before he got out of the car. He didn't look much like the sheriff.

A little on the squat side, Claud wasn't anywhere near as tall as Fuzz. Even with his hat covering his head, he was quite self-consciously aware of his receding hairline. He was only thirty years old to Fuzz's forty-three and the sheriff still had his full head of hair.

Claud's wife was too good a cook. That, combined with a frequent can of beer at the local hangout, had pushed his belly well beyond his belt buckle.

Putting his ear to the door, Claud listened. Fuzz hadn't said anything about a dog but he wasn't about to take any chances. He cared about as much for dogs as he did snooping around an allegedly haunted house.

As his hand grasped the door knob, a shiver slithered up his spine. Heat seared the back of his neck rocketing the tiny hairs on end. Breath hissed from his lungs as Claud spun around. There was nothing there. Unnerved, he chided himself for his foolishness.

True to his word, Fuzz had made sure he was the last to leave the house. The door was left open. Claud was glad he didn't have to take the time to pick the lock. The sooner he could have a quick look around and get out of there, the better he'd like it.

Wiping his feet on the doormat, Claud made sure there'd be no footprints to give himself away. Latex gloves would take care of any fingerprints.

Starting in the kitchen, he rummaged through all the drawers, cupboards and appliances. He stood on the table and peeked in the light fixture. Everything in the garbage was dumped into the sink, poked through, put back again. He rinsed and dried the sink with paper towels. The towels he shoved in his pocket.

He tapped walls for hiding places. He wiggled the stonework in the fireplaces checking for anything loose.

Nothing yet.

Baker took to the notion Fuzz had just sent him on a wild-goose chase. There was nothing weird going on here. It was just an old house given a bum wrap by superstitious locals but he lifted the lid to the toilet tank anyway. Took down the covers to the ceiling vents. He peeked behind the shower curtain. Even unscrewed the shower head and stuck his finger in the pipe.

He lifted Maggie's dolls one by one examining each for an opening in the antique bodies. Baker dumped Billy's stack of comic books onto the bed and ruffled through all the pages then carefully put them back in the exact order they were in.

Coming back out to the landing, Claud glanced up the attic stairs. He'd leave that for last. The empty rooms got a cursory once-over before he headed for Claire's bedroom. Opening the dresser drawers, Claud rifled through her few pieces of lingerie. A little black lace, a little red lace. No Victoria Secret or Fredericks of Hollywood. Disappointed, he shut the drawer and moved on to the closet.

Charles bristled as he forced himself to witness the violation before him. He wished no man's hands to sully his wife's intimate belongings. But he would bide his time. This little worm would rue the day he stepped one foot inside his house.

It took the better part of an hour and a half to reach the ranch. Nestled in the valley between two tree-covered mountains, it spread over hundreds of acres at the end of a scenic, winding road. Fuzz stopped the car a number of times for Claire to take pictures.

The ranch could accommodate about a hundred tents, travel trailers and even large RVs. Fuzz had told them Brett often rented the whole place out to different horse clubs so they could stay and ride for days at a time. He had a few camps set up here and there along the mountain trails.

Brett, a wiry little man no taller than Claire, was waiting for them under a sheltered overhang with four horses tethered to the corral fence. Two were quite a bit smaller than the rest. Claire was thankful for that. She really hadn't liked the idea of the children on the backs of huge sixteen-hand-high beasts.

Fuzz made the introductions as Brett started to tighten the girths. "Glad to meet you, ma'am." Claire grasped his outstretched hand and held it firmly. "Ever ridden before?" Taking in the supple length of her, Brett could see why his buddy would take a shine to the pretty little widow. He hadn't stretched the truth at all. Why, given the chance, he'd take a liking to her himself.

"Not in a long time," she admitted warily as she tried to see over the back of the horse he indicated would be hers to ride. "And nothing quite so big."

"Oh, this old girl's just like sitting atop a rocking chair," he smiled brightly. "Dottie here's just as liable to put you right to sleep." Claire had to agree the horse didn't seem too threatening. The giant black Appaloosa plodded lazily behind Brett as he led her a few times around the corral. A unique blanket of round white blotches covered her rump and spread down the outsides of both hind legs. The top half of her tail was white which blended in with black strands that swept the ground.

"Don't ever let anyone tell you horses are dumb animals. They can be mighty devilish if they've got a mind to it," Brett explained to the children as they followed him around the ring. "Sometimes they puff out their lungs with air." He demonstrated by taking in a long, noisy breath and sticking his chest as far out as he could possibly push it. "Then they let it out," air escaped his lungs in a whoosh, "most times when you're half ways swung up. Makes the saddle too loose, you see, when you go to get on and it slips down underneath their bellies. Found my head danglin' in the dirt more than once before I caught on. I swear I've heard them laughin' at me. That's why I walk them a bit before I double-check the cinches. Walking makes them forget to hold their breath."

"You sure are smart," Billy commented.

"Well, son," Brett beamed at the praise, "I've been called a lot of things, but I can't recall ever being called smart. What about you, little missy, you like horses?"

"I like the ones at the fair," Maggie chirped brightly.

"She means the merry-go-round," Billy clarified.

"Oh, I see. Well, I've got a real special little filly picked out just for you."

Maggie wasn't quite sure about this horse-riding business. "I think I'd rather ride with Mommy."

Billy wasn't surprised. "Oh, you baby! You're not going to fall off."

"Hold on now, son," Brett cut in. "If your sister doesn't want to ride by herself, that's okay." He reached out and gently tweaked her cheek. "It's okay, sweetie. Why, I rode in the same saddle as my daddy until I was a lot bigger than you are now."

Maggie hid her mouth with her hand and stuck her tongue out at her brother. Billy scrunched up his nose and glowered at her.

Claire missed the bickering. She had warned the children before they left, any squabbling and they'd be turning around and going right back home. Horses or no horses. The choice was theirs.

Horses cinched and ready to go, Brett helped Billy get his foot in the stirrup and swing his leg over the saddle of his little sorrell gelding. He shortened the stirrups after Billy was settled. "Just let Scooter have loose rein and he'll follow along behind," he instructed. "Hang on to this here horn if you need to keep your balance."

Standing with his head hung low, eyes almost closed, Scooter didn't seem to have much scoot in him. Even when Billy nudged him with his heels, the little horse didn't budge an inch. Rocking back and forth in the saddle, Billy asked, "Is he sleeping? Why won't he move?"

"He'll go with the others," Brett assured him. "He won't be left behind. Now little Rosie, here, she's going to be mighty sorry to be left behind." The little strawberry roan nickered at the sound of her name. "Come say hello to Rosie, Maggie. She really likes little girls."

As Maggie came near, Rosie strained her neck to get closer. Her nostrils flared as she tried to drink in the child's scent. "Hold your hand out so she can sniff you." Brett held tightly to her other hand so she wouldn't be frightened. "See . . . she likes you." Rosie's soft muzzle twitched against Maggie's outstretched palm.

Maggie giggled. "It tickles." Blowing warm, moist air, Rosie's nose moved to within an inch of Maggie's own. Maggie scratched the white star in the middle of her forehead. Pushing against her fingers, Rosie nudged closer. "She likes me," Maggie squealed with delight. "Can I ride her?"

"I thought you wanted to double with your mother?"

"She'd be lonely here all by herself, wouldn't she?"

"I can put her out in the pasture with all the others."

Maggie thought about that. Bravely, she shook her head. "No. I think she'd rather be with me."

"Well, lookee here!" Claud lifted the strongbox from the shelf in the closet and set it on the chair by the window. Opening the lid, he first lifted out the packet of letters and flipped impatiently through the stack. Then he unwound the tintypes and examined each one. They didn't mean a thing to him. He ruffled through the pages of Charles' journals reading a few of the entries. He supposed they were written by the Montgomery fellow that used to live there. Maybe that was what the sheriff was looking for.

Removing Clarissa's journal was a little more challenging. Unseen, Charles held it fast to the bottom of the box as if it were glued there. Muttering profanely, Claud struggled to get his fingers underneath not understanding what possibly could be making it stick. Then all of a sudden Charles pulled his hand away and the deputy lost his balance and fell to the floor. More cursing spewed from his mouth as Claud righted himself and reached again for the last book in the box.

Hot pain stung the top of Claud's hand as Charles slapped it. Claud pulled it quickly back as if he had been zapped by an electrical current. A look of pure astonishment covered his face as he rubbed away the sting. Peeking around the box, under the chair, he looked for any sign of a live wire touching the metal container. Nothing that he could see.

Once more he reached in. This time with cautious hesitation. The lid to the box slammed shut narrowly missing slicing off his fingers as he quickly pulled them back.

"Gawd A-mighty!" Claud tossed the letters, journals and photographs back into the box then unceremoniously threw it back onto the shelf in the closet. "If Fuzz wants to see what's in there, he's gonna have to see to it himself." He spoke aloud without really knowing why. There was no one else in the room to hear.

That strange prickly feeling crawled up his spine again and fiddled with the hairs on the back of his neck. However ridiculous it may have seemed, Claud could not get rid of the impression that there was another presence in the room. But he had a job to do and there was no way he was going back to the sheriff telling him he was too scared to search through a lady's boudoir.

Claud couldn't help himself from looking over his shoulder. Seeing nothing, he shook off the weird feeling then pulled Claire's duffle bag out from under the bed. It felt empty but he unzipped it to give it a quick once-over.

He ran his hands under the mattress being careful not to cut them on the springs and metal slats. Thinking he touched something, Claud lifted the edge of the mattress to get a better look. He opened the leather pouch he found there and watched wide-eyed as hundreds of golden coins spilled out onto the bed. "Pay dirt . . . Christ!"

This time it was not his mind playing tricks on him. Someone was breathing hot air down his neck. Swinging around he came face-to-face with a vaporous image of a man intently testing the sharpness of a sword with the tip of a finger.

As Claud cowered, a broad grin spread over Charles' face. Looking directly into the deputy's eyes, he mischievously whispered, "*Boo*," then instantly vanished from sight.

Since he knew the way, Fuzz took the lead on a big bay gelding Brett named Blaze. Scooter and Rosie followed with Dottie trudging dreamily along at the end of the line. It was difficult to carry on a conversation, but Claire was enjoying the peace and quiet of the wooded trail. She had already captured two deer on film, the rippling stream tumbling it's way down the mountain and a big grey squirrel scathingly chattering at them from a branch overhead.

Raising herself in the stirrups, Claire hitched up her backside hoping they'd be stopping for lunch soon. She was getting just a little too sore in places she'd rather not mention. Her poor old muscles had just barely recovered from their trek to the top of Hawksbill.

Brett was right. It was so quiet and serene in the hills, anyone on Dottie's back could very easily be lulled to sleep. Claire's head nodded more than once but she forced herself to stay somewhat alert to watch her children. They didn't have to worry about reining. Their ponies, even with shorter legs, seemed to step in Blaze's tracks as he gingerly picked his way up the uneven trail. Around trees, fallen logs and rocks, they zigged where he zigged . . . zagged where he zagged. All Billy and Maggie had to do was hold on.

Suddenly Claire felt Dottie's step falter and instinctively pulled up her head. A tingle ran up her spine as she realized a familiar presence had joined them. Perched behind on the horse's rump, she could feel Charles' arms lovingly encircling her as he nuzzled his nose into the delectable hollow of her neck.

"What are you doing?" Claire hissed aloud in surprise.

"What?" Maggie turned around almost losing her balance. "Wha . . . what did I do?"

"Nothing, sweetheart. You didn't do anything at all."

Billy and Fuzz had also turned to see what the matter was. "You okay back there?" Fuzz called.

Knowing no one else could see Charles, she added, "I was just talking to Dottie. She stumbled a bit, that's all." Turning her attention back to Charles, she whispered, "What are you doing here?"

"*You must leave with me now, my darling. This man is up to no good. He sent one of his lackeys to search the house.*"

"He did *what*?" Again she spoke too loudly.

Fuzz turned again. "Is there a problem?"

Claire forced a smile. "No. No problem." *Yet*, she added under her breath.

"*I'll take hold of the ponies and lead them down for the children.*" Charles was now walking beside Dottie.

As angry as she was, Claire was tempted to do that very thing. But she heard her daughter chatting happily to Rosie. Billy sat straight and tall in the saddle as if he had been riding all his short life. She didn't have the heart to spoil their day. She held Dottie back as the others rounded a bend in the trail. Charles appeared and Claire could speak a little freer.

"Charles, be reasonable. We can't leave now. The children will be heartbroken. They're really having fun. And Maggie's fallen right in love with Rosie. You saw her. She's having the time of her life. I can't take that away from her."

Charles had proudly regarded his young daughter's beaming face but he wouldn't be deterred. "We'll buy her a pony. We'll buy them each a pony. These very ones if they want. Just leave with me. Now."

With a heavy sigh, Claire said, "I know you're right. And we should. But I just can't disappoint them. It's not going to be easy, but we're just going to have to muddle through somehow for the rest of the day."

Fuzz was still far enough ahead. Curiosity got the better of her. "What happened at the house?" Claire asked. "Did he find anything?"

Nodding, Charles said, "Everything. The strongbox. The gold." He grinned mischievously. "And me."

SEVENTEEN

Every so often, Fuzz would look back to make sure he hadn't misplaced anyone. "The trail levels off just up here a bit more," he said. "We'll stop for lunch there."

"That sounds great," Claire called back to him. Miserably wiggling her numbing bottom, her mood blackened with each plodding step. Charles had vanished, but she knew he was still close by.

Fuzz's "bit more" turned out to be another half hour in the saddle. He offered to help Claire dismount but she insisted she could do it herself.

Loath to allow the cretin to lay a hand on his wife, Charles stepped between the horse and Fuzz as he, unseen, steadied Claire while she slid down Dottie's side.

As her feet once more hit solid ground, Claire was sure her legs would be permanently paralyzed. She rubbed her backside hoping to get the circulation going again.

"I'd be happy to do that for you, my dear." Charles whispered seductively into her ear as he gently massaged the fullness of her behind. Giggling, Claire quickly stepped away from his touch. She anguished over the idea of getting back in the saddle. Could walk down, she supposed, but even that would be tortuous. There was no doubt about it. She'd be even more sore by morning.

The clearing where they'd be having their lunch was a pretty little spot beside the brook they'd been following all morning. On the far side,

Brett had built a small corral where the horses could graze untethered. A lean-to set back into the trees was sheltered by tall pine and oak. A stone barbecue pit was dug into an open area out in front. Claire guessed the plank picnic table had to be at least eight to ten feet long.

Pointing to a worn trail leading up the hill behind the lean-to, Fuzz said, "The outhouse is up there, if you're so inclined."

Claire and the children headed up the path not quite sure what to expect when she got there. But she was quite pleasantly impressed. Although the outside of the little facility was built from rustic barn board, the inside was painted bright white and surprisingly clean. Only a few cobwebs and spiders. Nothing they couldn't handle. The side walls were open about a foot from the roof and covered with screening to provide both light and ventilation. There was even a real toilet seat and half-decent tissue.

Rinsing their hands in the icy water of the mountain stream, they shook them dry in the warm summer air.

Forcing politeness, Claire commented, "This is a lovely spot." She pointed her camera at the horses contentedly munching in the corral. Fuzz had loosened their girths and slipped the bits from their mouths.

"This is about the half-way point to the main camp on this side of the ranch. Brett's got a couple more rest spots like this one set up, but we'll head back down from here so we'll be sure to be back in lots of time before dark."

"That's a good idea since we didn't bring any camping stuff." Stifling a groan, Claire stiffly spread her plaid blanket from the car on a flat patch of grass beside the stream.

Fuzz regarded her quizzically. "If we did bring gear with us you'd have camped out?" He admired the curve of her hip as she bent to square up the edges . . . the swell of her breasts peeking out over the rounded neckline of the pretty red cotton tee-shirt she was wearing. He longed to taste the sweetness of her skin and feel its smoothness next to his own.

Knowing full well she wouldn't have come on her own, Fuzz resigned himself to the inconvenience of having her children along. One of these days, he'd catch her alone. One day very soon.

"Not on your life," Claire laughed. "I think we've had enough of camping to last us a very long time. Unless it's five-star. The Ritz. Hyatt. What the heck, I'd even take the Bates Motel over that cabin."

Quickly unpacking her backpack, Claire set out paper plates and plastic cutlery. Then she set containers full of cheese, cut up veggies, fruit, and home-made chocolate chip cookies on top of the plates to keep them from blowing away. Fuzz pulled the sandwiches from his pack.

"Come on, kids," Claire called to Billy and Maggie. "Lunch." The sooner they ate, the sooner they could get down this infernal mountain.

"I'm starving," Billy moaned pathetically as he flopped down beside his mother.

"Me, too," Fuzz agreed wholeheartedly. He had to admit Claire had a couple of cute kids, just annoyingly in the way all the time. Here he was trying to make time with their mother and she didn't seem to be taking the hint. Of course, he hadn't come right out and asked her for a date. Just the two of them. Occasionally, he had seen her car at the Jenkins' place when he was out on patrol. Maybe she could leave them there for a night. Or two.

But she had suddenly turned moody on him. A frown creased her brow as she knelt beside him picking up after lunch. This was not the same woman he left Shenandoah with a few hours ago.

"Is there anything wrong?" he finally asked. Reaching for a tendril of dark, curly hair that had escaped her hat, he meant only to tuck it away from her face. But before he could touch her, the back of his outstretched hand burned as if it had just been slapped.

"Wow," he squealed as he quickly withdrew. "That was some shock!"

Claire could not hold back a giggle. She had seen Charles rap the sheriff's knuckles. "There's a few thousand volts running through that force field," she warned mischievously.

"Whoa. What would happen if I kissed you?" He was willing to find out.

"Chances are you'd be electrocuted." She shivered at the thought of his lips touching hers.

There was a time she would have welcomed his affection. She would have investigated the man lounging beside her on the blanket with more than idle curiosity. This was the first time she had seen him in civilian clothing. His uniform fit him almost too tightly. The jeans and tee-shirt he wore today also left very little to the imagination. There was no doubt he was a perfect specimen of manhood.

Just not her man.

"Are you cold?" He couldn't imagine on a hot August day as this that anyone could possibly be chilly.

"No," she said curtly with a shake of her head. Billy and Maggie had changed into their swim suits and were happily splashing around in the frigid water of the mountain stream. Claire pointed to her children. "Just the thought of how cold that water must be made me shiver. I'm surprised they haven't turned blue."

"Nice save, my darling," Charles chuckled close to her ear. *"Why didn't you tell him what you were really thinking?"* Claire found it very difficult to suppress a smile.

Catching the hint of a grin, Fuzz commented, "You have a beautiful smile. You should do it more often."

"Thank you," was all she said as she focused on the children. "It's about time to come out and dry off, guys."

Discouraged by her dour attitude, Fuzz changed the subject. "You know you're the talk of the town, don't you? Staying in that house for so long."

"I didn't realize people were actually gossiping about us." Claire hated the idea of being the subject of gossip mongers.

"I wouldn't call it gossiping. More . . . curiosity."

"What are they saying?"

"Oh, nothing bad or anything. Just that they're surprised you seem to be the only one able to stick it out."

"It's just a house," she said with a shrug of her shoulder as the children ran up for their towels. Their lips had turned a sickly shade of purple. Just touching their skin made her shudder. Claire wrapped them each warmly with a hug and a kiss. "I'm surprised your fingers and toes don't fall off," she gently scolded. "You're so cold. Play in the sun for a bit and thaw out." Before they could scamper away, she pointed to their shoes. "Put them on, please."

"Do we have to?" Billy whined. "They're going to be sticky."

"Then put your socks on, too."

"My feet are still wet."

"Then dry them."

"Do as your mother asks, William," Charles said sternly. Both children looked up expecting to see Charles. No one appeared, but the sound of his voice was unmistakably clear to them.

"Charles is here!" Forgetting himself, Billy whooped with delight as he shoved his feet in his socks and shoes."

"Will you play with us?" Maggie begged. They were so excited that he had come along, neither child gave what they had just said another thought.

"Who's here?" Fuzz looked around but saw no one.

Claire couldn't think of a word of explanation for Fuzz. She couldn't believe that Charles would make himself known to the children at a time like this. She fumbled for words. Remembering something Rudy had told her, Claire said the first thing that came to mind. "Ummm . . . it's just a silly game they play. They have an imaginary friend." Hoping to gain a little sympathy, she dropped her eyes and sadly whispered, "Since their father died and all. You know how it is."

"Of course." Fuzz regarded her skeptically but decided to let it slide. He knew it wasn't unusual for children to pretend to have invisible playmates. His sister had one. Thankfully she quickly outgrew that phase. What he found strange was that both of Claire's children seemed to play with the same one. "We've never really talked about that."

"About what?" Claire offered the last cookie to Fuzz.

"Your husband." He took a bite then sucked chocolate from his fingertip. "If you don't mind me asking, how did he die?"

With a heavy sigh, Claire shrugged her shoulder. "I don't mind. I can talk about it now." Yet she took her time answering. "Stay where I can see you," she called after the children happily playing tag with Charles in the clearing near the lean-to. They now must be able to see him, too. She could only imagine how the display looked to Fuzz who, she noticed with amusement, was watching intently one eyebrow arched at a sharp angle.

The children were actually playing with a third person he couldn't see. They would reach out as if they were touching thin air, squeal, turn, and scurry away trying not to be tagged. Every so often, Charles would tackle one or the other rolling them on the ground. Finally tuckered, the children sprawled on their backs panting for air. Once more, Charles vanished.

"Ethan sailed out to set trawl for his lobster pots. His foot got tangled in the rope and . . . " There was a hitch in her voice. "And he was over the side before he even had a chance. We never saw him again," she said sadly.

"They never recovered . . . "

"His body? No."

"I'm sorry."

Claire had tried her best to be civil to Fuzz, but his deception preyed on her mind. What could he have possibly hoped to gain by sending his deputy to search the house? What had Charles done to the deputy? She had to find out before they left so she'd know what to expect when they got home.

Excusing herself to the privy, Claire knew Charles would follow. "You look ravishing, my darling," he crooned as he appeared nibbling at an ear. "Good enough to eat."

"Be serious," she demanded irritably pushing him away. "What were you thinking letting the children know you were here? The sheriff's suspicious enough already. You just fueled the flame."

"He'll be no problem, I assure you."

"Why?" Her eyes narrowed. "What are you going to do to him? What did you do to his deputy?"

Stricken with feigned innocence, Charles simply said, "I did nothing to him. He did it all to himself."

Groaning, Claire held her hand to her head. "Oh, no. What happened?"

With a smirk, Charles explained. "After he *thought* he saw me, he just let loose a howl that would make a banshee proud. He forgot all about the gold. He ran down the stairs so fast, I doubt he touched a single step. Such a skittish little fellow he was. It was all quite comical, really."

"So you didn't hurt him?"

"Why, my dear, I'm offended you'd even think that I would inflict harm on such a hapless being." He shook his head. "As I said, I did nothing. He backed his vehicle so fast he ran it right over the bank across the road. Well, if it didn't go and flip over just as pretty as you please."

"Was he hurt badly?" Claire could envision being convicted for inflicting injury on a police officer who was ordered by his superior to illegally break and enter on property she didn't even own. "Was he wearing his seatbelt?"

"I don't suspect so, being in such a hurry and all. Not to worry, my darling. He was coming around when the ambulance came."

The ramifications could possibly be serious, but Claire had no way of knowing what to expect. It was clearly an incident that probably would never even be mentioned in light of the fact there was no search warrant. Entry was unlawful. She'd just have to plead ignorance and see what developed.

By early afternoon, they were packed up and on their way back down the mountain. Her battered and bruised behind would need careful ministrations once they were home. Claire's thoughts wandered to an evening of tender caresses and loving touches. Charles was nowhere to be seen, but Claire knew he'd be keeping a watchful eye.

And it wasn't long before he made his presence known.

For no apparent reason, Fuzz suddenly toppled from Blaze's back landing on the ground with a sickening thud.

"Are you all right?" Stiffly dismounting, Claire wound Dottie's reins around a branch and ran passed the children to Fuzz.

Agitated, Rosie started to dance. *"Mommy?"* Maggie was starting to get scared.

"You're okay, Bijou. Just sit still, Margaret. She won't go anywhere." Charles was by her side calming the pony. *"Just pat her neck. She likes that."*

Grasping his shoulder in pain, Fuzz struggled to sit up.

"What happened?" Claire grabbed for Blaze's bridle before he had a chance to run off and tied him up as well.

"I don't know. One minute I was in the saddle. Next minute it felt like something plowed into me and here I sit." Fuzz tried to smile, but he failed to mask his agony.

"Is anything broken?" As she spoke, Claire searched the trees for Charles. That could be the only explanation. He had taken his revenge and knocked Fuzz out of the saddle.

"I'll be fine if you can just help me to my feet."

Fuzz bit back the pain as she tried to pull him up. Claire grimaced.

"Maybe the shoulder's dislocated," Fuzz finally admitted. "Do you think you can help me pop it back in?"

"A shoulder's the least of his worries," Charles warned menacingly.

Forgetting herself, Claire angrily swung to face him. "This is all *your* fault," she accused. "You could have waited until we were actually *down* the mountain."

Not knowing she wasn't speaking to him, Fuzz answered sheepishly. "I'm sorry. I really didn't plan this."

"No, I wasn't talking to you." She turned back to Charles and whispered vehemently, "You're going to have to help me do this."

"I'm not sure how much help I'm going to be," Fuzz panted in pain.

"Fuzz, I'm not talking to you."

"Then who are you talking to?" Sweat began to bead on his forehead as he struggled to look up at her. A confused look spread over his face. "Oh, no. Don't tell me you have an imaginary friend, too."

"Oh, don't be silly. I'm just praying to have the strength to do this right the first time. I don't want to hurt you any more than I have to."

Claire took his wrist and tried to straighten his arm as gently as she could. His face paled. His breathing became more shallow.

"Please . . . please . . . don't go into shock on me," she begged. She had only seen this done on television. One good pull and it should pop back into place. Placing one foot on his rib cage, Claire realized she wasn't tall enough to be very effective at all. His arm was almost as long as she was.

Charles stood close behind watching over her shoulder. "Take his wrist and give a hard yank when I tell you to," she ordered so just he could hear. "I'll pull from the elbow."

Regarding the less-than-law-abiding public servant with contempt, Charles sniffed, *"What if I don't want to?"*

"You'll want to unless you'd rather sleep alone in the attic tonight. And tomorrow night. Get the picture?"

With a sigh of resignation, Charles grasped Fuzz by the wrist. Without wasting any more time, Claire took hold and said, *"Now."* In unison, they sharply tugged. Fuzz tried not to cry out, but the pain was just too severe. With an audible popping sound, his shoulder moved into place. His breathing relaxed.

"Just sit still for a minute." Claire rummaged through her backpack for a couple capsules and what was left of her water. "This isn't much, but it may help with the pain." She took the children's towels and fashioned a sling to immobilize Fuzz's arm until she could get him to the hospital. "I know they're cold and wet, but it's the best I can come up with under the circumstances."

With Charles' unseen help she got Fuzz to his feet and into the saddle. If Charles had his way, he would have pushed him right on over, only Claire grabbed Fuzz by the leg to steady him. Wilting under Claire's withering glare, Charles stepped away from the horse, hands in the air conceding defeat.

As Fuzz swayed atop Blaze, he commented woozily, "You're one pretty amazing woman, you know that?"

"You just keep on thinking that."

EIGHTEEN

"Well now, this is my day for policemen." The x-ray technician positioned Fuzz under the lens.

"Yeah?" He flinched as she manipulated his arm to get the best angle.

"Your Deputy Baker was in here this morning."

"Baker?" Then he remembered the little escapade he had sent his man on earlier that morning.

"Huh huh. Keep still now." Stepping behind the lead shield, she pressed a button. Fuzz heard the machine whirr overhead.

Swearing under his breath, Fuzz angrily ground his teeth. "What happened?"

"He flipped your patrol car." Talking as she adjusted the machine for another shot, the technician continued, "Got himself a good concussion out of it. They're keeping him here tonight." Once more, the machine whirred. "Okay, Sheriff, just sit tight for a bit."

Fuzz had a few minutes to plan the next move, but he wanted to talk with Claud first to see if he had found anything.

Once the x-rays were developed, the technician examined them closely. "These look pretty clean. I'll just get the attending to have a look. You can put your shirt back on and take a seat in the waiting room."

Claire and the children were waiting for him, but Fuzz skirted around and went directly to the nurses' station. "I hear you have my deputy here. What room's he in?"

Taking the stairs to the third floor, Fuzz pushed open the door. He spotted Claud dozing in a bed by the window. There were three other men in the ward. One was softly snoring from his corner of the room. One was intently watching a silent television with an earphone stuck in his ear. The other man, a younger one, visited with a pretty girl. Wife or girlfriend, Fuzz didn't know. He didn't recognize any of them which was good. And no one seemed to take notice of him. Even better.

Nudging Claud awake with a quiet, "Hey, Bud," Fuzz pulled up a chair. Startled, Claud finally focused on the anxious face of his sheriff.

Leaning in closer, Fuzz whispered, "For chrissake, Baker, what happened?"

"Shit, Fuzz, you're not going to believe this." Claud shifted his weight to turn over on his side with his back to the others in the room. Still he glanced around to see if anyone might be listening. "I seen him, Fuzz. Large as life. Goddammit, he was going to *kill* me." In a panic, Baker's voice rose as he reached to grab Fuzz by the front of his shirt.

Fuzz scanned the room to see if anyone heard, then spoke softly trying to calm Claud. "Slow down, there. Take it easy." He pried Baker's fingers from the death grip he had on him and pushed his hand gently to the side of the bed. "Who was going to kill you? What are you talking about?"

"I did just like you said. Looked all around. Didn't see nothing out of sorts. Not until I got to *her* room."

"Whose room, the kid's or Claire's?"

"The big room at the front. As soon as I took a step in, it was like . . ." Claud shuddered violently wiggling his fingers up in the air, "hundreds of little bugs crawling all over my skin. It was creepy, I tell ya. Like somebody was watching me . . . breathing down my neck . . . ya know?" Fearfully peeking over his shoulder, the poor deputy half expected to see someone standing behind him. Relieved to see no one, he quickly turned back to Fuzz. "Then I found them."

This comment certainly peaked Fuzz's curiosity. Maybe it had been worthwhile after all. He inched closer. "What did you find?"

"*Gold.* Coins. *Thousands* of them." The man giggled like a little school girl. "We gotta get back in to get the gold. We gotta get back in . . ." A sobering look passed over his eyes as he turned away from Fuzz. "But *he's* there."

Gold? Fuzz couldn't believe his ears. Could Baker possibly mean the coin he had read about in that letter Claire was reading on the veranda that day? Where in blazes would there be gold in a house that's had countless owners over the past hundred years? He guessed it could be possible Claire had somehow accidentally stumbled upon it.

Fuzz shook his head. No, it couldn't be. His pathetic deputy had gone off his rocker.

"You must have been seeing things, Bud," Fuzz consoled as he tried to think it through at the same time.

"Honestly, Fuzz. It was there. I saw it. A whole bag full under her mattress." His voice rose again as he tried to convince the sheriff he hadn't been imagining things. Claud stuck his empty palm under the sheriff's nose. "I had them right here in my hand."

"Okay. Okay. Calm down," Fuzz hushed him. "Where are they now?"

Claud looked at him as if he had just crawled out from under a rock. "Well, *shit*, Fuzz. Like I was planning on sticking around engaging in niceties. I dropped them and high-tailed it out of there when he came at me with that sword of his. You gotta go back there and get them."

Sitting back heavily in the chair, Fuzz regarded his colleague skeptically. "Just what kind of medication they got you on?"

It was well passed suppertime when they finally made it home from the hospital in Front Royal. Tired and hungry, the cranky children bickered most of the way. Claire couldn't blame them. The day hadn't quite turned out the way she had planned. Still angry with Charles, she had advised him to keep out of her sight until she had a chance to calm down. Claire realized he had come from a time of chivalry where duels to the death were still practiced. Nowadays there were better ways of dealing with disagreements. But she wouldn't have known where to turn seeing as the local law enforcement was involved.

"Are you sure you'll be all right to get to your place?" Claire had insisted on driving from the ranch to the hospital and then to the house. "You'd better come in for a while until we see what those painkillers are going to do to you. Maybe they just haven't kicked in yet." And if

Charles didn't like it, he could just spend the evening in the attic for all she cared at the moment. At this point, she wasn't too concerned with his reaction. "The least I can do is feed you supper."

Charles bristled, but he should have realized pushing Fuzz out of the saddle wasn't the most brilliant idea he had ever come up with. Injuring the sheriff only made Claire feel responsible to take care of him.

Truth be known, Fuzz had palmed the painkillers the nurse gave him at the hospital. The shoulder wasn't aching so badly he couldn't tough it out. Besides, he wanted to have a clear head and his wits about him. Somehow he had to figure out a way to get upstairs before Claire had a chance to see the coin spilled all over her bed. That is if Claud was in his right mind and there was actually something to find.

Putting his hand to his brow, Fuzz grudgingly admitted, "I guess I do feel a bit lightheaded." He didn't overdo it, but hoped it was just enough to make her take pity on him. "If you don't mind, maybe I could lie down for a little while. Until my head clears."

"Of course." Once offered, Claire couldn't take it back. Biting her bottom lip, she glanced apprehensively toward the house hoping Charles would behave himself since he was the cause of this fiasco in the first place.

"Okay, let's get you to the house." Unlatching the trunk, she said to her children, "You guys bring in the backpacks, please, while I give Fuzz a hand."

Oblivious to his phony stagger, Claire supported him to the veranda and up the steps. As she reached for the door knob, she realized the door was still ajar after the deputy's frantic flight. The door swung open at her touch. Claire feigned surprise. "Fuzz, you were the last one out. You locked the door behind you?"

"Well, I sure thought I did." He could use the deputy's carelessness to his advantage. "Maybe we'd better have a look around." Somehow he'd have to get upstairs before Claire. "You check down here. If you see anything out of place, don't touch it. We'll dust for prints. I'll go upstairs."

Claire wasn't about to let Fuzz get away with it so easily. Maybe she could make him squirm just a little first. "Oh, you probably just didn't pull the door shut all the way. Sometimes the latch doesn't catch." She took a quick look around. "Everything seems to be okay down here. I doubt anything's missing. There's not much to steal anyway."

With a shrug of his shoulder, Fuzz conceded. "Probably you're right. But you and the kids stay here while I have a quick look around. Just to be sure."

"I'll check upstairs. You may lose your balance." Claire headed to the staircase only to have Fuzz hold her back.

"Somebody might still be up there. Let me go," he offered protectively as his foot hit the first step. "I'm not that dizzy. I won't fall."

"The coin is well hidden. Let him go, my darling. He'll find nothing," Charles whispered into her ear.

As upset with him as she was, just the sound of his voice was enough to melt her resolve. Claire stepped back.

Hearing his heavy footsteps overhead, she realized Fuzz had not even bothered to make a pretense of checking any room on the way to the front bedroom. Claire skipped silently up the stairs after him just to see the look on his face when he didn't find the treasure he was looking for. She knew Charles was already there.

Switching on the light, Fuzz immediately scanned the room. Nothing. Not even a stray penny. "Damn you, Claud," Fuzz muttered angrily under his breath. "You're a goddammed screwball." Disappointed, he looked under the bed just in case. Not so much as a fuzzy dust bunny. He ran his hand under the mattress.

"I don't think anyone's going to hide under my mattress," Claire chided with a grin. "What are you looking for?"

He was caught but not for long. "You know . . . " Fuzz straightened and turned with a silly little grin plastered all over his face. Scratching his head, he tried to cover his tracks. "I don't know why I did that. Habit, I guess. Looking for clues. Those pills have got me not thinking straight." That's it. He could blame it on the drugs. He could do *anything* and blame it on the drugs.

Reaching for her hand, Fuzz pulled her gently toward him. He licked his lips. With a salacious wink, he bobbed his head toward the bed. "Looks mighty inviting. Maybe you wouldn't mind if I took a bit of a nap right here. And since you're up here, too, maybe you could join me."

Claire could feel the electricity spark behind her as she stepped back and pulled her hand away with a nervous giggle. "Since we're up here and my children are downstairs waiting for supper, I think maybe not.

The sofa in the parlor is really quite comfortable. I'll get you a pillow and blanket."

His voice had taken on a distinct slur that wasn't there a moment ago. His eyes wandered vacantly. "Come on, Claire. You must know I'm attracted to you. Since the first time I saw you. Remember? When I came to chase the boogeyman away."

If Fuzz only knew that his boogeyman was standing nose-to-nose with him intently examining one eye and then the other. He sensed a warm puff of air wisp over his face. Fuzz stepped back a pace and brushed a hand across his cheek as if he had walked into a spider web.

Charles was between them. Claire wanted to reach out and steer him out of the way but she could see nothing to grasp onto. She knew she had to defuse this situation quickly before Charles once again lost his temper and did something stupid.

"Oh, Fuzz, you don't really mean that. It must be the painkillers talking. Didn't realize Tylenols were so strong."

"No. I'm very serious." Fuzz smiled sincerely and again reached out to pull her toward him. "I don't need drugs to tell you how beautiful you are. Or how much I've come to care for you . . . *and* the kids."

Ever so slightly, Claire's tone hardened as she drew her hand gently away. Whether he was stoned or not, she needn't antagonize the sheriff. Even so, her cheeks flushed with the slightest hint of pink at the compliment.

"You're a wonderful man." She heard Charles sputter behind her. "I'm flattered, really I am. And we've had a great vacation. But, as tempting as it is, I'm not prepared to start into a relationship that can't possibly go anywhere. We'll be leaving soon. In just a couple of weeks. I have to get the children home in time to get ready for school."

Disappointment, real or not, showed on Fuzz's face. With an impish pout, he stammered childishly, "But, you don't have to go. You can stay right here. With me."

"Oh, Clarry. This man is so irritating. He took no drug." Charles could barely contain his annoyance. *"Put a spell on him or something. Make him disappear."*

"What was that?" Fuzz straightened and looked around the room. "Did you hear that?"

A vague look washed over her face. "I didn't hear anything," she denied quickly.

"Are you sure you didn't hear anything? A man's voice?"

"Positive." Claire steered Fuzz toward the stairs. "Come on, it's been a long day. Let's get you something to eat."

"I could have sworn . . . " Giving his head a quick shake, Fuzz shrugged the incident off. "Must be hearing things." Maybe he hit his head when he fell off the horse.

Chafing against the temptation to trip him, Charles waited at the bottom of the staircase for his wife. Just before Fuzz caught up with her, he whispered, *"Tell him, my love. Tell him the truth. No one will believe him."*

Casting Charles a withering glare, Claire took the sheriff by the arm and sat him down in a kitchen chair. The children were already bathed and in their pyjamas, waiting impatiently, arguing over something or other. After popping some leftover lasagne in the microwave to warm, she excused herself to return to the foyer where Charles obediently waited pacing a small path in front of the door. Claire could only imagine he was trying to decide whether or not to pick Fuzz up by the scruff of the neck and heave him through it.

"Be reasonable, Charles," she whispered. "I can't tell him anything. He'll think I'm crazy."

"He's got to go, Clarry. I pride myself in being pretty even-tempered . . . " Claire snorted. *"But I just cannot tolerate this man being in my house. If you don't get rid of him, I will."*

Already dog-tired, Claire sighed envisioning yet another trip to the hospital. "Oh, please no," she begged. "What are you going to do?"

"I don't know yet."

"Just remember, it's your fault he's here in the first place. I'll feed him and he'll be on his way."

"He may need a little coaxing."

"You behave yourself," Claire warned. "I don't need any more trouble tonight, thank you very much." The timer buzzed. "Don't do anything stupid," she warned with a pointed finger and left him fuming at the door.

With a big yawn, Maggie was so sleepy her head nearly drooped into her bowl of ice cream. "Come on, missy, let's get you to bed." Figuring her little legs wouldn't hold up to the climb, Claire lifted her into her arms. "Billy will keep you company until I get back," she said to Fuzz. "I won't be long. Maggie, what do you say to Fuzz?"

With half-closed eyes, Maggie muttered sleepily, "Thanks, I had fun."

"You're welcome, Maggie." He would have had fun, too, if he hadn't been so clumsy and fallen off that blasted horse. Still didn't know how that happened. One minute he was headed down the mountain, the next he was ass-over-teakettle on the ground. He hated to admit it, but his shoulder was aching pretty badly. Giving in, he popped the pills he should have taken a long time ago.

Sipping his coffee, Fuzz watched Billy dawdle over his dessert. Kids sure knew how to drag out eating if it meant staying up a little longer. Pretty soon his ice cream would be milk. "You going to eat that stuff or drink it?" Fuzz laughed. Despite their childish squabbles and petty rivalries, Claire sure had some pretty good kids here. As far as kids go. He was the youngest of five in his family, so really hadn't had too much to do with little children. Fuzz figured he could handle them just fine.

"Hey, Billy, you like it here? Pretty nice place, isn't it?"

Billy didn't look up from his bowl. "Sure, it's okay."

"Would you like to stay here?" Maybe, with a real last-ditch effort, Fuzz could convince Claire to stay on by winning the kids over.

Shrugging noncommittally, Billy said, "I guess."

"Do you think we can convince your mom to stay?"

Another shrug. "Dunno. Maybe Charles can."

"Charles?" Where had he heard that name? Oh, yes. Up on the mountain. "Your make-believe friend?" The kid was too old for this game. "Come on, Billy, there's no such thing. You know that."

"We're not making him up," Billy insisted petulantly. "He's not make believe. He's a real live ghost. We found him here in the attic."

Taken aback, Fuzz was at a loss for words. He didn't know whether it was better to play along or if that would just give credence to their delusions? You seldom win against a child's logic. "Do you think I could meet your Casper friend?"

Billy peered just beyond the sheriff's shoulder. His eyes widened in surprise. "I don't think he likes being called Casper."

"Why do you say that?"

Billy pointed behind Fuzz. "Well, he sure don't look too happy."

Fuzz turned to follow Billy's gesture. For the briefest moment, appearing before his very eyes, was the apparition of a man brandishing a razor-sharp sword high above his head. Turning quickly away, a horrified gasp escaped his lips as he covered his face with his hands. Second guessing himself, Fuzz swung back around to take a second look. He saw nothing.

"Bedtime, Billy," Claire called from the top of the stairs.

With quick thanks to Fuzz, Billy scooted off leaving him alone in the kitchen.

Nervously, he glanced around once more. Fuzz noticed his heart was thumping just a little more quickly than it was a minute ago. "Idiot," he chided himself. "Get a grip." Probably just the medication kicking in. Had him a little spaced out. Pulling the bottle from his pocket, he read the label. *Do not drive. Do not operate heavy machinery. Do not take with alcohol.* The list of possible side effects didn't mention hallucinations.

Did somebody just blow in his ear? Fuzz twisted around covering the ear with his hand. As he sprang from the chair, he was sure he heard just a hint of laughter. Taunting laughter. Menacing. But he was alone.

Venturing into the dining room, Fuzz peeked through the French doors into the parlor. Nothing there. Movement from behind startled him and he stepped back in alarm.

He hadn't heard her come down the stairs. In her arms she held a blanket and pillow. "Hey, what's wrong?" Claire took one look at his ashen face and couldn't resist adding, "You okay? You look like you've seen a ghost."

From somewhere overhead an evil cackle emanated through the darkness.

"Did you hear that?" His voice cracked.

"Hear what?" Claire followed his gaze as he examined the ceiling. "Really, Fuzz. I think you'd better get some rest. You'll feel better in the morning."

Fuzz gradually nodded in agreement. "Yeah, you're right. This is ridiculous. I took those pain killers. Then Billy started talking about some ghost in the attic." He laughed. "It's stupid, really. I thought I saw something, that's all."

Claire barely suppressed a gasp, then giggled a little too quickly. "Oh, you saw the ghost? That is a good one."

Fuzz once more studied the ceiling. "Have you . . . ?" His voice trailed off as Claire shook her head.

"Nothing here's scaring us, Fuzz."

Exasperated, the sheriff asked, "Then how come you're the only ones who've been able to stay so long in this house? Everybody else has left screaming with their tails tucked between their legs."

He wasn't going to let up. With a heavy sigh, Claire resigned herself to the inevitable. The interrogation. The disbelief. The humiliation as Fuzz spread the story through the whole town. But what did it matter? Who would care? It would just be another fantastic story to add to the legend of the old haunted Montgomery house down by the river.

They could leave tomorrow. Or the next day. Except for Connie and Rudy, no one knew them. Not really. No one knew where they were from unless the sheriff thought to trace her licence plate number.

Anyway, maybe Fuzz was getting so loopy he wouldn't remember a thing by morning.

"Well, Fuzz, you may want to sit down for this one. It's an incredible story, really." As an afterthought, she asked politely, "Can I get you another cup of coffee?"

"No, thanks." Amused, his brow arched as Fuzz followed her into the parlor to take a seat on an antique brocade settee. "I'm all ears."

Claire dumped the bedding beside him. "Give me just a minute." Claire excused herself to run upstairs to get the tintypes. She came back holding them tightly against her chest and stood facing him.

"I know this is going to sound ridiculous, but here goes." Claire took a deep breath. "When we moved in here, Connie Jenkins . . . you probably know Connie . . ." Fuzz nodded. "Well, Connie told us about the house being haunted. And that nobody would stay here for very long. But I figured that was just a lot of bull. I wasn't going to fall for that nonsense."

She glanced at the photographs and bit her lower lip. "Then I found these." Claire handed them to Fuzz.

"I showed these to Connie's brother, Rudy."

"Yeah, I know him." Fuzz had grown up with the Freeman kids and had heard about Rudy's crazy obsession with ghosts.

"Apparently Clarissa Montgomery . . ." she pointed her out to Fuzz ". . . practiced black magic. She put spells on people. Rudy thinks

I'm Charles' . . ." she pointed again. "He thinks I'm his reincarnated wife."

Fuzz looked from the photographs to Claire. "You don't honestly believe that!"

"I didn't used to. But then it really made a little more sense once I let it sink in. I figure we've been able to stay here so long because the ghost likes us and wants us to be here . . . as his family."

Fuzz stared at her for what seemed like forever. He examined the tintypes from all angles. With all the elaborate computer software on the market today, anyone could have doctored up the photos to make them resemble Claire and her kids and to look old. For what purpose would anyone in the Shenandoah Valley want to scam Claire?

Fuzz finally cleared his throat. "You are joking, right?" He couldn't imagine she would be so gullible as to fall for the rumors and tales of a few superstitious locals and a raving lunatic spouting psychobabble.

"It's okay. I didn't want to believe it, either." Claire got up and headed toward the kitchen. "I've got dishes to clean up. You can spend the night on the sofa if you don't feel up to driving."

Darting after her, Fuzz caught Claire by the arm and pulled her back to face him. "Wait a minute . . ."

Staring at the white-knuckled fingers that clutched her arm, she added, "Please don't hold me like that. He gets very angry when anyone touches me."

"He . . . *What*?"

"Charles never did like people touching me," she repeated succinctly. Claire didn't like the notion that this man was thinking she was out of her mind and was having a hard time meeting his eyes, however, she forced herself to not look away. "You can ask him yourself. He's standing right beside you." Claire could see Charles glowering at the sheriff.

Fuzz wasn't falling for it this time, yet he dropped his hold on her. "Come on, Claire. Enough is enough. Are you and the kids deliberately trying to make a fool of me?"

"We're doing no such thing," she stated emphatically. "You asked for answers and I gave them."

"Well, it's crap and you know it," Fuzz muttered angrily. "You can't possibly make me believe this house is haunted." He outright refused to believe it even though what he thought he saw just moments ago was amazingly similar to the image Claud described.

"I'm not trying to," Claire insisted. "I don't believe this house is *haunted* at all. Nothing's trying to scare us away," she repeated. "I *do* believe there's a paranormal presence in here, though. And I've come to believe Charles has been waiting all this time for us to finally show up."

Quickly becoming convinced Claire and her children were all completely mad or playing him for a total moron, Fuzz tried to salvage a little bit of what was left of his own sanity.

"Okay, now . . . " Fuzz was trying his best to understand. "Just for the sake of argument, and, for the record, I don't believe a word of it, it was you who put a spell on this Montgomery guy to make him a ghost."

"In another lifetime."

"I see. And he's *allowing* you to stay here because . . . " he spiraled his hand prompting her to continue.

Claire finished the sentence for him. "Because I'm his reincarnated wife. Yes."

"Yes," Fuzz repeated incredulously. This was definitely too much for him to fathom. His brow arched sharply as he studied her intently. "And you actually expect me to *believe* this?" Was he the only sane one in this house?

"Believe it or not. It makes no never-mind to me."

Speechless, Fuzz stared at her again. Eyes unwavering, Claire glared back at him, chin tilted challengingly. However, she began to get a queasy feeling deep in the pit of her stomach. Maybe the truth hadn't been the way to go.

With a deep cleansing breath, Fuzz finally spoke. "Okay, either you're crazy or I'm crazy and I'm damn sure it's not me." Shaking his head, he made an annoying tsking sound. "I'm really disappointed in you, Claire. If you don't want to see me, all you had to do was come right out and tell me. You didn't have to come up with such bullshit. I could have taken the hint."

Fuzz pushed himself up and headed for the door. "I was under the impression you were a pretty level-headed person. Guess that goes to show you just how wrong you can be about someone. If you want to play house with Casper here . . . be my guest. It's time for me to leave."

In a presence unseen by her side, Charles whispered into her ear, *"Clarry, who the devil is this Casper person?"* But Claire chose to ignore him as she quickly became distressed by the sheriff's accusations.

As Fuzz hurried out the door, he spat accusingly, "I suggest you seriously look into professional help. The whole crazy lot of you are certifiable."

"Be gone with you, little pest." Charles dismissed Fuzz with a wave of his hand as he slammed the door behind him. If he had had his way, he would have sent Fuzz begging for mercy from fire and brimstone being hailed down upon him.

Fuzz fumed. He seethed. He muttered all the way to his car. He was convinced Claud had only imagined finding gold. Probably just seeing stars after hitting his head a little too hard.

The pictures aside, and as pretty as Claire was, he didn't need to get caught up in any kind of a relationship with a delusional woman. Best just cut his losses and leave the whole thing be.

Shame. Damn shame.

Tires spewed gravel as the sheriff sped from the drive.

NINETEEN

"I'm proud of you, my darling," Charles soothed as he wrapped his arms around his wife.

Claire wasn't quite so sure they handled it the proper way. "What if he causes trouble for us?"

"That pea-brain isn't worth your worry. Don't give him a second thought, my love."

Groaning miserably, Claire muttered, "I won't be able to show my face in town." She could almost hear the whispers and laughter behind her back. No doubt Fuzz would have her branded a crazy woman by morning. "What if he calls Children's Aid or whatever they call it down here and accuses me of being an unfit mother?" The color drained from her face at the thought of her children being dragged kicking and screaming from her. Especially in what was considered a foreign country. She had no idea what she'd have to go through to get them back. Kidnaping crossed her mind. Kidnaping and making a mad dash to the border. She plotted an escape route in her head.

"And just who would believe him? By his own admission, he took too much pain medication."

"I hope you're right." As she watched from the window, Fuzz's car lights disappeared over the knoll.

It had been an exhausting day for all of them. Muscles agonizingly sore, all she wanted was to soak for hours in a hot bath frothing with bubbles then snuggle in bed next to the man she loved.

Hoping she had taken care of the sheriff once and for all, Claire prayed she wouldn't have any more trouble. She had no idea what the deputy would do to try to convince him he had really seen gold in her room. But Fuzz found nothing and since he was the first to reach her bedroom after they got home, who else could have picked it up?

"You no longer smell of horse." He was waiting for her in bed as she painfully crawled in beside him. The bath felt wonderful but did blessed little to relieve her aching muscles. Hopefully her husband's loving hands would do the trick. If he could keep his mind on what he was supposed to be doing, that is.

"Massage, please," she reminded him with a giggle as he began to nibble playfully at her neck. "You're getting distracted."

"Begging your pardon, madam, but your scent is just too intoxicating."

"But I won't be able to walk for a month," she lamented. An earthy moan escaped her lips. He discovered the spot in the hollow just above her collarbone that always seemed to drive her wild. And the sound she made when he found it drove him mad with desire.

"Then it's a month you can spend right here with me," he whispered hoarsely.

"I don't have a month," she sighed unhappily.

"My darling, you have all eternity."

"Maybe you'll get sick of spending eternity with me."

"You are my life, not my life's sentence." He fondly kissed the tips of her fingers, one at a time.

She knew he was right. But when she passed away from this mortal life, Charles could be forced to wait another hundred years or so before a never-ending cycle of reincarnation brought them together. And once she found her way back to him, she may have to endure weeks of skepticism before he finally convinced her to believe in him.

What had she been thinking all those years ago putting this spell on them both? She had never expected her silly poem to actually work. Now her harmless little incantation may very well become a timeless curse.

She was human. He was not. She couldn't stay with him. Couldn't leave without him.

Somewhere between agony and ecstacy, Claire fell asleep. Charles lay beside her gently stroking the dark silky strands from her face. His wife peacefully slept in his arms while his soul was being torn apart.

He felt so alive and yet wasn't. He had substance, could touch, feel, be heard and seen, but had not the freedom to walk this earth at will.

Dawn broke with the birds twittering noisily to welcome the new day. Stirring from the depths of slumber, Charles stretched lazily. Softly murmuring, Claire snuggled closer to his side. As he became more alert, Charles realized he had awakened still holding her. He hadn't vanished through the night.

"Mmmm, you're still here," Claire mumbled groggily squeezing him fondly. "If this is a dream, I don't want to ever wake up."

"I'm not sure what's happening but I think I'm beginning to be able to stay visible for longer periods of time."

"That's wonderful!" Claire exclaimed happily then peered up into his downcast eyes. "Isn't it?"

With a shrug and a solemn nod, Charles hesitantly agreed. "But I'm still not human," he pointed out sadly. "When do you have to start for home?"

"A week from Thursday." The same response to the same question he had been asking for the past week.

"Clarry, we've got to figure this out before then." Charles rubbed his forehead as if the strain of the problem facing them was far too difficult to think about.

"Can't you come home with us?"

Disheartened Charles shrugged. As inviting as the offer was, he doubted he could make it work. "I seem to be tied somehow to this house. I always find myself back here when I can't stay in human form." He did manage a weak smile. "Anyway, how would the children explain me to their friends? 'Come on in and meet my new father . . . the ghost'."

Desperate for options, Claire boldly stated, "Well, then, I'll just have to put another spell on you. One that will bring you back once and for all. This one worked and all I did was make up a silly little poem to recite. I'll just make up another one."

"And wait another century to see if it comes to pass?" Sadly, Charles shook his head. "I don't think so."

There had to be a solution somewhere. A clue to the riddle. Clarissa had undoubtedly written down all she could remember in her journals. Claire had seen nothing there that she thought would be helpful. She studied the incantations Grandmama used so many years ago. Had she missed any that would have solved their predicament?

Claire lay quietly beside Charles mulling over another idea. It was a slim chance, but maybe he'd consider it. "We could talk with Rudy," she suggested barely above a whisper. "Maybe he has some answers."

Rudy had been back several times over the past few weeks, but Charles still wanted nothing to do with his study. He feared exposure. It was one thing to *think* paranormal beings existed, quite another to one hundred percent know it for sure. But he was running out of options. And time. Reluctantly, after much deliberation, he agreed.

✳   ✳   ✳

They hadn't heard them coming until it was too late to react. One after the other, Billy and Maggie burst into Claire's room and caught them red-handed. And very naked. Charles was leaning with his back against the old oak headboard of the bed with Claire snuggled to his chest. Thankfully, the sheet was already tucked up over her breasts with one side of it loosely draped across Charles' thighs.

Seeing no merit in vanishing at this point, Charles quickly adjusted the sheet to cover more of his exposed body. Neither of them had much time to think about it. The children pounced on the bed giggling with the exuberance of the new day.

Finding their mother in bed with a ghost didn't seem to phase them. A good thing, Claire thought, since she had no idea how she ever could have explained it to her young children. Thank God for the innocence of youth.

Squirming their way between Claire and Charles, the children competed for space almost dragging off the sheet precariously covering their mother's modesty. "Take it easy, guys," she laughed as she was jostled aside. "Watch the feet." Clutching the sheet to her chin, Claire wiggled over to give them room. Maggie assumed a place in Charles' arms.

Billy settled in beside his mother beaming up at her with a grin so big it was on the verge of splitting his face in two. "Guess you really do believe now, don' cha, Mom?" Just the way he asked, the teasing tone of his young voice made Claire suspect her son knew more about the facts of life than she was prepared to have him know.

"I guess maybe I do, Billy," she said with a playful tousle of his sandy hair.

"Are you going to be our new daddy?" Maggie peered longingly into Charles' eyes.

Charles didn't feel the need to explain that he had been their father ever since they were first conceived in the mid-eighteen hundreds, but he did need to say something. He was in bed with their mother without a stitch of clothing on. Chivalry warranted some kind of explanation.

Kissing the tip of her little upturned nose, he said truthfully, "I love your mother very much, sweetheart, and I love the two of you more than you could ever know."

"Are you getting married?" Billy asked in anticipation. "Can I be best man?"

Charles let out a hearty laugh. "My son, if anyone's going to be best man, it'll be you."

"All right!" Billy let out a whooping cry of delight.

"What can I be?" Maggie piped up not wanting to be left out. "I want to be somebody."

"Don't worry, Maggie," Claire assured her. "You'll definitely be somebody."

✳   ✳   ✳

"Charles, do you think it was a good idea to tell the children we're going to be married? Under the circumstances and all?"

"My darling, we're already married."

"Technically, but not officially anymore. Legally, I'm considered a widow. And you're . . . well . . . *dead*."

He laughed at her candor. "So we'll say our vows again in front of a preacher. Or a justice. Whatever will make you happy, my love."

"You'd allow yourself to be seen by an outsider?" He was having a hard enough time with his decision to make himself known to Rudy. Claire couldn't understand his rationale for this.

"If it would give our situation more credibility for the children, I . . ."

"And what if you happened to disappear right in the middle of the ceremony?" She interrupted him in mid-sentence. "What if you couldn't control—whatever it is that happens—and just vanished? How would I explain that one?"

He regarded her fondly and tweaked her chin. "Ah, my darling, I have faith in you. You'd think of something."

"*I'd* think of . . . ?" Flabbergasted, Claire brushed his hand away and stalked from the room. "*I'd think of something.*" Muttering all the way down the stairs, Claire wondered how she would explain something like that. How could it be explained? One minute he's there. The next, he's not. Simple explanation. He's a ghost. He does stuff like that.

Billy and Maggie already had breakfast started when Claire came into the kitchen. The cereal was in the bowls, not scattered on the table top. The milk wasn't spilled all over the floor. It was shaping up to be a good day.

Impressed, but suspicious, Claire stood in the middle of the room with her arms crossed over her chest. "And to what do I owe this pleasure?" Maggie slammed the fridge door. The butter dish almost slipped from her hands but she grabbed it before it hit the floor. Billy stood on a chair at the counter dropping bread into the toaster then bent over it watching the elements turn bright red. His nose almost touched the top.

"Billy, get your face away from that. It's going to pop up and hit you right in the eye." Then she noticed four settings placed at the table. "Are we expecting company?" she asked Maggie.

"No. Just Charles."

Confused, Claire said, "But he's never had breakfast with us before. Why set a place for him now?"

"Cuz he's going to be our dad. Daddy always ate breakfast with us." Maggie looked up expectantly, her big brown eyes full of hope.

If Claire's heart could have dropped to the floor, it couldn't have hurt any more. Ever since they assumed she and Charles were getting married she had a horrible feeling the children would get too excited and be thoroughly disappointed when they found out there was no way she could marry Charles. "Oh, sweetie, come on over here." She pulled out a chair to sit on and lifted Maggie onto her lap. Cuddling her little head close to her breast, Claire struggled for the right words.

"I know you miss your daddy. I do, too. And I have to admit, since I've met Charles, I've come to love him, too. Very much. But you know . . . he's not quite the same as us, don't you?"

"Yeeaaah." Without seeing it, Claire could tell by the sound of her voice that Maggie's bottom lip was about to tremble. But she couldn't let them think they were going to be one big, happy family and live happily ever after. They could very well be destined to repeat this very scene over and over. Millennium after millennium.

With a deep, agonizing breath, Claire continued, "And because Charles is a little, you know, *different* from us . . . since we're human and he's not . . . I'm not sure if it's possible for us to be a real family like we used to be with Daddy."

"But we can try, can't we?" Billy asked as he hopped down from the chair. Claire smiled at his optimism.

"Yes, Billy, we can try."

When the fog lifted from his brain, when the ache in his shoulder subsided, Fuzz went to take his deputy home from the hospital.

Fuzz felt badly for Baker. He had put him up to this shady operation and now look at him. His deputy was a pretty competent lawman, but even he had to admit he wasn't the brightest spark in the fire. "You must have been imagining things, Bud. There wasn't so much as a speck of dust in that room."

Shaking his head in disbelief, Claud already had a good reason why the gold was missing. "Then that ghost must have picked it up. Did you see him?" His voice rose sharply as did the stabbing pain in his temples from the concussion. "I tell ya, Fuzz, it was there. All kinds of it."

Claud was irritated, thoroughly frustrated and tired. Tired of explaining and trying to convince the sheriff he had seen what he'd seen. "You take me home. Get the woman and kids out of the way and I'll go back myself and get it."

"Let's just not worry about that right now." With all his protestation to the contrary, Fuzz still wasn't convinced Claud hadn't seen just what he said he did. Even Claire's irrational allegations seemed to corroborate Claud's story.

Uneasily, he remembered hearing sounds that may have been a man's voice coming out of nowhere. Remembered his own bleary-eyed vision. But Fuzz wasn't about to admit to anyone the remotest possibility of the existence of a paranormal being in that house. Just the thought of it was ridiculous. Not to mention it would make a shambles of his credibility in the community.

The woman had made a fool out of him. He had made a fool of himself by coming on to her the way he did. Better the whole thing just be dropped.

Rubbing his temples, Claud Baker was seriously beginning to have his own doubts. "But I saw *something*, Fuzz. I'm not making this up."

"Well, Claud, like I said before, maybe you dreamed the whole thing after you ran off the road and hit your head." He had to give Baker back a little faith in himself seeing it was his fault the deputy was in this mess in the first place. "Hey, it's possible, isn't it?" He slapped him solidly on the back.

Thinking about that for a bit, Claud finally forced out a sigh of resignation. After all his ranting, he'd better agree to something before the sheriff sent him for a psych evaluation. "Well. Guess it *could* be possible. I did take a pretty good wallop. But nightmare is more like it. It sure as hell was no dream."

TWENTY

Chase felt rather odd. Even after munching a couple more antacids, the indigestion persisted. Breakfast at that old greasy spoon off the highway just wasn't sitting well at all. The parking lot had been full of transports. A pretty good sign of decent food, he always thought. Maybe the sausage he inhaled was just a little passed its prime. Pulling off into the rest area, Chase got out to stretch his legs. A bit of a stroll may ease the pressure.

Normally he wouldn't have come this far north. Would have headed virtually due east from his parents' place near Tucson to his sister's on the outskirts of Savannah, Georgia. But, for some reason he couldn't understand, he gravitated back toward Virginia.

Chase couldn't understand the reason, but he knew what it was. He was simply having a devil of a time getting that crazy woman out of his mind. He felt compelled to see if she might still be there at that house by the Shenandoah River. Maybe she was. Or maybe she had already left and gone back to Canada. Chase really didn't want to cross that bridge right now.

The whole time he was at his parents' home, practically every waking minute, she had insinuated herself into his thoughts. More so now considering he was driving alone for hours on end.

His mother had noticed.

232

"You've spent the last two weeks moping around here, Chase," his mother said to him. "You seem so restless." She placed the steaming cup of coffee in front of him and handed him a spoon. "What's bothering you?"

"It's nothing, Mom. Really. I'm fine." Hunched gloomily over the table with his head leaning on his fist, Chase mindlessly stirred in sugar and milk. "I guess I'm just tired." It was the heavy sigh that gave him away.

"Are you worried about the operation, son?" She sat across the kitchen table from him resting her warm hand over his. "The doctor didn't keep anything from us, did he?"

"No, Mom. They told me the old ticker's working fine now. It's nothing to do with that."

"Ah," she nodded. "Then it must be a woman."

Startled by her intuitiveness, Chase bolted upright. "Just because I'm broody, you assume a woman's got something to do with it?"

"And you're about to tell me it's not?" Marion Tanner sniffed loudly as she snatched the spoon from his hand. "Give me that thing. You're going to scrape the glaze off the inside of that mug."

The oven timer rang. Marion excused herself to rescue her pie. The tantalizing aroma of apples and nutmeg had filled the kitchen for the past half hour.

Salivating for apple pie, Chase was only slightly disappointed when she came back with a hearty slab of chocolate cake. Food. The sweeter and more decadently rich, the better. A mother's remedy for all ills.

His eyes rolled back at the first bite. "You're bribing a confession out of me, are you now, Mom?"

"Of course I am, darling." Marion bluntly agreed plunging in with her own fork to keep him company.

Chase swallowed and stabbed another scoop of thick creamy icing.

"How many slices will it take?" Marion dabbed her lip with a napkin. "I only have one more and you're not getting it unless you come clean."

"But you have a whole pie."

She pointed her fork at him in warning. "*That's* for your father."

"He has something to confess?"

"Oh, he's always confessing something or other," she chuckled.

Chase clucked his tongue. "You drive a hard bargain, Marion Tanner."

His mother waited for him to continue yet Chase didn't volunteer anything further. Marion hated to pry but, as with all her children, she knew he would feel better once he talked about what was troubling him.

With an impatient sigh, Marion prodded, "You've forgotten how this game works? I bribe. You talk. So who is she and why does she have you all twisted up inside?"

Other than to tell her to just mind her own business, Chase knew the only way out was to leave the house. And he knew that wouldn't work. Not if he wanted to eat for the next week.

"Well, who she is . . . to be honest . . . I haven't a clue. Just like I don't know why it should matter." He pushed back his chair and brushed his hand over his face. "She could be a complete lunatic for all I know. But something about her just kind of . . . I don't know . . . *clicked*."

Chase went on to tell his mother about the woman's strange antics at the battlefield in Manassas.

"Stranger things have happened, son. Maybe she bumped her head a little harder than she thought. Poor dear was probably disoriented and frightened."

"But she seemed so troubled. I just feel badly I couldn't have done more for her."

"Sounds to me you did all you could. Didn't seem she wanted to accept anything else from you. You made sure she got to where she was going safely. That's more than most would do. Don't be so hard on yourself, darling. I'm sure she's fine."

In spite of himself, Chase smiled as he recalled the little lady plunked smack dab in the middle of the sloppy pathway.

"She was so pretty under all that dirt, Mom. The prettiest girl I've seen in a long time. Now I don't know who she is, or *where* she is. I just know I'm having one hell of a time getting her off my mind."

Marion regarded her son lovingly. She could see he was tormented. "So what are you going to do about it?"

"What can I do?" Chase muttered miserably. "She's probably not even still around there. I've no idea where she came from."

"I thought you told me Canada."

"Canada's a big country, Mom."

"But Nova Scotia is a little bitty province, I do believe. If I remember any of my Canadian geography at all."

"Yeah, that's a big help without a name or address." Chase shook his head. "It's useless to even think about it."

Marion sat back her brows knit in a frown. "You've got a good head on your shoulders. Use your imagination. Pretend you're a private eye. Be a super sleuth."

"You've been watching way too much TV, Mother."

"Then I guess it all boils down to one question. How badly do you want to find her?"

He asked himself that same question with each passing mile. Really, she was nothing like any other woman he had ever dated. He had his list of cons which he recited to convince himself she wasn't his type. She had dark hair. He preferred blondes. Her head barely reached his armpits. He'd just as soon not have to bend himself in half to hold a woman on the dance floor.

And there was that dreaded "k"-word. Chase definitely didn't consider himself father material but maybe kids weren't so bad after all. His brothers and sister all had two or three little hellions each. His own parents had raised four. What was there to be afraid of?

But none of that seemed to matter much as he headed northeast. He should've just acted like the randy male he usually was and got a name, address or even a phone number when he had the chance at Manassas. He'd kick himself from here to kingdom come if she had vanished without a trace.

But his mother had a point. Where there was a will, there was a way. He'd just have to find it.

Chase just passed Amarillo. Four or five more States to go. If he drove all night, he might make it to Front Royal by morning. Then . . . what?

"You've been so antsy all morning you're going to carve a path in that oak floor." Claire knew Charles was tense. Rudy was coming to visit just after lunch and neither of them knew what to expect from him.

Charles couldn't see how Rudy would be much help at all. But he was willing to put himself through it for Claire and the children. All they could do was trust he would keep their confidence. If not . . .

Claire knew only too well what Charles was capable of. She watched anxiously as he paced back and forth between the dining room and parlor. Same route he took while she endured the throes of childbirth—twice—in another lifetime, another century. "Can't you just sit down and be patient? Or go play with the children. Get your mind off it."

Charles turned to face her and smiled weakly. A pained expression crossed his face as he unconsciously rubbed a hand across his chest. His normally ruddy complexion was pallid. He was apprehensive and beginning to have second thoughts about meeting with Rudy.

But there was something else in the air that Charles couldn't explain. He was nervous. He would freely admit that. This anxiety he felt went beyond anything he had ever experienced. So much so that his chest hurt. Breathing became difficult, labored and shallow.

Ghosts shouldn't feel pain or at least he didn't think they should. He never had before. But there were so many anomalies in their particular case that any so-called normal theory of paranormal existence didn't seem to apply.

The pain was becoming relentless. Worse than he remembered when he was sliced by the saber in the war. He tried his best not to let it show. The last thing he wanted was to upset Claire. They had less than a week together. If Rudy had no answers . . . If Claire was forced to leave without him . . .

He couldn't—wouldn't—think of that now.

Sweat formed on Charles' brow. His hands felt cold and clammy. A profound sense of foreboding coursed through his entire being. Like *death* creeping up on him.

Was this what he had been waiting for all these years, to find his love then be torn from her again?

He must rise above the pain. He had to prepare Claire and the children for—something—anything. But he didn't know what.

Doubling in agony, he suddenly fell to his knees.

"Charles, what is it?" Panic filled Claire's voice as she rushed to his side. The pallor of his skin had not gone unnoticed nor the pain contorting his face.

Barely able to speak, Charles gasped for air. Then, with great effort, he drew a deep cleansing breath. The pain finally abated. "I'm all right now, my love," he panted.

"You're scaring me, Charles. What's happening?"

"I don't know, Clarry," he admitted honestly. "I've never felt pain like this since I passed over." With furrowed brow, he continued, "It was so intense, I really thought . . . Well, it's going to sound ridiculous, but I really thought I was about to *die*. Clarry," he said forlornly, "maybe my time's running out."

Claire couldn't accept that. "Charles . . . no." Tears welled in her eyes. "We can't let that happen."

Charles took her hand and brought it tenderly to his lips. "Oh, my darling, I fear we don't know how to stop it."

The first pain struck without notice piercing his chest with wrenching agony. Chase stifled a cry as he fought for control, his vehicle swerving erratically on the slick road before he finally managed to pull to the shoulder. Somewhere he found the presence of mind to turn off the key. An anvil had just been dropped on his lungs. They refused to inflate. The bone-crushing weight unbearable, Chase clawed at his chest. Sweat dripped from his forehead soaking through the cotton tee-shirt he wore. His fingers tingled. His arm had gone numb.

Chase struggled to stay conscious.

Rudy arrived shortly after one o'clock. Claire tried to remain calm as she led him into the parlor. Charles concealed himself behind the French doors dividing that room from the dining room. Try as he might, he hadn't been able to vanish all morning. There he would wait—listen—until the time seemed appropriate to make himself known. If at all. It would all depend on Rudy himself.

After offering him coffee or a cold drink, which Rudy was much too excited to accept, Claire sat next to him on the settee. He had seen the photos, the journals. It was his suspicion all along that she was the reincarnated wife of Charles Montgomery.

All Claire had to do was admit it. But not yet. Not without assurances.

A gentle morning rain made the humidity oppressive but, shaded by the large oaks around the property, inside the house stayed quite comfortable. Even so, Claire felt drops of nervous perspiration slip between her shoulder blades and trickle down her back.

"I'm so glad you called." Rudy broke the tension. "I wanted an excuse to see you before you headed back home." He could tell by the expression on her face that thought brought no pleasure. Quite prepared for just about anything, Rudy hoped Claire would be comfortable enough by now to share her secrets. She never did reveal too much whenever he had visited the attic over the past few weeks. Kept her guard up. But since she had made the invitation, he hoped the silence would be broken.

All morning Claire had rehearsed what she wanted to say but, now that the time had come, she had forgotten every word. She'd have to wing it and hope she didn't make a mess of it or reveal too much before she was ready.

"It certainly has been a very interesting experience. I've really learned a lot this summer. Much more than I had counted on."

Claire noticed Rudy's attention seemed to be riveted on the dining room. He didn't try to go any closer, but it appeared the effort was almost too much for him. If what he said was true, he could, no doubt, sense Charles' closeness. Could feel his presence on the other side of the wall.

There was little use in denying it. "I've talked with Charles," she blurted suddenly. "And I've seen him. Many times." There. She'd said it. Plain and simple.

Rudy sat quietly with his hands clasped between his knees. Digesting. Nodding his head ever so slightly. "He's here now, isn't he?" he whispered.

"In the next room."

"Will he let me see him?"

"Maybe." Claire took a deep breath. "It all depends on you, Rudy. It took a lot of convincing, but I believe what you said about me being Clarissa. I believe Charles is my husband and we're here because I thought I was being a smart-ass and put a spell on us all. Now we're really in a bind."

"You don't know where to go from here," Rudy stated sympathetically.

"Exactly," Claire sighed. "Charles is willing to speak with you, but only if you agree to keep this completely confidential. No news media flashes. No scientific papers. Nothing."

Without a moment's hesitation, Rudy nodded solemnly. "I had already decided as much. Really, who would believe me anyway?"

"I imagine Sylvia Browne and John Edwards would love to hear this story."

"I'm sure they would. Some say they're all smoke and mirrors. They somehow find out about a person, then tell them what they want to hear. I've met with both of them. If their so-called abilities are phoney, they've sure fooled me. They just know too many details that wouldn't be public knowledge. I'd believe them in an instant. But I'm not looking for that kind of notoriety."

"We have the photographs and the journals. You'd be famous."

"Not at the expense of my profession. It's too important to me. And there's no way I'm prepared to put all of you through that kind of scrutiny. It would be criminal."

"We have your word then?" Startled by his voice, Claire turned to see Charles peer cautiously into the parlor from behind the glass door. His tone was vibrant, his image clear.

Slack jawed, Rudy couldn't take his eyes from the life form staring back at him from the dining room. The intensity of his eyes was mesmerizing. It left him speechless . . . in awe.

This was no dream. It was true. Ghosts do exist and it was possible to converse with them. No gimmicks. No seance trickery. Here he was not ten feet away.

Rudy rose and walked cautiously toward Charles. Examining the apparition standing before him from head to toe and back up again, he just couldn't contain the joy he felt. Giggling like a silly school girl, Rudy reached out timidly and poked Charles on the arm. Solid flesh and bone. A look of wonder spread across his face.

As Claire watched, she tried her best to stifle the smile that crept across her lips. She doubted Charles took any delight in being prodded. The frown on his brow told that plainly enough as his eyes followed Rudy's finger. Yet he stoically held his ground. And his tongue.

She could only imagine what Rudy must be thinking. His actions reminded her of a child who was having a very difficult time containing his excitement. Biting his knuckle, Rudy's body trembled. He forced himself to keep his feet on the ground as if lead boots were glueing him to the floor so he couldn't bounce up and down in the air.

Rudy composed himself enough to speak. "This is amazing. Forgive me. I realize I'm acting foolishly. Please allow me a moment."

This was one personal triumph that would remain forever in secrecy, however, he had to gloat just a little. Rudy's life's work was now complete. He had confirmed the existence of paranormal beings even though he had to keep the discovery to himself. A victory, but Rudy felt no need of kudos. No need of worldly recognition. He could retire a happy man.

Clearing his throat, Rudy continued. "How can I help?"

Charles ventured closer. "Are we assured of your cooperation?"

"Most certainly." Grinning from ear to ear, Rudy again reached out his hand, this time to grasp Charles' in a firm handshake. "It's so absolutely wonderful to finally meet you, Charles."

Breathing a heavy sigh of relief, Charles returned his gesture with a wary nod of his head. Not knowing what to expect from this man, he realized he was putting his whole family in danger. For now at least, he agreed they could trust Freeman. They considered Breezie and Simon's offspring part of their extended family.

Rudy's heart was still pounding as he valiantly tried to appear professional. He took his place across from Claire on a twin settee as Charles sat beside his wife.

The whole story spilled from both Charles and Claire like a tag team. From the beginning with the spell. To the present as they now knew it. To the future, whatever that might entail. Back and forth, one after the other, they even finished each other's thoughts and sentences.

"I haven't been able to stay visible for any significant length of time," Charles explained.

"But this morning," Claire cut in, "he hasn't disappeared at all."

"Even when I tried," Charles concluded.

Rudy sat quietly absorbing all they told him. Unfortunately, he could offer no concrete answers. "Maybe your problem will solve itself," he speculated. "Maybe you'll be able to retain human form for longer periods the more time you spend together. Is that a possibility?"

"That seems to be the case," Charles agreed. "But I have to be certain. Rudy, I feel we're running out of time."

"How so?"

"Tell him everything, my darling." It wasn't the time to hold anything back if they expected Rudy to help. Claire continued when she realized Charles wasn't about to. "He felt pain in his chest, Rudy. It was bad. He said that's never happened before."

"Do you still feel it?" Rudy asked.

"No, it hasn't returned."

Rudy was struck by the intimacy they showed each other. Their hands were interlocked, their fingers entwined as if daring the world to pry them apart. As they looked at each other, their eyes fairly sparkled with adoration.

Contemplating for a moment, a thought occurred to Rudy. Tapping his finger against his chin, he said, "This is just a theory mind you, but it could be a possibility. You say you're staying visible longer. Maybe your body is undergoing some kind of physiological change. A metamorphosis that will revert you to human form."

Charles shrugged as he looked quizzically at Claire. Hesitantly, he agreed. "I suppose it's possible. We never thought of that. I just thought I was going to cease to exist."

"Maybe it's a process, though a painful one, that you'll just have to endure."

"So you suggest we just wait and see what happens?"

"What other option do you really have?" Rudy asked quite seriously. "It's not like any of us has any experience with this sort of thing."

"That's very true, Rudy. But we want to remarry and I really don't want us to get all the way home and all of a sudden Charles vanishes and ends up back here in Virginia." Claire's face was grim.

"Marriage?" Rudy queried more to himself than anyone. What would be the ramifications? Identification, social security number, blood test. What would a blood test of a ghost reveal? "Do you think that's wise?" he asked hesitantly.

"We're already married," Charles began as he rose to sit on the arm of the settee next to his wife. He placed his hand on her shoulder.

"In our hearts we always have been," Claire continued as she lovingly gazed upon her husband's solemn face.

"It would be mostly for . . . "

" . . . the children's sakes."

"We haven't even tried to explain much of this to them."

"Wouldn't know where to begin."

"They just seem to accept it all . . . "

" . . . without question."

Nodding once more, Rudy could understand the vague logic. But a legal marriage to a paranormal being?

"So I guess what we're really asking you, Rudy, is if you've come across any spells or incantations that you think might help us?" Claire pleaded hopefully.

"Unfortunately, I didn't delve into that particular area when I researched for my thesis." He saw the disappointment on their faces and thought harder. It was a long shot, but maybe some of the people he had interviewed who actively practiced the magic would have a suggestion or two. "It may take a couple days or so, but I can dig through my papers and come up with some contacts who may be able to help."

"Hopefully we still have a couple days," Claire said with a wan smile. "Anything at all you can think of may be helpful. I've gone all through the journals where I . . . *Clarissa* . . . wrote down Grandmama's spells. There was nothing . . . "

She stopped short.

Charles had suddenly left her side. The agitation had returned in full force. He couldn't keep still. "I feel it coming on again," he stated bluntly as the color drained from his face. Searing pain crushed his chest leaving him breathless.

"*Charles!*" Claire screamed as her husband crumpled to the floor and vanished.

TWENTY-ONE

So what the hell was that all about? Chase couldn't understand why his body had decided to play tricks on him and act up after all this time. His operation had been weeks ago. Now here he was out in the middle of godforsaken nowhere and he'd just had some kind of attack.

Couldn't be his heart. The doctors said all was well. He didn't figure he was under enough stress for an anxiety attack. He was on a mission and had no time or patience for that kind of foolishness.

As the miles dragged on, Chase totally convinced himself there couldn't be anything wrong with him. His body was probably just reacting to being over tired. Nothing at all to be concerned about. Mind over matter. Willpower over pain. If it happened again, he'd just tell himself to smarten up and stop being such a pussy.

Damn. Off in his own little world, Chase missed his exit off the Interstate. Now he'd have to backtrack. Irritated with himself, Chase focused his attention and stepped a little heavier on the accelerator.

But the further he drove, the more his thoughts wandered off the road and once again to that pretty little lady from Battlefield Park. Would she still be there at that house? Would she want anything to do with him or was this little detour just an exercise in futility?

She almost outright admitted she was single. Really, though, a beautiful woman like that with no companion? What would be the likelihood?

Zilch.

She was probably happily involved with some guy. The twinge of jealously caught Chase by surprise. Their conversation never really got into the nitty gritty. She hadn't been too forthcoming with personal information. Chase had been lucky to drag out of her what he did.

The more he thought of the woman, the more Chase realized all that he was missing from his life. A home. Wife. Family. Someone other than his mother and sister to write him letters when he was off doing his little part to save the world. Someone to welcome him home. Children to tuck into bed. To read stories to. Even if they weren't his own flesh and blood. He could love her children.

Chase knew he wasn't getting any younger. He'd better get on the ball and do something about it.

It would sure make his mom happy if he'd settle down soon. She constantly pestered about wanting more grandkids. Needed to use up her bits of leftover yarn to knit more mittens.

Mittens of many colors, she called them. Bright and gaudy. All her other grandchildren were grown and wouldn't be caught dead wearing them now.

Maybe he'd just have to start thinking about giving her something to do with her yarn.

All the way from Tucson, Chase had been trying to come up with ways to search for the woman if she had already left the house by the river. Someone would have to know who she was. Maybe she had been visiting friends.

More than likely those friends would tell Chase to jump off the nearest cliff and leave her alone, he thought pessimistically.

Pulling over for gas, Chase double-checked the road map. He'd be there soon and he was more than a little nervous. What would he say to her if she was there? What would he do if she wasn't?

Glancing at his reflection in the rear-view mirror made Chase grimace with embarrassment. Three days' growth of stubble shadowed his face. His tawny-brown hair plastered his scalp so sweat-slicked it had turned greasy black. Perspiration stained the armpits of his tee-shirt. Sniffing, Chase wrinkled his nose in disgust. He couldn't possibly present himself looking like such a scruffy slob.

Grabbing his duffle from the back seat, he made a dash to the restroom to clean himself up. A quick shave took care of the whiskers.

He'd forgotten his shampoo at his parents' house. The soap from the dispenser smelled like the antibacterial stuff but he did his best to wash and rinse his hair under the tap in the sink. Probably turn his hair orange, he silently grumbled. Orange or purple, it would still look better than it had. Stripping, he scrubbed and put on fresh clothes.

He smiled at the transformation. Shouldn't scare anyone off now.

Back in his Jeep and on his way, Chase tried to rehearse some plausible opening lines should he happen to find her still there. Everything he came up with sounded totally lame. Maybe he should just forget the whole thing and head back to Quantico. A couple, three hours would get him there.

Flexing his tingling fingers, Chase realized he had been gripping the steering wheel too tightly. Lost in thought, his body tense, he was barely breathing.

Gasping for air, Chase moaned as a stabbing pain shot through his chest. His vision blurred. Chase fought the steering wheel, but he was quickly losing control.

Veering sharply to the right, the front tire of his Jeep dropped off the pavement spinning into the loose gravel on the shoulder of the road. Catapulting over the ditch, the vehicle rolled end over end then sideways. Tires exploded. Windows imploded from the impact spewing glass over his arms and face nicking his flesh. A shard deeply pierced his arm.

A silent prayer flittered across bloodless lips. *Please God, don't let me die.*

❋   ❋   ❋

"*Charles.*" Panic stricken, Claire called again. No response. She could not even sense his presence in the room anymore.

"This has never happened before, Rudy. He could always still talk to me even when I couldn't see him." Tears sprang to Claire's eyes. "He's really gone this time. I know it."

The children had heard her scream and ran down from their rooms where they had been playing.

"Did you see Charles in the attic?" she demanded as the children skidded in their sock feet around the corner into the parlor. She clutched Billy by the shoulders. "Did he go up there?"

"We weren't in the attic," Billy said suddenly scared by the tremor in her voice. "What's wrong?"

"Go look. Quickly," his mother ordered brusquely turning him around and pushing him gently on his way.

But their search was fruitless. Charles was gone.

Rudy hadn't driven very far when he rounded a corner and was forced to slow. The road was blocked by two police cruisers. Only a few cars were stopped in front of him. The accident mustn't have happened very long ago.

He hadn't thought it wise to leave Claire so agitated, but she insisted his time would be wisest spent going through his boxes of research he had stored away many years ago. Thankfully he had kept it all as he tended to keep most everything related to the paranormal. His *X-Files* he liked to call them.

And if it were true, if Charles had vanished for all time, the search would be pointless. But he had promised Claire. The holdup would now delay him.

There seemed no way around for the time being. Straining to see what was happening, Rudy finally got out and wandered closer. He was a doctor with medical credentials. Maybe he could help in some way.

Only one vehicle seemed to be involved but the carnage from that littered both lanes. There wasn't much left of it. By the look of the car across the road, it had rolled several times and now rested against the fence. The ambulance had not yet arrived but police officers were trying to get to the victim. It was going to take more than their bare hands to get into that mangled mess.

"Hey, Doc." Fuzz waved to him from his cruiser. He held the victim's wallet he had managed to reach from his hip pocket and was examining the licence.

"Anything I can do to help, Fuzz?" Rudy offered congenially.

The sheriff shook his head. "Thanks, but I'd say he's pretty much a goner by the looks of him." Fuzz looked down at the little slip of paper he held in his hand. "What do you make of this?"

"Of what?"

Handing Rudy the paper, Fuzz filled him in. "I met this lady and her kids renting the old Montgomery place up the road a piece. This guy had that address tucked in his wallet. No name. No phone number. Just the address."

Rudy squinted through the bottom half of his bifocals. Scribbled on the scrap of paper was 13755 River Road. Claire's address. "Humph, I just left there."

"Yeah, she said she knew you." Fuzz said a little too pointedly.

Nodding, Rudy simply said, "My sister introduced us."

"Checking out the haunted house were you?" Fuzz laughed teasingly. No matter how much he ridiculed all the superstitious banter around town, never would he admit he thought he had seen the ghost. But if Rudy stuck around long enough, maybe he'd challenge him on Claire's ridiculous little story.

Rudy chuckled but didn't offer anything further. Changing the subject, he asked, "Who is this guy?"

Fuzz fished for the driver's licence and handed it to Rudy. "Name's Tanner. Chase Tanner. Mean anything to you?"

"Not that I can recall."

"Haven't run his ID yet. Guess it'll just be a case of notifying next of kin."

"Don't be too hasty, Sheriff. He's not dead yet, is he? I'll go have a look. See if there's anything I can do."

"Don't see much point. Might just as well call the coroner for this one."

Ignoring the sheriff, Rudy pushed passed the small crowd that had gathered. He couldn't just turn his back and not try to keep this guy live at least until the ambulance arrived.

Rudy caught a glimpse of the battered man still caught in the wreckage. Khakis. Short-sleeved plaid shirt. Clean shaven as far as he could tell under all the blood. The short hair reminded him of a military cut.

Rudy got the attention of the officers trying to extricate the victim from his vehicle. "Is he still alive?"

"Barely," one replied tersely. "Don't expect he'll be much longer if that ambulance doesn't get here soon."

They still had to get him out of the damaged car before the paramedics would have any hope of working on him. Rudy would be little to no help here. Yet he couldn't walk away.

He helped himself to a pair of disposable gloves from the medical box by the side of the road and stretched them over his thick hands. "Let me get in there to check his pulse." The officers stepped aside. Rudy reached through the window and pressed his fingers against Tanner's jugular. "Come on, you," he coaxed. "Tell me you've got a will to live."

Closing his eyes to block out the surrounding confusion, Rudy fought to concentrate and finally was rewarded with an unstable throb. Life's blood was all but flowing through Tanner's veins. His hope would fade quickly if he wasn't pulled from the mangled wreck soon.

Rudy turned to the deputies. "He's going to bleed out if we don't get it under control," he advised gravely. A rudimentary inspection showed numerous cuts and contusions to Tanner's head and face. Even though bleeding from these wounds was profuse, Rudy wasn't too concerned about that. The most disconcerting was the deep gash in Tanner's arm. Blood dripped down his limp fingers at an alarming rate. From the pool at his feet, Rudy judged loss of blood was already significant. Not much left to make the heart pump. Back, head and internal injuries were also suspect with this type of accident. Rudy couldn't reach Tanner's lower extremities to examine any further.

Swabbing the wound to get a better look, Rudy did what he could to stem the flow of blood from Tanner's arm. He could feel the imbedded glass and dressed around it. Removing it would just make him bleed more. He then pressed bandages against the cuts on his head and wrapped it with gauze to hold them in place.

Frustrated, Rudy put his own weight to pulling at the crumpled car door, but it refused to budge. He stretched through the window to check for pulse again.

Rudy gasped as Tanner's eyes suddenly shot open, his fingers clasping around Rudy's wrist. A gagging cough spit blood from his mouth while a violent shudder wracked his body. A whisper hissed through his lips. "*Clarissa.*" Tanner's eyes locked with Rudy's. Tormented. Pleading. Filled with pain. "*Clarissa.*"

Tanner's eyes rolled back. Sputtering, he gasped for air. *"Get . . . Clarry,"* was all he could manage before the blackness overtook him once more.

Stepping back, Rudy slipped his wrist from Tanner's grasp. There could be millions of women with the name Clarissa. Or Clarry. He stared at the unconscious man battered and bruised.

Could he have meant Claire?

Rudy heard the sirens wailing in the distance. Help was on the way. Trotting to his car as fast as he was able, Rudy turned the ignition, rammed it into gear and sped into a squealing turn.

It only took a moment to get back to the Montgomery house. Leaving the car running, Rudy huffed to the front door and burst through without knocking.

The ambulance lights strobed red and white as Claire carefully drove around the growing lineup of vehicles to get closer to the scene of the accident. She probably shouldn't have driven at all by herself she was shaking so badly, but she didn't want the children to be here to see the wreckage or an injured man.

Rudy couldn't tell her much. This Tanner fellow had said the name, Clarissa, and told him to go for Clarry. More likely just a simple coincidence that had absolutely nothing to do with anything at all.

But there had to be some connection. Rudy said he had their address in his wallet.

"Claire. What're you doing here?"

Startled by his voice, she turned to see Fuzz strolling toward her.

Claire shook her head and shrugged. "I'm not exactly sure," she replied honestly. "Rudy came to get me. He said the man in the accident was carrying my address in his wallet and thought I may recognize him if I saw him. But his name isn't familiar at all." She started walking toward the mangled wreck.

"Give us a hand," a paramedic called to the police officers standing around waiting to help. "We almost got him!"

The rescue team lifted off a section of crumpled roof that had to be cut away with a torch. The paramedics reached down to pull Tanner out. The officers stood ready to ease the victim to the ground.

"Can I see him?" The stricken look on her face revealed little. Claire was still very upset about Charles' disappearance.

"Guess there's no harm," Fuzz reluctantly agreed. "Hope you're not squeamish though. He's pretty banged up."

"I'll be all right," Claire hoped. She took a deep breath for courage.

As they moved closer, Fuzz cast her a sideways glance. He had acted reprehensibly and regretted the things he had said to her.

"Listen, Claire, about the other night . . . "

"Don't worry about it, Fuzz. You've every right to your opinion."

"Even so, I want to apologize. I had no call to say what I did. It's just that . . . well . . . I would have liked to get to know you better."

Feeling she had to say something to justify her irrational actions, Claire flew by the seat of her pants. "If it were under any other circumstances," she lied, "I would have liked that too. But, as it is, you know we can't stay here." She knew it would be useless to bring up his own deception. She just let it drop.

"I owe you an apology, too," Claire continued. "I shouldn't have let Rudy get to me. And I shouldn't have tried to scare you off with that ridiculous ghost story. It was childish, but I was really starting to like you. And I just didn't know how to tell you I didn't think I could see you anymore. You wouldn't have been the first person to think I was crazy."

"So it *was* all bullshit. The pictures?"

Claire hitched her shoulder and gave him a crooked little grin. "A little computer wizardry."

"I thought so."

"Look, there's no point in pursuing . . . "

He led her around some debris. "I realize that now," he cut in. "I was just . . . you know . . . kind of disappointed. Never had a woman turn me down for a ghost before."

Claire smiled. "Well, I guess there's a first time for everything." His laugh eased the tension.

As they neared the wreck, a thought occurred to Fuzz. "You know, the house is still on the market. Maybe he's just a guy who wants to see it and wrote down the address."

"Of course," she nodded with a feeble smile. "That's probably all it is. But, if it's all the same to you, I'd like to take a look at him anyway." She hadn't felt the need to mention Tanner had spoken to Rudy.

The police officers were just lowering the man onto a back board. A paramedic scrambled from the roof of the car jostling himself into position to check the victim's vitals before moving him to the ambulance.

Trying to keep from getting in the way, Claire glanced over his shoulder. Studying the man's features, Claire tried to imagine what he would look like without blood spattered all over his face. She sensed there was something familiar about him but she couldn't put her finger on just what it was.

"Do you recognize him?" Fuzz asked with a hint of impatience in his voice. There was more traffic backing up on both sides of the road. He had to get out there to move it along.

Claire craned her neck to get a better look. "Hmmm. He does look kind of familiar." Claire tried to place him though he just didn't register. "I think I may have seen him somewhere before, but I can't tell you where."

"No pulse here," the paramedic shouted.

Springing into action, the other paramedic immediately began CPR. Ripping open Tanner's shirt between thrusts, he paused when he saw the angry scar running the length of his torso. "Good Lord Almighty. What chainsaw ripped through him?"

Claire couldn't help but notice the jagged pattern running down the man's chest. The same scar she had traced with her finger more times than she could count. The saber wound from the Battle of Bull Run.

"Oh, God, *no*," she cried in horror. Claire turned frantically toward the sheriff. "That scar, Fuzz. I recognize that scar." There was no mistake about it. This was no stranger. She had no idea how it could be possible, but this was *Charles*. Blood drained from her brain. Claire struggled to keep from passing out. She all but collapsed into Fuzz's arms.

"Come on, Claire." She had seen enough. The sheriff tried to steer her away.

"*Nooo*," Claire howled ferociously as she pulled away from Fuzz and tried to kneel beside the lifeless body of her husband.

Fuzz grabbed her around the waist to hold her back. "Let them do their jobs, Claire. You can't help him."

"*Let me go!*" She fought with him to get away. "You don't understand. I have to go to him."

"Why? Who is he? How do you know him?"

Claire spun around to face the sheriff. "He's my *husband*."

"Your . . . *what?*" Fuzz was so surprised, he dropped his hold on her and took a step back. She was talking nonsense. When he had first met her, she said she was a widow. Her husband had drowned in a fishing accident. Then she claimed to be the reincarnated wife of a ghost. Now she was this dying guy's wife. That aside, all he could think to say was, "You said you were a widow."

Hesitating just a moment, she answered softly, "Not anymore."

"*Clear!*" warned a paramedic as he placed the paddles on Chase's bare chest and pushed the buttons. The defibrillator made him jerk as the electrical current coursed through his body. Still no rhythm. "Again. Up it. *Clear!*"

"Got something," said the other excitedly as he pressed his fingers against the jugular vein. Then just as suddenly, it slipped away. Shaking his head, he muttered, "Nope. It's gone."

"Once more. *Clear.*" Concentrating intently, he listened through the stethoscope. Nothing. "Okay, guys, that's it. I'm calling it." With a heavy sigh, he settled back on his heels making the hard decision to give it up. "We tried our best."

Standing out of the way, Claire had been praying silently. As she heard those dreaded words, she shot towards her husband lying so still on the cold ground. "Where are you going?" she demanded of the paramedics as they started packing up their equipment. "You can't just leave him."

"Look, lady, we've done all we can. He's dead."

Stricken, Claire's eyes welled with tears. "No, he's *not*," she hissed through clenched teeth. "He can't be dead. You've got to try again." Pleading, she pulled the paramedic by the arm back toward Chase. There was nothing left of her resolve. Tears spilled from her eyes. Nearing hysteria, Claire implored the men to do something. Anything.

"Listen. There's no point. Even if we got a pulse now, it's been too long. He'd be brain-dead. A vegetable."

"*No,*" she insisted madly pulling at him. "Check again. Please." He tried to pry her hands away but she wouldn't budge.

Finally she realized the futility of fighting with these non-believers. With a fiery swing of her head, she snarled, "Then get away from him. Give me those paddles. I'll do it *myself!*"

Roughly pushing the other paramedic away from Chase, Claire frantically fumbled with the leads to the defibrillator. She didn't know how to work it.

She didn't know how to help him. He wasn't breathing. His heart was not pumping precious blood through his veins.

Grief overwhelmed her as Claire flung herself across his lifeless body cradling him in her arms and rocking him as she would a little child. She wept bitterly. His skin was already waxy and grey. Cold to the touch. Cold as *death.* Nothing like what he had been such a short time ago.

"Claire . . . " Fuzz knelt quietly beside her and tried to ease her away. "Please. Come with me," he implored gently. "He's gone."

"Don't *touch* me," she screamed viciously. "Get *away* from me. Leave us *alone.*"

Fuzz backed off leaving Claire to her grief.

Claire had told him her husband had drowned at sea. Had he miraculously survived? She had recognized that horrendous scar. Why not his face? Maybe, for some reason, he had altered his appearance because he didn't want to be found.

Fuzz didn't begin to understand their story. Didn't have time to analyze it at the moment. He had a job to do getting this mess cleared up and the road open again. There'd be time to launch an investigation. Tanner wasn't going anywhere anytime soon.

Drawing Chase's head to her breast, Claire whispered distraughtly into his ear. "We've waited so long, my darling. Don't you dare leave me again. Not now. Not like this. You've got to fight. Fight like you've never fought before." She slid her hand down his chest following the path of the angry scar. "The Yankees couldn't stop you. Don't let this."

Just then the sun broke through the misty clouds. The warmth of its rays ignited Claire's spirit. A sudden calm flooded through her as she raised her face to the sunlight. Thoughts formed into words. As if she were captive of a trance, Claire began to chant at a frenetic pace. She didn't know where the words came from or what she was saying.

"From time everlasting, Immortal your soul, Draw hither your spirit, In this life be whole. From time everlasting, Immortal your soul, Draw hither your spirit, In this life be whole. From time everlasting, Immortal your soul, Draw hither your spirit, In this life be whole."

Claire repeated the spell as she cradled his body close to her own.

One of the paramedics asked Fuzz, "What the hell is she saying to him?" as they stood back and watched the pitiful scene.

"Beats me. She's talking so fast I can't make out the words. Maybe French. She's from Canada."

"Did you get a load of that scar?"

"Yeah. Looks like somebody tried to saw him in half." Fuzz cringed at the thought.

"Can't you get her out of there? We've got a date at the morgue."

"Just give her a minute more. We've got to wait for the coroner anyway."

"Can't we at least get him in a body bag?"

Fuzz snorted. *"You* try and move her!" He turned away to flag the tow-truck driver back towards the wreck. They'd done all their photographs and measurements, all their angles and speculations. It would be up to the autopsy to show actual cause of death.

Emotional exertion slicked her skin with a fine sheen of perspiration. Heat swept through her body like wildfire. Still chanting, Claire again began to feel faint. As she leaned her cheek against Chase's forehead to keep her balance, she imagined she felt warmth to his skin. But Claire reasoned her own skin was so flushed it would make anything she touched feel warm.

Then only a moment later, the slightest puff of breath escaped his nostrils followed by a feeble twitch.

Falling back, Claire exclaimed excitedly, *"He moved! He moved!"*

One of the paramedics had been observing her closely. Overwrought family members occasionally collapsed in tragic situations. Just in case he had stayed near ready with oxygen. He was close enough to witness the index finger wiggle on Chase's left hand but he wasn't about to tell her . . . not yet . . . that it may only be the reflex action of a dying muscle.

The paramedic laid his fingers against Chase's jugular, then placed a stethoscope on his chest and listened intently as Claire scrutinized his every move.

"I don't believe it! *We've got sinus rhythm!*" he shouted jubilantly as he positioned the oxygen mask over his patient's nose and mouth.

Tears of relief flowed freely. Claire stood back to allow the paramedic to confirm a steady pulse. Taking charge, he called out, "Let's roll." With swift precision, Tanner was lifted into the ambulance. Claire climbed into the back still tightly clasping his hand.

As the ambulance careened out of sight, sirens blaring, lights flashing, Fuzz stood back and watched it go.

Totally perplexed, his deputy asked, "What just happened here, Sheriff?"

Fuzz just shook his head. "I don't think we want to know."

TWENTY-TWO

Sirens shattered the stillness of that balmy summer afternoon as the ambulance sped toward the hospital. Claire studied the unconscious man lying on the stretcher in front of her. A sudden wave of doubt flowed through her.

Who was this man . . . really? The man she had grown to love more than life itself or a complete stranger? There was a certain familiarity about him. Maybe their paths had crossed somewhere before yet Claire still couldn't place him.

If she concentrated hard enough, she could see a hint of Charles in a clean cut sort of way. Rawboned features. Long straight nose. Strong angular chin with the slightest of dimples. Light-brown hair cropped just shy of a buzz cut. Much shorter than Charles' tied-back ponytail.

Brazenly, she swept her eyes over what she could see of his body. Brawny, like Charles. Broad shoulders. Well-toned, rippled chest. Powerful arms. Narrow hips.

Claire tried to picture Charles without his mustache . . . his soft, shamefully kissable lips. Tanner's were not quite so full. Were they kissable? And what of his eyes? Were they the soft green of her husband's eyes which sparkled jovially when he smiled?

Monitors beeped reassuringly. The paramedic checked his patient's vitals every moment or two. With each passing minute, Chase seemed to grow stronger.

And with each passing minute, Claire tried to make sense of what was happening. Charles' scar suddenly appearing on Tanner's chest. Had she just imagined the similarity? Did she want this man to be her missing husband so desperately that she could actually convince herself of such a fanciful notion?

Just a few short weeks ago she would never in her wildest dreams ever believe such a possibility. Yet here she was tossed into her very own science-fiction mystery.

Without warning, Chase gasped for air. Clawing at the oxygen mask covering his nose and mouth, he writhed. Startled, Claire leaned as far back in her seat as she could while the paramedic tried to keep him still. She thought she heard him speak.

"What did he say?" she asked.

At the sound of her voice, Chase calmed and turned toward her, his bleary eyes searching for her face. His hand groped towards hers. Claire clasped it immediately and bent toward him.

"Clarry?" His eyes closed and he drifted off once more. Any doubt in her mind vanished.

The hospital staff had been alerted and Chase was immediately rushed to a trauma room. Quickly triaged, the attending physician ordered an operating room readied. Transfusions were begun to replace lost blood. A vascular surgeon was called to remove the glass from his arm and repair the damaged artery.

Without thinking, Claire introduced herself as the wife even though she had no idea if this man was already married. She refused to leave his side during the barrage of testing and x-rays or as the nurses meticulously plucked each embedded bit of glass from his skin. Only when he was on his way to surgery did she dare slip away to call Rudy.

Too exhausted to explain, all Claire told him was to meet her at the hospital. Rudy made arrangements with Connie to pick him up to get his car which Claire had left beside the road at the accident scene. Then his sister would take the children back to her house so Rudy could meet with Claire.

Released from post-op, Chase was being settled into ICU when Rudy finally arrived. Claire was fussing with the bedding and pillows trying to make him more comfortable. Not that he would have known. The doctors suspected it would be a few more hours before he fully regained consciousness. Claire just needed something to do.

She kept up a steady stream of conversation. Quiet, reassuring words about nothing in particular. Claire wanted him to hear the sound of her voice. He was beyond communicating with her, but he knew she was there. She was sure of it. The ever-so-slight squeeze of his hand told her so. And the way the corners of his mouth rose, barely perceptible, when she tried to be funny.

Claire looked up as Rudy stepped in beside her. "Do you know him?" he whispered.

Claire's eyes immediately welled with tears. It had been a very long day. Her nerves had been stretched beyond the breaking point. Suddenly overwhelmed, she struggled to speak. "It's a miracle, Rudy. I don't know how, but he's Charles. It's not his body, but it's Charles in there. In Chase Tanner's body."

"Are you certain?" Rudy asked skeptically as he peered over her shoulder at the sleeping man.

"Of course I am. Look." She carefully pulled down the sheet that was tucked tightly across his chest. "Look at that." With a feathery touch, she traced the scar. "Charles was wounded at Manassas. This is exactly the same scar that he has. I know it is. There can't be another one like that in the whole universe."

"Absolutely amazing," Rudy whispered. He examined the scar closely. "Well, it certainly had to be an old sawbones who stitched him up. Primitive conditions. No decent supplies. Shove the guts back in, sew them up and send them back to the front lines. No respectable surgeon nowadays worth his weight would leave a patient looking like that."

Claire understood the deplorable conditions early army surgeons had to endure. Blood. Filth. Infection and disease running rampant. She hated the thought that Charles was subjected to such atrocities.

In his letters to Clarissa, Charles had passed off the injury as a mere inconvenience. Clarissa had strongly suspected otherwise, but letting on how concerned she actually was would have just upset him more.

She didn't want him worrying over her. "I'm just glad he survived it," Claire said gravely.

The attending physician was beginning his rounds. Rudy stepped out of the way, but Claire hovered close by. Finishing his examination, he told Claire how lucky her husband was. There was no debilitating head trauma as was seen so often in rollover accidents such as his. A couple broken ribs, probably from the impact from the steering wheel, showed up in the x-ray. Other than the punctured artery, only a few nicks and bruises. Very lucky indeed.

The doctor, as well, mentioned the unsightly scar. From Tanner's medical records that were faxed from Quantico, he was aware of recent bypass surgery. What he couldn't understand was why the incision was much longer than it needed to be. Or why it hadn't healed neatly.

Not knowing the slightest thing about Chase Tanner's medical history, Claire held her tongue. Couldn't offer information or explanation until she could find out more about this person she believed with all her heart hosted her husband.

They still didn't know what may have caused Chase to lose control of his vehicle. Possibly he fell asleep at the wheel. Or maybe he swerved to avoid an animal on the road. They were just speculating at this point and wouldn't know until Chase woke. For now, all they knew was that he was very fortunate to be alive. The doctor had tests scheduled to rule out further heart problems.

Visiting hours were long over. Rudy brought Claire something to eat from the cafeteria. "You're going to have to bring me a bedpan, too, Rudy. I'm not leaving him," she insisted stubbornly.

"You're not going to do him any good so exhausted you can't see straight. He's going to be out of it for quite a while yet. Go home. Get some rest. Come back in the morning."

"I'll sleep standing up if I have to. I'm not going."

He knew there'd be no winning this argument. "Suit yourself," he relented.

"I just want to be here when he wakes up," she whispered wearily.

"I know you do." Rudy patted her hand sympathetically. "What'll I tell the children?"

Claire shook her head. "I don't know. Nothing much yet, I guess. I'll have to think of something. They'll probably be asleep by now anyway."

"I'll just tell them you'll see them tomorrow."

"Thanks, Rudy. And thank Connie for me. I'll call in the morning."

He started to leave, thought better of it and turned around. "Tread lightly, Claire," he cautioned. "When he wakes, it may not be Charles. You have to be prepared for that possibility."

"But it is," Claire replied with conviction. "He said my name in the ambulance. Said it to you, too." Her voice faded to a whisper. "It has to be."

Rudy nodded. "Try to get some rest," he advised and slipped quietly from the room.

But Claire would fret more than rest. The monitors beeped strong and steady. The nurses assured her his vitals remained stable. But she knew any number of complications could once more take the life of her husband.

Claire gently stroked Chase's still arm. "Sleep soundly, my darling."

❋   ❋   ❋

Chase forced open one eye. Then the other. He ached all over. His head pounded unbearably. It hurt to breathe. Needles punctured the backs of both hands. Tubes snaked from every quadrant of his body.

Where the hell was he? What happened? Chase tried to remember but it was just too painful to even think.

Not daring to move his head for fear it would fall off, he scanned the room within his limited line of vision. He sniffed.

Hospital.

He knew all too well the smell and sound of one. Monitors beeped way too loudly. He'd kiss someone for a set of earplugs.

A soft sigh drew his attention. Rolling his eyes downward, Chase was surprised to see a mass of dark curls nestled against his thigh. A finely boned hand lay limply on the bed beside him.

It definitely wasn't his mother. His sister was red-headed. Nurse perhaps? He shifted his weight and groaned at the effort.

Her head shot up. "You're awake." Her voice was sweet. Soothing. A smile of relief brightened her face. "How do you feel?" She reached for his hand. Her grip tightened possessively. Lovingly.

His brain was still fuzzy from anesthesia. His tongue was thick and unwilling to form words the way he knew he should. Chase slurred, "Like I just jumped out of a plane without a parachute." Words echoed in his head sounding strange and far away. Sputtering to suppress a sneeze, Chase's eyes watered with pain. "Oh, damn." He panted for breath.

Claire pushed the call button for a nurse. As she reached out, Chase caught a better glimpse of her. He couldn't believe his eyes. Here was the lady he had been searching for. There by his hospital bed. What were the odds?

"It's you!" he hissed through swollen lips. Mercy, even his teeth hurt. He closed his heavy eyes. Reopened them. "You're really here?"

"You recognize me?" Elated, Claire rose so he could see her more easily. She gently stroked his bruised cheek relishing the feel of his unshaven stubble. Never again would she complain of whisker burn. "I was so afraid you wouldn't know me. I'm not sure how this happened, but we'll figure it out."

The familiarity of her touch took him by surprise but he couldn't act indignant even if he wanted to. He had been craving her caress ever since he left Tucson. Chase wished he could enjoy it, but he hurt too damn much.

"I know you don't look the same," she continued, "but . . . "

He gasped, "I don't?" Chase tried to raise his hand to his face, but it just wouldn't go. "Dammit, am I all cut up?"

"No, not so bad. Just a few bumps, bruises. Nicks from the windshield glass." Claire gently indicated a few specks that were already scabbing over. "Some deeper than others, but not to worry." She smiled tenderly.

A mumble of relief. "Oh, thank God." He had his share of battle scars, however, it wasn't an urgent goal of his to collect any more.

"I was getting rather used to the mustache, though." Claire tweaked his upper lip playfully.

"Mustache?" Chase ran his tongue along his upper lip. He experimented with a beard in college, but that was years ago.

"And I'll miss running my fingers through your hair." Chuckling, Claire patted his arm. "But it's okay. You're still very handsome. Just . . . different."

"Thank you . . . I think."

She ignored his confusion. "What do you remember?" she asked gently.

"Nothing really. Just an awful pain in my chest."

"You were having pain on and off throughout the day."

Chase just stared at her. How the hell would she know that? "Guess I was," he finally agreed.

"There was a piece of glass in your arm. Cut into an artery. You had surgery to repair that. And they figure the steering wheel cracked a couple, three ribs. You were in very serious condition when they found you. We almost lost you," she said gravely. A tear glistened in her eye.

Claire sat beside him on the edge of the bed and lay her hand over his heart. Another familiar gesture that startled him. For a lady he could barely pull two words out of just a few short weeks ago, she certainly was mighty friendly all of a sudden.

Now she wanted to be chatty just when his brains were about to explode into a million pieces. His arm throbbed unmercifully from surgery. His heart pounded against cracked ribs. And he just plain wanted to be left alone at the moment. "Listen . . . "

Before Chase could say another word, a nurse appeared at his side to check his vitals. "It's good to see you awake, Mr. Tanner," she said brightly. "How are we feeling?"

"I don't know about you," Chase responded miserably. "But I feel like shit."

His choice of words caught Claire's attention. It wasn't like Charles to resort to crude language.

The nurse nodded compassionately. "Well, that's to be expected for a little while at least. I've got your meds right here."

Before she had a chance to administer them, Dr. Beaton, the resident cardiologist, stopped by to check on his patient.

Chase listened to the doctor's prognosis but little registered. The rumbling in his stomach could no longer be ignored. Chase had not eaten for many hours. Managing a crooked grin, he whispered raspily, "I'm hungry."

It surprised Claire to hear Charles ask for something to eat. But she guessed it would be rational that he could eat if he were really human once more.

With a hearty laugh, the doctor said, "Well, Mr. Tanner, that's a good sign." He patted Chase on the shoulder. "We'll see what we can do about that."

The doctor continued on his rounds. The nurse set about rustling up a meal.

"You're hungry?" Claire laughed planting a kiss on Chase's forehead. "Your first food in . . . what? A hundred years or so?"

"Not quite that long," he tried to chuckle, "but sure seems like it." On duty, Chase was used to not eating for long stretches at a time. Medical leave had spoiled him, along with his mother's cooking.

The nurse returned with a light meal tray. Chase inhaled the toast and fruit fantasizing about the steak he promised himself when he was released.

"The doctor ordered me to slip you a little something to help you sleep more comfortably." She inserted a syringe into the intravenous line.

"How about a lot of that little something?"

"Now, now," she giggled. "We mustn't be greedy." Turning to Claire, she said, "This should kick in quickly, Mrs. Tanner. He'll be pretty groggy in just a few minutes. Why don't you take a break? The cafeteria food really isn't that bad."

"Thank you. I'll wait until he's asleep."

Chase heard the words, Mrs. Tanner, but they just didn't sink in. The drugs started to work their magic almost immediately. Eyes growing heavy, Chase fought to keep them open but it was fast becoming a losing battle. His head bobbed. He felt punch-drunk. Giddy.

Even so, he grasped her hand in his. "I'm so glad you're here. I didn't think I'd ever see you again."

"Neither did I." Claire brushed the hair back from his forehead. "When you disappeared from the house . . . "

"Disappeared?"

"Yup. Just vanished. Ppffft . . . ," she waved her hand, " . . . into thin air. Scared us to death."

Chase didn't have the wherewithal to get his head around what she meant by that, but by that point he just didn't care. His eyes were closed now. Words came haltingly. Dreamily. "But . . . you found me."

"Actually, Rudy found you."

She said it as if he should know who she was talking about. "Rudy?" He tried to open his eyes but failed. Arched his brow instead. Chase fought to conjure up a face but he was sure he didn't know anyone by that name.

Claire nodded. "He came on the accident and you told him to come get me."

"I did?"

"Uh huh." She stroked his cheek soothingly.

"But . . . " Chase was quickly becoming incoherent.

"Shhh," Claire urged. "We'll talk more later."

"But . . . " He struggled to open his eyes. Swallowed hard to clear his throat.

"But, what?" She indulged him.

"I . . . couldn't've." His head swayed but Chase managed to get his eyes blearily pointed in her direction. "Didn't know . . . if you'd still be here. Took a . . . chance. Just couldn't get you . . . off my mind. Tried like hell to, but . . . the more I tried to forget you . . . the more I had to see if I could . . . find you."

Something was wrong. "Pardon?" Something was seriously, drastically wrong. Claire stepped back. Withdrew her hand.

"Ever since I saw you . . ." He giggled. ". . . that first day."

"At Richmond?" She hoped with all her heart. "The Harvest Ball?"

"Hmmpp. No, silly. Manassas. Remember? You were having a rather . . . bad day."

Searching his features once more, recognition finally set in. Her voice flattened. "Yes, I remember you now," she agreed in a hushed tone. The man who helped her from the battlefield. A terrible feeling began to gnaw at her stomach. She turned away from him wanting to sit down until she felt steadier.

"You said my name to Rudy, then called me Clarry in the ambulance." The words came in a flurry catching in her throat.

"Can't see . . . how . . . "

Claire panicked, grasping at straws. "You had my address in your wallet."

"Oh, yeah. That. I followed you."

"You followed me? From Manassas?"

"Yup. To make sure you got . . . home . . . okay. Was hoping you'd still be there. I wanted to . . . " He took a deep breath and panted. *Oh God,* it hurt to talk. " . . . to see you . . . again," he huffed heavily. "But you never . . . told me . . . your name."

Claire braced herself against the back of the chair. Leaning forward, she forced slow, shallow breaths to try to relieve the horrible pressure building in her chest. She didn't understand. Hadn't this man called her by name? Hadn't he called her Clarry? Not to mention the scar. What about the scar?

Tears filled her dispirited eyes. One spilled down her cheek. Pressing a hand to her lips, she held it there until she felt she could speak once more. "Um . . . Claire," she whispered. "My name is Claire."

"Mmmm, beautiful . . . name. Nice to . . . meet you . . . Claire." Finally giving in, Chase slept.

Devastated, Claire couldn't believe she had made such a mistake. This man was not her Charles.

TWENTY-THREE

Sleep held no healing escape for Chase Tanner. Somewhere deep within, a battle raged. Sword against sword. Soul against soul. Each knew only too well the toll of war. Each in his own time.

Cavalry. Infantry. Cannon fire. Chase could smell the stink of battle. Hear the sounds. See the horrors. Entirely too familiar.

Every dream started with a battle. Chase stood alone in the midst of the chaos around him. Out of the smoke from thousands of spent rounds of ammunition, a figure would stride towards him. A captain in Robert E. Lee's army bedecked in gold braid with a gleaming sword swinging at his side.

Even though Chase outranked him, he felt inclined to salute. The captain was dressed in a uniform of years gone by. Chase in desert camouflage. Each a soldier. Each defending his own.

The Confederate officer assumed an offensive position as Chase stood defenseless before him.

With hands at each other's throat, Chase came to accept this as a battle of a different sort. Of wills to survive. To dominate.

Neither would surrender. Neither would be defeated.

Therefore, no one could win. Even so, he felt no threat to his life. No hatred.

Chase would not forget the look of steely determination in his adversary's eyes. Or his grimly set mouth framed by a drooping mustache. Or his long hair pulled back tightly held at the nape of his neck by a worn leather thong. Wisps about his face had escaped its binding to blow in the befouled breeze.

Once an eternity seemed to have passed in deadlock, the soldier would suddenly step back letting his hands drop to his sides. Lifting his arm once more, he'd present Chase with a yellow rose. "Take this to her," he'd say. "Yellow is her favorite."

"Take it to whom?" Chase would ask.

Before the soldier could answer, he would fade into the haze only to reappear atop a knoll overlooking a river. Chase would find himself next to the officer in a tiny cemetery plot where four granite headstones stood side by side. Chase tried to make out the inscriptions chiseled on them, however, a fine mist obscured the names. The little plot was meticulously kept, its white picket border strong. Surrounding the interior of the little fence, bushes of yellow roses bloomed profusely.

"There lies the key to our immortality," the soldier spoke reverently. "Our family. Yours and mine."

Chase could not argue the validity of that statement. He pointed to the graves. "Our immortality? They do not live," he heard himself say. His own voice echoed with an eerie resonance.

"You are mistaken."

Laughter rose from the meadow below. Chase turned to see two children chasing each other in a game of tag. Their innocent voices sang in the summer sunshine. On a blanket nearby, a woman wearing a gown of shimmering emerald velvet sat under a parasol shading herself from the sun's blistering heat. As the sound of their voices caught her attention, she turned toward them and waved. Her smile dazzled them both.

Chase recognized the woman. "Claire," he whispered.

"Clarissa," the soldier corrected. "My wife. And our children, William and Margaret. Taken from me too soon. Awaiting my return once more."

Turning his back on the soldier, Chase watched the woman in the meadow now playing and laughing with the children. His heart suddenly filled with the profound sense of longing and of loss. He, himself, felt the anguish. Shared the grief.

Chase wanted to wake up, to end this nightmare, but he was powerless to do so. Captive to this soldier's will, he could do nothing but surrender to his mercy. Where he led, Chase was obliged to follow.

"Isn't she beautiful?" Chase heard him speak in a hushed tone. Reverently. Lovingly. "My enchantress. From the moment we met, Clarissa took my breath away. Then she stole my heart."

The soldier rested his hand on Chase's shoulder. In a blink, Chase knew their past. From the spilled punch dribbling down Clarissa's bodice to that terrible day when news came of her death. Devastation. Prison. Sweet revenge.

When he opened his eyes, Chase was still in that little cemetery. This time when he focused on the stones, he could see the names clearly. Clarissa, the children. Falling to his knees, he wept. "I'm too late," Chase cried bitterly. "I came for her, but it's too late."

He felt the soldier squeeze his shoulder compassionately. "All is not lost."

"What can I do?" Chase sought comfort in the eyes of the soldier. He was met with firm decisiveness.

"We must join forces. Unite. Or we shall both cease to exist."

"How can this be?"

"Our courses were charted long ago. Through no fault or wrong doing on anyone's part, your route—and mine—has been chosen. You're not merely a means to an end, young Tanner." The soldier, speaking clearly and in complete control, was determined to convince. "Both our lives depend on your acceptance. Time is fleeting. You must allow me to emerge or we shall both die."

Fear. Panic. Something was congesting Chase's lungs, the pressure rising beyond misery. "Why should I just hand you over the keys to my life?" he hissed defiantly through tight lips.

The soldier dropped his hand and stepped back. "Don't be a pig-headed fool," he stated irately. "You *know* you need me. We need each other to survive. We *must* become one."

Deep within his soul, Chase realized the soldier spoke the truth, but he was loath to give up what little control he still possessed. Though he dreamt, Chase felt the capability to survive on his own was rapidly being snatched from him. His defenses breached, he could offer no more resistance. Defeat compelled him to ask, "But what will happen . . . to *me*?"

"It's not my intention to dominate. How can I explain this so you will understand?" The soldier threaded leathery fingers through his wind-blown hair. Placing one hand over Chase's heart, the other over his own, he spoke patiently. "Hearts and minds can be bound together. We will still preserve our own individuality yet it has become necessary that we rely on each other to sustain life. We must put our faith and trust in this to survive."

Chase looked back down the knoll where the woman and the children played in the meadow. From some unknown dimension, confusion turned to resolve. "How much time do I have?"

"You will know she speaks the truth. Heed her words, my young friend. You must decide quickly."

The alarm alerted the nurses. Forced abruptly from sleep, the dream dissipated and was all but forgotten. Suffocating, Chase grabbed his chest.

✳   ✳   ✳

"It was *horrible*, Rudy," Claire wept into the phone. "He's not Charles. He's just some guy I met at Manassas. He doesn't *know* me. Not really." She hunched over the receiver trying to shield herself from passersby. "Now what do I do?"

"First you need to calm down," Rudy urged softly. "Take a deep breath."

"I don't want to breathe," she cried mournfully. "I just want to curl up and disappear. You tried to warn me. You warned me it may not be him. But, oh no, I wouldn't listen."

"Claire." Rudy had to speak louder to make himself heard over her sobbing. "I'm coming to pick you up. We'll check the house again. Maybe Charles is there."

As they pulled into the driveway, Claire searched the attic windows for any sign of Charles. Even a shadow would have given her hope. Anything.

When she pushed open the front door, Claire knew Charles had not returned. There was no energy in the house, no spark, just empty rooms.

Tears glistened Claire's weary eyes. She hated being reduced to a sniveling crybaby. Through everything this past year, she had been so stoic, so strong. But ever since she came to Virginia, to this peaceful

Shenandoah Valley, it seemed Claire could not escape constant turmoil. It was too much to bear.

She hadn't thought much about it before, but all of a sudden she felt homesick for her little sleepy town by the ocean.

Claire let her purse slip from her fingers and drop to the floor. She wandered blindly into the kitchen, sat at the table and lay her head on its cool flat surface.

Rudy followed and filled the kettle for tea. "You haven't eaten anything, have you?" he asked quietly. Claire shook her head. He rustled through the fridge for bread, butter, and jam. Maybe she'd manage some toast.

The kettle whistled. Rudy dropped a couple tea bags into the pot and poured the boiled water in to steep. He buttered the toast when it popped and cut it into quarters. Scrounging around in the cupboards, he found peanut butter.

Neither spoke. Neither looked at each other. Rudy had to nudge Claire's arms with the plate to get her to raise her head.

Despondent, Claire could only mutter a sullen word of thanks. She nibbled absently just to keep Rudy off her back. She had no appetite even though it had been hours since she had last eaten anything of substance.

Rudy poured two cups of tea. Into hers, he added milk and sugar. His, he left black. The chair legs scratched against the floor as he pulled it out to sit beside her.

All night he had been thinking long and hard about Charles. About this Tanner fellow, too. Rudy had come up with a theory of sorts.

"I know what I heard at the accident, Claire."

"Apparently we were both mistaken," she responded blandly.

"Possibly, but I really don't think so. I've given this a great deal of thought. There's too many coincidences."

"He already explained the address in his wallet."

"But could he explain the scarring?"

"Didn't ask him."

"Well, I think we should. And I also think we should show him the journals and letters."

"Oh, what for?" Claire asked snippily. "He doesn't know anything about our history."

"But neither did you when you first came to Virginia."

Claire sighed deeply. "No. But it's not the same."

"Why is it not?"

"I was drawn here because of Charles. Tanner only came back to see if he could get into my pants." Petulantly, Claire pushed herself away from the table. "Like I was some bimbo he could pick up at a bar."

"Oh, you really don't believe that."

"I don't know what to believe anymore." Claire picked up the teapot. "Want more tea?" When Rudy shook his head, she stacked the cups on the plate and unceremoniously dumped everything into the sink. Nothing broke.

Rudy chose his next words cautiously. "What if . . . What if he just needs convincing? Like you did when you came."

Claire mulled that idea over for a moment or two. "Maybe," she finally agreed. "But I had those old tintypes to push me in the right direction. Tanner doesn't even look like Charles."

"We know he had by-pass surgery, but that scar is certainly unique to say the least."

"Oh, it's probably just some cruel coincidence," she muttered.

"But surely Tanner would know if it's different."

"One would surely think so if he ever looks in a mirror."

"Then let's take him a mirror."

❋   ❋   ❋

Armed with her briefcase full of letters, journals and the old tintypes, Claire returned, more than a little apprehensively, to the hospital. Rudy may be onto something, but she wasn't hopeful. The less she expected, the less she'd be hurt. As if she wasn't hurting enough already. Another husband had vanished leaving her and the children alone once more.

With an aching heart, Claire had to tell the children Charles still had not reappeared. She saw no point in telling them about Chase Tanner.

Wanting to get her argument in order, Claire took her time walking through the hospital, passed emergency, then up the flight of stairs to Intensive Care. She stared at the door for a full minute, took a deep breath for courage, then pushed her way through.

Claire stood there gaping at the fresh linens stretched neatly on the bed. It took a moment for it to sink in. She hadn't expected to see Chase's cubicle empty. No monitors beeped. No intravenous lines. No body. Fear squeezed the breath from her lungs.

Claire swung around looking for a nurse. She spied a young orderly preparing a patient on a gurney. Laying a hand on his arm, she asked hastily, "Do you know where Mr. Tanner is?"

"Gone," he stated tersely.

"Gone?" She whispered aloud more to herself than anyone. Every drop of blood drained from her face. "You mean . . . he's dead?"

A nurse came up behind them. She took Claire by the arm and led her to a chair. "No, hon." She gave her hand a few sharp pats to put a little color back into her ashen skin. "He's just down the hall having some tests done. Don't you worry none. He'll be back in a few minutes. You can wait right here."

Turning toward the orderly, the nurse clucked her tongue. "Jonathan . . . you quit scaring folks. You're going to have to learn a better bed-side manner if you're planning to work in my unit. Add a few more words to your sentences."

"Sorry, ma'am," Jonathan said as he flew out the door.

Relieved, Claire let out a deep breath. At least the kid knew how to put two words together. Any more than that, she didn't know.

Claire used the time to go over her strategy. Just tell it like she saw it. That was her plan. Put the ball in his court. Let the chips fall where they may. Scrunching her nose, Claire tried to think of another, but she had run out of clichés.

She thought she had her composure under control, but when Chase was wheeled into the room, her resolve unraveled. Her whole carefully rehearsed argument slipped from her thoughts.

Chase smiled when he saw her. "You're back. I missed you when I woke up."

Even though she quaked so fiercely she could almost hear her bones rattle, Claire tried to put a cheerful look on her face. "Sorry, had to slip out for a while. Didn't want to wake you."

Once he was settled, she asked, "What were the tests for?"

Chase's smile wiped away the fleeting furrowing of his brow. "Oh, this and that. Routine heart stuff. No big deal."

"Is everything okay?" Had she not felt so heavy-hearted, she would have shown more concern.

Chase shrugged not mentioning the pain. "Don't have the results. I don't feel quite so out of it this morning. A little more coherent. Brain's not quite so cloudy."

"Bet you'll still feel pretty sore for quite a while yet."

Chase snorted. "That's an understatement. Oh, I almost forgot." It took some concerted effort on his part, but Chase managed to reach the bedside stand. Pulling a flower from the drawer, he presented it to Claire.

Surprised, she asked, "And what would this be?"

The corner of his mouth rose slightly. "A rose, I think," he replied dryly.

Claire clucked her tongue and grinned. "I can see that. But why?"

Chase shrugged. "I don't know. Just thought you might like it."

"Yes, I do." She held it to her nose drinking in its fragrance. "And yellow, too. My favorite. How did you know?"

He shrugged and winced. "Just a hunch. Had them send it up from the gift shop."

"Well, it's beautiful. Thank you." One more sniff then she set the bloom aside. Of all the shades, he chose yellow. "Listen, I should have asked if there's anyone you'd like me to call for you. Your parents, perhaps? Wife?" It was as good a delay tactic as any.

"Ha! No wife. But thanks, anyway. Someone called my parents yesterday when I got out of surgery. And I called myself a couple hours ago."

"Oh." Claire looked around the ICU. All the cubicles were occupied. Family members hovered. Some held hands with their loved ones. Others flipped through magazines biding time while their patient slept. Chase seemed the most mobile and alert of the lot. But there wouldn't be much privacy here for what she intended to say. "Are they coming?"

"My parents?" Chase shook his head. "No. My dad doesn't travel well anymore. And my mom wouldn't come on her own. Anyway, I told them I'd be well taken care of. After all," he reached for her hand, "I have you."

Claire took his hand in hers, though hesitantly. "You told them about me?"

"I told Mom, but I'm sure Dad knows by now, too." Chase rubbed his hand over his chest. He pressed his eyes closed to concentrate as he tried out a couple shallow breaths followed by a deeper one. "Damn broken ribs. I'm thinking it hurts more now than after the bypass. And of all times, now they want to wean me off the morphine."

Suddenly guilty for making him talk so much, Claire said, "I'm sorry. Maybe I should just go so you can rest." She started to rise.

Chase tightened his grip and clasped his other hand on top to make sure she didn't get away. "No, please don't. It'll be a hell of a long day here all by myself." As an afterthought, he added, "Unless you have other things to do."

She wished she could think of something. "No," Claire said vaguely. "Nothing that can't wait."

"Good. I'd really like the company. They're sending me to a different room soon. Guess I'm not sick enough to be taking up space here anymore."

"Another room," Claire repeated. She'd gladly wait until then to make him think she was crazy. In the meantime, she could certainly keep him occupied with idle chitchat that wouldn't tax his strength. He was going to need all that he could muster.

A couple naps later and Chase was moved to the cardiac wing where the staff was better trained to monitor the bouts of pain he was experiencing. He felt guilty for drifting off while he had a visitor, but he was powerless to fight the weariness. Though sleep brought him precious little rest. The same dream plagued him each time he drifted off.

Bits and pieces, Chase yearned to remember. The atrocities he desperately wrestled to forget. Drug induced or not, he had to remind himself they were merely nightmares.

But try as he might to convince himself of the contrary, Chase had a sneaky suspicion he'd just survived a terrible wreck only to step right into hell.

Somewhere just below the level of consciousness, his journey was about to begin.

TWENTY-FOUR

She stood in the misty shadows. Hidden. Yet he knew she was there. "Tell me your purpose, young Tanner." Her voice sounded strange. Oddly exotic. "Why have you come at this time?"

Chase noticed she had referred to him in the same manner as the soldier. "I came to find you." He spoke softly. Optimistically.

"For what purpose?"

Chase searched for her in the darkness. She eluded his sight. "To give you my heart."

"Can you unconditionally accept what your heart tells you no matter how unrealistic it seems?"

Peering into the fog, Chase spoke with conviction. "I believe I can."

"And can you love me, love my children, knowing *my* heart will forever be pledged to another?"

"Yes," Chase vowed sincerely. "I know I can."

Stepping toward him, she turned into the light. The electricity passing through the core of his being burned as one long sizzle from head to foot and back again. At first glimpse, Chase was reminded of Claire, of the way she looked as he awoke with her at his bedside. This woman, a mirror image, was equally as lovely. Yet even as he knew he dreamt, Chase realized this woman had been dead for well over a century.

Chase stood still as she slowly stepped toward him. He saw a solitary tear glisten as it slipped from her eye. He touched her face.

"Why do you cry?" he asked tenderly. As the droplet touched Chase's finger, his heart almost stopped as another surge of electricity sparked through his veins.

"We're coming to the end of it, one way or the other. Look hard at the consequences. Make your choice wisely. It will secure your future or extinguish it for all time."

Chase had already decided he could love her. He stated adamantly, "I know what I want."

Compassionately, she smiled for the first time. "Your coming here to this place . . . at this time . . . was destined long ago."

Chase shook his head. "I don't believe in destiny."

"I know. The thought of your life already planned displeases you." She turned her back to him and stepped away.

"Please . . . wait." He reached out to touch her once more.

"You must be wholehearted in your resolve, young Tanner. She and I are one as you and he will be."

"I am aware," he declared hastily as her essence slipped through his fingertips.

A coughing fit brought Chase fully awake. The spasm tore at his chest causing him to clutch his ribs. "Merciful heaven," he groaned miserably. As his eyes began to focus, Chase noticed Claire standing beside him. Her hand was poised to touch him though never did.

He longed for her to rub away the pain, but didn't dare ask. Regrettably, the easy familiarity Chase felt when he came to after surgery was gone.

"Are you okay?" Concern creased her brow.

"Nothing a gun wouldn't fix," he wheezed.

"Should I get the nurse?"

"Naw. They won't give me any more of the good stuff anyway. Sorry," he yawned. "Can't seem to help drifting off. Must be the tail end of the narcotics they've had me pumped full of. I'll try to be a better host," Chase promised.

"For heaven's sake, you don't need to apologize to me," Claire admonished. "It's only been a day. Don't push yourself so hard. Lie back and relax. Close your eyes if you need to."

She took a deep breath. Then another. Before she totally lost her nerve, she flat out plunged right in. "If you're up to it, there's a little story I'd like to tell you."

"Hey." Chase jerked his head toward all the tubes and monitor leads. "You've got a captive audience here. What kind of story is it? A bedtime story?"

"Guess it will be if I bore you to sleep."

"Somehow I'm thinking you're not the boring type."

"And how would you know that?"

"Well, what I've seen so far has been anything but." He smiled teasingly picturing Claire running amok around the battlefield at Manassas. "I've been intrigued since the first day I laid eyes on you."

"Oh, yeah," she grinned sheepishly. "One of my better days. I can only imagine you were pretty close to calling the asylum."

"Mmmm, I admit the thought did cross my mind."

"Well, after what I'm about to tell you, I'm sure that it'll cross again." Claire took another deep breath. She looked seriously into his eyes. "I need you to keep an open mind. I need you to keep a *very* open mind. Can you do that for me?"

"Well, I've always considered myself a pretty liberal sort of guy."

"Good, because what I'm about to tell you may make you run screaming out of here."

Chase tried unsuccessfully to hitch himself into a more comfortable position. "Lady, I've been to hell and back more times than I care to think about. Even if I could get out of this bed, I doubt there's anything you could say to me that would scare me much."

"We'll just see about that." Stalling, Claire began fussing with his pillows. "Do you need anything? A drink, maybe?"

"A stiff one would be great, but I doubt you've got anything smuggled in that purse of yours." Chase didn't bother to hide his amusement even though he saw a frown shadow her face. In his opinion, Claire had the prettiest pout he had ever seen. But his attempts at humor were failing badly. Playfully, he squeezed her hand to stop her from fidgeting. "Come on, it can't be all that bad."

Claire sighed heavily. "I think we both could use that stiff drink."

"I'll settle for a smile," he coaxed gently tweaking her lip with his finger.

If only to accommodate his wishes, Claire feigned a weak grin. She was too nervous to smile. "I don't know where to begin," she admitted gravely. Claire had so much to tell him, but she couldn't afford for this man to think she was nuts. Fuzz, she didn't care about. Not really anyway. But this man could very well hold all their lives in his hands.

"Well, as I recall, don't most bedtime stories begin with 'Once upon a time . . . '?"

Claire tried to relax. "Okay," she began with a bit more animation. "Let's go that way." She paused to get her thoughts in order. "Once upon a time . . . there was a witch."

"A witch?" Chase arched his brow with interest. "An old, ugly witch with a big hairy, green wart on her nose?"

Claire curled her lip. "No," she shook her head, "not an old, well . . . okay . . . older, but certainly not ugly."

"Then she was a sexy witch. I like my bedtime stories about sexy witches."

Annoyed, Claire pulled her hand away from his to whack at his arm. "No, not a sexy witch, either." She paused. "Granted, she was quite the beauty in her day, but I can't picture her as sexy." Claire stiffened to present a regal bearing. "Grandmama was a high priestess." She searched for the right word as she drew her hand up with a grand gesture. "Elegant," Claire stated sophisticatedly.

"Grandmama?"

"Yes, Grandmama," Claire repeated. "Listen. I'm going to find a dirty old sock to stuff in your mouth if you're going to keep interrupting me," she threatened.

"Sorry." Chase stifled a snicker with a moan. It hurt too much to laugh. "Grandmama was an elegant, high-priestess witch. Continue."

Claire silenced him with a withering glare. "Grandmama was from the bayous of Louisiana and she practiced the magic."

"Magic? Like black magic? Voodoo dolls and stuff?"

"Yes, casting spells, incantations, the works."

"Did she ever turn anyone into a jackass?"

"I can find that sock," Claire sputtered in exasperation.

Chase apologized. "Sorry. Just trying to grasp the gist of where this may be going."

"I'm not sure if there will be a gist." Claire wrung her hands. "Oh, I've made such a mess of everything already. I know where I want to go with this, but I don't know how to get there in any kind of logical order. There's nothing logical about it at all."

"Well, then just spit it out and we'll sort through it later," Chase suggested. "But don't expect me to sit here like a bump on a log. I don't think I'll be able to keep my mouth shut. You've got me all a-twitter."

Self-consciously, Claire turned away. "I'm trying to be serious here and you're making fun of me."

Chase had underestimated her nervousness. "No, really I'm not." Claire's hand trembled in his. If he dared lay his hand against her breast, he could only imagine her heart would be wildly beating. "Are you saying this is a true story?"

Biting her lip, Claire took her time answering. "Yeah," she finally admitted. "I believe so." She was still unable to meet his eyes.

"And since you're telling me this story, somehow I figure into it?"

"Yes, I'm thinking so." Not waiting for him to respond, Claire steeled her resolve and forged ahead. "Did you ever see that old black-and-white movie, *The Ghost and Mrs. Muir*? I can't remember who was in it. Rex Harrison, I think, but I'm not sure. Doesn't matter anyway. Years later they made it into a TV sitcom."

"Can't say it's anything I've seen."

"Well, anyway, this widow and her daughter moved into a dead sea-captain's house. Only the captain, it turns out, wasn't ready to give it up. He was still there . . . as a ghost." Claire leaped up and began to pace. When she reached the door, she turned to face him. "Do you believe in ghosts, Chase? Do you believe in the spirit world?"

"Can't say that I've given it a whole lot of thought. But I'm not about to say they don't exist."

Bolstered by a spate of confidence, Claire continued. "Then you're far more accepting than I was. I didn't believe at all. No way. No how. My mind was closed to even the possibility of an afterlife." Claire rifled through her briefcase and pulled out the tintypes. "The agent I rented the house through told me it was haunted. Well, I figured that was a big joke. But after we moved in, I started having dreams. Dreams that seemed familiar to me. Like I had already experienced what I dreamt about. A whole lot of other strange stuff started happening, too. And with the kids . . . well, that's another story."

Claire perched on the end of her chair and fiddled with the photos shuffling them around until she found the one of Charles. "I dreamt about this man." She turned the picture around and handed it to Chase.

Chase sharply drew in his breath. "No way." Closing his eyes, he lay his head back on the pillow.

"What is it? Are you okay?"

"You had dreams about *this* guy?"

"Yes, I did. Every single night since we moved in."

"*After* you saw the picture, right?"

"No." Claire shook her head. "Before I found it."

Chase studied the photo again. Inspected it closer. Uncertainty edged his voice. "I've seen him, too, I think."

"Really?" Claire sat up straighter. "Where?"

"I'm sure he's the soldier I'm fighting with in *my* dreams. Every time I close my damn eyes, he's got his bloody hands around my throat."

"Oh, that's *wonderful*!" Claire could barely contain her excitement. If Charles was appearing to Chase, then surely he must still exist on some level.

Taken aback, Chase snapped, "Wonderful that this maniac could very well strangle me in my sleep?"

"I know they seem real," Claire mollified. "I know only too well. But they're only dreams." She added defensively, "He can't and *won't* hurt you."

"You're just a little too okay with this, I think. Just who the hell is he?"

Claire reached for the photo and gazed at it lovingly. "This is Charles Montgomery. My husband."

Chase stared at her not knowing how to respond. He tried to find the words to call her a bloody lunatic, but the brand remained lodged somewhere between his gut instinct and his vocal cords. Just when he thought he might want to spend the rest of his life with this woman, his earlier impression of her came creeping back. She was insane.

Unless she had gone to extreme lengths to fabricate an elaborate scam. But why drag him into such a harebrained scheme? Extensive military training always made Chase wary of conspiracies. He'd show her. He was too well trained for brainwashing. Accusation tickled the tip of his tongue. He bit it back.

He looked deeply into Claire's eyes. There, with thick dark lashes framing the biggest, brightest pupils he had ever seen, he could read nothing corrupt.

Chase couldn't come up with a motive. He swallowed the incriminating remarks he was contemplating and nearly choked on them. For the life of him, he couldn't grasp why he should believe any of what she was feeding him. But, undeniably, he did.

Torn between the possibility of a sinister plot for his sanity and his own predilection toward believing the haunting dreams, Chase vowed to keep his wits about him. Until he could prove otherwise, he'd play along.

"Come on, Claire," he chided. "This really is a lot to swallow."

"Boy, don't I know it," Claire agreed sincerely. "What do you remember dreaming?"

Chase closed his eyes. His head was beginning to pound. "Not much," he admitted wearily. "A war. Explosions. Fighting. Always a fight. With that man trying to kill me, but I guess he must think better of it and leads me to some graves instead. I think he was crying." Then Chase remembered his own pain. "Or maybe it was me," he whispered in afterthought. "And then I see a woman and her children. And the woman looks . . . " He opened his eyes and turned toward her. "She looks . . . like you."

"And the children? Could you recognize the children?" She set the other photos side by side on his lap.

Before him lay the images of the lady and children also in his dreams. "Clarissa," he uttered absently. "William and Margaret."

Claire shot him a keen look. "I never told you their names."

Totally unnerved, Chase glanced up at Claire. "No, you didn't." He jabbed at the picture of Charles. "*He* did." Chase realized what he had said. "Shit. Now you've got me talking about him like he really exists."

"Oh, he does," Claire stated confidently. "And do you know what's even more amazing?"

Lost for an answer, Chase simply shrugged hoping it was a rhetorical question.

Removing small pictures of her children from her wallet, Claire set the other photos in front of him. "You could hold a mirror to my Billy and Maggie and see them in these old pictures."

He looked again at the photos. "William and Margaret. Same names as your kids."

"Identical in every way," Claire admitted. She pulled out the journals handing him the first one. "Let me back up a ways. I found the pictures and these in a strongbox under the floorboards in the bedroom I'm using. The more I read, the more they seemed familiar. Like I said about the dreams, I felt I had experienced—first hand—everything that was written here."

As Claire talked, Chase began leafing through Clarissa's journal. The very first paragraph caught his attention. "*It is currently the year of our Lord 1863 and I write these words in the hope that the one who follows through the portals of time will know me . . . will know us. I say 'us' for we are one.*" Recalling the words spoken to him by Clarissa in the dream, Chase absently whispered aloud, "She and I are one."

"Pardon?"

Chase waved the journal. "*My* dream. In my dream, she said '*she and I are one*'. But there was more. I'm sure of it." With crinkled brow, Chase fought to remember, then shrugged. "I don't know. It's gone now." He set the journal aside to pick up the other tintype. "Who are these other people?"

"Breezie and Simon Freeman and their children. Clarissa bought them from slavers and freed them. They worked with the Montgomerys."

Chase rubbed his aching forehead. "I'm not following."

"Let me try the condensed version." She squirmed in her chair tugging it closer to the bed. "Clarissa's grandmother taught her the magic though Clarissa, herself, never really believed in it all that much. But when Charles decided to enlist in the war, the Civil War, Clarissa put a spell on him that would keep them always together. Charles survived the war, but Clarissa and the children didn't. And the spell . . . well, it worked on Charles and he remained in a state of limbo for all these years waiting for Clarissa to return to him."

Uneasily, Chase couldn't help but ask. "And did she return?"

"I'm getting to that. I know it's a far-fetched tale," Claire acknowledged.

Chase's temper flared. "No, it's freakin' *unbelievable*. That's what it is."

Claire ignored his outburst. "I know. And I had one hell of a time coming to terms with it myself. I even went so far as to call a psychologist who specializes in the paranormal. He came in with all his meters and scanned the house for high levels of electromagnetic and ion readings. Even checked the local area for any seismic activity. He believed there was a definite spiritual presence in the house. But Rudy—Doctor Freeman—is a descendent of Breezie and Simon. He had his own theory."

"What was that?"

Claire took her time answering trying to gauge Chase's possible response. She said slowly, "That I'm the . . . reincarnation . . . of Clarissa."

Now Chase did choke. With a pained grimace, he folded his arms across his chest to keep his broken ribs from puncturing a lung. "Okay, now," he finally wheezed. "Dreams, magic . . . ghosts. Now reincarnation. You're actually telling me you believe in that spell stuff?"

"Never in my wildest dreams would I ever have, but now, not only do I believe in them . . . " Claire leaned toward him looking him straight in the eye. "Sweetheart," she said sassily, "I've cast them."

TWENTY-FIVE

The way she looked at him that instant . . . with a smile just the naughty side of wicked . . . he'd have believed her without hesitation.

You will know she speaks the truth.

Chase swallowed hard. Grimaced. Rubbed his chest.

"You honestly believe this?" It was more a remark than question.

"Now I do. Yes," Claire stated for certain. "Sure, I was having dreams that would make a sailor blush." Embarrassed, Claire averted her eyes. "Not just once . . . " Her blood ran hot just thinking about them. "But pretty much the same dream every night. Then I started hearing and seeing an entity the children had been telling me existed all along. Moreover, I found myself having actual conversations with it myself. It took reading those journals all the way through to finally make me realize that I had reincarnated. When I read the letter to Charles telling him of our deaths, well," her voice hitched and filled with emotion, "I felt I was experiencing it all over again. Charles appeared. Held me. It must have taken that deep a trauma to make me remember everything."

Claire could see there were questions clouding Chase's eyes. He regarded her skeptically and opened his mouth to say something, but she cut him off. "Just bear with me a little longer." On a roll, she spoke more quickly wanting to finish before she lost her train of thought.

"When you saw me in Manassas, I had just witnessed the First Battle of Bull Run. The whole thing in all of just a few minutes. I thought it was some re-enactment. I even snapped a whole roll of film. When I went to talk with some of the actors, I realized it wasn't a performance. There were real dead soldiers on that field. I saw bodies scattered as far as I could see. It was horrifying." Claire closed her eyes and tapped her fists against her temples. "I wish I could get the images out of my head, but I can still see the blood and the dismembered limbs. I can smell the gunpowder.

"Then I found Charles. He was cut so badly. I don't know how he survived, but he did. Maybe it was divine intervention. Maybe it was Clarissa's spell.

"When you had the accident, no one thought for a moment you would come through it. The paramedics gave up on you. You had no pulse, had stopped breathing. They tried to shock you back, but it didn't work."

Bracing herself for his reaction, her voice faltered. "Then I saw the scar." Claire gently moved Chase's arms aside and lifted the sheet covering his chest. With the lightest of motions, she traced the whitened trail with her fingertip.

Moaning spontaneously from her feathery touch, Chase closed his eyes. He was certain he could feel the sparks surge directly to his heart while his brain immediately turned to mush.

Chase conjured up just enough breath to mutter, "The scar?" Claire's hand still rested on his body. He treasured its warmth and was in no hurry for her to move it. Even so, he involuntarily tucked his chin into his chest trying to look down, but he was just too stiff and sore.

"This scar isn't from your surgery. I've seen it on Charles so many times in my dreams. And when he's appeared to me. I've touched it. I've committed it to memory. I can't even begin to understand how it could happen. All I know is it's appeared on you. And when I saw this scar . . ." Claire slid a velvety finger along his chest once more sending a swift shiver deep within. "I just knew—no, I *truly believed* with all my heart—Charles had somehow entered your body."

Eyes widening in disbelief, Chase tried to speak—to scoff—but Claire quickly moved her hand to cover his lips with her fingers. The flame extinguished in his chest only to scorch his mouth. "Let me finish," she insisted.

"I know it sounds preposterous," Claire conceded. "*Completely* ludicrous. But I genuinely believed you were Charles. And, by all accounts, you were . . . *dead*."

Chase heard her voice soften to a whisper. A quivering sob threatened to silence her. His soul screamed to comfort, yet he was powerless to utter a word.

Pausing a moment to collect herself, Claire rolled a bedside table across Chase's lap. The hinged top raised to reveal a mirror underneath. She positioned it at just the proper angle for Chase to see his chest.

He could have been looking at the image of a stranger's body. The scar reflected in the mirror was not the neat and tidy healed incision he had left the base hospital with, but the remnants of some hideously barbaric butchery. Chase gaped at the jagged trail then gingerly touched it with his own fingers.

Raising his eyes to anchor on Claire's, Chase remained speechless. He tried to make sense of it all, but couldn't come up with any sane hypothesis.

Sensing his silence as a shift in Chase's reticence, a tentative smile bowed Claire's pallid lips as she clasped his hand in hers drawing it to her own heart. "The paramedics had already pronounced you dead," she repeated. "I was beside myself. I didn't know what to do. I felt so helpless. In my mind, I had lost Charles all over again."

Tears flooded her eyes. Claire swept them away swallowing to clear her throat. "I held . . . you . . . in my arms. All of a sudden, I started chanting. I don't know where the words came from. They just spilled out of my mouth. Over and over. I didn't know what to expect. I just knew I had to try something . . . *anything*. Sure, I don't deny it could have been coincidence you came back on your own. Miracles can happen. In any event," Claire spread her hands in front of her, "here you are."

As his gaze remained locked on hers, Chase drew from her strength. Could he accept such conviction? She truly believed what she was saying. Spell or miracle. Either way, he had survived to live another day.

And the scar? He examined it once more in the mirror. It definitely had changed in appearance. Chase had no way to explain it.

God, his head hurt. He felt one long ache from head to toe. Chase longed to fall asleep so he could wake up again and pass all this nonsense off as a bad dream. He had to decide which was the lesser of two evils:

Stay awake and be captivated by Claire's ridiculous story or endure that blasted recurring nightmare.

He pushed back the pain and forced his eyes to stay open.

Whistling a breath through his teeth, Chase shook his head. "So you're saying I have you to thank for saving my life?"

Claire hitched her shoulder. "I'd never know for certain, but I'd like to think so."

"Huh. I . . . don't know what to say," he said slowly. "I guess . . . thank you . . . would be in order." He grew quiet. Pensive. God, he had . . . *ceased to exist*. It sounded familiar. Ominous.

"Are you okay?"

Chase sighed annoyed by the queasy pressure growing in his chest. "It's kind of a shock to hear you've actually been . . . *dead*. I know I was on a heart-lung machine during the bypass, but that was kind of different."

He suddenly felt so small and insignificant in this vast universe. All his adult life, Chase had been the one in authority. He chose his own direction. Held no one but himself responsible for those choices. Now his self-control was slipping away from him. And deep down, Chase knew he was powerless to stop it.

"I don't think it's so much a fear of dying," he continued hesitantly. "I wouldn't be in the type of job I have if I were afraid." Chase searched for an explanation. To even think was agonizing. He sucked in a deep raspy breath. "Every time I was deployed on a tour of duty. The Gulf. Afghanistan. I was in Iraq when my heart started acting up. Every mission there's always that feeling of . . . I guess it would be . . . *dread* . . . that something may happen that I've got no control over. And now, damn it," he added adamantly, "I'm just not ready to give up whatever little control I've got left."

Regardless of his resolution, a sense of foreboding washed over him. *Time is fleeting. We shall both cease to exist.* Chase couldn't help dwelling on those words. He struggled to remember more of what he had dreamt.

Chase drew his hand over the bizarre scar. He was still having a hard time accepting the possibility of being possessed by a paranormal being. Weren't they considered demonic spirits?

"Shouldn't I be calling a priest to perform an exorcism or something?"

"You think *Charles* is a *demon*?" Claire threw back her head and laughed. "You feel something *evil* inside you?"

It was good to hear her laugh though it miffed him that she would make fun of him. But just for an instant. It was no more than he had done to her.

Smiling himself, Chase hesitated then shook his head. "That's just it. I don't feel *anything*. Shouldn't I feel different . . . like two people?" He rubbed his chest. "Wouldn't I *know* if I had another personality lurking inside me someplace?"

Claire tipped her head and replied seriously. "I wish I could answer that. In my case, I don't consider myself two people. I just remember my past life."

Keeping his eyes on Claire's, Chase was fascinated by what he saw there. Dreams of days long ago mingled with despondency of the present and hope for the future. Did she hope that her future would involve him?

"What if we called Rudy?" Claire suggested. "Maybe he could hypnotize you and see . . . "

"If your dead husband is rattling around in my head somewhere?" Chase cut in more sarcastically than he intended. "I'm not so sure I'm ready for that."

"I'm sorry." His words stung even though she sensed Chase was on the verge of believing. So close that she longed to take him by the shoulders and give him a good shake to hurry him up. But she couldn't be impatient. Claire could understand he would have difficulty accepting such a concept. She certainly took her own sweet time doing so.

Smiling, Claire stroked his arm soothingly but there was no joy behind it. Yet the spot she touched threatened to catch fire.

Chase could see disappointment etched in her face. But he, too, was disheartened. He had traveled all this way to suggest making a life together. Chase sighed and finally spoke aloud the thoughts he harbored for so many miles. "Is the thought of being with me so unbearable?"

Claire was caught off guard by the question but recovered quickly. "Oh, Chase, of course not." She spoke the words credibly enough, but Chase heard no conviction in her voice.

To snuff the flame that was about to ignite, he stilled her hand under his own. It did nothing to quell his increasing affection for her. This woman seemed to be everything he dreamt about. Everything he needed.

"I could provide for you," he offered sincerely. "And for the children. I could love you with all my heart."

"I've no doubt of it." Her voice trailed off. "But . . . "

"I know," Chase said with a hint of bitterness. "Your heart belongs to another."

Catching her breath, Claire stammered, "How . . . how did you know I was going to say that?"

"Clarissa beat you to it."

"Clarissa appeared in your dreams, too?"

"Either her or . . . Was it you? If you're supposed to be this Clarissa person, don't you know you've been messing with my head?"

She sat back trying to recall some little inkling that might lead her to think she had a part in Chase's dreams, but couldn't come up with anything. "Clarissa must still have some latent powers of her own. But you seem to be remembering more," Claire prompted gently.

"Bits and pieces seem to pop up now and again," Chase admitted guardedly.

Our family. Yours and mine.

Startled, he glanced around fully expecting to find someone whispering in his ear. His brow puckered, voice faltered. "Bits and pieces out of nowhere." The fluttering of his heart, twitching and churning inside, unnerved him. How the hell was he supposed to handle this? With all the resolve he could muster, Chase tried to bury the peculiar anxiety but failed miserably.

Yellow roses, the laughter of children at play, muddy trenches, thundering hooves, rat-infested prisons, hunger, pain.

Chase couldn't escape the chaotic confusion pervading his thoughts.

We're coming to the end. Time is fleeting. We must become one.

Focused at the center of all the turmoil—the one saving grace.

Claire.

I know what I want.

Reaching to tuck an errant curl behind her ear, Chase challenged Claire's heart. "Tell me something." He spoke hopefully. "If this *husband* of yours . . . If Charles were lost to you forever, could you love me for the person I am?"

She countered with a question of her own. "If I said yes, would you believe me or think I was just saying it because I'm convinced you're hosting Charles' spirit?"

"Touché." Chase pouted, but just for a moment.

She and I are one as you and he will be.

The words echoed. His voice brightened masking the pressure building in his chest. "So I guess if this Charles of yours and I are supposed to somehow become one person, that would already make you *my* wife, too?"

With a smile, Claire tilted her head and nodded. "So it would seem."

"Okay. Then just for the sake of argument, let's say I'm inclined to believe this foolishness."

Consequences.

"What happens next?"

On impulse, she leaned toward him. With her eyes fastened to his, Claire traced the scar. Chase was positive flames flickered from her fingertips.

Then her sultry mouth was on his. The sensation took him by surprise.

Claire pulled back and watched his eyes alter with awareness. In Claire's dark, broody eyes, Chase was sure he caught a flash of triumph. She knew. Moreover, she knew he knew. She stepped forward once more to murmur softly into his ear. He heard nothing but the deafening drumming of his own blood beating wildly, savagely, in his mind, soul, loins. Had she been chanting the most fearsome incantation, he'd have been no less spellbound.

Chase forced breath back into his lungs. Claire's kiss had depleted every cubic milliliter. Though he definitely wasn't complaining. "What did you say to me?" He rubbed his hand over his eyes to clear his blurry vision. And make sure his face had not melted clean off. "My mind was definitely elsewhere."

"I said," she repeated bewitchingly, "that it would be a pleasure to get to know you." Her breath, just above a whisper, blistered his ear. Chase could have sworn he detected a sulphuric flavor as her mouth once again possessed his.

Chase blew out one long consummating wave of hot breath. He shuddered stiffly fighting for air. Fought to overcome the excruciating misery devouring his mortality.

But it was too great. Too much to bear.

The time had come to make his final choice. If he chose to believe that he was somehow linked with the spirit of Charles Montgomery, he'd have to trust Charles would be true to his word and allow him to be part of a new existence.

Love me, love my children.

Chase realized the futility of resisting this woman he had waited for all his life. He could have her. He could have it all.

Love trusts.

He could let go.

His lips still tingled as Claire released him.

Throat parched, he panted, "My *God*, woman. You *could* raise the dead."

That *voice*. Claire leapt back. Astonished, the name stuck in her throat. "Charles?" she gasped reaching toward him, yet not quite daring to touch his face.

He smiled up at her. "Yes, my love."

Claire flung her arms around his neck. Intravenous lines, monitor leads be damned. "Oh, my darling." Holding him tightly, tears flowed freely. "But . . . How . . . ?"

"You kissed him once. Do you honestly think I was going to allow him an encore?"

First wiping her own face with the corner of his sheet, Claire dabbed dry her tears from his. "I truly believed I was kissing *you*," she sniffled joyously.

He enjoyed her angst only for a moment. "I certainly hope so, my dear." Heartily, he laughed aloud. "A stubborn one, that Chase Tanner.

It was enough of a distraction to his defenses for me to come forward. And just in time, too."

"Why do you say that?" Her brow shot upwards. His fingers soothed it back down again then swept gently along the curve of her cheek.

"I'm sorry, Clarry, but young Tanner's heart was not healthy enough to withstand another seizure."

A pang of sorrow filled Claire's soul. "Oh. Oh, my. I was just getting to know him." A dreadful thought suddenly occurred to her. Agitated, she cried, "My God. I shouldn't have kissed him like that." Her hand flew to cover her mouth. "I *killed* him."

Amusement sparkled in Charles' eyes. "No, Clarry. Your charms are powerful, but, trust me, you're not *that* good." He laughed aloud at the indignant expression that crossed her face.

"You didn't, by any chance . . . *cause* . . . the accident, did you?" She felt uncomfortable asking such a question, but the suspicion would forever prey on her mind if she didn't.

"I assure you, my love, the man was drawing his last breath as I entered his body. He'll live on through me. I've given my word."

"You spoke to him through the dreams." Claire smiled with understanding. "Just like you did with me."

"Well, almost," Charles smiled mischievously. "Not quite so . . . *hands on* . . . so to speak."

"He said you tried to strangle him."

"Had to get his attention."

"It was you who spoke to Rudy and me?"

Reflectively, he nodded. "I tried to break through, but I was just too weak to stay in control." Energy depleted, Charles remained repressed behind Tanner's strong will to survive.

"The feeling was inexplicable, Clarry." He whispered in case someone happened by to overhear. "One second I was with you and Rudy at the house. The next I was lying out there in the rain. I felt like I was being smothered. I couldn't breathe."

A violent shudder wracked his body. He squeezed her hand for comfort. "I was so frightened. I had no idea what had happened. Then I heard your voice pulling me from some terrible darkness deep within." He tenderly kissed her fingertips. "You brought me back, my darling."

"I didn't know what I was doing," Claire admitted solemnly. "Something just came over me. I don't even remember what I said."

"It doesn't matter, my love. Whatever you said, it worked." His eyes misted as he thought of the alternative. Emotionally overwhelmed, his voice broke as he whispered, "Thank you."

Charles pulled her into his arms tightening his embrace. "My greatest fear was existing an eternity without ever seeing you again." His voice cracked. "This was a close second."

Swiping at her own tearful eyes, Claire nestled closely. "I wasn't going to let you get away so easily. Not if I could help it anyway."

For all intents and purposes, Charles would assume the life of Chase Tanner. Two beings occupying the same body, he and Chase were now one.

TWENTY-SIX

Claire reluctantly left Charles to rest while she called to check in with Connie and the children. Rudy was anxiously waiting to hear from her. He dashed out the door before she could hang up the phone. Connie would bring the children in the morning.

The door to his room propped open, Charles happened to notice movement in the hallway. He recognized the surgeon. With his spectacles perched on his nose, Doctor Beaton, an older, more-seasoned man with greying temples, strolled into the room followed by a posse of students. The three youngsters in freshly starched lab coats were new faces.

Charles regarded each of them. A queasiness flipped his stomach as grim faces stared back at him. Something didn't bode well.

"I'll get right to the point." Doctor Beaton began bluntly as he flipped through the chart. "Your test results don't look good."

"That's not possible," Charles simply stated.

With a patronizing glance over the top of his glasses, Doctor Beaton simply ignored him and carried on with his diagnosis. "The initial work-up done when you were admitted after the accident failed to catch a small leak in the sutures connecting the main bypass vein feeding your heart. I'm afraid it's been on a slow drip for quite some time now. If you hadn't been experiencing pain prior to the accident, I might have suspected a tear from one of the broken ribs."

"They're preparing the operating room," a student continued. His short, dark hair reminded Charles of his old horse, Diablo, hot with sweat from a long, vigorous ride.

"Whoa. Just back up a minute." His eyes darted from one to the others. "You're recommending open-heart again?"

Another student cut in. "Fluid is draining into the chest cavity surrounding your heart," he was saying. "If we don't go in to repair it now, it could lead to congestive heart failure."

"The buildup has been causing your pain and shortness of breath," Dr. Beaton concluded.

"Really?" Rejecting their learned evaluation, Charles demonstrated by rapping firmly on his chest. "No pain," he stated emphatically. Took a deep breath for good measure. "Better lung capacity than I've had for years."

Dr. Beaton removed his glasses and regarded him a little more condescendingly than Charles normally would have tolerated. "You can be in denial all you want, Mr. Tanner, but these test results don't lie. You need this surgery. And the sooner, the better," the doctor urged.

"I want a second opinion," Charles demanded.

"Second opinion about what?" Claire had walked in with Rudy close behind.

Charles waved his hand in dismissal. "Oh, they want to open me up again," he explained impatiently. "I told them there was no need. Tell them, Rudy."

Rudy stepped forward. Offering his hand to the doctors, he introduced himself. "Gentlemen, I'm Doctor Rudy Freeman." He reached for Chase's chart and gave it a quick once-over. "If you'd just give us a moment, I'd like to speak with Mr. Tanner."

"We've got the OR booked in two hours. The ultimate decision is his, of course, but I wouldn't be doing my job if I didn't point out how critical this is. See if you can talk some sense into him."

Grinning, Rudy nodded. "I'll see what I can do." Turning to Charles, the smile just kept growing wider until it bloomed into a full-blown laugh. "Claire explained everything. Welcome back, my man."

Charles, still hindered by the intravenous lines, grasped his outstretched hand. "These bells and whistles can come off me now, Rudy. I've no use for them."

"Let's not be in a hurry," Claire suggested gravely.

"Doctors," Charles muttered tersely. "They think they know everything." Then, in retrospect, he added, "No offence, Rudy."

Still chuckling, Rudy fully expected his cheeks to explode, he was so intrigued by Charles. What a case study this would have made. Despite the thousands of witnesses who would be willing to swear they had their own experiences, society as a whole was just not ready to embrace the paranormal reality. Rudy no longer had a burning passion to convince the world. Seeing for himself was satisfaction enough.

"They're not going to find anything, Rudy," Charles stated adamantly. "The heart is not Tanner's. It's healthy once more."

"It wouldn't hurt to have the tests run again," Rudy suggested prudently. "Just for good measure. That way the hospital can cover its ass."

Lips set in a determined line, Charles looked up at Claire who was holding his hand tightly. With an ever-so-slight nod of her head, she silently pleaded for his cooperation. "Oh, all right," he reluctantly consented. "So long as they don't cut me open," he grumbled dryly.

The tests were redone. Stymied by the bewildering results, the cardio team ordered yet another round. Aside from evidence of Chase's bypass surgery and the cracked ribs, there were no other abnormalities.

While they waited for Charles to return to his room, Rudy dragged Claire out into the courtyard for some fresh air. Her eyes, blackened from lack of sleep and worry, closed against the bright sunlight. Finding an empty bench under a weeping willow, Claire slumped herself down. Her head fell wearily into her hands. She sighed heavily. "This has just been too much to take in."

Rudy rubbed her back comfortingly. "You've had to deal with a lot in a short period of time," he consoled.

"He looks so . . . *different*," Claire confided. "I know it's Charles, but . . . I don't know. I guess I feel like a . . . *bigamist*. There's two men in there." She giggled in spite of herself.

"You know, Claire, you don't have to do anything you're not comfortable with. No one's going to hold you to anything. You're not committed to spend the rest of your life with . . . "

"Oh, I know that, Rudy. My brain's telling me not to rush into anything but my heart's telling me I'm Charles' wife no matter how you look at it." Her voice faded away. "It's the children I'm worried about."

Rudy could understand her anxiety. Billy and Maggie had just recently lost their own father. Then Charles whom they had grown to love. Now they would be expected to accept this bizarre transfiguration.

"Kids have this wonderfully amazing ability to roll with the punches," Rudy projected wisely. "They were the ones who tried to convince you that a ghost was living in your attic. They're smart. Let's give them a little credit."

※　　　※　　　※

Exhausted from the battery of examinations, Charles was returned to his room where Claire and Rudy nervously waited.

Pushing Charles' wheelchair into the room, another doctor greeted them. "I'm Dr. Jeffries. Head of Cardiology." He locked the wheels while Charles crawled back into bed. "Mr. Tanner here has pretty much baffled us," he explained. "I'd say *miracle*, but I'm rather hesitant to admit it. So we're going to go with the best two out of three results and spring him in the morning so long as there's no change in his condition."

To Charles, he said, "The ribs will cause you some grief for a few weeks. And you'll have to get the stitches removed from your arm. But, other than that, you'll be good to go."

Frustrated, Charles asked, "Why not now? You really have no cause to detain me."

Laughing, Dr. Jeffries agreed. "No, this isn't a prison. We're just being cautious."

Fearing a confrontation, Claire stepped up. "Thank you, Doctor. Tomorrow's just fine," she interjected giving Charles' arm a decisive squeeze. "Just to be on the safe side."

"Traitor." Charles muttered the lighthearted accusation when Dr. Jeffries was out of earshot.

But when he tried to shift to a more comfortable position, his obstinate muscles rebelled. "I haven't felt this sore in . . . a few years." His body hurt. It was irritating. But it felt . . . *human*. With a pathetic groan, he begrudgingly relented. "Maybe one more night isn't such a bad idea."

"Traitor, eh?" Claire winked at Rudy. "Maybe doctors do know something after all."

"I'm sure they were all first in their classes," Charles sneered haughtily.

"Well, not all of them," Rudy laughed. "Some of us scraped through by the grace of God."

"Then we'll thank God you were here for us," Claire said sincerely. "I'm not sure what we would have done without you."

Rudy dismissed the praise. "I can't take any credit. Believe me, this has been a learning experience for all of us."

So many coincidences contributed to the phenomena playing out the way they did. Above all . . . faith. Faith in an undying love strong enough to span time eternal.

Charles laid his head back and closed his eyes. Rudy took that as his cue to leave.

Worried that he was hiding something from her, Claire asked once more, "Are you sure you're all right?"

"Remember when I fell off the roof of the house? That day the rain was so heavy we ran out of pails to catch all the leaks?"

"I thought you had broken every bone in your body."

"Sure felt like it," he agreed. "I'm fine, Clarry. Just sore," Charles yawned. Fatigue overwhelmed him. "And *tired*."

Claire straightened his blankets. "You should get some rest," she urged.

Charles shook his head. "We've lost too much time already."

Stretching out beside him, Claire cradled him in her arms. Stroking his forehead, she soothed his fears. "Sleep, my darling. We have all the time in the world."

❄   ❄   ❄

Morning dawned bright and beautiful. Charles was anxious to escape and go home with his family. The monitors were disconnected. The intravenous lines removed from his veins. He stared at the bruises the needles left on the backs of his hands. "All this fuss and bother for a few nicks and scrapes."

"Just imagine how many lives this fuss and bother would have saved years ago," Claire reminded him. "Not to mention the morphine you fell in love with."

Charles sighed with profound pleasure. "Maybe they'll let me take some home with me."

"Don't count on it," Claire laughed. "I don't want to have to deal with an addict on top of everything else."

He playfully tweaked her chin. "Don't fret so, my love. What do you have to worry your pretty little head about other than planning the perfect wedding?"

"And where would you like me to start?"

Charles could see by the creases in her forehead that she was very serious. He hated to see her so uneasy and would move heaven and earth to allay her fears. He pulled her towards him patting the side of the bed. It was his turn to comfort. "What bothers you the most, my love?"

She nuzzled her nose into his neck. A familiar gesture of closeness she cherished. "How are we going to explain this to his family?" Claire wondered apprehensively.

"We're not even going to try," Charles replied. "It's such a strange feeling, Clarry. I know all about the man."

Quirking a brow, she sounded dubious. "Everything?"

"Just like you knew of Clarissa."

"But this situation isn't quite the same."

Reassuringly, Charles patted her hand. "I know, my love," he agreed. "We'll just have to work it out the best we can, Clarry. I guaranteed Tanner would not lose his identity. But I must remain in control. If he comes forward, we may both die."

Something more to worry about. Claire wondered if it would ever end. "How can you stop him from emerging? Wouldn't your healthy heart support him, too?"

"I don't know that, Clarry. We can't take the chance. I'll just have to stay strong and not let down my guard. So . . . from now on . . . we must make a concerted effort to lead his life. I must keep my promise. I must become Chase Tanner."

"But you talk so differently from Chase. More formal speech. Your mannerisms. Body language."

"I'm sure I can learn a Texan accent." Charles cleared his throat and attempted to impersonate Chase's voice. "Speak more crassly . . . like a Marine," he barked. "Try to be like Tanner. And we must refer to him in the first person. Starting right now."

Noticing Claire's dismayed expression, he ran his hand affectionately through her silken curls. "Don't dredge up trouble before it happens, Clarry. No one will notice. Tanner will guide me."

Claire still wasn't convinced. "What if I slip up and call you Charles instead of Chase?"

"No matter. His legal name is Charles. His father is Charles Senior. They called him Chase to distinguish between them."

"So when his mom yelled they knew which one of them was in trouble?"

Charles laughed. "You've got it. So, if you call me Charles instead, everyone will just think I've done something to annoy you." Then Charles smiled, a leisurely, lazy curling of lips that never failed to set her insides all aflutter and obliterate any rational thought. He always had that effect on her even in a stranger's body.

❋   ❋   ❋

Chase Tanner had three siblings. Two brothers, one there in Virginia, the other in Michigan. A sister in Georgia. All born and raised in the Texan cattle country not far outside Austin.

Tanner had no wife, ex-wives or children. No competition. No sibling rivalry other than between her own two kids. That would certainly make it much easier when he showed up with a complete, ready-made family.

Claire had gone from her little one-parent family of three to more in-laws than she could count. "Do you think they'll accept us?" she asked anxiously. "You know, some parents don't think much of their sons marrying single moms with kids."

"You worry too much." With a comforting chuckle, Charles held her hand to his lips. "My dear, who wouldn't love you? Mom is going to be so tickled pink to have more grandchildren to spoil. And she's going to adore you. Otherwise she wouldn't have tried so hard to get me to come back to see if I could find you. But you'll have to watch her. She'll try to feed you to death.

"Angie . . . who knows? She's female. As for Rick and Tyler, my charming brothers? Blatant womanizers, the pair of them. Quite frankly, I'm going to have to keep a real close eye on those two.

"Dad's pretty quiet. Probably won't say too much. But if he offers to fix something for you, you'll know you're a hit."

"Well, I'm looking forward to meeting everyone." Claire tried to sound optimistic. "Hope I can remember everyone's names." She snuggled closer relishing his warmth.

"Be patient, Clarry. No one will expect you to know everything about them right off," Charles assured her. And he, himself, would have to make a concerted effort to sort out Tanner's life from his own past. He wouldn't want to make the mistake of bringing up something from another century.

"What else can you tell me?"

"You already know some from the medical file. *I*," Charles emphasized, "am a major in the military. The Marines."

"Hmmm, a promotion from captain. Why couldn't you have gone into banking like your father? Something simple. And safe."

"Where's the excitement in that?" Charles joked with a twinkle in his eye. "I'm a 'go-forth-and-conquer' kind of fellow." A low growl rumbled deep in Charles' throat as he nuzzled his lips deeply into the curve of her neck drinking in her delectable scent. "Each and every conquest is pure delight, my love. I can't wait for the next."

Laughing, Claire tried to wiggle away. "You must be feeling better." She slapped his hand as he tried to sneak it up the front of her shirt. "Behave, you. Tell me some more. How are you going to explain how we met?"

"I guess we can't very well go with the truth." He thought for a moment. "I'm sure Mom has already told everyone you're the mad woman I met at Manassas."

"Oh, that's just *great*," Claire groaned indignantly. "That'll make a good impression, I'm sure."

"Mom knows about your fall and hitting your head. She was sympathetic," Charles assured her. "Clucked like an old mother hen." He remembered the park. "What a sight you were, covered in mud and all. You . . . ," he chuckled in spite of himself, ". . . really were a mess," but groaned as the effort pulled at various strained muscles.

"You're going to be pretty stiff and sore for quite a while, I imagine." Claire gently massaged his chest and arms provoking a surge of searing heat through every quadrant of his body.

Charles eyed her wickedly. "Keep that up and I'll show you just how stiff I can get."

301

"Be serious." Claire rolled away to put a little distance between them.

"Believe me, I am." Sobering, Charles threw up his hands in defeat as her keep-your-hands-off-me look squinted back at him. "Okay, we'll think about something else." Rolling his eyes to the ceiling, Charles tapped his finger against his chin. "Nope. Not working. All I want is your naked body in this bed with me." He flipped up the sheet then, just as quickly, flung it back down again.

A somber cloud threatened his humor. "What about the way I look? Do you find this Tanner person's body attractive? I know you miss the mustache, but I can grow that back."

Sidling flirtatiously up to him, Claire lifted the sheet and sneaked an appraising peek underneath. "Well, from what I've seen so far, I'd say he's quite appealing. As long as I know you're in there someplace, I imagine I can grow to tolerate it," she teased. "It'll be like making love to a whole new person."

Charles frowned, eyed her narrowly. "I'm not sure I'm in favor of *that* idea," he muttered miserably.

She couldn't resist the temptation. "Isn't that a man's fantasy? Make love with two women at the same time. I think turn around is fair play, don't you? I could be making love with two men . . . "

"Maybe it's some men's fantasy." He cut her off short. "Certainly not mine. One of you is all I can handle."

TWENTY-SEVEN

"Remember," Rudy warned. "You can't say anything to anyone, Connie." He slathered jam over the quarter inch of peanut butter already spread on the toast.

Huffing indignantly, Connie planted her fists on her generous hips and turned from the sink to stare at him. Her cocked head shook ever so slightly. "Don't you *dare* turn all peacock on me, Rudy Freeman." She tsked her tongue. "I'm the one who told you there was something fishy about that house in the first place."

"I know it. And I also know how you like to gossip with your friends, one-upping each other and all."

"And *who* put Claire in touch with *you*?" She jabbed a chubby finger at her own ample bosom. "I do believe that would be *me*." With feigned disgust, Connie waved him off. "You just go on about your own business now. I've got children to get dressed. Claire will be here in a few minutes."

"I thought you were taking them to the hospital."

"Well, I'm not. She changed her mind. Wanted a bit of time to themselves to get them used to the idea."

Rudy helped himself to another slice of toast. "Makes sense."

"I'm so glad you approve."

But even after driving all the way to the Jenkins' house from Front Royal, Claire wasn't sure how to broach the subject. She still hadn't decided when she pulled into the driveway.

The children met her at the door excited to finally get to go see Charles. Rudy and Connie had said little to them except for what Claire thought best for the moment, that Charles left the house to help a friend and they were in an accident. He was going to be just fine but needed to stay in the hospital for a day or two.

Not knowing how they'd react when they saw him, Claire wanted to take this alone time to explain that Charles would not look the same as he did at home a couple days ago.

"So how come he looks different?" Billy asked.

"Well, that's a pretty hard question to answer. It's complicated and we really don't know ourselves exactly how it happened." An explanation they might be able to understand suddenly dawned on her. "You know in your Scooby-Doo cartoons when a ghost or monster seems to get inside another person and make them do all sorts of funny stuff? Well, it's kind of like that. His friend was sick and Charles went to live in his body to help keep him alive. Now he can be with us for a long, long time."

"What about the friend?"

"He was really hurt, Billy, but he's going to be like a silent partner," Claire said solemnly. "Charles will do all the talking for him now."

Claire checked for traffic, then signaled to turn into the hospital parking lot. "And he'll help Charles know what to do when he has to." She looked over at her frowning son. "Does that help any?"

Billy hitched his shoulder as he scrunched his nose. "I hope he's not a geek."

"No, Billy, he's not a geek. He's actually very handsome."

Maggie asked, "As handsome as Charles?"

"I think so, sweetheart. In his own way. He looks different, but he's still the same Charles inside."

"I know, Mom," Billy piped up. "Let's pretend he's a secret agent and he had to get a new face so he wouldn't get caught by the bad guys." He looked over the back of the seat at his sister. "We can pretend, eh, Mags? It'll be fun."

Billy to the rescue. He was such a bright boy for all his eight years. "That's a great idea. Can we all do that?" Silence from the back seat. "Maggie?" Claire looked in the rear-view mirror at Maggie's sullen face as she peered blindly out the window.

Claire understood it was a lot to pile on Maggie's little shoulders. Now her little girl had to get used to yet another change in her young life. The resilience of youth, Claire kept reminding herself. She sure hoped it was true.

Claire held the door to Charles' room open for them. For all his bravado, Billy balked. Hesitantly, he poked his head through the door quickly scanning the room before spotting a man in the bed.

Not expecting him to stop, Maggie bumped into his back pushing them both into the room. The man who was supposed to be Charles rested with his eyes closed but sat up when he heard the commotion. Maggie gave him a cautious once-over but moved no closer.

"Hey, guys." A broad smile brightened Charles' face. "Come on in."

Taking the children by the hands, Claire all but dragged them to his bedside.

He sounded like Charles, Maggie thought. She quirked her brow and studied the man more closely.

"It's okay, *Bijou*. You don't have to be afraid. It's me." Charles winked at her. He opened his arms wide inviting them both in.

That's all it took. The children clambered onto the bed. Enveloping them both at once in his strong embrace, Charles kissed each fondly. "Oh, my darlings," was all he could muster before the tears flowed down his cheeks. Rocking back and forth, he cradled Billy and Maggie as they desperately clung to him.

Maggie sniffed loudly as she fought back her own tears. Swiping the sleeve of her sweater under her runny little nose, she whispered haltingly, "You're going to be my daddy now, right?"

"Yes, Margaret, I am." Charles stroked her thin sun-bronzed arms.

"Will we be Tanners, too?" Claire had told them they would have to get used to calling Charles by the name of Chase Tanner instead of Charles Montgomery.

Charles beamed at his little girl. "Would you like that, Margaret?" Her curly head bobbed emphatically. Legally adopting the children would seem the most logical thing to do. Unless Claire had some reason against it, there was no one to object.

"What do you think, William?"

Billy threw up his hands in exasperation. "Will it stop you calling me *William*?" he pleaded hopefully.

With a laugh, Charles shook his head. "Probably not."

"Can we make a deal then? Can you *please* call me Billy when my friends come over?"

Old habits were hard to break. After all, he had called him William for so many years. But Charles would do just about anything at this point to make him happy. "Deal. I'll do my best to remember. Forgive me if I might slip from time to time. I am an old man, you know."

Billy giggled as he rolled his eyes. "Are you ever!"

Wiggling out of Charles' arms, Maggie drew herself up so she could look at him directly. "Do we have to call you Chase? Can't we call you Daddy?"

Touched, his heart couldn't have melted any quicker. Charles was hoping that would be the natural progression of living under the same roof, but didn't think it would be this soon. "I'd like that very much."

Claire glanced at Charles. A frown had suddenly wrinkled his brow.

"You okay?" Many horrendous scenarios had played out in her mind over the last couple of days. She had hoped she could put those to rest.

"Yes, I'm fine," Charles assured her with feigned levity. "Better than fine. I'm fantastic." He gently roughhoused with Billy then drew Maggie to him for a resounding kiss on her forehead.

She wasn't convinced. Digging into her purse, Claire pulled out a handful of loose change. "Here, Billy. Take Maggie and get a couple drinks. There's a vending machine in the sun room at the end of the hall. Come right back."

As they disappeared around the corner, a guttural chuckle rumbled in his throat as Charles caught her by the hand and pulled her closer. "Well, my dear. Alone at last."

Claire allowed herself to be pulled into his arms. He brushed soft kisses over her face then buried his face in her hair.

She smelled of bright, sunny days. Cool, fresh breezes. Fragrant roses. He drank in the perfume that was Claire.

Charles tucked her head onto his shoulder, circled his arms comfortably around her. Gradually relaxing against him, she sat in silence. Soothed by the stillness, Claire sank into the solace of his embrace. Yet he seemed restless.

"What's bothering you, Charles?"

Charles hitched his shoulder muttering, "I don't know." His voice cracked which proved he was lying. With a heavy sigh, he came clean. "I worry about how all this will affect you."

Claire tucked his hand into her own, kissed his fingertips. "What do you mean, sweetheart?"

"Well, the children don't seem to have a problem with becoming Tanners," he said. "Do you think you can get used to the name?"

Reassuringly, Claire smiled and patted his hand. "As long as you're in my life, I can be Claire Tanner just as well as Claire LePaige or Clarissa Montgomery. It's just a name."

❊   ❊   ❊

August twenty-fifth. It was a good day. Claire had remembered even after all these years. Waiting for them at the house was a cake. A welcome-home cake. A birthday cake. Charles' birthday.

"There wasn't room for a hundred and seventy-six candles, so we settled for one big sparkler."

"The biggest one we could find," Maggie chirped happily.

Amazingly, neither child had ever questioned again why Charles looked differently than he did a couple days ago. He was just Charles. Maybe their innocent acceptance came part and parcel with the original spell Clarissa had chanted so many years ago. And they seemed truly excited about the idea of a new family.

Rudy and the Jenkins family visited briefly for cake and ice cream. Connie had never met Charles in spirit or flesh. She nearly burst from all the questions pent up inside. But to her credit, she did well not to ask any of them within earshot of her husband, Arthur.

To her way of thinking, Connie saved the most important question for Claire when they were alone gathering up plates and glasses from all over the house. The others were outside. While the children played on the river bank, the men watched them and exchanged war stories.

"Child, I would have signed myself into the nut house by now. How are you keeping your sanity around all this?"

"I'm sane?" Claire laughed that nervous little giggle she resorted to whenever she didn't know what else to say right away. "I don't know.

Maybe I *am* crazy. I used to try to convince myself this was all a dream. And now I keep thinking I'm going to wake up back home in my own little bed. And if I woke up and it wasn't real . . . I think my heart just might break right in two."

It took more than a few nudges to get everyone out the door that evening. The children were tucked into their beds played out from a day of celebration. The dishes were washed, dried, and put away. Cake crumbs swept up. Ice cream mopped off the kitchen floor. She and Charles were alone. And Claire was nervous.

He'd be waiting. Waiting for her to come to him. To give herself to him as she had done so many nights before.

Initially, she had been filled with excited anticipation. Now she was just downright terrified. Terrified that she would not be able to respond to Chase as she had with Charles.

When it came right down to it, Claire hoped that Clarissa's spell would help her accept Charles' new look as easily as the children did. It wasn't that Chase Tanner wasn't attractive. She was sure he had turned his share of heads. And she knew she was being rather silly. But she couldn't shake the feeling that she would be somehow unfaithful to Charles if she . . . *appreciated* . . . Tanner's body.

She could plead exhaustion. She definitely did need sleep, there was no denying that.

Claire had no time to think of another excuse.

He was behind her . . . nuzzling into her back . . . sliding his body into an amazing fit against her. Managing a skittish laugh, Claire tried to slink from his grasp, but only succeeded in making him tighten his hold. Lowering his mouth, he nipped at her jaw. Another nibble, tantalizing and soft. Claire stiffened. Charles stepped back. Swung her around.

"What is it, Clarry? You're trembling."

Her hands shot up to press firmly against his chest. "It's just . . . I don't think . . . "

"Then let's not think." He caught her by the bottom lip. Skimmed his fingertips along her collarbone.

"No, Charles." Claire tried to push him away but it would have been easier to move a brick wall. "You just got out of the hospital. We're both exhausted. I just don't think it's a good thing. Not tonight."

Charles eyed her narrowly, then to her complete chagrin, threw back his head and laughed. "Always looking out for my welfare, aren't you, my darling? Feeling it would be completely irresponsible of you to come upstairs and have your way with me?"

The sudden gleam in his eyes had her resolve wavering. "Well . . . I . . . You just . . . "

"Didn't your Grandmama ever teach you that you should never say no to your husband?" Recklessly capturing her mouth, Charles reveled in the taste of her. His intension was only to taste, to treasure the moment, but it quickly ran beyond any good intention.

His kiss. Scalding. Skillful. Claire moaned, her world tilting precariously. Even as she slid toward surrender, Claire twisted her fingers in the front of Charles' shirt and held fast.

He whispered something. Claire didn't know what. The blood pounding in her ears drowned out all sound.

Pulling away, Charles waited for her eyes to open. To focus. When they did, the look in her eyes . . . glazed with a fusion of turmoil and delight . . . nearly knocked him to his knees.

And as he drew away, Claire lifted her hand to her burning lips. How could a kiss be so tender and searing at the same time? She cleared her throat. "I can't breathe."

"I'm a mite breathless myself."

"What a kiss!" Lightheaded, she giggled.

Charles agreed wholeheartedly. "It was a *great* kiss. If one of us were a toad, there could have been serious trouble."

Temptation enveloped her. Claire's reservations vanished.

"Make love with me, my darling. Tonight. Right here." He munched eagerly at the nape of her neck gliding her to the floor in one fluid motion.

"Mmmm." She all but gave in then suddenly bolted upright. "Here? On the kitchen floor?"

Her reaction amused him, but Charles refused to let the mood be shattered. His mouth explored her face. He repeated gently, "Right here, my love. On the kitchen floor."

"What if . . . the children . . . "

"The children are asleep." His hands moved over her body. His lips followed.

The floor was so cool. Invitingly cool. And the heat from his body was intoxicating. "I need you, Clarry. I'll need you forever."

Claire opened her mouth to vainly protest but whispered promises silenced her. The tenderness of his touch stole any sense of modesty. His stroking hands heated her skin to a feverish pitch.

Suddenly there was nobody else in the entire world but the two of them.

Slipping off her shoes, Charles flitted a finger along the arch of her bare foot. The tickle entrapped the breath in her throat. Swallowing proved difficult.

"You've such pretty feet." Offhandedly, he said it, with laughter in his voice as he began to nibble her toes. The breath that was trapped burst out, her fingernails piercing his back like talons.

The electricity drizzled through her veins until everything inside her tingled. Charles leisurely worked kisses up the side of her neck to her cheek. His mouth skirted hers, teasing, awakening the hunger of her own desires.

Sliding her hands up his back, Claire dreamily curved her body to his. Her head fell back in surrender.

The sound of her sighs filled his head. The kisses grew longer. More intense. His tongue devoured her taste, sweet and feminine. Unequivocally perfect.

Charles worked himself out of his shirt. As her hands wandered over his back, kneaded his rigid muscles, a low sound of enjoyment rumbled in her throat.

His heart skipped a beat or two. Maybe more. Those leisurely timid strokes of her hands were exhilarating. Incredible.

Claire languidly allowed Charles to undress her. Let his hands trace and dawdle where they pleased. He showered her skin with slow tenderhearted kisses that sent it quivering.

Claire lost herself in her husband taking delight in a lightheaded blend of sensations and wonderment. Her body began to rock. Taking control of the pace, Claire took pleasure in his body as he matched her rhythm.

She felt him thrust helplessly. Listened as his breath suppressed a gasp. Then, carried away with her effect on him, allowed herself liberation until the splendor of it flared through her.

"Charles." His name moaned through Claire's lips as he coaxed her up to that first rippling summit. So intense was her release . . . so unexpected . . . that her earlier hesitation instantly erupted into tiny, little particles of spent energy and simply evaporated from her thought.

Charles did say she worried too much.

TWENTY-EIGHT

Claire was concerned that maybe they were trying to cram too much into such a short time. A birthday party, wedding, packing. And a long drive back to Canada. But Charles insisted he was up to the challenge.

Connie would take care of the arrangements for them to buy back their house which they would use on vacation for the time being, then as a retirement home once Charles resigned from service.

The whole formality of the real estate process irked Charles. It was their property. Always had been. Why should he have to buy back his own home? But it could be bought for a wink and a whistle. They did have the gold which would ease many burdens and give them a comfortable life once they could exchange it for useable money. Claire had already contacted a number of rare coin dealers.

Closing up a house for the winter was no easy chore. Getting a head start packing away a few things, Claire busily puttered here and there. Overhead in the attic, Charles was making a clatter rummaging around. Hearing a strange thumping noise, Claire went to investigate. She soon found it was Charles dragging something down the narrow attic stairs. The heavy wooden crate bounced as it hit step by step.

"Broken ribs, remember? Stitches in your arm. Let me help."

Shaking his head, Charles replied breathlessly, "I can manage."

Hefting the box into his arms, he waddled under its weight to their room. "God bless the inventor of cardboard."

"Stubborn man. You shouldn't be lifting that!" she scolded.

"Out of my way, woman, before this thing falls on the both of us."

"Well, don't use up all your strength," Claire whispered seductively. "I'm going to want some of that later." Playfully, she sidled up next to him nipping at his earlobe.

Unceremoniously, he dumped the crate on the bed. "Recognize this?" Charles asked tenderly as he pried off the lid and stepped back.

Hands cupping his face, Claire planted a loving kiss on his lips after she dug deeply through layers of tissue and discovered the treasure buried beneath. "I never thought I'd ever see this again," she squealed with delight. Although tinged ivory with age, the gown she lifted from the crate had survived the years. Yard upon yard of silk and lace was still soft and supple. "I can't believe you saved it. It never even occurred to me to ask. I just assumed it was long gone."

"It was well hidden."

"Ah, the secret nooks and crannies. Simon was a genius, wasn't he?"

Under her gown and enormous mounds of crinoline, lay the very same uniform Charles wore at the officer's ball just before he left for war almost a century and a half ago. Still crisp and unspoiled, the wool miraculously hadn't faded or been infested by moths. Tucked at the side of the box was his ceremonial sword, a gift from his father.

Claire grew pensive as she lightly slid a finger down the sterling blade. "Will this all be here next time?" she whispered softly. "Will there be a next time?"

"We can only trust, my love, that there will be."

Claire quickly changed the subject before her bottom lip had a chance to start trembling. "I'm sorry your parents aren't feeling up to coming for the wedding. Are they disappointed?"

"They've been to three. Missing one won't hurt them. Anyway, they said we can make it up to them. They want to throw us a good old fashioned Texan shindig even though they've deserted to Arizona. Show you off to all their friends."

"That sounds like fun. Maybe we can go over the Christmas break."

"We could," Charles agreed. "Or we could go to Arizona now before we head back to Canada."

Trying to work it through in her head, Claire carefully set the sword on the bed. "I'm sure it's the right thing to do, Charles, but it's Maggie's first day of school," she said quietly. "She'll be so disappointed. It's been all she's talked about the past year."

"She'll still have a first day. It just won't be this Tuesday." Drawing her hand to his lips, Charles then switched his attention from her fingers to that sensitive spot just below her ear. He could feel her knees slacken as he knew they would. It made him grin and tilt his head to gaze adoringly down at her.

Knowing full well what he was about, Claire cursed herself for being so predictable. A nibble anywhere in that general vicinity of her neck and she would rarely refuse him anything. And now her legs wouldn't move.

Billy would be okay being a little late back to school, she had no doubt. She wasn't so sure about Maggie. "Let's talk with them," Claire suggested breathlessly. She leaned her back against him. "We won't leave a decision like that up to the children, but I want to discuss it with them."

Weaving romantic notions around in her head, Claire felt her temperature rise. It was her own fault. He stirred something in her that no one else ever could and she hadn't the sense to move out of his reach. "I'm sure we can entice them to want to meet their new grandparents."

"We can fly." Charles loosened the buttons of her blouse pulling the neck of it back. His lips flitted across her shoulder. "Have they ever been on a plane?"

"No, they haven't." Her head dropped back while a purr escaped her lips. "Maybe that will be just the ticket."

Then she smiled lovingly at him. "Move the box."

They hadn't heard the vehicles pull up the drive. Two minivans and a Ford Explorer. The incessant pounding on the door startled them.

The children ran from the attic. Claire pulled her hands out of the dishwater and caught the drips on the kitchen towel. Charles peeked out the window then threw open the door. One by one, they converged. All six of them.

"Well, I'll be damned. Look what the cat dragged in," he shouted in delight. "Clarry, come see who's here."

"I know, Chase. I know. We should have called . . . " Rick began.

"But we wanted to surprise you," Tyler finished.

"Well, a surprise it is," Charles laughed, grabbing at hands, slapping at backs. Angie and the sisters-in-law got a peck on the cheek and hug.

Time for the acid test. They knew it would happen sooner or later. A little more practice would have been good. He'd have to rely on Chase to pull this off.

"It's good to see all of you." His greeting was genuine, but he'd forgotten the Texan accent. Glancing from face to face, he realized it had gone unnoticed in all the commotion.

Angie muscled her way over to plant herself in front of him. She examined his face studying each bruise and scratch. "Mom said you had an accident."

"Yup. Totaled the old Jeep."

"You okay? We promised we'd make sure you were okay. They can't come see for themselves, you know."

"Didn't expect them to." Hitching his shoulder, Charles made light of the injuries. "A few stitches, a couple cracked ribs. Nothing I can't handle. Going to miss that Jeep, though. It was a classic."

"It was ready for the museum, that's what it was," Rick laughed. "I still think you stole it from the motor pool."

"Well," Angie broke in. "Since Mom and Dad can't be here for the wedding, we're representing the clan. Farmed the kids out so they won't be underfoot."

"So *we* could have a good time for once," Leanne chimed in.

"Couldn't have our baby brother jumping into the fire without us here to give him a little shove." Tyler punched his arm. Hard.

"We just wanted to see for ourselves," Allan said. "Make sure you actually went through with it."

"Should have happened sooner as far as I'm concerned," Nicole muttered.

Tyler cracked. "I'm surprised it's happening at all."

Charles cocked his head toward the kitchen and winked. "Believe me, it was worth the wait." He grinned as Claire came out of the kitchen.

With second nature, she lifted her hand to make sure her hair was still tidy. Presentable for company. A familiar gesture that made Charles fancy mussing it all up again.

Rick nearly choked. "Definitely worth the wait," he repeated just under his breath. First reaction? He was as stunned as she was lovely. Refined. Pure class. Out of his brother's league to be sure. How the hell did *he* end up with *her*?

They all started toward her at once. Caught off guard, Claire barely had time to react before she was engulfed by arms. So many arms and just as many lips. An experience she wasn't at all used to.

Charles quickly came to her rescue. "Back off, you maniacs," Charles ordered as he eased Claire from the fracas. "You're smothering the poor woman."

"Just getting to know our new sister-in-law." Tyler gave her an appraising once over.

"Well, at least let me introduce you before you have your way with her." To Claire, he whispered loudly enough to be heard by them all, "Didn't I warn you about the brothers?"

"Hey!"

Claire laughed at the offended expressions on the men's faces. With a chance to get her wits about her, she relaxed and held out her hand to each in turn as Charles rhymed off their names. "My sister, Angie. Allan. Tyler and Leanne. Rick and Nicole."

Lost in the shuffle, Billy and Maggie squeezed through the maze of bodies. "Hey, everyone," Charles called to get their attention as he took the children by their hands. "Here's Billy and Maggie." Charles winked at them. It would be hard. He was sure he'd slip up. But he'd try to keep his promise to Billy.

Two surprised children stared back at him. Billy couldn't believe his ears. "*Yes,*" he shouted pulling his fist triumphantly through the air.

The women took to the kitchen to get acquainted with Claire and the children. The men ventured out to the veranda.

Allan cut right to the chase. "Hey, what about that blushing bride of yours?" He looked around for Angie as if Charles would reveal some sultry secret.

Shaking his head, Rick added, "I can't believe you actually found someone to agree to marry the likes of you."

"Mom said you found her in a park."

"Yeah. Manassas. I followed her home."

Rick and Tyler exchanged astounded looks. "And she didn't have you arrested?" They shook their heads. "Silly, silly girl."

Claire brought out a tray of sandwiches and lemonade and set it down on the veranda floor beside Charles' chair.

"Ah, bless you, Claire." Tyler dove for a salmon. Patting his rounded belly, he groaned, "I'm near enough to wasting away."

Not knowing him well enough for what she'd like to come back with, Claire's lips twitched trying to restrain the giggle. "I can see that. A mere shadow of your former magnificent self, to be sure." She bent to graze a quick kiss along Charles' forehead. "Let me know if you'd like anything else."

"Don't you have any beer?" Tyler shamelessly asked frowning toward the lemonade.

Struck by his boldness, Claire found it comical. With just enough muscle behind it to make Tyler sit up and take notice, Claire patted him sharply on the cheek. "We didn't know you were coming now, did we?" She smiled mischievously. "But I'm sure I could conjure up something else, if you'd rather."

Envisioning both brothers in a state less than human, Charles quickly took Claire by the hand and drew her away. "Lemonade's just fine, sweetheart. Thank you."

Claire sashayed to the door, then flashed Tyler an amused glance over her shoulder. With a wink, she disappeared.

Instantly entranced, Tyler nearly choked on his sandwich. "Oh, Chase," he wheezed, "you're going to have your hands full with that one."

"And she's all mine, you old reprobate. You'll do well to remember that."

Rick stood and peered up into the mountains. There was a hint of fall in the air. A brightly colored leaf here and there. The promise of beauty to come.

They were a closely knit family despite being spread out over half the country. And a squabble here and there never caused any long-lasting rift. Chase had thrashed him on more than one occasion. He'd chance a fist wouldn't find his face.

They had all discussed it the night before at the motel. Even so, he was hesitant to bring it up. Rick didn't turn around as he spoke for them all. "Seriously, though, Chase. Don't you think you're moving just a little too fast? You've only known her for . . . what . . . all of two minutes?"

In another lifetime, the brother's mistrust of Chase's judgement would have sparked a brawl. More mature, Charles pushed back Tanner's combative instinct. "I know it seems like that. But I feel I've known her all my life. Okay," he conceded thinking they'd be expecting some kind of Chase-worthy rationale. "I know my life was just fine the way it was. Or so I thought. Until I found what I was missing."

"And you think it's this woman? What do you really know about her?"

"All I need to know." That the sun rose and set in her smile. In her touch. That a day without her by his side was sheer torture. "Everything I need to know."

Rick wasn't getting through to him. "But wouldn't it be best to give it a bit of time before jumping in head first? Chase, you're our brother. We just want you to be happy."

"I've plans to stay that way."

"But . . . "

Growing tired of the negativity, Charles quickly cut Rick off. "No buts. That's the end of it. Be happy for me or go the hell home." He was sure they meant well, but they'd just have to give it up. Nothing could dissuade him from legally taking Claire as his wife.

Death couldn't stop him. These mere mortals weren't about to.

Knowing better than to get between the two, Tyler sat back hoping to enjoy a free-for-all that didn't happen. Happily chewing away on his sandwich, he swallowed and washed it down with the tart drink. Puckering his face, he wished there was something a little more potent mixed in with it to make it drinkable.

The door creaked as Billy inched it open. His face awash with sheer boredom, he slipped through the crack onto the veranda.

"Come on out and join the men, son."

Billy silenced Charles with a wave of his hand. "Shhh. I don't want them to come looking for me." He glanced nervously over his shoulder and whispered, "I can't stand it in there. It's awful. Nothing but stupid *girl* talk. Now they want me to wear a suit. *And* be nice to Maggie."

The women helped Claire pull together a simple wedding. With a few flowery garlands, two or three potted plants and a candle here and there, their small parlor was transformed into a romantic chapel.

A crunch of gravel told them Rudy had arrived with the Justice.

The children were scrubbed and dressed. Maggie looked adorable in a simple pale yellow sun dress while Billy acted quite the little gentleman in a borrowed navy suit from one of Connie's boys.

And Charles had warned him. No stunts like he pulled last week to spoil this day for his mother. No frogs or worms down the back of Maggie's dress.

Charles looked dashing dressed in his Confederate uniform. Undoubtedly it would raise an eyebrow or two in the family. They were beyond caring at this point. They'd take it as it came. Make it up along the way when they had to. One day at a time.

Straightening the golden braid through the fringed epaulet on his shoulder, Charles turned as he sensed movement behind him. His heart skipped a beat as he witnessed the vision of loveliness before him.

In the same gown she wore so many years before, Claire radiated genuine beauty. Beauty of the eternal soul. A bouquet of yellow roses cut from her garden completed the vision.

Hair piled in ebony curls atop her head, Claire could have stepped out of the exact photograph taken at their wedding over a century ago. Yet something was different and he just couldn't put his finger on it.

Claire followed his gaze downward. With his brow sharply arched, she could tell he was trying to figure out what wasn't quite right. "It's the crinolines," she finally admitted with an apologetic sigh. "I'm sorry. I know you wanted it just like the first time, but the crinolines had to go." Her pout was sorrowful, yet the twinkle in her eye held no remorse.

Amusement softened his face. "It's a beautiful gown either way, my love." He tenderly kissed the tip of her nose. "And you make it even more beautiful. It's a brand new life we're headed into. Full of wonders and surprises. We'll make new memories."

Charles reached for his bride's hand and drew her towards him. Eyes misting as she graced him with a loving smile, Charles would be forever thankful for every minute he was forced to exist without her if it meant another chance at a full lifetime together.

Suddenly he swept her up in his arms and muffled her surprised gasp with his mouth. Carrying her down the old servants' staircase,

Charles evaded their guests and snuck out the back door. Setting her down, he took her by the hand and hustled her toward the river.

"They'll be looking for us, Charles." Her sandals slipped on the dewy grass.

"We've got a minute." He steadied her as they hurried down the bank where the hammock rocked gently in the morning breeze. The pungent odor of the cedars clung in the air.

"You're not about to muss me all up, are you?" The thought intrigued and irritated her at the same time.

"That would be my first choice." The smile he sent her was meant to charm, but all he got back was a shriveling glare. Amused more than disappointed, he cleared his throat. "But . . . no. I just needed to talk with you alone. Without being interrupted."

Charles pulled a tiny blue velvet box from his pocket. "I didn't have a chance to buy you a new ring. I guess this will have do." Opening it, he was delighted by the surprise he saw in her eyes.

"*My ring*," she squealed. The very ring he had slipped on her finger so many years ago. The sparkling blue sapphire his father, William, had given his mother, then made a present of it to Charles for their own wedding.

Tempted to snatch the box from his hand, it took all the restraint Claire could muster to simply reach out and touch it with her finger. Make sure it was real. "Aren't you just full of wonders?"

"I didn't want to take you unawares in front of everyone."

"And smart, too." She jumped when Charles snapped the velvet box shut and tucked it away.

"There's just one more thing that needs doing before we go back in." He reached behind the cedar tree where he had stashed a bottle of wine and two crystal goblets.

"What's this?"

His face lit up in a devilish grin as he poured rosy red wine into the glasses. "Just a little pre-wedding toast."

Holding her glass to the sunlight reflecting off the river, Claire examined the brew suspiciously. "Have you been playing with the spell book?" She sniffed its rich bouquet searching for unidentifiable scents of powders and potions.

"It's just wine—honestly—no bat's wings or toad's warts. Anyway, the spell's already been cast. What's the harm in repeating it?"

Raising his glass, the ping of fine crystal rang out as he tapped it against Claire's. "Say it, Clarry."

Their eyes met with the fixation of boundless love as she recited the words that so long ago sealed their fate.

ABOUT THE AUTHOR

From an early age, Ann Charlotte has been writing stories. Encouraged by her Creative Writing professor, she has pursued her dream of a career as an author. A short story has been published by *Reader's Digest* (Canadian Edition) and a work of poetry has been published in an anthology of verse. Of three full-length novels completed thus far, *Spellbound*, is the first to be professionally produced. She is currently working on a children's book, *The Adventures of Skeeter Marie*.

Originally from Nova Scotia, Ann Charlotte was raised in Ontario, Canada. She is the mother of two children, Jeremy and Jenni Lynn, and currently lives in Missouri, U.S.A., with her husband, Ken.

CPSIA information can be obtained at www.ICGtesting.com
Printed in the USA
LVOW111206121012

302505LV00001B/6/P

9 781420 827491